JENS LAPIDUS

TOP DOG

Jens Lapidus is a criminal defense lawyer who represents some of Sweden's most notorious underworld criminals. He is the author of the Stockholm Noir trilogy, three of the bestselling Swedish novels of this past decade: *Easy Money*, *Never Fuck Up*, and *Life Deluxe*. He lives in Stockholm with his wife.

D0711174

ALSO BY JENS LAPIDUS

TOP DOG

TOP DOG

JENS LAPIDUS

Translated from the Swedish by Alice Menzies

Vintage Crime/Black Lizard

VINTAGE BOOKS

A Division of Penguin Random House LLC | New York

Library of Congress Cataloging-in-Publication Data
Names: Lapidus, Jens, 1974– author. | Menzies, Alice, translator.
Title: Top dog / by Jens Lapidus ;
translated from the Swedish by Alice Menzies.
Other titles: Top dogg. English
Description: New York : Vintage Crime/Black Lizard, November 2018.
Identifiers: LCCN 2018005472 | ISBN 9780525431732 (pbk. : alk. paper)
Subjects: LCSH: Women lawyers—Sweden—Fiction. | Murder—
Investigation—Sweden—Fiction. | Suspense fiction. | Mystery fiction.
Classification: LCC PT9877.22.A65 T6713 2018 | DDC 839.73/8—dc23
LC record available at https://lccn.loc.gov/2018005472

Vintage Crime/Black Lizard Trade Paperback ISBN: 978-0-525-43173-2
eBook ISBN: 978-0-525-43174-9

www.blacklizardcrime.com

Printed in the United States of America
10 9 8 7 6 5 4 3 2 1

TOP DOG

SWEDISH WOMEN'S WEEKLY
EXCLUSIVE MINGLE AT BUCHARDS EXHIBITION

CoolArt and Buchards threw an exclusive launch party last night, in celebration of their unique art. The event saw Prince Carl Philip and his graphic designer friend Joakim Andersson mingling alongside Stockholm society and the big names of the art world.

Our reporter also spotted a couple of newcomers to the Stockholm collectors' scene: youthful financier Hugo Pederson and his beautiful wife, Louise. The stylish pair are said to have a keen interest in art, and sources tell us that they have built up a sizable collection of contemporary pieces despite having only been collecting for two years.

"I've always loved the fragile, the complex," Mr. Pederson cheerily told our reporter.

Mr. Pederson works for investment firm Fortem, and has rapidly become a great patron of a number of artists.

"If you're lucky enough to earn a bit of money, you also have to give back," he continued, heading off to mingle alongside his equally engaged wife.

Johan W. Lindvall, 2007

Prologue

Adan dragged the aluminum ladder over to the back of the building and peered up at the balcony. The apartment was on Nystadsgatan: first floor—it shouldn't be too hard to unfold the ladder, lean it against the balcony, and climb up. But still, fuck—he felt like he was about to shit himself. Genuinely. He could just see it: him at the very top of the bastard ladder with a brown stain on his ass.

He had actually stopped doing jobs like this. He was nineteen now and too old for break-ins: it was the kind of thing they used to do at the end of high school. Plus: it was beneath him now. But what was he meant to do? If Surri told you to do something, you did it.

They had known each other since kindergarten, lived on the same block, played on the same teams—their fathers had even been neighbors back in the old country. "We were like everyone else in Bakool. We didn't care about one another more than we needed to," Adan's old man used to say. "But everyone here thinks we're like family, like we're the same person."

His father was both right and wrong: Surri *was* a brother. But he still acted like a dick.

Adan could feel the chill of the ladder through his gripper gloves. Gloves: he had kept that part of the routine from before—his prints were guaranteed to be saved in a database somewhere. He braced himself; there was a lot of him to haul over the railing: he had to weigh at least 240 pounds. Still, the screwdriver was light in his hand, and the grip felt comfortable—as though his fingers had actually been longing to use it, despite his living a completely ordinary life these days. Drove a delivery van for his dad's boss, ate popcorn and watched *Luke Cage* and *Fauda* with his girl at night. It was just that two weeks earlier, he had been asked if he wanted to earn a little extra dough. Nothing illegal, just a one-day job for old times' sake. You were crazy if you said no to that kind of thing.

It was all those German bastards' fault. What Surri had wanted was for Adan to travel down to Hamburg and pick up one of the new 7 Series BMWs. It was a done deal: you could get a 730d for under 100,000 euros there, then sell it without any trouble for 150,000 back in Sweden. The only problem: you couldn't register too many cars to yourself in any given year, otherwise the tax authorities would come sniffing. And that was where Adan came in.

He had taken the train down to the southern tip of Denmark; a one-way ticket was 599 kronor, and he had spent the entire journey listening to Spotify on his new Beats headphones, keeping a tight grip on the fanny pack Surri had given him, and staring out of the window. A million kronor in euro notes weighed almost nothing. He had never spent so long on a train before, but it was actually pretty sweet. He never got bored of watching the scenery outside. It flew by: frosty fields, wooded areas, and small towns where people seemed to collect rusty wrecks and old planks of wood. He wondered how they made a living.

He'd had no trouble finding the car place, signing the documents, and negotiating with the salesman, who even spoke a bit of Arabic—it wasn't Adan's language, but he knew enough to be able to say a few friendly phrases. It felt sweet to sink back in the black leather seat, start the engine, and cruise back to Sweden. He drove different pickups every day, but never BMWs. This car didn't just *look* like it had class—you could feel the quality in the details, too. The smell of leather, the feeling when he ran his fingers over the dashboard, the weight of the doors, and the faint, comforting sound when they closed. He had thought about Surri, the guy did everything with style—even his balaclavas came from sick French designers. One day, Adan might even be able to afford a car like this. But, right then, his plan had been to drive all evening and night. He wanted to get the BMW home without having to check in to a motel.

It was on the highway outside of Jönköping that he first heard it: a hollow scraping noise that definitely didn't sound good. He had pulled over two miles later. Climbed out, inspected everything, but he couldn't see a thing. The sound had returned the minute he pulled away. After another twelve or so miles, a warning light had come on. "Brake Fault." What did that mean? Shit—he didn't know if he could even keep driving. He had slowed down, causing a line of traffic behind him; he was going forty in the seventy-five lane. The car sounded terrible. Another five or so miles later, he had pulled into a gas station and asked if the assistant could come out and check the car. The kid had spots all over his face and looked like he was five years younger than Adan, but he had immediately started shining a flashlight at the rims of the tires.

"Looks like your brake pads are pretty much gone," he had said. "You can't drive another inch in this car. Shame with such a sick ride, by the way."

That had been the end of the upside: Adan had had to pay a recovery van to tow the car to the next garage. It had taken five weeks to fix and cost forty grand. But there was also a risk it was pulling to one side, they said. Adan had called the seller in Germany and yelled at him, but the guy had pretended he didn't even speak English. In the end, Surri had a valuation on the piece of crap car: he wouldn't even get six hundred thousand for it.

"How could you be so thick not to even check the car before you signed?"

———

The lock on the balcony door gave way with a click and Adan pushed it open. Surri had been clear: "The cops are keeping our guy who rented the place in custody, but they haven't found the shit there. So if you break in and find what's mine, we can write off half your debt. You know how much I blew on that car."

Adan had squirmed. "Is anyone living there?"

"Fuck that. There won't be anyone home tomorrow night, either way."

Adan thought back to one day in the yard when they were younger. Surri had fallen from the jungle gym, dropped like a little rock and cut his knee. To them, it seemed like a river of blood had come flooding out, and the cut was full of gravel. His friend wouldn't stop crying. "I'll help you. C'mon, let's go to my place, I think my dad's there," Adan had said in as gentle a voice as he could. They were six at the time, and Adan knew that his father could mend Surri's knee. Sure enough, he had—his father had cleaned the wound and applied the biggest Band-Aid they had ever seen. As they drank chocolate milk, ate cookies, and watched *Toy Story* on DVD afterward, Surri had said: "Your dad's better at that than mine."

It was a two-bedroom apartment. Adan switched on the light in what had to be the living room and saw a green sofa, a glass-topped coffee table, and a bookcase. There was also what looked like a projector of some kind. In both bedrooms, there were narrow, unmade beds. People had to be living there—why else would there be newspapers on the coffee table and a T-shirt hanging over the back of a chair?

At the same time, the place was also barely furnished, so maybe they just slept over here every now and then. He picked up the garbage can in the kitchen, peered down at an empty milk carton, and caught the scent of something he definitely recognized: stubbed-out weed.

He went through the kitchen cabinets and the fridge. The person or persons living there had plenty of chips and sour cream, but no normal food. He peered into the oven and the dishwasher, got down onto the floor and shone his flashlight beneath the sink and behind the fridge. It was dusty.

People could be imaginative sometimes, but he didn't find a thing. He lifted the cushions from the sofa, ran his hand beneath the sheets and the mattresses in the beds. There was a bag on the floor in one of the bedrooms, and he rifled through it—spotted a few more T-shirts, four pairs of boxers, and some socks. He climbed onto the coffee table and shone his flashlight into the air vent in the wall. Nothing.

He couldn't see a thing.

Back in the living room. Adan got down onto all fours and peered beneath the sofa, shone the flashlight behind the bookcase.

The guy who rented the place before these people must have screwed Surri over—there was nothing here, or maybe the cops had found it after all. It wasn't really Adan's problem anymore. Not that Surri would see it that way.

And then he heard something. A noise from the hallway.

No, it was in the stairwell, on the other side of the door. He could hear voices out there.

Before Adan had time to think, he heard the key rattling in the lock. *Shit*—someone was on their way into the apartment. He turned out the lights in the living room.

He could hear people talking in the hallway now. Two voices, a girl's and a guy's. Maybe he should just jump out and beat them up, whoever they were. But no—he wasn't like Surri. He wasn't a *tough* guy.

He crawled behind the sofa.

The voices grew clearer. The girl was talking about someone called Billie. The guy mumbled something about a party. "Almost party time."

Adan lay perfectly still, trying to keep calm and quiet. He should go back to Hamburg and kill that BMW salesman with his own bare hands—this was all his fault.

Then he heard a door close. It sounded like it might have been the bathroom door, judging by the distance. Was this his chance? He could hear only the girl's voice now; she was humming some tune. The guy was probably in the toilet. It sounded like the girl had come into the living room. Then silence. Adan wasn't even breathing, just trying to listen. The padding of feet. Puffing sounds. Then more footsteps, out, toward one of the bedrooms.

Now.

He got up: the living room was empty. He took two long strides toward the balcony door. He wasn't thinking, wasn't reflecting. Just acting. He tore open the door. Didn't look back. Stepped out onto the balcony. Closed the door behind him. Sucked in the fresh air.

He jumped over the railing.

He threw himself down. No, he fell.

Like Surri from the jungle gym.

The darkness felt safe, but it was far too cold out. His gloves were as thin as paper.

Adan leaned against the tree. He was trying not to put any weight on his right foot, which he had really hurt in the fall—the bastard might even be broken. All the same, he didn't want to leave. The ladder was lying on the ground in front of him: he had dragged it behind him as he limped away over the snow. Surri would go crazy when he told him he hadn't found anything. Still: it had to have been Surri's own guy who'd screwed him over. Adan *had* searched everywhere.

He had been standing here for four hours now. Just waiting. Hoping the pain in his foot would go away. The lights were on in the apartment. Strange colors lit up the walls, and the music poured out from the balcony doors, which opened every now and then. There were so many people inside—he could see them through the windows like blurry backup dancers on some televised talent show.

At some point tonight, the idiots in there would have to leave, or at least go to bed. At some point, the chips and dip would run out. Then he would put the ladder back in place and climb up onto the balcony again. Search the place one last time.

He wouldn't be able to stand here all night—his foot was in too much pain—but he could hold out a while longer.

He wasn't really a warrior.

But he could wait.

There were nineteen people in the little living room, but they had invited at least as many more. Roksana really wanted the place to be packed tonight—for her and Z's housewarming. She hoped people would think it was a good opportunity to party. They would come, wouldn't they?

Young Thug tunes thundered out of the sound system she had borrowed from Billie—and which Z had linked up to SoundCloud on his phone. Thuggy delivered—his listless, droning voice in a melodious riddim rap. It was a full-body experience, a dive into a warm, swirling, glittering sea of styles and sounds. Roksana glanced around the room again: Did people like the tunes? Were they having fun? Was the atmosphere good?

People had brought their own drinks. Bottles of sparkling wine lined up on the coffee table. Roksana had explicitly asked for it in her Messenger invite: *Bring bubbles! Roksana & Z will supply the tunes, party, and nibbles.* She hoped it hadn't sounded too forward.

The nibbles consisted of peanuts and chips, but Roksana had dribbled some truffle oil into the sour cream—and everyone said it was the best dip they had ever tasted. Still, the food wasn't exactly the main event—the focus was on the party, and the party was fueled by the music. The sound system, the choice of songs, the mix. Z had even managed to get ahold of a smoke machine and a mini-laser show. They hadn't had time to put up any pictures or posters, so it was perfect, the best use for a white wall. The ironic smoke hung around the sofa like a cloud, and Roksana thought it felt like she was in a club, a super exclusive one. The only difference was that they were missing a DJ booth and that the people still arriving would have to wade through a hallway full of Roshe Runs and retro-inspired Vans. It was Z who had insisted on the no-shoe policy. "If we're going to do this, we need to limit the amount of cleaning we have to do afterward. Because I suck at cleaning. Have I ever mentioned that?"

Roksana didn't know what Z had or hadn't said—they hadn't exactly planned to move in together. Still, it should work out. Z was a good guy.

She checked Instagram and Snapchat to see whether anyone had uploaded anything from the party. But no, so far their event hadn't made it into that territory. Please, people, she thought, you like the party, don't you? Can't you just dance, even a little bit, a few of you, at least? And take some photos.

The apartment was pretty big, 560 square feet, but it was on Nystadsgatan in Akalla, which was pretty far out from central Stockholm and from Södertörn University, where she was studying. But Roksana hadn't had any other choice. She had been renting a room from Billie before, on Verkstadsgatan in Hornstull, until Billie had decided to become polyamorous and have three of her partners living there at the same time. Z had suggested that they rename that part of town Whore-nstull. But for Roksana, it wasn't a joke; there just hadn't been room for her—plus, she couldn't cope with one of the guys playing cheesy Swedish pop on Billie's stereo all day, not even ironically. As luck would have it, Z had been kicked out of his sublet that same week. He had spent three days sleeping on his gran's sofa and had been an inch away from a serious mental breakdown.

Roksana was standing between Z and Billie. All around her, the guests were mingling. A few were rocking gently in time with the music. She didn't want to watch them too openly—it would be too obvious. She checked Instagram and Snapchat again. Maybe they thought she was boring, just sticking with her besties; maybe her besties thought she was beige for just sticking with them.

She had her hair up in honor of the evening, and she was wearing her new silver Birkenstocks. Other than that, she was wearing her usual blue jeans and a white T-shirt she had found at her mom and dad's place. Billie moaned about it sometimes, but Roksana stuck to her usual look; her style icons were George Costanza and practically everyone from *Beverly Hills, 90210*. The whole thing was a middle finger to trends and fashion ideals.

Billie was in a great mood—that was a good sign. She was wearing Adidas pants, a loose long-sleeved T-shirt, a choker, and a soft Gucci cap on top of her pink hair. She had even dyed her underarm hair pink—"To celebrate you guys," she claimed. It was hard to believe that she would be starting a law degree in just a few days' time. Roksana was glad that Billie had left all her boyfriends and girlfriends at home—she was always more relaxed without them. She was Roksana's oldest and probably closest friend, but after their recent problems, she didn't really know quite where they stood.

Billie pulled out a carton of cigarettes. "What's the deal here? Do I have to go out to the balcony, or is it OK if I smoke in here?"

Z looked up again. "Hell no. The smoke gets into the curtains and bedsheets. Roksy and I have talked about this."

Billie rolled her eyes. "But you don't even have any curtains."

Z was firm. "Makes no difference. Smoking indoors isn't cool."

"Is this going to be some kind of clean living place or what?"

Roksana laughed. "Yeah, only plant-based, organic food. Forks over knives, you know the drill. And no plastic sets foot inside the front door."

Z pulled out a ziplock bag and a pack of OCB Slims.

"Anyone want their own joint? I've got plenty." He held up the bag. "You know there's a golden rule when it comes to marijuana.

Keep sativa and indica separate. Both are subspecies of canna-bis, but the plants look completely different, different thicknesses of leaves and all that, but who cares. The important thing is the effect: it's like night and day. Indica's your regular couch stoner variety. Like, it gives the right high for someone who wants a Play-Station and chill feeling. But this is a twenty-four-month sativa, the Châteauneuf-du-Pape of weed. It doesn't get any better than this."

Z carefully separated the grass on the rolling paper. "You smoke this, you get high. Then you smoke some more and get even higher. There's no ceiling, I swear."

That was all beginner's bullshit. The difference between sativa and indica wasn't always clear, but Z loved putting words to things, chatting away. It was who he was: he couldn't just keep up with the world—he had to be able to describe what was going on, narrow it down, understand it in terms of categories and structures. Some-times, it felt more like a competition.

Roksana took the joint Z held out to her and took a deep puff. "Have you finished mansplaining yet?"

They laughed, Z too. "You know what I'm like," he said.

Z was nice, in his own special way: he saw patriarchal structures as clearly as he saw the principles of weed; he didn't just under-stand society's patterns, he was also aware of his own position in the power hierarchy. A man who explained things to women. A man who always knew what was what. A man who began 90 per-cent of his remarks with the words "So, it's like this . . ."

The hours passed. Erik Lundin mixed nicely with Lil B in a sweet fade to Rihanna—a bit unexpected, but shiiit, she was good—and then something completely different that only Z knew about: apparently their name was Hubbabubbaklubb. People were bounc-ing on the floor, free spirit dancing in the corners, bobbing in time with the music. Z's little laser show beamed geometric shapes onto the walls. There were empty plastic glasses and broken chips all over the table. Rizla papers and wine bottles strewn on every other surface. She might even have seen a rolled-up banknote—people were too obvious sometimes; it wasn't cool.

They had to be having fun now? Roksana checked her phone for the two hundredth time. The only thing that had been uploaded was a screenshot of Z's playlist, accompanied by a cigarette emoji and the words *smoke w every day*.

Roksana had warned the neighbors, so they should be okay, she and Z weren't exactly planning to have parties like this every weekend. Plus, for some reason, she got the impression that the guy they were subletting the place from, David, didn't care all that much. So long as he got his money, he was happy, though the strong smell of weed that was probably lingering in the stairwell might raise questions. One of the neighbors had told her that the guy who lived in the apartment before them had caught the police's attention. They had apparently arrested him and raided the place a few weeks earlier, but then they had handed the apartment back over to David. Roksana didn't care; David had said they could live there for as long as they wanted, so she didn't care who had been in the apartment before, or what they'd used it for. The important thing was that people thought she and Z were doing things right now.

That it was a good start to her mini collective with him.

A good start to the term.

Her friends had gone. Too early, it felt like. Roksana tried to stop the thoughts swirling through her head: Had she been too much of a cliché when she told them she was thinking of studying in Berlin? Hadn't she been nice enough?

The living room looked like a war zone. The rug in the kitchen was damp; there was weed on the windowsill. She wondered how Z would cope with the cleaning afterward.

Billie said: "Shit, everyone just disappeared, including my ride. Guess a lot of them wanted to see Ida Engberg."

Z was on the sofa. "Ida Engberg, she's the absolute bomb.

Maybe we should go, too?" Z was so high on his so-called twenty-four-month sativa that he probably couldn't even stand up straight.

"We need to clean and air this place. But you go if you want. It's cool with me," said Roksana.

Billie's pupils were as big as the cosmos. "I can help you clean up the worst of it."

"How were you planning to get home, then? Taxi?"

"Nope."

"First metro into town?"

"Nope."

"Kayak?"

Billie laughed.

Roksana opened the balcony doors wide. She didn't feel drunk anymore, and only a little bit high, but the cool, fresh air still came as a surprise—it was like her mind had been rinsed with mineral water. She peered out at the shadowy trees: the apartment was on the first floor—it wasn't all that far to the ground. She could make out a thin dusting of snow down there, but right beneath the balcony it looked like someone had torn up the grass, and she could see footsteps leading away in the darkness.

Billie could get home however she wanted; it wasn't Roksana's problem.

"I saw that you had a fold-up bed in the closet. Can I sleep here?"

Roksana turned around. The room really was a mess; someone had knocked over a bong, and the water had seeped out beneath the coffee table—but she couldn't stop her heart from skipping a beat: Billie wanted to stay over.

"Don't you have to get home to Fia, Pia, Cia, Olle, and whatever they're called?"

"You sound a bit heteronormative right now and fascist."

"I didn't mean it like that. But you did actually kick me out of your place. And now you want to sleep here."

"We have to question the prevailing norms, and that also applies to the way we speak. Words are authoritarian instruments in the gender power balance . . ." Billie grinned at herself. Her mouth was crooked; it always had been. "But I'm so sleepy. And it's ages since we had breakfast together."

They opened the closet door. A musty smell hit Roksana. There wasn't a light inside, but Z used the flashlight on his phone to shine a beam of light over a cardigan and a denim jacket that Roksana had hung up. He was okay with Billie staying over, too.

There was something off about the closet. Roksana didn't know what it was, but it gave her bad vibes.

"Can I borrow your phone?" She shone the light onto the wall. The closet was almost empty, with nothing but the bed, her two pieces of clothing, and a few abandoned hangers dangling from the clothes rail inside. The smell wasn't actually musty; it was more like old wood and stale air. But she suddenly realized why the space had given her a bad feeling—and it wasn't the booze or the weed she had smoked. No, something wasn't right. The bathroom had to be on the other side of the wall, but, if that was the case, the closet should have been bigger. The angles were all wrong. The architect must've been tripping. Something was built weirdly in there.

And then she started to knock. Even now, she realized that she wouldn't have done it if she hadn't had the cocktail of drink and drugs that she'd had earlier. She knocked on the inner wall. She knocked everywhere, at the bottom, in the middle, higher up—like she was searching for hidden treasure somewhere. Roksana stood on her tiptoes and felt the top of the plywood sheet behind the clothes rail. She managed to push her fingers in above it. It creaked.

"Z, help me with this. I think this wall is loose."

Z staggered into the closet. Billie watched them from outside.

Z: high *and* tall.

"Pull it a bit," said Roksana.

Z yanked the wooden sheet. It moved. The entire wall came loose and fell down on top of them.

Roksana managed to raise her hands in time; somehow she had

been expecting that very thing to happen. The board was thin and light, not even half an inch thick.

"What the?" Z groaned. It had hit him on the head.

They peered into the space that had opened up in front of them: narrow, maybe five square feet in total. There were two boxes inside.

Roksana suddenly felt focused, sober: the fresh air from the open balcony doors had made it all the way inside. Cool. Clarifying. What was this hidden space?

She bent down and picked up the box closest to her, which was roughly eleven by eleven inches wide.

Z was on his feet now. "Is this some kind of self-storage place or what?"

She placed the box on the living room floor.

It was easier to see in there. The cardboard box wasn't taped shut.

Z leaned forward. Billie did, too. Roksana bent down and folded back the flaps.

They all stared at the contents.

What the fuck?

PART I

JANUARY

1

The only good thing about this meeting was that it was with the same caseworker who had helped Teddy when he was first released. Her name was Isa, and she looked just like she had when they first met: Still around forty, still dressed like some kind of hybrid bohemian Södermalm woman and blingy Östermalm lady. Still wearing brightly colored scarves and weird wrist warmers alongside small diamond earrings, which weren't actually that small.

"Hi, Teddy! It's been a while," said Isa. Small dimples appeared on her cheeks when she smiled. For some reason, Teddy liked her, even though her only role was to put him to work.

"Yeah, time flies," he said, trying to seem friendly in return. The whole thing was really just embarrassing.

When he first got out of prison, he hadn't thought he would need to sit here. And certainly not several years later. He had thought he would come out to a different Sweden, that he would be on a different level. He had been motivated, ready to work hard and to give up his time. He really had changed: he was ready to take the hard route, to leave all the crap behind him. But being ready was one thing—actually changing was another. Reality had quickly caught up with him. There was an eight-year black hole in his CV, and by now he had almost become accustomed to people's suspicion. Though only *almost*.

"Well, let's go over how the past few years have been, job-wise," Isa suggested.

"Where do you want to start?"

"I know you found a job at a law firm?"

Teddy wanted to keep this brief. "Yeah, I took a few assignments as a special investigator for a firm called Leijon."

"Special investigator, what does that mean?"

"It's kind of hard to explain, but the partner in charge, Magnus Hassel, he called me a *fixer*."

Teddy thought back to how many of those jobs had led to violence, and how he had risked becoming the Teddy he no longer wanted to be. He hadn't worked for the firm for more than a year now, ever since the whole Mats Emanuelsson case.

Isa asked a few questions about wages, work experience, and whether he had taken any training courses. "And after the law firm?" she wondered. "What did you do then?"

"Since then it's been tricky. I've taken some Krami courses."

Isa looked down at her papers. He knew she wouldn't just be able to see that he had taken all of the guidance courses and group activities run by Krami, but also that he had completed at least five practical placements. None of them had led to a permanent position.

Krami was an initiative run by the Public Employment Service and the prison authorities, aiming to help guys like him—people with a so-called criminal history—find and, above all, *hold down* a job. He didn't know why it never worked out for him.

Isa talked about guidance courses and work plans. Her desk was made of pale wood. The floor was linoleum, the walls covered in white textured paper, and the chairs felt plastic. Behind her, there was a glass panel through which Teddy could see other employment officers and his own reflection. He was tall and always felt like his hair was invisible somehow: ash blond, shortish—or maybe it was mid-length.

With the exception of Isa's earrings, everything in the room reminded him of prison. It wasn't a personal room, it wasn't Isa's own office, it was a meeting cell, a place that looked in to the employment service but not out onto reality.

Though maybe Teddy did know what his problem was. After all those years in prison and his subsequent years of freedom, he still didn't know anyone but the people he had met inside and those he had known before he was sent down, people who belonged to his old life. He could count the number of people he was close to on one hand: his sister, Linda, and her son, Nikola. Dejan, from the past. Tagg and Loke, from his corridor in Hall Prison. Those were the people he felt comfortable around. It was in their company that he could be himself. Then there was Emelie, of course, but he didn't want to think about her right now. In any case, none of them could offer him a job, other than possibly Dejan. But that work would hardly contribute any tax to the Swedish state. In fact, there was a risk it would actually lead to increased costs for the country—in the form of a greater burden on the law enforcement agencies investigating whatever Dejan was up to.

Maybe he should just accept his predicament: realize that he didn't fit in. Teddy would never be a part of the Sweden that he had longed for while he was inside, ever the outsider. But that wasn't the same thing as saying he wanted to be a criminal again.

"Are you listening, Teddy? You have to listen, otherwise I can't help you."

Teddy stretched out his legs beneath the table. They had almost gone stiff from sitting still for so long. "Sorry. I was just thinking about a friend who might be able to help me find a job."

It was a long shot. But what was he meant to do? None of the courses, placements, or group seminars had led anywhere. Dejan was bound to be able to help him, for old times' sake. Isa tapped away at the keyboard as Teddy told her about his friend's construction company. Then she cocked her head and gave him a serious look.

"I'm sorry, Teddy, but I think it could be tricky with your friend.

I don't want to sound judgmental, but his firm has a very modest turnover, and he hasn't declared any income for the past ten years. I don't think he can offer you a real job. Not a job that I can approve, anyway."

Isa was right.

But she was also wrong.

2

It was six in the morning, and the crazy thing was that Nikola didn't even feel grumpy. George Samuel, his boss, had a particular way of smiling, which meant that his entire face crumpled up around his eyes. Nikola wondered whether George could even see when he smiled.

"Morning, Nicko, know what we're doing today?" he said as Nikola stepped into the cramped office.

Nikola put on his tool belt. "Yep. We're starting our biggest ever job. You haven't talked about anything else for a week."

They walked out to the van together: *George Samuel Electrical* in elaborate script on both sides. His tool belt jangled. Nikola didn't have his own ride, which was why he always met his boss at work and traveled with him to their jobs. Plus, it gave them a good opportunity to chat.

It was his mother, Linda, who had found him this placement with George Samuel. And now Nikola worked like any other Swede: five days a week. Up with the first radio broadcasts, lunch at eleven thirty on the dot, then back home before it even got dark in winter. Sometimes, he slept for an hour before dinner, just so he could manage to stay up past nine.

An unfinished shopping center rose up out of nothing in Flemingsberg, tucked between the train tracks and the court—like someone had buried an enormous concrete egg there, and it had only just started to hatch. It really was a huge job. George Samuel wasn't the only electrician who had been contracted, but for him and his apprentice, it meant ten months of full-time work all the same. A guaranteed customer for almost a year—that was invaluable, Nikola knew.

They stood side by side: worked as a team. Single-phase, three-phase, junction boxes. Cables, fuses, and amps. Nikola's technical vocabulary had swollen so much that he knew more electrical words than he did slang terms for drugs. Sometimes, it felt like his job meant more to him than the rest of his life put together, but that was okay—he liked it, aside from when the workmen started drilling in the distance. That sound reminded him of the explosion.

Eighteen months earlier, he had been on his way inside his uncle Teddy's place. When he turned the handle to open the door, a bomb had exploded, throwing Nikola against the opposite wall. He had suffered injuries to his abdomen, chest, and hands, which, out of sheer reflex, he had used to cover his face. It had meant a week in intensive care followed by a month on the ward. His mom and Teddy had been there every day, but the girl he was dating at the time, Paulina, had dumped him. It was just as well—clearly she wasn't worth his time.

Like always, George had set up his dusty old radio on the floor. They listened to Mix Megapol—Bebe Rexha's cocky voice was singing the same line over and over again. It was like working to a particular rhythm.

George turned down the volume. "You know that next week, you'll have done your sixteen hundred hours?"

"Really?"

"Yes, really. You've been doing really well, Nicko. I'll help you finish your certification. Your apprenticeship's over, the board'll approve you straightaway. You'll be a qualified electrician. What do you say about that?"

George Samuel chuckled—his eyes narrowed again, and Nikola

couldn't help it: he had to laugh, too. He had to laugh hysterically. George Samuel, blind from laughter—Nikola, almost an electrician. It made sense. He would have a real job. A real wage.

Who would have believed that eighteen months ago? While he was lying in intensive care after the explosion and Linda was beside herself with worry about him being on the wrong track. Who would have believed that life could be good? Who would have believed that it might actually be *really* good?

They were all proud of him. Teddy, who had found him his apartment, patted him on the shoulder every time they met: "Glad you're not following in my footsteps, Nicko." His grandpa still tried to make him go to church, but now he just smiled when Nikola refused. "You're on the right track, *moje malo zlato.* Your grandmother would have cried tears of joy." Even the boss of Spillersboda Young Offenders' Institute had called to congratulate him on his change of lifestyle: as though Nikola had uncovered three identical symbols on the millionaire scratch card.

But it was his mom who was happiest of all.

"Do you know what I think's so good?" she had said one day that spring, when he was still attending classes at the adult education college and had told her his grades. They had been walking along the canal, and Nikola had glanced over toward Södertälje Centrum. The birds were twittering like crazy, and there was dog shit on the path.

"That I broke away from my old life?" he tried.

"No, actually. The best thing is that change is possible. I was worried while you were in Spillersboda, you know, and even more once you got arrested and after the explosion. But now we have proof. That people can change."

Linda had a salon tan and was wearing Ray-Bans that covered half of her face, but Nikola could hear it in her trembling voice all the same: she might have been shedding a tear or two behind her glasses.

"You know, Nicko, you don't need to believe that you have to be someone anymore, that you have to strive for status and that kind of thing," Linda had said, pausing for effect. "Because you're already someone."

They had stopped at a park bench. Nikola had turned to her. She was wearing a Houdini fleece and walking pants of some kind: they didn't really go with her tan and glasses. Body: outdoorsy Swede. Head: MILF warning. Ahh, strike that last part—that wasn't the kind of thing you thought about your own mother.

The ground beneath the bench had been covered in seed shells. *Albuzur*—sunflower seeds. Nikola was a big fan. It meant that someone had spent a while sitting there before them, thinking things through. He had sat down. "I've got my Swedish exam next Thursday, and I have to submit an essay."

"Exciting. What's the essay on?"

"*The Count of Monte Cristo.* Have you read it?"

"No."

"It's one of Grandpa's favorites, you know."

"I can imagine. He's a big reader. It'll be fine, I know it."

Nikola's grandfather was a reading wizard: a man who had moved to Sweden from Belgrade sometime long ago and who had always taken Nikola seriously. He remembered his grandpa sitting on the edge of the bed, reading aloud from "the classics," as he called them. *The Jungle Book, The Three Musketeers, The Count of Monte Cristo.*

At the same time, his grandpa had also raised Uncle Teddy— one of southern Stockholm's legends in his day. Nikola couldn't reconcile the two in his mind.

Chamon's Audi A7 was parked in the middle of all the construction machinery outside the half-finished shopping center. Like always: his friend's collection of parking fines was fatter than one of Escobar's wads of cash. Not that Chamon cared—the car wasn't registered in his name. They never were. *Vorsprung durch Technik*—or, as Chamon liked to say, "Forward through Babso." That was the name of the guy who had four hundred cars registered to him in Södertälje.

It was Thursday, but Nikola wouldn't be working tomorrow. In other words: it was the weekend. George Samuel had agreed to let Nikola go at two thirty. They would see one another again on Monday, like usual.

Chamon started the engine. "You heard that Audi's releasing a new flagship model, the Q8?"

"Yeah, I read about it. It's gonna have the V8 engine. But weren't you talking about getting the new Lexus, the LS?"

Chamon stared at him. "Are you kidding me? I'm from Södertälje. I only drive German."

Things were going well for Chamon—clearly—and his car was the strongest evidence of that. Then the watch, then the other jewelry, then where he went on vacation; people didn't care where you lived. They never talked about where Chamon got his money from—even if Nikola knew that he dealt to chalk-white inner-city kids at their insanely wild rave clubs. You didn't talk about that kind of thing, even with your best friend—especially not if that person wasn't part of *The Life* themselves. Nikola did sometimes long for it: for what he'd once had. The freedom. The lack of control.

They went back to his place, watched a few episodes of *Narcos* for the second time: loved it when Escobar inspected the coke factories in Medellín. They went down to buy kebabs. Chamon pulled out a couple of grams of weed, which they smoked in Nikola's hookah—Nikola needed these chill moments. Ever since the explosion, something had happened to him, even if he couldn't quite put his finger on what.

He and Chamon laughed. Listened to music. Leaned back on the sofa and just chatted.

After a few hours, Chamon looked up. "Nicko, do you believe in God?"

"Nah, not really." This was classic Chamon crap talk. "I believe in fate. And my *dachri*."

But Chamon didn't laugh. "Do you believe in God or not?"

"Shit, man, I don't know."

Chamon drew on the pipe, then he kissed the thick gold cross that hung around his neck on an even fatter chain. "I do."

"Why?"

His friend's eyes were glossy. " 'Cause there's got to be something other than this."

"Than what?"

"Bro, I don't get any sleep at night. I wake up every fifteen minutes and peer round the curtains. If I hear a noise on the street behind me, I drop to the ground. The minute I see a car I don't recognize, my stomach turns. I'm getting fucking ulcers."

"But you're free. You don't have to get up at five every morning like I do."

"I dunno, man, maybe you don't have it so bad. It's hard to explain, but sometimes I feel like I can't do it anymore, like I'm tired of the whole thing, I don't have any power. You know how many people've been killed these past few years? You know how many brothers have vanished? But the people making the decisions don't give a shit. They're all such whores, you know. I want to do something else sometime. Travel, you know? Or try out music or something. You know what I mean?"

"Music?" Nikola didn't recognize his friend: *want to do something else sometime*—that sounded more like his mom's nagging than Chamon.

"I mean, I'd like to learn an instrument. I was playing football for a while, but my mom always said I had an ear for music, that if I heard a tune once, I could sing it back perfectly later. She said I was musicalistic, or whatever it's called. But *dachri,* these days all the undercover cops and snitches are fucking my head so much, I can't hear a thing in there. Won't be long before there's none of me left. Not even sweet tunes."

Nikola tried to work out how serious this conversation was. He thought about George Samuel and about how the most difficult thing he'd done today was to pull four insulated copper wires through a conduit.

And Nikola knew: he had made the right decision. Almost an electrician.

The Life wasn't for him.

3

Emelie got up, smoothed the creases in her pants, and went out to greet Marcus. Anneli, the secretary she and the other lawyers shared, had already buzzed him in through the door downstairs. If Marcus had taken the stairs, he should be ringing the buzzer in approximately seven seconds. But if he had gone for the elevator, it would be a few more. It was a kind of litmus test, Marcus's first. Emelie's own inclination was always to take the stairs, regardless of how heavy the files in her briefcase were. Not that it really made much difference; she had already offered him a probationary position as a lawyer. There was no denying that it was a big step. Emelie had been running her own firm for just under eighteen months now, but the number of cases had exceeded expectations. She no longer had time to handle everything herself, which she knew was a luxury. Still, it was a risk—from today on, she wouldn't just be responsible for paying her own salary. From now on, Emelie Jansson Legal Services AB would have to bring in enough money to cover two wages every month, one which came before her own. The curse of the small business owner, she thought. If Marcus was ever unwell or unable to handle the work, or if he simply didn't manage to invoice properly, it was the firm that would suffer, and it might not survive. Her dream might come crashing down. But she needed someone to lighten her load all the same: in that sense, it was a must. She had too much to do.

———

Marcus was tall and well built, with a thin, neat beard, and as they shook hands, Emelie noticed that he smelled good. He had probably taken the stairs. For a brief moment, she had thought he was expecting a hug, but she was his boss and employer now, even if there were only two years between them. Besides, she wasn't the hugging type.

"Please, come in. I'm so glad you could start today."

Marcus was wearing a navy suit, and his slacks were slightly too short, but that was just the fashion right now. The top button of his shirt was undone, and he wasn't wearing a tie, which was fine, given that he wouldn't be in court today. To begin with, he would just be getting to grips with everything. The way he moved reminded her of Teddy, she thought: calm and deliberate.

"Let's go to my office," said Emelie. "Would you like anything to drink?"

She had asked Anneli to make sure there was freshly brewed coffee in the machine, and a couple of bottles of Ramlösa water in the fridge.

"Please. You wouldn't have any caffeine-free tea?" Marcus asked.

Caffeine-free tea, Emelie thought. That sounded quite unlawyerlike, though maybe it was just something else that was trendy right now. She turned to Anneli and passed on the request.

"Nope, afraid we're a bit low on the caffeine-free today," the secretary said with a wry smile. The only thing Emelie and the other lawyers drank was coffee, coffee, and more coffee.

They went into her office. On one wall, she had a framed Mark Rothko painting. It was a poster, of course, a flat expanse of red that faded to brown and then something close to yellow. Emelie liked it; she thought it brought a sense of calm to the room, even if the fact it was only a poster reminded her of her previous employer, Leijon. Magnus Hassel, the partner she had worked with there, collected contemporary art, and he had both Warhol and Karin "Mamma" Andersson canvases hanging next to works by Giacometti and Bror Hjorth in his office. But that was history now. She had resigned from Leijon because they wouldn't agree to her taking on a defense case. And then she had taken what had to be seen as a giant leap into the world of law: from being employed by one of Europe's best corporate firms to renting an office and a quarter of a secretary's time in a space she shared with three old human rights lawyers. Her former colleagues at Leijon had raised their eyebrows. A downgrade, a desperate fall from the elite to the D-list. She could, at least, have applied for a position with one of the renowned criminal firms, worked for the courts or with the Swedish Prosecution Agency, if what she wanted was to work on human-centric cases like that? It was just that it didn't suit Emelie—she wanted to be left to her own devices, that felt important, she'd had enough of bosses getting involved. And she knew she could be one of the best.

Marcus placed his bag on the floor. It was made from dark green canvas and looked pretty expensive. She didn't know much about his background; all she knew was that he had gone to high school in Kärrtorp, in the suburbs, and now lived centrally, in trendy Södermalm. The salary she had offered him was one thousand kronor less than he had been getting from the small-family law firm where he had been working before—and the fact that he had agreed to it was proof of his commitment. If he was as good as she hoped he was, he would soon be on commission.

"So," she said, pushing a laptop over to him. "This is your computer. You'll need to choose a password and that kind of thing. You'll be in the room next door. I've ordered you a desk and a chair, but they're not being delivered until next week. Sorry about that, but until then you can work in here. Hope that's okay."

"Absolutely, but would it be okay if we turned off the light?"

Emelie looked up. She didn't understand.

"It's just, I'm allergic to electricity. I can't handle it. I prefer to work by candlelight or with a paraffin lamp, and I like to use a pen and paper rather than a computer."

Emelie stared at the young lawyer in front of her. She had made up her mind about Marcus Engvall immediately after her interview with him: he had top grades from his placements and kind words from his previous employers, and he was passionate about people-centric law. He also seemed to have a sense of humor, a good temper, and courage—the former were important for the clients, and the latter essential for this type of work. Courage: not many people talked about it, but it was the most important quality in a defense lawyer. But now: her suspicions should have been raised at caffeine-free tea. What was this? Allergic to electricity? That wasn't even a thing.

Marcus smiled, winked. "Don't worry, I'm just kidding. I'm happy to work in here. With the lights on."

He placed his phone on the desk. The screen was cracked.

"And I don't have anything against electrical devices. In fact, I'm a bit of a tech nerd."

Emelie laughed. Marcus did, too. So he did have a sense of humor.

It was actually Magnus Hassel who had given her Marcus's name a few months earlier. Emelie had been waiting for Josephine, who still worked at Leijon, at a restaurant called Pocket City when she heard someone say her name. She had turned around and realized that two of her old bosses were sitting at the next table. Magnus Hassel and Anders Henriksson. How could she have missed them? Back when she was at Leijon, they were the ones responsible for her yearly development meetings, something she didn't exactly miss. She remembered them well.

Anders Henriksson was somewhere north of fifty, but he probably dyed his hair and Botoxed his forehead to make himself look closer to thirty. A few years earlier, he had married a secretary twenty-five years his junior, and yet the transformation wasn't quite complete: he still thought Zara Larsson was a Spanish clothing brand and saw Harvey Weinstein as a hero. But that wasn't his claim to fame, nor was his so-called EQ—in that respect, it was probably fair to talk about him being exceptionally challenged. Where Anders Henriksson really shone was in his performance. He was behind several of Sweden's most respected M&A deals, known for not winding down despite approaching retirement age, and listed in all the most important rankings as *"A brilliant analyst—creative and authoritative."*

Magnus Hassel, on the other hand, had never needed any further introduction. He was Mr. M&A in Sweden; anyone who was anyone in the Swedish business world knew who he was, and not just the lawyers. He had held the hand of the biggest business leaders, MDs, and industry giants, and led them to even greater riches. According to *Dagens Industri*, Magnus Hassel had brought in twenty-five million kronor in bonuses in the last year alone.

But all that belonged to her old life. Emelie had entered a new arena now. Far removed from the flashy offices, billionaire clients, and exotic jurisdictions. And with half the income.

It was Magnus who had forced her to resign, who had turned up while she was defending Benjamin Emanuelsson in court and spent an entire day listening to her in the public gallery. She should hate him. And yet she knew he had a high opinion of her and that he really had tried to make her change her mind, to stay at Leijon. Emelie couldn't dislike him 100 percent. Only 98.

"I didn't think you came to these parts anymore," Magnus had said. He was casually dressed: a green tweed jacket, jeans, and a pink shirt. Jeans—during her three years at Leijon, Emelie couldn't remember ever having seen him in anything so casual. "I thought people like you stuck to Kungsholmen and the satellites."

Technically, he was right. The majority of Stockholm's criminal law firms were based in Kungsholmen. Its proximity to the Stockholm district court, police HQ, and the main custodial prison made it the natural neighborhood for anyone who liked to be able to walk to their meetings, interviews, and hearings. She spent much of the rest of her time at the district courts in Södertorn and Attunda, or the smaller custodial prisons in Huddinge and Sollentuna.

"The satellites," as Magnus called the inner suburbs, made Emelie think of the Eastern Europe of the past. Satellite countries, Soviet vassals.

"I'm meeting Jossan," Emelie had said. "And she doesn't like straying far from sanctuary."

Magnus had laughed. Anders Henriksson, on the other hand, hadn't reacted. Emelie had thought back to his scarlet face when he and Magnus first confronted her about taking on the Emanuelsson defense.

"I've heard things are going well for you," Magnus had said, raising his glass as though to toast her.

"Yeah, I actually have a bit too much to do. I should probably hire an assistant."

"You should be happy, then. But you still can't be earning as much as you were with us?"

Emelie had wondered whether his mocking was friendly or whether he was genuinely trying to provoke her. She had raised her still-empty glass to him. "You pay a price for being at the top."

Anders Henriksson's face had changed color at her last remarks. But Magnus just laughed.

"Listen," he had said, leaning forward. "I actually think I know a kid who would be a great fit for you. He applied for a job with us last week, he's a newly qualified lawyer, he's been in court, seems smart, hardworking, like you."

"Why didn't you hire him, then? I thought you liked workaholics?"

Magnus had leaned even closer, his mouth practically brushing her ear. "He talked about working for the rights of the individual and defending a system that should provide support to everyone. He actually sounded worryingly like you. He's a vegan, too, and there's no trusting people who don't want to eat dead things."

Emelie leaned back and studied Magnus. His eyes glittered.

"Tell him to send me an application," she said.

Back at the office. Anneli called through. "I've got a woman on the line for you. She sounds really desperate," she said, transferring the call.

"Is this Emelie Jansson?" asked a bright voice on the other end.

"Yes, speaking."

"Good, great. My name is Katja. I need to meet you. Today."

Emelie leaned back in her chair. Marcus was sitting in silence opposite her, fiddling with his computer.

Everyone always thought that their case was particularly urgent. Perhaps that wasn't so strange—if you had been accused of something or were the victim of a crime, it was almost certainly a traumatic experience, something you wanted to deal with immediately.

"I'm fully booked today, and my new lawyer has just started. Would you have time for a meeting next week?"

"No, no. We need to meet right away. It can't wait."

"Could I ask what this is regarding?"

The other end of the line went silent.

Emelie repeated her question. "What is this regarding?"

She heard Katja take a deep breath. When she next spoke, her voice seemed to tremble. "It's not something I can talk about over the phone. So when can you meet?"

There was something in the tone of the woman's voice that caught Emelie's attention, rather than what she actually said.

"Could we do Monday? I don't usually arrange meetings for Saturdays and Sundays."

"I don't know. You absolutely can't tell anyone that you've spoken to me."

"We have strict confidentiality rules here."

Emelie wondered what this was about. The young woman had barely said anything, but the stress in her voice was clear.

"I really need to see you as soon as possible—could it happen before Monday?" Katja asked.

Emelie knew that you had to stick to your principles where clients were involved, otherwise there was a risk they would eat you alive. But something felt particularly urgent here, and so she said: "Okay. Let's meet tomorrow."

4

Saturday dinner at Mom and Dad's house in Kista. Baba was depressed again, Mom said, and Roksana wanted to find some way to help him, but first he had to accept that he needed other people, that he wasn't alone in this.

She was sitting on one sofa and Caspar on the other, the same leather sofas they had fought on as children. The glass table that Roksana had once fallen onto, when she was seven or eight, was in the middle of the thick Persian rug. Her father had had a fit when that happened, because he had been convinced it was broken. Roksana thought about that sometimes: hadn't Baba been afraid that *Roksana* might be broken? The brass tray of teacups was on the table, same routine as always—bringing in the tray was the first thing her mother had done, before Roksana even had time to take off her coat in the hallway.

Some things never changed.

There was a football match on TV. The curtains were half-drawn and the cushions on the sofa were plumped up in color order: red in one corner, green in the other. The wooden display cabinet was full of golden carafes, brass trays, and vases; Roksana could have closed her eyes and still described exactly how they were set out. Her mother's most prized possessions were the candlesticks she had been given by her father. "*Dokhtaram,* these are the most valuable items I own," she often said. "Not because we might get a lot for them at auction, but because they were your grandmother's family's dowry to Grandad. They're the only memory I have of my mother's family."

Caspar's eyes were glued to the TV. He was older than Roksana, but he still lived at home—not that that particular fact was something they discussed. They weren't allowed to mention it—Caspar might feel degraded otherwise.

Baba came in and Roksana hugged him. "I'm glad you're here," he said in her ear. He smelled of Aramis, like always. "It's the perfume of all perfumes, the original, the father of all male scents," he had once said when Roksana asked why he wore "old man perfume." Not that she had put it like that.

He was wearing a white short-sleeved shirt tucked into a pair of jeans. They were actually pretty nice, very norm core, as Z would say, but that wasn't the kind of thing Dad was aware of. When he sat down on the sofa, he said only one word: "Caspar . . ."

Both Caspar and Roksana knew what that meant—Baba wanted to change the channel.

"But Man U are playing. Zlatan, for God's sake," Caspar hissed.

Their father took the remote control and switched off the TV. "Football is nice when Team Melli play. Do you remember that match?"

Roksana knew what he was talking about—they had been there when Iran played an international against Sweden at the Friends Arena in 2015, alongside forty thousand other Swedish-Iranians. It was a memory she would keep for life, a party, and the only time she had ever seen her father in that mood—Iran had lost 3–1, and he had bawled. But Roksana had been able to see that they weren't just tears of sorrow—there had been something else in there. And the truth was that Roksana had cried, too; that match had woken something in her that she didn't quite understand—a sense of pride, and a longing for something she thought only her mother went on about, a sense of belonging to something that she and the forty thousand others all shared.

Her thoughts turned to what they had found in the apartment. She, Z, and Billie had stared down at the contents of the box from behind the fake wall in the closet. A space probably constructed for one single purpose.

The box had been full of bags, and through the transparent plastic, they could see the contents. The bigger bags contained smaller ones, all filled with white powder.

They had sat down on the sofa. Z was a pro; he had cut a small hole in the corner of one bag and shaken a tiny amount of powder onto a glass plate. Billie had said: "I think we should turn the lights off. I mean, since I'm going to be a lawyer and everything."

She was right, even if they'd had the mother of all parties less than an hour earlier, there was a difference between a bit of weed and the bags they had just found. They might be looking at more than ten kilos of the stuff.

All three of them had bent down. Z had licked his little finger and dipped it into the chalky white pile of powder. Held it up in front of his face.

"Looks pretty crystalline."

Roksana had noticed that, too. The powder reminded her more of sea salt than cocaine or baking powder.

A white tablecloth—nothing beat her mom and dad's food. The ornate floral plates that they had brought with them from Tehran were carefully set out, with forks and spoons—but no knives; at Mom and Dad's, you didn't use knives. Roksana always used to put out knives for her Swedish friends whenever they came over as children.

There was mountains of food: ghormeh sabzi and a special vegetarian version for Roksana, saffron rice, salad, and green beans. When their mother brought out the plate of tahdig, both Roksana and Caspar leaped forward. Tahdig: when Roksana was younger, she had always wanted to help line the bottom of the pan with potatoes, before the rice was added on top, and then make holes for the steam to escape more easily. Her mother was always responsible for turning the whole thing upside down so that the potatoes on the bottom came out on top: a crunchy rice cake, probably the most delicious thing Roksana could think of.

"How are your studies, Roksana *joonam*?" Dad asked in his eighties Farsi. Roksana had never thought about it before the previous summer, when her cousins from Tehran had laughed at his old-fashioned way of speaking during a visit to Sweden.

Roksana knew roughly what was coming, and she always replied in Swedish. "It's going fine."

He took a sip of his wine, which her mother had only poured herself and her husband. Caspar and Roksana were still both expected to drink Coca-Cola, even though both were well over twenty. "Behavioral Science, that's the name of the course? Isn't it?"

"Yes."

"And it's like an easier version of the psychology course?"

"I don't know if you could say that, but I'll be able to work in many of the same areas. It feels good."

"But you could have been a psychologist."

"I didn't have the grades, Baba, you know that. The psychology degree at Stockholm University is probably the most difficult course to get into in Sweden. You need something like a score of 22.3, or at least a 1.9 on the aptitude test."

Her father put down his wineglass with a thud. "You could have achieved a 22.3 if you had knuckled down rather than running off to parties all the time. You're intelligent, Roksana. You're smart. Your mother and I have raised you well. Look at your brother: he will be a dentist. It's a profession that has good jobs. He'll be a doctor. You could have also . . ."

"But I didn't want to be a dentist. I'm not interested in people's mouths. They're boring and smell terrible."

"Come on, now . . ." said her mother. "No fighting. Will you be able to call yourself doctor, too?"

"No, Mom. I won't be a doctor. I'll be a behavioral scientist."

"But you know how we see it, *azizam*. We moved here for *your* sakes. We've worked hard for *your* sakes. We've toiled so that *you* can choose the best jobs and live the best life. We don't want you to waste your talents. Have you applied for the aptitude test? You have the ability to get into the psychology course, your father and I both know that."

Caspar poured more cola for himself; the bubbles fizzed in the glass and came close to spilling over. "Stop guilt-tripping Roksana. She's not like you. You just need to respect that."

Their mother opened her mouth to say something before closing it again. Their father impaled a couple of peas on his fork. Roksana poked at her rice. She *had* applied for the aptitude test, to see whether she could improve her results—but she wasn't going to tell them that.

After a while, Mom poured some more wine. "You know, this is a Shiraz, and I heard that it's called that because the grapes originally come from Shiraz, your grandfather's hometown."

Roksana didn't say anything. Everyone at the table had heard the Shiraz theory at least 150 times before.

"Look what I've got," Z had said, smiling his best luxury-estate-agent smile. He held up a small box, roughly the size of a paperback. "You're lucky you ended up living with such an expert. We can check what this white powder is."

EZ Test, said the top of the box. "I bought this kit online last year. It was just lying at the bottom of the bag I still haven't unpacked. So good to have when you need to know what you're taking."

Z had opened the box as, like always, he explained what was what. "This thing calculates the composition of different substances with real precision, only cost sixty-nine kronor. You won't find one any cheaper."

He had held up a small ampoule that was transparent at the bottom. There was some kind of liquid inside it. "You take a sample the size of a pinhead," he read aloud in English from the minimal instruction sheet, scooping a pile of powder the size of a fingernail onto a teaspoon.

Roksana had studied the description on the packaging. "That's too much. That's not a *pinhead*."

Z had turned to her. "Which of us is the expert here? That's about a nail's worth."

"Yeah, but *pinhead* doesn't mean nail. Though maybe you thought the instructions were in Azerbaijani? Because in Azerbaijani, it means testicle."

Z had mumbled something as he Googled the word *pinhead* on his phone. "Okay, you're right," he managed to say, shaking off some of the powder. Next, he had tipped what was left on the spoon into the ampoule and screwed on the lid. He shook it. Roksana had thought about Ray, her chemistry teacher from high school. He'd had a yellow mustache and wore leather waistcoats, and he'd had violent outbursts at some of the guys in her class practically every lesson. But he had always calmed down quickly and continued the lesson with untiring enthusiasm—and he had loved Roksana's curiosity.

"Okay, that's been two minutes. The reaction should be done and we can compare it to the color chart." Z had held the ampoule up to the light with the instruction sheet next to it. Roksana had studied the different colors. Red: ketamine. Greenish yellow: amphetamine. Blue: cocaine. Purple: MDMA. Yellow: Ritalin. Burgundy: PMA.

The color of the liquid in the ampoule was clear to see—it was red.

"It's ketamine," Roksana had said.

"I've always wanted to try it," Billie replied.

"They say it's better than DXM," said Z.

"*They*'re usually right," said Billie.

"Who's *they*?" Roksana had asked.

"No idea," Billie had replied. "But who cares. We're trying it."

Stockholm County Police Authority
Case #: dnr 0104-K3941

OFFICIAL NOTES

The following are extracts from a selection of telephone conversations and SMS messages between suspect Hugo Pederson and a number of other individuals. The monitored phones have the following subscriber numbers: 0733-475734 and 0704-343222. The conversations were recorded between 2005 and 2006.

TELEPHONE CONVERSATION 1

To: Hugo Pederson
From: Louise Pederson (wife)
Date: 23 September 2005
Time: 21:34

LOUISE: Where are you?

HUGO: At work.

LOUISE: Do you think you'll be back before I go to sleep?

HUGO: Mousey, that depends when you go to sleep. If you doze off in front of *Sex and the City* like usual, you'll be snoring like a little pig when I get home, because I've got loads to do here.

LOUISE: Aha, like usual then. Oh, by the way, I talked to Isabelle today, and I got so annoyed. Do you know what they're doing?

HUGO: No.

LOUISE: They're using Stacek for their renovation.

HUGO: That's good, isn't it? I mean we're using him too.

LOUISE: Exactly, but they're planning on getting him in before us. And they're going to gut the whole place, tutti banutti, Isabelle went on for half an hour about Dornbracht taps, Kvänum kitchens, Gaggenau ovens, limestone in the hallway and recessed spotlights in the ceiling.

HUGO: Good for them, so long as it doesn't overlap with when we were planning on doing our thing.

LOUISE: Our thing, our thing, Hugo, our thing isn't even a thing compared to what they've got planned. We're just changing the kitchen and repainting the bedroom. Our thing is a poor budget version, a cheap joke. I think we should redo the bathroom as well, and at least get the wiring redone. It'll be embarrassing otherwise. Everyone else is redoing everything, and we're just fiddling with the kitchen worktops.

HUGO: Everyone is not redoing everything.

LOUISE: Isabelle and Anders are doing everything, and you know that Ebba and Pierre completely renovated their villa last year, they even built an extension. Anna and Carl-Johan fixed up their entire apartment in London, too. So yes, everyone is doing everything. Except us.

HUGO: But our bathroom's perfect. Why do we need to redo it? The previous owners only renovated it two years ago. They changed everything, every last tile.

LOUISE: You just said it, it's already two years old. It's 2005 now and I hate those terracotta tiles. And the freestanding toilet. No one has freestanding toilets anymore, they need to be fixed to the wall, otherwise you might as well have a compost toilet.

HUGO: But I think we should wait, the place was expensive enough as it was.

LOUISE: Hugo . . .

HUGO: What?

LOUISE: I'm ashamed of our home.

HUGO: Mousey, come on . . .

LOUISE: No, I think it's embarrassing. I barely even want to invite people over when it looks like something out of an Ikea catalogue. Good night.

TELEPHONE CONVERSATION 2

To: Carl Trolle (friend)
From: Hugo Pederson
Date: 23 September 2005
Time: 22:42

HUGO: Hey, man, it's me.

CARL: I can see that. What're you up to?

HUGO: Fixing.

CARL: Mmm.

HUGO: Night shift for me.

CARL: But you love that. I'm at home.

HUGO: I'm not just going to sit still and wait for business, that's hard work. Did you do a half day today?

CARL: Ha, ha, funny. Fredrika's eating out at Teatergrillen with work, so she's probably having a good time, but I . . .

HUGO: You're doing what you do best, I bet. Chafing your palm.

CARL: Honestly though, have you seen Porn Hub? What a site, you can click your way to anything.

HUGO: What'd you say it was called?

CARL: Porn Hub

HUGO: I'll give it a go.

CARL: Now? At work?

HUGO: Nah, I'm not like you.

CARL: We put in an offer on an apartment, by the way.

HUGO: Yeah? Where?

CARL: Kommendörsgatan. Eighteen hundred square feet.

HUGO: What do they want for it?

CARL: Sixty-five thousand per square foot. This city's sick.

HUGO: You need to do anything to it?

CARL: Yeah, of course. Fredrika wants to gut the place, open plan, Carrara in the bathroom, she wants it bright and fresh, etc. It's actually pretty cool.

HUGO: Aha.

CARL: But we don't know if we'll get it.

HUGO: Nah. So you're going big on the renovation.

CARL: Of course, I told you. You've got to. You want to make it your own, you know? You don't just want to move into someone else's world. So I completely understand Fredrika. It's a bit embarrassing not to do it these days, if you ask me. It's not like it's rented.

HUGO: Nah, that's true.

CARL: Exactly.

HUGO: Listen, I've gotta go. Speak later, man. Speak later.

CARL: Ciao.

5

There was a sign above the garage: *Car Wash, Reconditioning—Central and South Stockholm*. On the flags fluttering alongside it: *Unbeatable Prices* and *Rental Cars Available*.

Teddy was in the passenger seat next to Dejan. Dejan's dog, the Mauler, was in the back. They weren't here for the comprehensive car wash or the unbeatable prices, even if Dejan did have a new ride: a Tesla Model X. When he first told Teddy he had ordered the Tesla, Teddy hadn't believed him. "Are you going all eco-warrior in your old age?"

Dejan had replied with dead eyes. "Just wait till you test drive it." There were certain things you just didn't joke about with Dejan: his dog was one of them, his cars another. And his friend had been right about the car, even if it did look like an overgrown Peugeot. The Tesla felt so high-tech inside that it reminded Teddy more of a tablet computer than a car. The falcon wings—or back doors, as they were known to ordinary people—opened upward, like on a Merca SLR, with the one difference that this was a four-wheel drive beast that didn't use a drop of petrol. Craziest of all was one of the settings on the touch screen: *Ludicrous Speed*. The thing could do 0–60 in three seconds flat—without any gears. The sickest part about that experience was the silence—it was like leaping into a precipice, with nothing but the wind in your ears. Teddy's

hand instinctively sought out the handle above the passenger-side
door; he needed to hold on to something, to limit the height of
the fall, and his stomach felt like it was an inch away from being
turned inside out. Dejan, on the other hand, was shouting loudly:
"Whooah!"

When they pulled over in Flemingsberg, his friend had explained:
"It's over one G, apparently. This little beauty accelerates faster than
if we'd fallen out of a plane."

Teddy nodded, swallowed—that explained his near-puking-death
experience. "Maybe I should become a tree hugger, too," he said,
leaning his head back against the headrest. "When I can afford it."

He hoped Dejan would take it a little easier on the way back.

There was no way Dejan's car would fit through the narrow
garage doors, but he was here on a different kind of business.
Teddy was with him for the simple reason that on the kind of
business Dejan wanted to do, you didn't want to be alone. Not
even Dejan. Teddy was his friend's backup. His life insurance. His
parachute. This was just the kind of job with Dejan that Isa from
the employment service didn't want Teddy to take. He understood her. But what was he supposed to do?

They rang the buzzer on the metal garage door. Though it was
only three in the afternoon, darkness had fallen. The *bzzz* sound
was loud: they barely heard the click of the lock—but there was
clearly a surveillance camera above them somewhere. Dejan pulled
open the door, and they walked down the ramp inside.

Concrete floor, Ditec signs on the walls, posters for maintenance products, service packages, equipment, polish, and wax. The
garage was gloomy, and it smelled of exhaust fumes. There were
five cars parked along one wall: battered rust buckets of unflashy
makes. Dejan's space car would have felt uncomfortable inside, like
a prince among paupers, or whatever the expression was. On the
other side, there was a stud wall that formed an internal room,

probably some kind of office space. Otherwise: a hydraulic lift on the floor and plenty of equipment—probably all the kinds of things you needed for this kind of outfit.

But, again, Dejan was here on a different kind of business.

Teddy turned his head, scanned the place. He couldn't see any movement. But then they heard a voice from inside the office. "Dejan, you little Serb, come in."

A man with a neat beard, a hoodie, and sweatpants came out of the office. Teddy felt like a dwarf in comparison, despite being almost six and a half feet tall. He had seen plenty of big guys in his time, in the prison gym, in the circle around Mazern, the task force cops who had crushed him when he was arrested. Guys who worked their asses off on the bench press every day, or who hung from the pull-up bar only to end up with necks that looked like spaghetti in comparison to the lump in front of him now.

Dejan and the giant shook hands. Mumbled to one another. "So where's Abdel Kadir?"

The man led them toward the office. Dejan nodded in the direction of the guy and hissed to Teddy in Serbian: *"Hajduk."*

They stepped into the office. There was another man sitting behind the desk, also dressed in casual sporty clothes. His beard, however, was far from neat; it looked more like it could belong to Santa. He had a white crocheted hat on his head. His name was Abdel Kadir—the Beard Man.

The room was bigger than it looked from the outside, and there was some kind of curtain hanging behind the desk. There were pictures of various cars on the walls, alongside Arabic text. Dejan sat down opposite Abdel Kadir. "It's been a while."

No chairs for Teddy and the giant; they would have to hover in the background.

"Four years. I blew a hundred grand that night, did you know that?" Abdel Kadir's voice was soft, but his eyes were cold. "But I don't gamble anymore. Don't drink, either."

The giant stepped over to the curtain and pulled it to one side. Abdel Kadir held out a hand. "This is the factory."

"Okay, smaller than I thought," said Dejan.

"It doesn't need to be any bigger." Abdel Kadir bared his teeth—he was probably smiling behind his beard. "This is the actual printer," he continued, pointing to one of the machines. "It's not printing the driving licenses that's the difficult thing. What takes experience and skill is achieving the right paper quality." He gestured to the next machine, which was smaller. "That's a holo-gram printer. You'll never have any problems there, it takes care of itself, and no one even checks the holograms on ID cards these days, anyway."

The next piece of equipment was the biggest. "We use this for laminating. No problems here, either." He pointed to the last machine, which looked like an ordinary computer. "Let's put it like this, you could buy the rest of the stuff online for two grand apiece, but what we've got in this box here, that's taken us three years to build up. It's the program and the database. That's what you're paying for."

Dejan ran a finger over the gray lid of the printer. "But it's a package deal. Not just the stuff here, but the other thing we talked about, too. The thing we agreed on."

"Of course. I promised you everything, and you'll get every-thing. Not just the machines and the database. You can take over the payment system, several manuals, all of our contacts, even the chat."

"How's the payment system work?"

"We use *hawala*. It's the most secure."

"*Hawala*? What are you talking about? You'll have the CIA and FRA up your ass at the slightest whiff of a fart. Why don't you just use Forex or Swish or something?"

"The customers deposit the money here, and our *hawala* guy in Dubai makes deposits into our banks, Abu Dhabi Commercial

Bank or Emirates Islamic Bank. The cash never even leaves Sweden, that's the point. *Hawala* is based on trust. It couldn't be any more secure. You understand?"

"What do they take?"

"Five percent in total, three percent to the recipient here, and two to the mother organization in Dubai."

"So I'd have to open an account in Dubai?"

"It's not a problem. Norwegian flies there for four thousand return. You don't even need to stay overnight."

Dejan mumbled something that Teddy didn't catch. The mood had turned; Dejan was annoyed about something. The gorilla frowned. Abdel Kadir, on the other hand, seemed oblivious to the shift—he held up a stack of papers and talked about the advantages of the *hawala* system. If the deal went through, the Beard would soon have 1.2 million reasons to be happy.

Teddy couldn't help but think of Nikola. On the whole, things seemed to be going well for his nephew. He would soon be an electrician and might be able to keep raising his grades on the side. Going forward, he might even be able to apply to university. But sometimes, it was as though Nikola couldn't quite be happy that his life was on the right track. Maybe it was the explosion—he was different somehow, like he had developed a hard shell inside himself. And Emelie? She was hard inside, too. All Teddy knew was that she was running her own law firm these days. He had tried calling her a few times after the Emanuelsson trial. He had even sent her a letter. She never replied. He didn't know why. It wasn't like they needed to get married and live the rest of their lives together. But they could have gone on a few dates, hung out a bit over the summer? Now it was like they had entered something that would never reach any kind of conclusion.

Dejan spun on his chair and turned toward Abdel Kadir. "Why are you selling up, if everything's so damn good?"

The Beard Man got up. "I've made plenty of money from this. It's time to move on. I'm going abroad."

"Where?"

"Doesn't matter. I'm not the same man I was four years ago. I've found my real self."

"*Zakat*, what's that?"

Abdel Kadir breathed out through his nose, making his mustache flutter. "What difference does it make?"

"I'm looking at a receipt here, from Dubai. Three percent plus two percent, you said, but then there's 2.5 percent *zakat*. The hell's that?"

Even the Beard paused now: the atmosphere was terrible. The corners of his mouth turned down. The gorilla's eyes darted back and forth between Dejan and Teddy, as though he were following a tennis match in aggression.

Abdel Kadir got to his feet. "You ask too many pointless questions, my friend."

Dejan followed him up. "You told me you paid three percent to the middleman here in Sweden and two percent to the guy in the desert. Then I see another two point five percent."

"Let me explain, rather than you shouting."

"I'm not shouting." Dejan took a step toward Abdel Kadir, both men breathing through their noses now.

"*Zakat* means alms."

"And what are alms?"

"A donation, a gift. It's a Muslim thing, nothing you'll have to pay."

"So where does this donation go?"

"Religious organizations, but that doesn't affect you, kafir. There's no need to worry."

Dejan's nostrils flared. The hissing sound of his breathing was like someone frying meat. Abdel Kadir glared. Things were close to getting out of hand now.

Teddy moved forward, closer. The gorilla followed him with his gaze. Took a step forward himself. Teddy tensed. His fingers reached for the spring coil baton Dejan had handed him in the car.

This was *exactly* the kind of job Isa *didn't* want him to take.

Every movement now: he saw everything.

The gorilla's hand on something inside his hoodie.

Dejan moving jerkily.

Abdel Kadir positioning his feet farther apart.

Damn it.

"Abdel, I liked you better when you drank, gambled, and did drugs. I'm not going to ask what kind of organizations you've been financing, but let me say this: I'm not interested in doing business with bearded cunts."

Dejan turned on his heel and left. Teddy followed him.

He didn't breathe out until they were back on the street.

"You need to chill out," Teddy said to Dejan once they were back in the car.

"Why should I chill out?"

"Because that could've ended really badly."

"Listen, Teddy. I've been a thief all my life. I've burnt down restaurants and set cars on fire. I've imported everything you could imagine. I've kidnapped people and beaten people to a pulp. But that doesn't mean I don't have honor. Not like those bearded guys: they don't know what right and wrong are. Because God knows one thing: everyone I've ever fucked up has deserved it."

"Even Mats Emanuelsson? Who you and I kidnapped?"

Dejan's hands were relaxed on the wheel. "That was over ten years ago, and Emanuelsson was a money launderer and criminal. If you're in the game, you know the rules. But I'm still sorry you had to do eight years for it."

They drove by enormous advertising boards for newly built residential areas. *Dalénum, Unum, Lyceum—modern design, high ceilings and bespoke kitchens. A unique place to live.* But if all these luxury apartments were unique, why did they all have roughly the same name? Teddy himself lived in Alby, which was where he was heading now. Home.

His phone started to ring. He glanced down at the display: Emelie.

He hesitated, wondering whether he should answer. She didn't give in—the display kept flashing: *Emelie cell.* It tore at his eyes, ears, and fingers.

Dejan turned toward him. "You gonna answer that?"

He really wanted to.

And yet he rejected the call. "Nah, it's nothing important."

6

Weekend hang: Nikola and Chamon were having lunch at Steak-house Bar. Nikola went for a burger. Chamon cut his New York strip into three equal chunks.

"You going to the gym later?"

Nikola swallowed his food before he replied in Chamon's own language. "Bro, you won't be up to it. What you do doesn't count as eating. You just make the meat disappear from the plate by opening your mouth three times. You can't work out for at least five hours after that."

Chamon laughed. "In that case we can just chill, Biblosh."

Biblosh—that was his nickname among the boys. It sounded weird, like he was some kind of religious nut, but he knew where it came from. He knew their language, and they thought he spoke Syriac like someone from the old books. Biblosh, the Bible Man: that was him—a Swede with Serbian roots who had grown up in a neighborhood where everyone spoke Arabic and Syriac. Their language was his.

They climbed out of Chamon's car outside the gym.

Nikola felt something he didn't want to feel. The tiny Spider-Man tingles came first: the headache. He grabbed his forehead.

Chamon recognized the gesture. "Painful?"

It was cool of Chamon to ask. The headaches were one of the aftereffects of *what happened:* the explosion. That shit was still attacking him. The doctors said that everything had healed— everything but this, which came back at regular intervals. Which sometimes thundered away like a death metal band had taken up residence in his skull and decided to split open his head from the inside.

The police had shut down the bomb investigation after just a few months. *No leads have been made. Illegal activity cannot be ruled out,* they wrote in the letter they sent to Nikola, as though nothing criminal had even happened. Chamon had snorted when he found out. "Unexpected, man. The pigs have never made an effort when it comes to you. Except when they wanted to put you behind bars." Maybe his friend was right. But somewhere, deep down, Nikola hoped that they would have looked at him differently if it happened today.

As they walked toward the entrance to the gym, it was as though the tingling feeling in his forehead turned into small lightning bolts. Like a tiny voice was trying to tell him something, but he couldn't understand what.

He opened the heavy door. Heard the familiar sound of groans, shouts, and feet on mats.

All Training MMA. Basement gym. Temple of violence. Fighting Mecca with a capital "M." The floor was soft, the concrete walls painted white. Punch bags and balls hanging from the ceiling. Mitts, fight gloves, and jump ropes by the entrance. Mixed martial arts was almost as big as football here: the real sport of the people.

There were teenage boys grappling on the floor. A coach in sweatpants and a hoodie who looked like Snoop Dogg was hovering around them, giving instruction. The principle was simple: use the laws of physics and the build of your body to do as much damage to your opponent as possible. Sweat, adrenaline, and blood. A sociologist with enough interest and a keen sense of smell could have written an entire thesis on the scents and the guys in these parts—forced to fight their way through life.

Chamon and Nikola sat down against the wall at the very back of the gym. There was a mini version of the octagon set up, with bars, ads for various fighting brands and everything. But it was empty—the kids were panting on the floor outside of it today.

"I think Yusuf's coming," said Chamon.

"Sweet, haven't seen him in months."

"Yep, and you know, he's practically a bodyguard for the boss these days. And Isak's nephew trains here, so maybe Mr. One'll come down, too."

Nikola tried to play cool. He occasionally saw Yusuf, who often gave Chamon jobs. But Isak.

The myth. The legend. The icon. Isak: the role model for everyone who knew that Tony Montana was living and thriving in Sweden. He just went by a different name: ISAK.

Then the lightning came back. The piercing, blinding pain in Nikola's head. And the little voice started shouting again. What the hell was this? This ringing. The white glow. Like he was scared. It sounded like it was longing for fresh air, to get away from here.

They turned up after an hour and a half, probably crazy late. Chamon didn't complain.

Yusuf greeted them like usual, a hugged thump on the back and a laugh. Isak nodded almost imperceptibly and winked. He was wearing Adidas pants and a North Face coat—looked like any other dude. Still, the fighters stared at Mr. One like God himself had come down into the temple of sweat.

"Nicko, Biblosh." Yusuf spoke with his usual drawling, unclear voice. "You're an electrician now, right?"

Nikola glanced at Mr. One. Maybe he thought Nikola had

betrayed them by no longer working for Yusuf and, indirectly, him. That he had abandoned the family.

"No, not yet. Almost, though, maybe next week, and I've got my grades up, too."

Isak took a step closer. His voice was hoarse. "Grades? You're gonna get a real job afterward, right?"

"I don't know. Being an electrician's cool."

Isak raised his voice slightly. "Nah, like hell it is. I want to see you becoming a lawyer or a professor or a doctor or something. Believe me, man, leave this shit behind if you can. You might as well."

"But being an electrician's a good job, and it's not easy . . ."

"Nothing's easy. But you've always liked reading, haven't you? Your uncle did, anyway. How is Björne these days, by the way?"

Isak and Teddy: friends from *waaaaay* back. Nikola didn't know anyone else who called him Björne—Bear. He didn't know whether they had seen one another during the past ten years, either while Teddy was inside or afterward. But still.

"He's doing good, I guess," said Nikola. "But I think he needs a woman."

Isak opened his mouth and exploded into a fit of laughter. He was bent double, spitting saliva, laughing so hard that he was about to suffocate. "Tell him I said hi, in that case," the boss panted between guffaws. "And if he wants a woman, he'll have to come to Vegas next time. The hookers over there are out of this world."

After a while, Isak, Yusuf, and Chamon went into some kind of office.

Nikola stayed where he was, watching the others. Some of them were pretty good. The bad vibes were still bothering him— his blinding headache was still lingering. He didn't know why Mr. One and his boys were taking so long in there.

Not long later, three men came down the steps. Chamon was still in the office with Yusuf and Isak. Nikola wondered what they were doing in there. The guys had no bags or backpacks with them, so they probably weren't here to train. Their hoods were up, and they had a kind of *stiff* way of walking.

One of them opened his mouth: "Ey, whores, where are they?"

The guys on the floor stopped; they were fighters—not exactly used to being talked to like that. Then Nikola saw it: the three guys' arms were relaxed. Each of them had a weapon in his hand.

DACHRI.

The kids on the mats didn't understand a thing. "Who d'you mean?"

But the new arrivals weren't interested in any more talk. They headed straight for the door of the little office—the room where Chamon, Isak, and Yusuf were having their meeting.

Nikola shouted as loudly as he could, "What are you doing?"

The door opened, and Chamon stuck out his head—his eyes widened. He saw the three men. Fifteen feet away.

It was too late.

Chamon took a step forward. The men stopped.

Chamon, completely unafraid: "Who're you, fatty? And what do you think you're doing?"

Nikola could see now, his friend also had something in his hand. It was a Glock.

The guys on the mat had gotten up; they were all staring. The sweat glistened on their faces. A few backed away. They might be tough in the ring, but right now they didn't have the balls to do *nada.* Just like Nikola.

Chamon aimed the Glock. Nikola hadn't realized that his friend carried a gun.

The guy at the front pulled a face. His pistol was still hanging by his leg. Probably surprised that Chamon had pulled out his own piece so quickly.

Chamon was glaring. There was zero chance this would end well. The guy at the very front didn't back down: his eyes were as dark as a fucking elevator shaft in a power outage.

Chamon took another step forward. Nikola saw one of the other guys twitch.

Bad move by Chamon.

Nikola shouted: "Watch out!"

But it was Chamon who fired. The shot sounded like an atomic bomb in the gym.

The guy who had been trying to raise his weapon threw himself to one side.

Nikola leaped forward, tried to punch the guy at the front in the stomach. It was like hitting a tree—he must have been wearing a flak vest under his hoodie. The fighters on the mats had started running now. Where was Yusuf? Where was Isak? Were they just hiding out in the office?

The noise was insane—Chamon fired his Glock again.

But the guy at the front had also had time to pull out his weapon.

BAM.

Chamon didn't shout. He didn't make a sound. He just fell, back into the office.

As though in slow motion. Like some C-rated action film. The others just stared like wild monkeys.

Yusuf and Isak came rushing out now. Yusuf was waving a pistol. Yelling at the intruders to clear off, that they were going to die, that he would fuck their mothers.

The guys backed away, up the stairs.

Nikola leaned forward, saw it clearly now: Chamon was on the floor.

His jaw. It wasn't there anymore.

The bottom section of his friend's face was gone.

Nikola squatted down.

In the background, everyone was shouting.

He didn't dare lift Chamon up. He just took his hand.

Tried to hold his gaze.

Come on, man, don't leave me now.

I want to do something else sometime.

Chamon's own words.

I want to do something else sometime.

Brother.

Don't die on me.

Please.

7

Emelie couldn't understand why he wasn't answering. She had called Teddy at least fifteen times over the past few hours, and he had rejected her every single time. She needed to talk to him—it was about the meeting she had just had with Katja, the young woman who had called the office.

It had all happened so quickly. She thought about how the intercom had buzzed and a soft voice had asked if she could come up. It struck Emelie that she hadn't asked Katja her surname. She should have taken it down, if for no other reason than to check for conflicts of interest. Katja could be the partner of an existing client, for example, or feature in some other case.

Marcus had been there, working over the weekend—a good lawyer; he was sitting with a fraud charge in which the prosecutor had, among other things, cited what he called general evidence to show that their client had previously engaged in identity theft. "It should be possible to get that evidence thrown out," Emelie had told him. "It's got nothing to do with the current charge, and that's not okay, in my eyes. Dig up everything you can find, all precedence and doctrine relating to Chapter 35 of the Penal Code. Then I want your own views and recommendations, too."

Emelie had heard the door open out in reception, followed by Marcus greeting someone. Almost immediately, Emelie's phone had rung: "They're here now."

" 'They'?"

"Yeah, she's here with someone. They don't even want to take off their coats and sit down to wait. Real gems, if you ask me."

The young woman was wearing a short leather jacket that looked like it belonged in another decade. There was a man in the seat next to her. His worn denim jacket looked like it had once had a number of patches sewn onto it—there were darker areas of material on the arms and the back. He kept glancing around as though he was expecting an ambush of some kind. Emelie had wondered if he was the girl's father; he looked like he must be in his midforties. The girl's eyes were mostly fixed on the floor; she was clearly uncertain.

Emelie had held out a hand to her. "Hi, you must be Katja."

The young girl had looked up. Her skin was so pale and thin that Emelie thought she could make out the blood vessels beneath it.

The man had stepped between them and held out a hand. "Yes, this is Katja. And I'm Adam. Boyfriend, cohabitee, fiancé. Many names to many people, if you like. Thanks for seeing us so quickly."

Emelie had noticed that he had incredibly small teeth. Adam, like a little rodent—a rat.

They crowded into Emelie's office. She was on one side of the desk, with Katja and Adam opposite her, and Marcus at the very end. "This is my assistant lawyer, Marcus Engvall. I thought he might join us."

Katja had glanced at Adam, and when she opened her mouth to speak, Emelie had realized that they were the first words she had uttered since they arrived. "It's all so sensitive. I would rather not have any outsiders involved."

Emelie had cleared her throat. "Marcus is absolutely not an outsider. He works for me and is subject to the same rules of confidentiality as I am. But, if you feel uncomfortable, it isn't a problem."

Adam had placed a hand on Katja's arm. "Nah, we don't want to cause any trouble. He can stay."

Emelie had turned to Katja. "*You*'re the one who decides."

The young woman's voice was almost inaudible. "It's fine by me."

"Okay, then. What did you want to tell me?"

The same silence as when they had spoken on the phone. Katja had glanced at Adam. Neither of them said anything, but Emelie had studied her body language: her shoulders were hunched, practically up to her ears; her fingers were drumming the table, her breathing irregular.

"Or would you rather I asked you some questions?"

Katja had closed her eyes for a few seconds. "No, it's fine. I want to do this myself." She moved her hands into her lap. "The police want to interview me. But I don't want to be interviewed."

She fell silent again. Adam had taken her hand and held it in his own, wrapping his fingers around her little fist. "You need to start from the beginning, you know that."

It almost seemed like she was gasping for air. "It's not easy, it's really not. I'm not used to talking about it."

"It's okay. Go at your own speed," Emelie had told her. "And start however you like."

It looked like Katja wanted curl up in the fetal position on the floor. But, instead, she started to talk.

"Okay, it was just over ten years ago. I was thirteen and I was difficult, I had all kinds of problems, was taken into care and put in a home. Then, through . . . someone who I . . . who I . . . trusted, I was put in touch with a man who made a suggestion. We would meet, and I would be given money."

Katja had paused. It looked like Adam was squeezing her hand.

She went on: "The man was friendly and pretty gentle when we met, but he was allowed to do whatever he wanted. He gave me five hundred kronor afterward. That was a lot of money to me at the time, and I didn't really think about what had just happened—

some of the other girls at the home did similar stuff and they talked about it all the time, almost like they were boasting. The man got in touch again after a few weeks, and we met for a second time. I saw him several times after that, and on one occasion he asked if it would be okay if one of his friends came along. I agreed to it because I thought I'd get paid more."

Katja had trailed off and glanced at Adam. "I was so young, but no one understood. It's hard to explain."

"You don't need to explain," Emelie told her.

"It was like they took my sense of self away. And I've never found it again."

Katja's eyes were fixed on the window behind Emelie.

Adam said: "Keep going, now. I'm sure the lawyer doesn't have all day."

She had taken a deep breath. "After that, I said I didn't want to do it anymore, that they'd gone too far, but then he said he would tell my mom, the staff at the home, my dad. I didn't care about the staff, and I might not even have cared about my mom, plus my dad was dead. But I really didn't want my grandma and grandad, who were still alive at the time, to find out. I knew I couldn't cope with that—so I kept quiet. Didn't say a word to anyone. I met the man and his friends again and again that year. I can't tell you what they did to me, because I don't have the words for that. It was like I was living in a fog, I started smoking hash and heroin, I tried to kill myself, ran away from the home four times. But it kept happening.

"By the end of that year, I had a breakdown, I just remember crying on the bathroom floor. The man seemed worried that I'd tell someone, that I wouldn't manage to keep quiet about what they'd done to me. He told me that they had filmed me several times, and then he showed me a clip of myself. He said: 'If you don't stop screaming, we'll upload this to the Internet so everyone can see what a little slut you are.'

"Eventually, I was moved to another home, up in Norrland this time. It was probably a sheer coincidence, or maybe the staff could see that Stockholm was no good for me. Anyway, it was a real stroke of luck. I say luck, but maybe it would've been better if I'd ended my life then."

Katja had met Emelie's gaze for the first time. Her eyes looked almost transparent. "Someone handed in a hard drive full of the films they made to the police. The police tried to work out who was in those awful videos, and somehow they managed to identify me, even though I was only thirteen at the time. Now they want me to go in and talk about all this, but all I've done these past ten years is try to forget."

Emelie had felt herself shiver, and she hoped that neither Katja nor Adam nor Marcus had noticed. A hard drive full of abuse. It sounded all too familiar. The hard drive had first come to light during the Benjamin Emanuelsson case and had eventually been handed over to the police by Benjamin's father, Mats. She and Teddy had dug as deep into that horror as they could, but they had never managed to find out exactly who was behind it, had never managed to come up with any names. They had never managed to work out who was involved in the group of men who had abused girls and forced Mats Emanuelsson into a life on the run. But now the police had clearly had a breakthrough.

That had made her think about the fact that she hadn't heard from Teddy in more than a year. After everything that had happened, the two of them had actually tried dating. They had just finished a meal in a restaurant and were probably about to head back to her place when she had asked the question that was still whirling around her mind: "Teddy, are you going to get a normal job now, after Leijon?"

"I don't know."

But she kept pressing him. "Are you going to change now?"

He had wiped his mouth with his napkin. When he spoke, his voice was barely audible, but the content of what he said was clear. "Tell me what you mean."

"I mean, are you going to be civilized?"

"Believe me, Emelie. Ever since I got out, I've been trying to make it in society. But no, I'm never going to *change* who I am."

Emelie had wiped her mouth, too. Then she had asked for the bill. It was the last time they had seen one another.

Back in the office, she had turned to Katja. "I actually know quite a bit about this case."

"I know."

"Why did you call me, of all people?"

Katja had made a pained groan. "Because when I told the police I didn't want to go in and talk to them, they said I could have a lawyer to help me, a counsel for the injured party. And you're the person they recommended."

Emelie had tried to smile. "Well, that explains it. The police know that I'm already relatively up to speed on this. And I know it's difficult to bring up all these old memories, Katja, but it might actually do you good to talk to the police, to help them find the people responsible for hurting you so badly, those pigs."

Emelie immediately regretted using those last words—she had never been good at expressing herself.

Adam had cleared his throat. "No, we don't think Katja should testify. She's already suffered enough from what they did to her."

Emelie had leaned forward. "As it happens, there's an obligation to give evidence in Sweden, so the decision isn't entirely yours. But I do completely understand your situation, Katja. Let's look into it, and see whether there's any way to make things easier for you."

She had glanced at Marcus, who nodded.

Adam got to his feet. Katja followed him.

"I think it's best if we leave now, so the lawyers can work in peace. The police want to talk to Katja soon, possibly even on Monday, so there's a bit of a rush to work out how she should handle this, if I can put it like that." Adam had bent down and placed a business card on the desk.

They shook hands. The whole thing felt so abrupt. Emelie didn't even have time to follow them out.

She had turned to Marcus, who handed her Adam's business card. She studied it.

Adam Tagrin
K Tagrin Import AB
0733-56 89 00
- *Making pleasure easy* -

Before Emelie had time to do anything, Marcus had held up his phone.

The crack was like a shadow over the text, but she could still clearly read what was on the home page Marcus had found.

K Tagrin Import AB
Adult films and erotic events

"Porn," said Marcus. "That bastard owns a company that deals in porn."

And it was then that Emelie heard a name echo through her mind. The name of someone she needed to talk to now.

Teddy.

8

After dinner, Roksana helped to clear the table. Caspar was back in front of the TV. Dad was still sitting at the table, not helping. If he was feeling like Mom said he was, then he was excused. Her mother brought out the bowl of fruit that was always carefully organized: oranges at the bottom, then apples, and grapes on top.

"Is that organic fruit?"

"I don't know, but they're Kishmish grapes, from Iran."

"I think you should have a better idea of what you're buying."

Her father cleared his throat. "So what is the course you're taking now called?"

Roksana didn't have the energy for another round of this, but she told him the truth. "It's called Gender, Power, and Ethnicity."

"Aha, and what kind of job can you get after that course?"

Roksana didn't reply. She couldn't argue with him. He was fifty-eight. That was too young to have stopped working, too young to spend all day at home, doing nothing. Dedication to his job with the council had been his pride and joy, ever since Mom and Dad arrived in Sweden in 1985, Roksana knew that. Work first. Always.

"I could have become an engineer here," he said, as though he wanted to move on to a new topic. "It would've been better for my back."

Roksana knew that, too. Baba had been studying to become a civil engineer at university in Tehran, but he'd had to pause his studies when they fled. When the shah fell, they had believed in a better society. But the fundamentalists had won, and Dad never graduated.

Roksana went over to the kitchen counter and started looking through his cassette tapes. The labels were faded, but she knew what was on them all the same: Googoosh, Dariush, Vigen. All old men and women, but Roksana still liked them. "You know all this is on Spotify now? We can throw away these tapes."

Her father glared at her. He got up and grabbed one of the tapes: the BASF logo on the side wasn't even visible any longer, they were so well used. "Are you crazy? These are sacred. You don't touch my cassettes."

They filled the dishwasher. Mom served more tea. Roksana placed a bowl of pistachios in front of Caspar.

"Roksy, they're right."

"Huh?"

"You would get into the psychology course if you made an effort."

She sat down next to him without replying. Her thoughts were drifting again, back to a few days earlier.

Thirty milligrams, maybe, no more than that. Z had spent ten minutes searching online forums before he worked out the right amount. They had each helped themselves to a hit and then snorted it—like some kind of super potent coke. That was how you did it, according to the Internet, if you didn't want to take it orally or intravenously. Roksana had tried E and speed a few times before; they both made her jittery and gave her a creative feeling, but there were things she would rather take. It was four thirty in the morning.

The first effects had appeared only a few minutes later.

At first, it had felt just like E, only a little softer and cozier: Roksana's body faded away and the sofa started to feel endlessly soft, like she was sinking and sinking into the cushions, and both Billie and Z immediately seemed to be a few yards away from her, then tens of yards, then the room stretched out and her body felt like jelly, like soft, warm slime, and for a brief moment she was worried she would panic, but then she didn't know whether her eyes were open or closed, and everything felt flexible, the wall, the door into the kitchen, and the balcony doors floated together to become one great big swirling, twinkling light that blinked in time with her heart in rhythm with her entire being and with Billie and Z and the cosmos like a light, which grew stronger and stronger and eventually filled her entire field of vision and she couldn't see anything but its white glow and she wanted to go over there, she wanted to swim in the air through the tunnel of light and she was on her way through the end of life and maybe she was about to die but at the same time she knew she was going with the flow and then she saw Billie again upside down in negative in black-and-white and then she was no longer in the apartment, she was upside down below the balcony on the frozen grass but there was nothing wrong with that because the chill was cozy and warm and she melted into the ground and became part of the earth and the roots and Z started to laugh and said that Roksana looked like an elk though he himself looked like an apple, a green and glossy apple, and she just laughed and Z laughed and Billie laughed and it felt so good that they were all just laughing without feeling like she needed to fit in and without all the rules to follow and Roksana rolled around on the sofa and said "can we draw something?" and Billie suggested they draw robots because they were robots and then Roksana realized why Baba never threw her up in the air the way she had seen other dads do when she was a child, and then the peak was over and Roksana had sat up on the sofa and everyone had laughed, she had tried to get up but was so unsteady that she sat down again.

Ten minutes later, they had been back to normal. Z was sitting with his phone in his hand, Googling, searching. "I just had the trip of the year," he said.

Billie got to her feet. She hadn't been unsteady at all. "That was the best thing I've felt. *Ever.*"

When Roksana got back from her parents' house, Z was watching a documentary about Lance Armstrong's rise and fall on his computer. Z was like that—he liked learning, possessing a surprising amount of knowledge about a narrow subject. People saw it as a good thing. Ironic nerdery.

"Have you eaten? I've got some food from Mom and Dad's if you want it."

"You're kidding, that's great. Is it lamb stew or vegetarian?"

"Ghormeh sabzi, Mom's original, not my vegetarian one."

"Best food on earth. I'd love some."

Roksana sat down next to him on the sofa. She thought back to their recent find. They had rebuilt the fake wall in the closet and hidden the bags of ketamine behind it—though they deliberately hadn't driven in the nails very far.

After a while, she and Z switched to a different documentary, which was essentially just a long interview with Susan Sontag. *"What pornography is really about, ultimately, isn't sex but death,"* Sontag said. Though she was Jewish, she actually looked very Persian.

"I feel like going to Dusky," said Z.

Roksana knew of the illegal club: it was huge and had taken place several times now, out in the Ulvsunda industrial estate. "Atmospheric and always innovative," Billie had said. They often had sweet headline DJs. Exclusive guest lists—it was the Ora Flesh collective behind the event. Ora Flesh: the twenty-two-year-old model who was married to the photographer with the full beard and ADHD, who had praised the Bagarmossen area in his latest art project—which was as right as it could be.

"Yeah, me too," said Roksana. "But I wasn't invited."

"Me neither. Maybe Billie can help? Could you give her a call? Tell her we'll bring some of the fun powder for her to try again."

"The really important thing is not to reject anything," Susan Sontag said on-screen.

Roksana pulled out her phone. She had to think about what she was going to say to Billie. How she could make the degradation of begging seem like something completely different.

9

Evening now, on the way home from a job with Dejan. Teddy was in his own car.

"Yeah, hello?" he answered, his voice deliberately expectant. This was probably the twentieth time Emelie had called him today. This time, he didn't reject her call—he had to satisfy his curiosity, even if he was disappointed in her.

"Hi, it's me."

"Yeah, I can see and hear that. Oddly enough I still have your number saved. Why are you bothering me?"

He stepped on the accelerator. Though he had recently used the wipers to wash it, the windshield was dirty. For some reason, it was constantly being flecked with dirty drops of liquid, even though it wasn't raining and the closest car was at least fifty yards ahead. It was a mystery, as though the dirty water on the road were trying to get to him but was thwarted by the glass on its way.

"Teddy, something's happened."

He lifted his foot from the accelerator. He didn't want to lose the driving license he had only recently regained—he had been without one for ten years and was happy that Dejan had been willing to step up as his instructor.

"What's going on?"

Emelie said: "We need to meet."

He was close to stamping on the brakes now. "Why?"

"I don't want to get into it over the phone. Can we meet? It could be about our old case."

Teddy had made up his mind to avoid digging any deeper in anything to do with the Emanuelsson family. He and Emelie had done what they could and then some. Everyone had thought that Mats—the man Teddy and Dejan had kidnapped ten years earlier—had killed himself, but when a mutilated body was found out in the Värmdö woods eighteen months earlier, Mats Emanuelsson's son, Benjamin, had found himself suspected of murder. Teddy and Emelie had eventually found out that Mats was actually alive but that he had been forced into hiding because of what he knew about a child abuse ring. They had even established that certain police officers had been involved in preventing the truth from coming out. Eventually, Mats had had no choice but to show his face in order to stop his son from being convicted, and that was when he had handed the hard drive of abuse over to the police. In the end, Teddy and Emelie had failed to track down any of those responsible. The trail had gone cold with a man who called himself Peder Hult. The men were still out there somewhere. They might still be doing it.

Despite that, Teddy had come up with a principle around the whole case: everything has its time—and he wasn't going to look back. Enough was enough.

And yet he also heard his own voice replying to Emelie now, as though it were coming from someone else: "I'm on my way. Now."

Half an hour later, he was standing outside a wooden door on the second floor of an old building on Hantverkargatan. There were four nameplates: Martin Koor Law Firm, Kjell Ahlblom Legal Services, Sami Gutierrez Law Firm, and, finally, Emelie Jansson Legal Services. Teddy wondered why they didn't have a joint name, like *one* single company.

Emelie opened the door the minute he buzzed, as though she had been waiting for him on the other side. Her office was almost completely dark, but he couldn't help but notice how attractively she moved. The way she pushed her hair behind her ears with her middle and ring fingers. How she shifted her weight from one foot to the other, making it look like she was rocking to some internal rhythm.

They didn't hug.

Only the desk lamp was switched on in her office, and there was a half-eaten box of sushi at one end of the desk. At the other, she had a computer screen and a keyboard. Other than a notepad and a couple of pens, that was all.

"So this is your new office? Why don't you have more artwork on the walls?" he tried to joke as he sat down. What he really wanted to know was how she was, how running her own law firm was going. Whether she had met anyone who was a better fit for her life than him.

Emelie turned to one side, not looking at him as she spoke. "Now's not the time, Teddy. I'm going to be representing a woman who was abused by *them*."

She told him about Katja.

"So I was wondering if you could help me. Because I have the feeling she's going to need a lot of support."

The office fell silent. The sound of a bus struggling up Hantverkargatan made its way in through the window.

"Emelie, isn't it better to let the police do their job?"

"They haven't exactly done all that well so far—they've had those films for over a year now. Plus, it was probably this Peder Hult man who tried to blow up you and your apartment eighteen months ago, when Nikola got hurt."

The Mats Emanuelsson case, Teddy thought, it followed him through life. So Katja was one of the girls abused by the predators.

There was something steely in Emelie's eye. "You have to help me, Teddy. Help me pick up where we left off."

"Why me?"

"You know people I can't reach otherwise. You can do things

I can't. I know you want to move on with your life, and I respect that. But we never found the people who were really behind all this. The people who hurt your nephew. We gave up halfway."

Teddy knew now what he had seen in Emelie's eyes. She had no intention of giving in.

But him?

Would he?

10

Small metal dispensers of hand sanitizer everywhere. A mecca for drunks: go to the hospital, take an empty bottle and a pump. Get yourself wasted on disinfectant. Free is good.

Nikola made his way in. The automatic doors whirred continuously. There was a line at the information desk. The color codings on the walls were harder to read than if they were written in Amharic.

When he and Yusuf had arrived with Chamon three days earlier, he had watched them wheel his friend away and close the doors. "Only relatives allowed, I'm afraid." No one knew what was going to happen—the image of Chamon's broken face on repeat. The sound of his gurgling on a loop.

But now Nikola was back.

The robotic woman's voice in the elevator announced that he had reached the third floor. Nikola checked the signs. Ward 345. This was the right place; Chamon's dad had told Nikola where Chamon was—otherwise, he never would have known.

The doors into the ward swung open with a whirring sound. Chamon had been transferred from intensive care to a normal ward, meaning you could just walk straight in. Nikola wondered what the police and the hospital knew about how Chamon had really sustained his injuries—he hadn't said a thing, in any case, and he seriously doubted anyone else from the gym would have, either. The golden rule: no talking to the pigs.

The hallway was full of medical equipment on carts. The clusters of doctors and nurses in Birkenstocks and green hospital scrubs seemed mostly to be chilling. The bluish plastic floor was polished and reflected almost everything going on in the hallway. In the distance, there was a sign with a crossed-out cell phone.

Nikola stepped inside. He didn't know which room Chamon was in, but he could just look around, he thought. One of Isak's guys was supposed to be keeping watch outside, but he could also be in the room itself.

The ward smelled like boiled potato. An older man with a bandage over his mouth was shuffling down the corridor, looking really creepy—like a mummy who had come alive in one of the operating rooms. But the old man also reminded him of Bojan, his grandfather. Lately, he had also started dragging his feet, as though he didn't have the energy to walk. It meant that he sounded different when he moved, more shuffling, sluggish, a trudging style that didn't seem right. Grandpa was a strongman—or at least that was how Nikola had always thought of him.

A nurse hurried past. There was a red light blinking above one of the doors farther down the hallway. In all likelihood: I need help taking a shit, I need help turning over in bed, I need someone to jerk me off—because I can't manage it myself.

"Hi, sorry, I'm looking for Chamon Hanna," said Nikola.

The nurse replied: "Turn left over there, then it's the second room on the right. But I think he's asleep right now."

The door had an extra-large handle, or at least that was how it felt. Nikola stepped inside: the lightning had started flashing in his head. He needed to stop; maybe he would have to sit down. Flashbacks from the room where he had been bed bound after the explosion. The bluish-gray curtains over the window, the glass of juice on the table next to the bed. His mother's anxious glances from the armchair in the corner. He had to cover his eyes with his hand. Get away from the memories: the lightning. Then he looked up, focused on *this* room. On Chamon. His friend's face was bandaged, with dressings covering his chin—probably from the operation, and there were bruises around his nose and on his cheeks. His gold chain and cross were missing from around his neck—Nikola wondered what had happened to them. The bed's wheels were locked, and there was a drip stand to one side, its tubes leading directly into Chamon's arm. His friend probably couldn't eat.

Nikola sat down in the only chair. Chamon seemed to be sleeping. Gym redux: the shouts from the bastards who had attacked, the crack of the pistol shot. Chamon's jaw in pieces, hyperventilating. The blood on the wall. Nikola's own heart rate at 180. The fragments of bone that had caught on his sweater.

Then it hit Nikola, like a bomb. WTF—there was no one here. There was no one keeping watch on the ward. No one sitting either outside or here in the room. Anyone could walk right in, just like he had. His friend wouldn't even wake up before someone had time to do something. The nurses outside wouldn't have time to notice that anything had happened.

Nikola pulled out his phone and called Yusuf. No answer. He sent a message: *Am with C now. Why's there no one here keeping an eye on him? Send someone. Bello or whoever. /N*

Bello was a good guy. When they were in high school, he, Nikola, and Chamon used to drive hot ATVs down by Igelstaviken. Nikola didn't know what his real name was; everyone just called him Bello—and no one seemed to remember why.

He waited a few minutes. Chamon was quiet. Nikola leaned in toward him. Was his friend breathing? He couldn't hear anything. He leaned even closer, tried to listen. Look. Feel.

He saw Chamon's chest rising. Slowly upward. Slowly downward. Good.

His phone beeped. A reply from Yusuf: *I was there before, it seemed cool.*

Nikola wrote: *Someone should still be here.*

The reply came a few seconds later: *They were probably after Mr. 1. Not C.*

Nikola understood his point: no one was after Chamon; that seemed logical. But still. He took out his phone again. Wrote to a few guys. After ten minutes, he had managed to get ahold of Isak's private number. He called it—the first time he had ever contacted Mr. One directly.

The ring signal sounded like it was coming from abroad. "The king speaking," the boss eventually answered.

"Isak," Nikola spoke in Syriac. "I'm at the hospital with my boy."

"How's he doing?"

"I don't know. He's alive. They've operated on him."

"I heard. Thank God. He's got a present waiting for him."

Nikola had heard about that. Isak had sent a curved, seventy-eight-inch Samsung to Chamon's place—the sickest TV on the market—but what was his friend going to do with that right now, while he was stuck here?

"Listen, Isak, there's something that doesn't seem right."

"What?"

Nikola went over to the window. How should he put it to Mr. One, without making a mistake? Without being disrespectful. Down below, he could see the main entrance into the hospital. There were people everywhere. This was probably Stockholm's biggest hospital: pensioners, immigrant families; tired, broken people who might not really need to be here. But the people he could see still didn't feel like a representative sample of Sweden—they were what Grandpa called *radnička klasa,* the working class. Where were the others? Where were the inner-city people and the brats? Maybe they had their own hospitals now, or maybe they just didn't get ill quite so often.

Nikola said what was on his mind. "Isak, there's no one here keeping watch. Anyone could get in."

"Ah shit, that's no good. I'll send someone."

It sounded like Isak was eating something—the chewing noise was almost deafening.

Nikola tried to explain.

Mr. One continued to chew.

"I can't stay here all day, so it'd be good if someone could come pretty soon."

"Got you. How long can you stick around?" It was hard to hear what Isak was saying. What was the boss eating? Oatmeal?

"Two hours max, then I've gotta get to work. I promised my boss, and I need the hours to get my electrician's certificate."

"I'll get someone there by then."

Nikola turned around and looked at Chamon. One of Isak's faithful. A man who always had his back. Never chickened out. Who hadn't dropped out the way Nikola had. A blood brother. A soldier.

"Chabibi." A faint, rough voice.

Nikola turned around. Chamon's eyes were open. Nikola sat down. "You can talk?"

What little he could see of Chamon's face crumpled in pain when he tried to move his mouth. Nikola could tell that his friend was wondering who he had been talking to.

"Ignore me," he said. "Just a joke."

Chamon reached for a notepad from the bedside table. He grabbed a pen and wrote in slow, spindly letters. *I'll write instead. Hurts so fucking much to speak.*

"Okay, got it."

The pigs tried to interview me yesterday. Pretended I was too groggy to understand what they were saying.

"Okay."

Yusuf was just here.

"But he's not here now."

I dunno where he is. Do you know who the shooters were?

"No idea. What did the cops say?"

Fuck all. Just that they wanted to know if I knew who'd shot me. And then they wanted to know who else was there. They want to interview you all.

"Did you tell them?"

Nah. We don't talk to them like that.

"No, I know. So they have no idea, either?"

Don't think so.

"They'll try to interview you again."

I know. Plenty of people would've said more than I did.

Nikola didn't understand that last part. "What do you mean?"

Chamon's hand was on the covers again. The pen rolled onto the floor, and Nikola bent down to pick it up for him. His friend was clearly exhausted, but Chamon still held the pen steady as he wrote two new lines. *You can't trust anyone. I want out.*

Nikola studied that last sentence.

Chamon's eyelids fluttered. Then he turned away and seemed to fall asleep.

Just over two hours later. No one had turned up to take over from Nikola. Chamon was still sleeping. Nikola had pulled the chair over to the window and was looking down at the constant stream of people coming and going through the entrance. He had bought a couple of cans of Red Bull from the vending machine by the elevators and was trying not to drift off. To hell with George Samuel today; Chamon was more important—he just didn't know why his replacement hadn't shown up.

Then he saw the very thing he didn't want to see. Three floors down.

Two men in sunglasses, even though it was an overcast day; two men moving a little faster than everyone else. There was something about their movements, their stiff gait. Even though Nikola couldn't see their faces, he was sure—*they* were here, the same guys who had been at the gym. They were here to finish the job—there was no doubt about it.

Fucking hell.

He opened the door to the hallway and saw two women in white hospital scrubs talking to each other.

"Can you help me?"

The older of the two women turned to him: plastic glasses and a name badge—apparently her name was Britt Fuentes.

"You have to help me get my friend out of here," Nikola said.

"What do you mean?"

"Britt, please. My friend can't be on this ward right now. We need to move him somewhere else."

Britt Fuentes's furrowed brow looked like crumpled paper.

"No. No, absolutely not. We don't move patients like that."

The men shouldn't have known which ward to find Chamon on—but the speed of their movements suggested otherwise.

"It makes no difference what you normally do. You have to help me. Otherwise I'll move him myself."

He went back into the room, loosened the brakes on the bed, and started to roll it out. Britt and the other woman blocked the doorway. Grumbled, tried to talk him around. They just didn't get it. He readied himself, gave the bed a real shove. Pushed it into them: "What do you think you're doing?!"

He rolled on, out into the hallway. There was a thud behind him—the drip had fallen over. He backed up, stood it upright again. Pushed Chamon toward the exit. He looked down at his friend. Still sleeping.

A man in scrubs came running toward them. He smiled tensely. "What's going on here?"

Nikola tore the drip line from Chamon's arm—he would survive without it for a few minutes.

"My friend needs to leave the ward." He continued pushing the bed.

"No, no, I don't think so," the nurse protested, also blocking his way.

Enough now.

"Look, there are two men on their way up here to kill him, so lay off!" Nikola shouted.

Britt and the others grabbed at the bed. Shouted at him. Nikola gesticulated with his arms. The lights on the ceiling looked like the white lines on a highway.

At the end of the hallway, the doors opened and Nikola saw them: the two men stepped inside. He knew what they wanted to do now—what he *didn't* know was how to stop it. Everything seemed to happen in ultraslow motion after that, like someone was showing all the agitated people frame by frame. Angry frowns. Flushed red cheeks. Confused, irritated eyes.

The men were still wearing their sunglasses. They swung their arms, turned their heads like T. rexes on the prowl.

Nikola shouted. "No, no!"

They stepped closer, toward the bed where Chamon was lying. The nurses, or whoever they were, still didn't understand a thing. They continued to pull at the bed.

The men had almost reached them now, and Nikola could see that one of them had a gun in his hand. Ten feet away. Britt Fuentes cried out; she finally understood what was going on. Nikola reacted instinctively: he pushed the bed as hard as he could, sent it rolling as far as possible toward the doors, past the two intruders.

The man with the gun hissed something, but Nikola didn't catch what he said. Then he turned around, raised his pistol, and headed after the bed. Nikola threw himself at him, one last effort.

People were screaming. Maybe there would be a bang now: a bullet to the head. It didn't matter. Nikola tried to grab the gun. Lashed out all around him. He hit something hard—the pistol flew out of the man's hand.

"Cunt!" the man shouted, looking like he had just woken up from a dream. Maybe he realized that without the gun, it would all go to shit. He started hurrying away. The older of the two did the same, shoving one of the women to get past and practically knocking Britt Fuentes to the floor. But he was moving more slowly, and he paused as he reached Chamon's bed. Britt Fuentes pulled at him the way a toddler pulls at their mother. There was a bang. They fumbled for a few seconds, and the man managed to throw her off. Then he vanished through the doors.

Nikola took a deep breath. Was it over now?

The nurses continued to shout. People were running around him like headless chickens. Britt's face was completely red. It looked like Chamon was moving in bed. A doctor came running and started to push him away. Someone who looked like a security guard grabbed the gun from the floor.

Nikola caught up with the bed. Looked down at Chamon. He was no longer moving. The doctor's hands were pressed to Chamon's stomach. Then Nikola saw it: the covers around his hands were red and sticky. What had happened? Deep down, he already knew. He saw the doctor trying to stem the bleeding—it was already surrounding Chamon like a sea. The man who had fought with Britt must have done it—shot him in the stomach.

Nikola saw his friend's peaceful face.

He shouted at him: "Can you hear me?"

Chamon was still.

Chamon wasn't breathing.

Chamon.

11

Riche: classy, stylish, great people watching. Stockholm's premiere lunch spot for generations, and, come night—the timeless bar numero uno in town.

Even when she worked in the area, Emelie had never quite felt comfortable there, but Josephine, aka Jossan, loved Riche, so she obediently caught the bus over whenever they had lunch plans together. It was okay—like going on a day trip to some animal park you used to visit as a child. Emelie thought back to when she had bumped into Magnus Hassel and Anders Henriksson in a restaurant nearby, when Magnus had recommended that she hire Marcus.

The glasses hung in circles above the bar—promising success in the so-called divorce bar—and there were upside-down lilies above each of the tables. A contrast: after lunch here, she would be accompanying Katja to her second police interview. Emelie had also been there for the first.

They had met at the main entrance to police HQ on Polhems-gatan. Adam was there, too. The roof by the entrance stuck out like a long bridge over the tall glass doors, and you could make out the guard booths and security doors inside, preventing anyone without authority from getting in. The truth was that Emelie had never used that entrance before. She was normally involved in criminal cases of far less importance, which meant that the suspects were interviewed at local police stations, at Kungsholmsgatan 39 or in custody. But now she was acting as counsel for the injured party, not a defender, and the policewoman they were meeting worked for NOA—the Department of National Operations, previously known as CID.

"She doesn't want to go in," Adam immediately said after they shook hands.

Emelie had placed a hand on Katja's shoulder; it felt frail and bony. Her leather jacket seemed far too thin for the cool weather.

"I looked into it, Katja, and if you don't turn up to these interviews, then they can ultimately put out a warrant for you. That's not to say I think you should go into this without making certain demands. And I'll be with you the whole time, making sure you feel okay."

"She still doesn't want to," Adam had said.

"Adam," Emelie replied, her voice louder than before. "You won't be allowed to sit in on the interview—you know that, don't you? So it's better if you let Katja speak for herself. What do you say, Katja?"

Katja had looked down at the pavement. "It's okay."

It didn't sound like she felt even close to being okay.

Chief Inspector Nina Ley had introduced herself. Somehow, her short dark hair didn't seem to fit with her broad face and narrow eyes; it was like she was missing something to make it all hang together, a pair of glasses, for example. She led them down hallways and along passages as though someone was watching every step she took, as though she thought she was part of some photo reportage where her poses were more important than making any progress. The way she walked had reminded Emelie of several of her clients.

Some parts of the police station seemed relatively modern, with glass partitions from floor to ceiling, but others were old, with

dark, wooden wall panels. They had passed enormous men in uniform who fit the stereotype of the crude muscle machines in the
National Task Force; older men in cardigans, with glasses hanging around their necks; middle-aged women with cropped hair and
exercise monitors on their wrists. Probably all police officers. Eventually, Nina had shown them down a set of stairs and punched a
code into a keypad next to a metal door. They came into a smaller
room with some kind of reception desk. "This is such a sensitive
case that I'd like you to leave your phones, computers, and any
smart watches you might be wearing here." Nina had pointed to
two ziplock bags.

Emelie had squirmed. "But Katja is the injured party, not a
suspect."

"Absolutely. But, like I said, the unit working on this case is special within NOA, and we have our principles." Nina had opened
one of the bags and held it out. She wasn't particularly accommo-
dating, this officer.

The interview room had no visible windows, just curtains. There
was a carafe of water and a thermos of coffee on the table. A large
mirror on one of the walls—a one-way mirror, in all likelihood,
meaning they could be watched from the other side.

"Make yourselves comfortable," Nina had said. "I'm just going
to fetch the recording equipment."

Katja's fingers drummed the table.

"Are you feeling okay?" Emelie had asked. "You just need to let
me know if you want a break, you know that."

Katja had continued her drumming. It sounded muffled, as
though the room was built for screams that wouldn't be overheard. Emelie thought of Teddy; he had been locked up behind
high walls and barred windows. And though he pretended to live
a life adapted to society, he was still affected by the person he had
once been—or by the way the world saw *him*, at the very least.

Nina had returned. She poured water for Katja and coffee for Emelie.

"Katja, I'm so pleased you could come in. You're very important to us."

"Before we get going," Emelie had spoken up, "I just want to assure myself of a few things."

There was a deadly serious look on Nina's face. Emelie had continued: "We understand that it's a special unit handling this case, but considering the background of what happened earlier, in linked cases—and I'm thinking primarily of Benjamin Emanuelsson's case here, where we know that at least one police officer, Joakim Sundén, was involved—I'd like to know how you will be maintaining confidentiality within the force."

Nina Ley hadn't seemed the least bit surprised by Emelie's words.

"That's a relevant question, and what I can say is that this case was opened by CU, the Stockholm Police authority's internal investigation department, but that when the hard drive containing the films was handed in, it was passed to NOA. What we call our *Great Wall*—internal confidentiality, in other words—is even stricter here than if CU had been leading the investigation. It means that all material is handled by separate units requiring different passwords and verifications than for the usual IT system. No other officers can access our investigation—we're even based out of different stations, as you can see—and it might be over-the-top to say it, but Katja herself is classified, so her name won't appear in any of the documents."

Nina had gone on to explain the internal processes and reasons why Katja could trust her. Emelie couldn't help but agree—this really was a special unit: an authority within the authority.

"So, can we begin?" Nina had asked once she was done.

Katja's fingers hadn't stopped drumming the table the entire time.

"No, there's just one more point I'd like to make," Emelie replied. "As I'm sure you can imagine, this risks tearing open an enormous wound and bringing up painful memories for my client. I want us to agree, before we begin, that the minute my client requests a break or to pause the interview, we will do that."

Nina had poured more water. Her eyes were different colors: one blue and the other green. "I accept that. But Katja must also understand that it's important that I'm able to ask my questions. We're here to investigate a particularly serious crime, and, if I may say so, Katja is not the only victim. Within the framework of this investigation, I've identified more than thirty-two girls who have been abused by various men, sometimes by up to eight at a time. In total, there seem to be around fifteen men involved, and we refer to them as 'the network.' The films are dated from different points in time, but they stretch over a period of at least twelve months, though my understanding is that it went on for longer than that."

Nina fell silent. The air-conditioning hummed.

"If I'm perfectly honest, I fear it's still ongoing. That the network is still active."

Emelie had crossed her arms. "That doesn't make the situation any less sensitive for my client."

The interview had taken almost three hours. Nina began by explaining that they had analyzed the people in the films using various pieces of facial recognition software. "Unfortunately, the men's heads are rarely visible, and when they are, their faces are very blurry. We haven't managed to identify a single one of them. We're continuing to work on a number of other leads, though I can't say any more about that right now."

Katja had also had to talk. She repeated the same things she had told Emelie during their first meeting, but with more detail this time. Which home she had been living in, how she had met the man for the first time, which hotel by Stockholm Central Station they had met at—she couldn't actually remember the name, but she remembered that it had a reception that was lit from beneath with blue lights. She had spoken about how he offered her Coca-Cola with whiskey and asked her whether she was a virgin, then told her a long story about his first time, how nervous he had been but also how good he felt afterward, and how he had then taken her to bed while repeating how sweet and sexy she was. As she lay on the bed covers, he had asked whether he could massage her breasts. She said that she had been slightly giddy from the whiskey, but that before she had time to reply the man's hands were beneath her top. She hadn't actually thought that was too dangerous at the time, because he seemed so gentle and actually pretty wimpish, but later, after she'd had a few more sips of her drink and the man had gone on about her breasts, after he had hinted at how tough she was and placed the five hundred kronor he would pay her on the bedside table, he had asked whether he could have sex with her. "The minute you feel uncomfortable, you just tell me," he had said in a bright, almost childlike voice; he had worn a condom and it had all happened very quickly, and after a while, when she asked him to stop, he had. But then, once they were done, he wouldn't even look at her. He had dressed quickly and then left the room before her. The five-hundred-kronor note was still there, waiting for her. She had spent every last öre of it on new clothes in H&M.

"Did he tell you his name?"

"He called himself Henrik, but he never said his surname."

"Did he ever use a different name?"

"No, I only heard Henrik."

"Did you tell him how old you were?"

"No, but I said I was in the seventh grade."

"When did you say that?"

"I don't know, it might have been later, when the other stuff started."

Nina's questions were direct, not introducing any leading information unnecessarily. She hadn't worked Katja; she had just allowed her to go on. An interviewing pro.

"Did you meet him again?"

"What happened then?"

"How did you agree when to meet?"

"Do you remember what your phone number was at the time?"

"Do you remember *his* phone number?"

She had occasionally taken shorter breaks between questions, but then she got going again. "Do you still have your bank account with Nordea?"

"Have you ever spoken to anyone about this?"

"Did anyone earn money from it?"

"Do you know whether they filmed that?"

On several occasions, Katja had paused and looked down at the table. Emelie had assumed she wanted to stop; she had even asked her. But Katja had raised her head, her voice suddenly steadier. "Now that I'm here, I might as well speak."

The question was whether it would make any difference. Some of the events were nothing but vague memories now, and others even looser fragments. She was often incoherent, mixing up events and people. It was probably a completely normal psychological defense mechanism—if she had to remember everything she had been subjected to, she would go crazy. But Emelie knew how it would look in the interview transcript all the same. She still couldn't comprehend why Nina and her team had been unable to identify a single man from the films in more than a year—what kind of bunglers were they, exactly?

What Katja had been through hadn't ended then. It had escalated. Driven her to the depths, to hell. She spoke about how she had been taken out to a country estate, dressed up in bunny underwear, and, alongside a couple of other girls, been expected to flaunt herself in front of a group of old men.

Later, she and a few other girls had been taken down to an underground apartment of some kind, and Katja had been led into a cold room with a lonely bed in the middle. Next to the bed, on the floor, there had been a number of different objects: leather straps, whips, dildos, handcuffs.

Emelie had recognized what she was talking about: a mansion full of old men. Mats Emanuelsson had mentioned the very same thing, only from a different perspective.

Katja went on: "I mean, I realized someone would come in and have sex with me, but I . . . I . . ."

Emelie had been surprised that Katja had managed to say as much as she already had without a break. But it was as though the words no longer wanted to cooperate. "They tied me to the bed, with my arms out . . . there were so many . . ." She had continued to talk, incoherently, uncontrolled. Emelie could still grasp enough of it to understand. "Urine . . . excrement . . . I shouted no, no, stop . . . the dildo in my buttocks, they hurt me so much, I wanted to die . . ."

Emelie had put down her pen. "Even though you haven't asked for it, Katja, I think we should take a break."

The room fell silent. Nina's face had been as gray as the curtains along the wall. Katja had started to shake, her hands covering her face. Emelie put an arm around her.

Nina broke the silence: "I think what you've just mentioned appears in one of the films. And I'm afraid we'll have to show you it. You might be able to identify some of the men. Anything you can remember is valuable to us. The names of the other girls, for example, or any other information about them."

Josephine strutted into the bar. Emelie's train of thought was broken, just like the interview with Katja. There hadn't been any more questions after that, but they would start up again today.

On the way over to Emelie's table, Jossan kissed at least five people on the cheek. To her, this wasn't just lunch with a friend, it was a vital networking, cluster-building, face-time opportunity. She was building up a client base for the long term. Acquisition. Again: the contrast—one moment, Katja's story; the next, this.

"Pippa, how goes it?" Jossan always called Emelie Pippa; she was convinced that Emelie looked a lot like Pippa Middleton.

They hugged like normal people—to Emelie, cheek kisses were alien, particularly with a close friend.

"I heard you hired a fully qualified assistant lawyer. You're starting to grow, sounds fantastic," said Josephine.

"Yeah, I actually got ahold of him through Magnus Hassel. I bumped into him and Anders Henriksson while I was waiting for you in Pocket City a few months ago."

"Anders, though. He's so shady. He's such a nerd."

"I know, but why's he shady?"

Jossan sat down. "I've always thought that nerds are hiding some kind of exceptional talent, like the whole nerd thing is just a facade; they're compensating for their nerdiness by being incredibly smart or incredibly kind, for example, only no one ever finds out because they never make any friends. But Anders Henriksson, he's neither. He's *just* a nerd—there's nothing else to him."

"He's managed to become partner."

"Anyone who's willing to work eighty-hour weeks and die twenty years early can do that."

Their food arrived. Panko-coated pollock with soy and ginger crème for Emelie, and grilled pike with roe beurre blanc for Jossan, minus the pomme puree that was supposed to come with it. Emelie started to drop her thoughts of Katja's interview.

Jossan pulled a small metal tub from her designer handbag and placed it on the table. "I don't eat any food with starch in it," she announced, opening the tub. There was something green inside; it looked like wilted salad leaves. Jossan scooped a few onto her plate using her fork. "I've started a new supplement diet, too."

"Exciting. What is it?"

"Algae. You've got to try it. Chock-full of minerals, vitamins, and antioxidants. Makes your hair better, and it boosts your immune system, too. I haven't had a headache in two weeks. And look at my skin, it's like a baby's."

Emelie took a bite of her fish—it tasted fantastic even without the addition of aquatic plants. She couldn't help but like Josephine, despite how self-obsessed she was and despite her talking about Tinder dates and Little Liffner bags far more often than important things. She always made Emelie laugh.

A while later, Emelie felt her inside pocket buzz. She pulled out her phone and saw an unknown number. It was Katja. From her voice, Emelie immediately knew something was wrong.

"I don't know if I'm going to go," Katja said.

"You mean you don't want to go to the police interview today?"

"I don't know if I can."

"Has something happened?"

"Yes."

"What?"

"I can't say over the phone."

"Do you want to talk about it?"

It sounded like Katja whimpered. "Yes, that would be good."

"Can you come to my office?"

"I'd rather not. I just want to be at home. Can you come to our apartment? Maybe we can go to the interview together afterward. If I decide to go."

Katja and Adam lived in Axelsberg, on Gösta Ekmans väg. The brown buildings looked like huge Lego bricks. Flat roofs, ninety-degree angles, nothing unnecessary sticking out. Jossan had raised an eyebrow when Emelie told her what she was doing. It wasn't exactly custom for a lawyer to go over to their client's house like this, but it also wasn't forbidden. And if the client wanted it, then why not?

Josephine had footed the bill for lunch, and they had agreed to meet again soon.

The snippet of film Emelie and Katja had been forced to watch at the station was playing on her mind—it was the worst thing she had ever seen. But there was something else to it, something she couldn't quite put her finger on—as though she recognized the girls being abused. Maybe it was just that they all looked so normal, beneath the makeup, the bizarre underwear, and their tormented faces. They could have been her or any of her friends fifteen years ago.

The elevator had double doors, in line with some new regulation—first an ordinary door, then two automatic doors that completely sealed the metal box. The only indication that you were being carried upward was the roller-coaster-like sensation in your stomach. It was Adam's name on the mailbox: Tagrin. Emelie wondered how much older than Katja he was; it was something she should ask Marcus to look into.

The doorbell was a classic, a small black button on the door itself. She rang it.

No one answered.

Emelie pressed her ear to the door: she couldn't hear a sound from inside the apartment.

For some reason, she took hold of the handle. The door was unlocked.

She had an extremely bad feeling about this. "Hello, Katja?"

No reply.

The hallway was messy. There was a flimsy throw rug on the floor and shoes on the shoe rack, several of them probably Katja's.

"Adam?" she tried.

No reply.

The light in the hallway looked old, brass and glass. It was on.

Emelie raised her voice. "Hello, is anyone home?"

She didn't bother taking off her shoes. Something wasn't right; she could feel it with every inch of her body.

There was a poster on one wall, depicting an old-fashioned map. *Bacon's Standard Europe,* it said at the top, and Emelie had time to see that Yugoslavia was still one big country. To the left was a bedroom, but something was pulling Emelie to the right. A living room. A brown sofa, a coffee table covered in newspapers and remote controls, two floor cushions, some dry houseplants in the window.

And a body on the floor.

At first, Emelie couldn't work out what the sound she was hearing was—then she realized that it was her, that she was screaming.

Katja was lying on the floor.

There was blood everywhere.

She didn't need to bend down to understand.

Someone had killed Katja. Stabbed her to death.

Emelie looked up at the wall.

Huge letters, written in blood.

It said: WHORE.

TELEPHONE CONVERSATION 3

To: Hugo Pederson

From: Göran Blixt (boss)

Date: 12 October 2005

Time: 10:10

GÖRAN: Could you come in half an hour before lunch?

HUGO: Sure.

GÖRAN: Good. I'm on my way from the golf course now, but I'll be back by then. We'll go through the analysis. Lots of interesting stuff there, Hugo. We could probably kill the little Dane. But we need to do it good and proper. The price is around 140 today.

HUGO: I know. But it's going down, believe me, it's going down. It's just a question of timing.

GÖRAN: Like always. Anyway, we'll talk about it later. I need you to sign the new policy document Michaela and I have produced, too. We need everyone to agree to these rules.

HUGO: Okay, no problem. Wasn't the old agreement enough?

GÖRAN: Yeah, but this one's clearer and better, even though the content is virtually the same. No conflicts of interest, no private business and so on.

HUGO: I'd happily go in on the Dane myself if it came down 3 or 4 percent.

GÖRAN: I understand, but you know the rules. No private business, we can't have that. Your time needs to be spent analyzing what we should be doing at Fortem Capital, that's all. I own your brain, Hugo, haven't you realized that?

HUGO: Ha, yeah, my brain understood that long ago.

GÖRAN: Good, glad to hear it. See you soon. Bye.

TELEPHONE CONVERSATION 4

To: Pierre Danielsson (co-suspect)

From: Hugo Pederson

Date: 12 October 2005

Time: 13:10

HUGO: Little Pille, little Pille, liked to pull on his willy.

PIERRE: Very funny.

HUGO: Things are happening now, little Pille.

PIERRE: What?

HUGO: With the Dane.

PIERRE: Okay, then maybe we should call on the burners?

HUGO: Okay, I'll call you.

TELEPHONE CONVERSATION 5

To: Pierre Danielsson (co-suspect)

From: Hugo Pederson

Date: 12 October 2005

Time: 13:11

HUGO: Little Pierre, little Pierre, scratched his hairy derriere . . .

PIERRE: You're very funny, everyone knows. Truly. And you sing like Céline Dion.

HUGO: Good job for these prepaid Telias . . .

PIERRE: Better safe than sorry, right? You never know, these burners are just to keep on the safe side. So, what's going on?

HUGO: I've been analyzing Danfoss for two weeks now. They've been at it for years, but they're still miles from the top. They're the Arabs of the North, the Danes. But if you bring about some changes to the leadership, make the business more efficient and overhaul the capital structure, huge amounts could be paid out to the shareholders. We've checked over ten factories and gone through all their provider contracts. I know that firm like I know my own dick. And now for the fun part.

PIERRE: What does Göran say?

HUGO: Exactly. I presented the case to him at lunch and he said: "We're going in." So Fortem'll be going in as a new owner. We'll start taking position from tomorrow, Fortem's going to take at least ten percent. So the price is going to . . .

PIERRE: The Danes are gonna fly. Shit man, nice. What do we do, then?

HUGO: You do what you want, so long as you do it right. No big, obvious positions, try to get as many blocks on the outside as possible, outside the market exchange systems. You're using your guy in Switzerland, right?

PIERRE: Yeah, yeah.

HUGO: Good, speak later.

PIERRE: Yeah, hey listen . . .

HUGO: What?

PIERRE: Greed is good.

HUGO: Exactly. Ciao.

TELEPHONE CONVERSATION 6
To: Jesper Ringblad (stockbroker, Nordea)
From: Hugo Pederson
Date: 12 October 2005
Time: 13:17

HUGO: 'Sup, Jeppe. It's Hugo P.

JESPER: Mr. Pederson, good to hear from you.

HUGO: Yup, let's hope so.

JESPER: Ha.

HUGO: I want to buy Danfoss A/S B shares.

JESPER: The Danish heat pumps?

HUGO: Yes indeedy. I want one hundred thousand.

JESPER: Okay, wait a second . . . right, Danfoss B . . . it's being traded on the Copenhagen Stock Exchange and the Dow Jones.

HUGO: I know.

JESPER: And you want to buy at what price?

HUGO: What's it at now? In the U.S.?

JESPER: They haven't opened yet.

HUGO: Of course. Copenhagen, then.

JESPER: Roughly 123.7, 123.8 Swedish kronor.

HUGO: Listen, go for two hundred thousand. I've got a feeling about this. Something's going on there.

JESPER: Really? Two hundred thousand?

HUGO: Yeah, and it needs to happen pronto, you understand?

JESPER: Okay, I'll try as quickly as possible. What's your limit?

HUGO: One hundred twenty-four.

JESPER: Okay, I'll get going then.

HUGO: No, wait. There's one more thing: you can only buy in blocks, nothing from the market's electronic systems. Only direct from your contacts. It's important.

JESPER: Then it might be a bit tricky getting so many.

HUGO: Yeah, yeah, but you'll be well paid for it. It's your job, man, isn't it?

JESPER: Yes, of course. I'll try.

HUGO: Perfect. I'll call you later.

TELEPHONE CONVERSATION 7

To: Jesper Ringblad (stockbroker, Nordea)

From: Hugo Pederson

Date: 12 October 2005

Time: 14:08

HUGO: How's it going?

JESPER: I've managed one hundred thousand.

HUGO: Then you need to pick up the pace a bit now. And listen, I want another one hundred thousand.

JESPER: Are you really sure, three hundred thousand Danfoss B in all?

HUGO: I've never been more sure.

JESPER: You don't have the funds in your account.

HUGO: You know what Mahatma Gandhi always said, right?

JESPER: No . . .

HUGO: *Greed is good.* I'll borrow it.

JESPER: Mahatma Gan . . . ?

HUGO: Or whoever the hell it was. Doesn't matter. All you need to do is haul in three hundred thousand of those Danish bastards. And if there's not enough dough in the account, lend it.

TELEPHONE CONVERSATION 8

To: Hugo Pederson

From: Jesper Ringblad (stockbroker, Nordea)

Date: 12 October 2005

Time: 16:40

JESPER: Hey, it's Jesper.

HUGO: Hey, hey.

JESPER: It's done now. All the shares are in your account. Three hundred thousand.

HUGO: All in blocks?

JESPER: Yep, everything.

HUGO: Thanks, you've done a great job.

JESPER: I'm glad you're glad. That's the most important thing.

HUGO: Hell no, the most important thing is that I make money on this.

TELEPHONE CONVERSATION 9

To: Louise Pederson (wife)
From: Hugo Pederson
Date: 12 October 2005
Time: 18:40

HUGO: Hey, baby.

LOUISE: Hi.

HUGO: What are you doing?

LOUISE: I've been to the gym, was just going to stop somewhere to get some dinner.

HUGO: Let's go out to eat, you and me?

LOUISE: Can you?

HUGO: Yeah, of course. Where do you want to go? Should I try to book us a table at Sturecompagniet for seven?

LOUISE: Sure.

HUGO: Oh, and one more thing, Mousey. We'll redo the bathroom, and the rest. We'll do the whole thing.

LOUISE: But you said we couldn't afford it.

HUGO: It'll be okay.

LOUISE: You're wonderful. You know that? Kisses.

12

Roksana and Z were in a car on the way to Dusky. An UberPool, of course—they couldn't afford anything else.

"If you bring some of the stuff I tried at your place," Billie had laughed over the phone when Roksana called her to ask about the event as subtly as she could. The address had arrived in an SMS a few hours later. The whole thing was classed as a private party, and Roksana knew it took more than paying the entry fee to be let in. The Ora Flesh collective was exclusive: everyone there was carefully chosen.

There was a food truck parked outside the industrial building. It wasn't open yet; it was only twelve thirty, but people were guaranteed to be hungry in a few hours' time. Above the door: a small banner covered in emojis.

They could hear music coming from inside the building. *Untz-untz-untz,* a powerful bass line, a rhythm echoing out into the entrance. Shit, this was going to be great.

Roksana and Z walked down a long hallway, concrete walls, people standing around in groups—maybe they hadn't been let in. It was warmer here. The sound grew louder. After a minute or so, they saw a couple of figures standing by a metal door. The music was drumming against their eardrums now. Two girls in faux fur were each holding an iPad, checking people off the guest list. Roksana hoped they weren't about to run into problems, but one of the girls just smiled when she said her name. "You're Billie's friend, right?"

"I think it's an old turbine hall," Z said, barely audible over the music. It pulsed through Roksana's body in shock waves. She could see huge fan heaters next to the towers of speakers. Lasers created light shows in the air: hearts, geometric shapes, explosions of color. Glowing, psychedelic UV adornments hung on one of the walls. On the largest, she could see the emojis again.

"They've got a really sweet vibe going on here," Z shouted, which meant that the level of irony was perfect.

Shit, it was nice.

"Can you see who's playing?"

Roksana glanced over to the DJ booth. She was no connoisseur, but she recognized Ora Flesh herself: the model married to the photographer. The hottest couple in town. It couldn't get any better.

There were three, possibly four hundred people in the turbine hall. The vast majority were Roksana's age. The free spirit hippies were at one end of the room, shaking their long hair as though they were at some kind of shaman festival, but, for the most part, the people crowding the dance floor looked normal. She recognized a few of them: Billie's friends, Billie's friends' friends, and even two girls who had come to her and Z's housewarming party. She tried to wave to them, but they didn't seem to recognize her. There were a few older people, too, even a number of old men with wrinkled faces. Keith Richards clones, almost. She assumed they were old photographers, stylists, art directors, and that kind of thing.

The music was seamless, each mix blending into the next. Roksana scrunched her North Face coat into a ball and shoved it into the bag on her back. She had bought the coat from Humana Second Hand on Timmermansgatan.

Z went over to the bar and bought two balloons and two lagers. They took a few sips of beer and then inhaled the nitrous. It made

Roksana's head tingle, and she laughed like a madwoman when Z broke out some extreme liquid and digits dance moves. His entire body was like a giant flow of energy. She could never have come here without him.

She spotted Billie and the two girls again, across the dance floor. Roksana glanced at Z: Shouldn't they go over? But Z seemed completely lost in himself now, Roksana was dancing, too. Her arms were like electric cables in the air. She was sweating. She was breathing. She checked her watch: they had been there an hour now. She saw Billie making out with a guy who looked like Elijah Wood. The laser beams drew art on the walls. The underground feeling was intense, even though the organizers were some of the most well-known names in Stockholm. She wished she could afford a new pair of sneakers—her feet were soaking, and the soles had started to ache. Most of all, she wished that some of the people who had been at their housewarming would come over and say that the party had been sick.

"Want to go through to the other bar?" Z shouted. "Where the sofas are."

The bar in the room where the sofas were was oddly quiet. "That's new sound system technology—I saw a documentary about it," Z began, about to launch into a lecture that Roksana managed to stop.

"I know," she said.

There were sun loungers lined up next to the old sofas. Fabric on the walls. There was sand on the floor and incense burning on the bar, spreading its fragrant scent and positive vibes.

"It's called *Satya Sai Baba Nag Champa*," Z said, setting off again.

"Nice, very nice," said Roksana. "Especially the sand."

Billie was already sitting next to a group of people. "Heeey, Roksy. Come and sit."

They made small talk for a while.

"Anyone got anything good?" a girl asked after a while.

A cute guy laughed. "I have, but I paid two grand per tablet, so I'd have to charge you."

Roksana took off her backpack and felt for the plastic bag inside.

Billie turned to her. "*Ey, bish,* did you and Z bring the stuff?"

Billie always wanted to sound like she came from the suburbs, even though she had grown up in the heart of bohemian Södermalm.

Roksana told the truth: "Yeah."

Billie pouted. "Girl, I love you. For real. Can I have a hit?"

Half an hour later, they came down from their high. The music from the dance floor thudded faintly against the walls.

Billie shouted out with happiness, "Even better than last time!" Her partners laughed like mad. They had been crawling around in the sand during the rush, thinking they were dwarf hamsters.

The cute guy who wanted to sell E had a smile so wide that it threatened to split his face in two. He blinked at Roksana. "That stuff. I mean, it's incredible. What's your name?"

"I'm Roksy."

"Aha, were you the one who had the housewarming last week?"

"Yeah."

"Did you have fun?"

Roksana wondered why he was asking. What had he heard?

"Yeah, we had fun."

The cute guy pushed his hair out of his eyes. In the gloom of the bar, he almost looked like Archie from *Riverdale.*

"Only *fun*? 'Cause I heard it was completely insane, off-the-hook crazy."

The cute guy blinked with those big eyes of his. Then he cleared his throat and shouted across the chill room: "Hey, everyone! Roksy here's my new queen. She's the best."

A bubbling feeling in her body. It wasn't the ketamine. Roksana knew it was something else—it was the buzz of being on the way up.

13

Teddy was on his way to meet Emelie and Jan at the apartment where she had found Katja's body. Emelie had called him immediately. Her voice was composed, despite the fact that she should still be more or less in shock.

Axelsberg, Gösta Ekmans väg. Teddy's father lived nearby. The area had changed while Teddy was in prison. In the past, it had been home to normal, working-class Swedes and migrant workers, but now: Axelsberg, Örnsberg, Aspudden—they were all small, wannabe versions of Södermalm. The same trendy black rolled-up beanie hats; the same brown laced boots. The same kids called Harriet and Folke.

Teddy was early. He studied himself in the rearview mirror. His hair was mid-length. For the first few years after he got out, he had barely wanted to cut it at all, but now he kept it neat. His nose was stubby, his eyes big. They looked even bigger in the mirror, like black holes where the mirror effect disappeared.

He didn't know what they were hoping to find out here, but it was worth a visit all the same. Maybe one of them would spot something the police hadn't noticed.

He had met Nikola at an Espresso House by Södertälje Station a few days earlier. It was the middle of the day, and the place had been half-empty. Nikola went for an energy drink; Teddy ordered a coffee with milk. The cashier had given him a searching look. "What kind of coffee?"

"Just an ordinary coffee, please."

She had put her hands on her hips. "We've got flat white, macchiato, or cappuccino; we've got caffe latte, fudge latte, frapino, and single estate filter coffee from Lubanda, Monte Alegre, Monte de Dios, and Sidamo. Then there are the special brews."

Teddy had tried to process all that information. "You choose," he eventually said. "So long as I can have milk."

"Okay. Would you like lactose-free, almond milk, or organic oat milk?"

Teddy didn't know whether he should laugh or scream. "Do you have normal milk? White, runny? From a cow."

He and Nikola had sat down in a quiet corner. The leather armchairs had an artificial patina on them, but they were comfortable. Teddy had noticed an oily layer floating on top of his coffee. Nikola was moving slowly, as though he was in pain. Teddy had just heard from Linda that Chamon had been shot and killed two days earlier.

"Nicko, I'm so sorry."

Nikola took a sip of his energy drink.

"How're you holding up?"

His nephew was wearing a Stone Island cap pulled low on his forehead. "I'm cool." But Teddy could see that his nephew was far from cool. His shoulders were tense, his face pale, his nails in bad shape. That was one of the things his father, Nikola's grandpa, liked to say: you can always judge a man by his nails.

"It's okay to feel broken. He was your friend," Teddy said.

"I'm done grieving."

"It doesn't work that quickly."

"What would you know?"

For the first time, he had noticed Nikola's eyes beneath the brim of his cap. They weren't just full of pain; there was something else there, too. They were burning, smoldering. The look Nikola gave him could have killed—it blazed with rage.

"I know how much Chamon meant to you, believe me. But don't do anything stupid, Nicko. Promise me that. Don't do anything stupid."

Nikola had pulled out his phone and turned it off. Then he had dragged his armchair closer to Teddy's. "Teddy, *Ujak,* how could they kill a helpless man in the hospital? What happened to honor?"

Teddy tried to think of an answer. "Same thing, I'm afraid," he said, "that's going on across the world right now. The idiots are taking over. They want to replace anything complicated with something simple, something easier for the bastards to live by. But if the world's upside down, that doesn't mean you have to be."

"I can't live like that, though. Can you help me? Find these bastards."

"I don't think that's a good idea. Please, Nicko, stay away. Don't start anything. Don't do anything you'll regret."

Nikola's voice had been hard when he replied. "But I need to get something back."

"It's too late."

"So you're not going to help me?"

"Not to get revenge, no."

When Nikola looked up, his eyes hadn't even been blazing any longer—they had just been full of darkness. "Teddy, you were my hero. You're the one who taught me about honor." Nikola had crushed the empty can without even realizing he had done it. "You remember what you used to say when I was a kid, when I came to visit you inside?"

Teddy shook his head.

"You said that sometimes, you have to walk through the fire to come out clean on the other side. But you're not who you were, *Ujak.* You're not who I thought."

There was a knock on his car window. It was Emelie, accompanied by Jan from Redwood Security—the ex-cop turned private security consultant who had helped them with investigations in the past. Jan was wearing some kind of shiny coat, something that was probably meant to both look presentable and keep out the rain and snow. He had been a huge help on the Emanuelsson case, spotting things other people had missed. Teddy gave him a hug. "Jan the man," he said. Then he approached Emelie.

"How are you?" She deserved a hug after what she had been through, but she took a deliberate step back.

"Not okay. But we need to get to work." There were dark circles beneath her eyes.

Teddy scratched his forehead, his fingertips feeling the frown lines there; they seemed to have grown exponentially since he learned that Emelie had found Katja dead.

"How do we get into the apartment?" he asked.

Jan shrugged. "What don't we do in this line of work?" He held up what looked like a small screwdriver. A skeleton key.

"Did Katja live here alone?"

"No, she shared the apartment with her partner, Adam, and occasionally his son."

"And where's Adam now?"

"He's the main suspect. But they haven't managed to track him down yet. There's a warrant out for his arrest."

"And the son? Where's he?"

"He lives with foster parents," Emelie said, stepping out of the elevator doors, which had opened with an ominous creaking sound.

There was no sign that the police had gone through the apartment with a magnifying glass or that a brutal murder had taken place there just a few days earlier.

Emelie's silhouette was tense.

"Everything okay?" Teddy tried to ask her, but she disappeared into the living room as though she hadn't heard him.

"In here," she said loudly. "She was lying here."

The brown sofa, the coffee table, the solitary straggling plant in the window. On closer inspection, the place seemed to have been carefully cleaned; Teddy could barely see any possessions.

Jan got to work. Teddy had seen him in action before. Though the apartment was bright, he used a small pocket flashlight. He poked at certain surfaces with his little cotton swabs, crawled around on the floor like some kind of Sherlock Holmes with a magnifying glass. Teddy knew he shouldn't touch anything he didn't need to touch and that he shouldn't bother Jan with stupid questions. He just walked through the various rooms and looked around.

The hallway. The kitchen, with two unwashed coffee cups. A bedroom with an unmade double bed and the curtains closed. A teenager's room with its own TV and a PS4. A bathroom with a cracked sink and a dirty tub.

Teddy peered out through the windows. Gray skies. Three below zero out there. The building on the other side of the yard was identical to the one they were in. He wondered how many apartments there could be in each of them, at least a hundred. The uniform rectangles, the flat roofs, the monotonous colors—people's lives would be housed in similar shapes.

Down below, a car was trying to parallel park in front of Teddy's Volvo. Everything was so quiet around here. But there was something moving in the distance; something flapping around, disturbing the peace.

Teddy glanced over to the other building. Birds. There were too many birds on the opposite roof.

"I'm going out for a bit," he said.

The other building had the same entry code as Katja's, and he took the elevator to the top floor. Once there, he found a set of stairs that led up to a roof hatch. It was locked with a padlock. Teddy went back down to his car. He didn't drive around with a full toolbox, but he always kept a few things in the car—things like a Stanley knife, for example.

The padlock wasn't an especially sturdy specimen, and he jammed the knife into the lock and applied pressure. The lock held, but the fastening on the hatch didn't. Teddy climbed up the metal ladder to the roof and immediately spotted the flock of birds in the distance. The roof was covered in snow and ice, but it was also completely flat, so it was just a matter of walking over there. There were ventilation shafts rising up here and there.

Magpies and crows: birds that didn't have the sense to leave Sweden over winter. Teddy felt the draft from their wings as they frantically flapped away. He was close to the edge now, where the birds he had seen from Katja and Adam's apartment had been gathered.

There was something on the roof. He moved closer.

It was a backpack.

There was a tear in one corner, a huge hole, probably from an animal biting or ripping it open. All around it, he could see crumbs of some kind. Teddy bent down. He yanked the stiff zipper and pulled out the contents.

Power Bar wrappers and a thermos flask. He continued to rifle through the bag. Found something hard and black. He held up the object. It was a pair of binoculars.

The windshield wipers squeaked. Emelie was sitting next to Teddy in the passenger seat. The car was still cold, and it had started to snow.

"So whoever was lying up there had energy bars and coffee," he said.

Teddy had called Emelie and Jan, and they had come up to the roof to see what he had found. Afterward, Emelie had phoned a police officer called Nina Ley.

"The coffee in the thermos is ice-cold," Jan had explained. "Rats or birds have probably bitten a hole in the bag. But someone was up on that roof, using those binoculars. You can see straight into Katja and Adam's living room and kitchen from up there. And I think that whoever was up there also put the padlock on the hatch. It doesn't look like the type normally used on that kind of thing."

The car was hot now, warm air pouring out of the vents. It was six o'clock, and they had been waiting for the forensic team who was now examining everything on the roof. Jan had already gone.

"What are you doing now?" Teddy asked.

"Going home to do the same as the past few days."

"Trying to sleep, having nightmares?"

"Basically."

"You don't want to get dinner with me, then?"

The rhythmic whining of the windshield wipers was almost hypnotic.

"I'm guessing your finances aren't rock-solid, but are you offering?"

"I thought business was going well?"

"That was before someone started killing my clients." Emelie smiled—for the first time all afternoon. It sent a heat wave through Teddy.

They sat down at Raw Sushi & Grill. Teddy had managed to find a parking space right outside Emelie's place. "They're endangered. As rare as pandas," Emelie had said.

She thought sushi was a perfect choice; Teddy was just happy that they had niku on the menu—different types of grilled skewers. The plates were square and the tables black. He ordered a beer. Emelie went for half a bottle of white. He wanted to ask how she was doing, talk more about Katja's apartment and the murder scene, but the people at the next table were too close; it felt like they would hear every word.

Instead, he said: "So how's your firm really doing?"

"Managing. I actually hired another lawyer. He's insanely ambitious, often stays later than me at night."

"You two in a relationship?"

"Come on."

He sipped his beer. Emelie picked up a maki with her chopsticks and held it in the air.

"What about you, what are you doing these days?"

"I've been helping my old friend Dejan with a few things."

"I remember him. Isn't he . . . ?"

Teddy put down his glass. "I know what you're going to say. You sound just like my caseworker at the Public Employment Service. You both think Dejan's a criminal, and by that you mean he's not clean."

"I don't know what I mean."

"He's done a lot of bad things, I'll give you that. Just like I have. And he's not completely aboveboard now, either, at least not on the financial side. But somehow, I don't see him as the big criminal anymore, not when I read in the paper that the owner of Ikea and thousands of other filthy rich Swedes don't pay any tax at all. The people with the most pay least, isn't that strange?"

Emelie topped up her glass.

"And they're the people you used to help, when you were at Leijon," he continued.

"If you're going to sit there and provoke me, then we might as well ask for the bill right now."

Teddy didn't want to attack Emelie; it was just that he had felt like this before: she saw him as improper. He was someone she would never introduce to her friends.

Two hours later, they got up. Emelie had drunk two more glasses of wine, Teddy three beers. He didn't feel drunk, but he was definitely light-headed.

"You can't drive home," she said, hanging her bag from the crook of her arm. "Can you take the train? Karlberg Station is pretty close."

"No, there's no train out to Alby. And taxis cost a fortune from here."

"Aha."

He opened the door for her. The cold was even worse now. Maybe she was slightly unsteady.

"Aren't you coming up, then? For coffee, as they say?"

Teddy could just imagine her softly lit bedroom, her scent. He pictured Emelie's body before him, not wearing any clothes.

"No," he said. "I don't think of us like that. Or rather, *you* don't."

14

The funeral: there were more than a thousand people there, possibly even two. Nikola didn't know. All he knew was that Saint Aphrem Syriac Orthodox Church was spacious, that the Hanna family was large, and that they had a lot of friends. People were crowded onto the pews—the women on one side, the men on the other. Others were standing along the walls. Some hadn't even made it in: Nikola knew there were people waiting outside.

It was his first funeral, and the first time he had ever been to a Syriac church. He had been to Saint Sava in Enskede a few times, with Grandpa, but that was Serbian Orthodox, and as small as a caravan compared to this.

Choirs and incense. Men in black suits and ties, older women with shawls covering their heads. Nikola was in the third row. He wasn't family, wasn't blood. But still—Chamon had been his best friend. Nikola was glad his mom was there, too, even if she was sitting on the other side of the aisle.

The coffin was at the very front, surrounded by a sea of red and white roses. There was a framed picture of Chamon on a chair, with a black silk ribbon draped over one corner. Tall candles on either side.

Up on the podium, there were several people wearing capes and small hats. The man in the middle had a huge beard, and he was holding a golden scepter. Nikola assumed they were all bishops and priests. They said mass, everyone sang along, someone spoke in a powerful voice. A younger priest translated certain things into Swedish. Two boys played the violin and piano. The women cried. The men hugged one another. It was all so sick. He couldn't make sense of it: Chamon.

Gone.

Nikola had been released two days after the murder. For some reason, they had initially thought he was involved. That was always the way: if you came from Ronna—the most ghettoized area in Södertälje—you were an automatic suspect. The cell they put him in had given him flashbacks to his time in custody for the Ica Maxi job. The minute Nikola touched the walls, it felt like his body was about to shatter. He had curled up in the fetal position on the green PVC-coated mattress: the thing was like Hästens' most luxurious model in reverse form. The plastic mattress from hell was only two inches thick, and the floor felt like the coldest thing on earth. Apparently the state's generosity was limited: yet again, he hadn't been given a pillow, not even anything to put on his feet. The cement walls were covered in graffiti, and the concrete floor stunk of piss. No toilet, no TV, no phone, nothing to read other than the carvings on the walls. Just him and his panic. His devastation. His anxiety.

He had failed to save his best friend, and the cops were refusing to even tell him whether any of the killers had been caught.

They had put handcuffs on him and led him to the interview room the next morning. He still didn't know why they had taken his freedom: he was a witness, not a killer. The doctors and nurses: surely they could confirm that he hadn't been part of the death squad that attacked Chamon?

He had shuffled out into the hallway with the guard behind him. The interview room was exactly how he remembered it. The same dirty plastic floor with the same simple table screwed to it. The same bare, grayish-white walls.

The door had opened and Simon Murray had come in: the cop who had arrested him at the hospital, the plainclothes officer who had been after Nikola and his crew ever since they were kids. Who had pulled them over, harassed their girlfriends and stopped off to see their parents when they still lived at home. He was part of Project Hippogriff—the joint initiative in southern Stockholm working toward a safer city. Murray's hair was short and blond. Black boots and a heart rate monitor around his wrist. He looked like he always had: a cop from birth. There must be something in his blood, in his DNA. Nikola didn't know how the man could work undercover when it was so obvious to everyone what he was.

"Hi, Nicko," Murray said, gesturing as though he wanted to embrace Nikola.

Nikola had sat down. He wasn't "Nicko" with this cop. Didn't Murray realize that he was grieving?

"I'm sorry. They couldn't save Chamon, he died quickly."

Nikola had looked out of the window, toward the walls. The sky was the same color as the concrete. He already knew Chamon was dead; Nikola had seen his friend's stomach close-up.

"I know this must be extremely difficult for you, I know how close you were to Chamon," Murray had said. "But I have to interview you. I'm sure that you, more than anyone, know why things turned out like this."

Nikola didn't have the energy to move. Though the room was warmer than his cell, he was still freezing. But he had wanted to go back there all the same. Away from this.

"Come on, Nikola. Give me something. At least tell me who was there when he was shot the first time."

Nikola had pulled his legs up beneath him. He shivered. He and Yusuf had driven Chamon to the hospital from the gym, and they had agreed simply to hand over their friend—not to say a word to anyone about what had happened.

Murray said: "Do you remember when I arrested you and Chamon for the first time? You were only eleven. We had to drive you home to your parents. You'd been stealing baseball caps from Intersport in Södertälje and then selling them at school. Do you remember what your mom said when I handed you over?"

Nikola hadn't replied.

Murray continued: "She said, 'Nikola isn't like that.' That was what she said: 'My son isn't like that.' Do you remember that?"

Nikola remembered. Linda had been disappointed in him so many times. But somehow, she continued to believe in him. Pictures had flown through his mind. All the times she had made dinner for him and Chamon, all the times he and his friend had kicked the ball around in the inner courtyard on Robert Anbergs väg, how Chamon had come up with his own little songs about their lame teachers.

Nikola had realized that he was about to start shaking. He opened his mouth. Murray grasped the situation immediately, fell silent—waited for Nikola to start talking.

He had considered just doing it, telling the cops what happened. Forgetting his honor. Spilling what little he knew—saying that the first crap had gone down at the gym, that Yusuf, Isak, and a load of MMA guys had seen the bastard who shot Chamon. But at the same time: How did the police actually work? Why should he show them the way?

"Come on, Nikola. Say something. You're a Swede, for God's sake, not a Syrian. Don't be like them. Just give me something."

Nikola had had to hold himself back then, a hairbreadth from flying at Murray: the racist. The cop who wanted everything but gave nothing in return.

He had cleared his throat. Built up some saliva—defended the holy principles. Spat straight into Simon bastard Murray's face.

"I'll never be Swedish the way you mean. And I don't talk to cops."

The gold ornamentation around the columns and the painted icons on the walls. Huge ceiling lamps as big as Smart cars hanging above the churchgoers. The marble floor glistened. He saw Chamon's father, Emanuel, his mother, and his siblings; he saw Yusuf and Isak. He saw Bello and the rest of the boys spread out among the others, sitting next to their fathers. He saw people he only vaguely recognized.

The priests held out their hands in front of them, their palms turned up. Gold and silver crosses around their necks. The melodies sounded ancient. It was Linda who had bought him his suit.

It was time to file past the coffin. There were a few men standing on one side of it, and a few women on the other: the core of the Hanna family.

Nikola saw how the majority held their right hands over their hearts, and he did the same. He also saw that no one was stopping to talk to anyone from Chamon's family, they were just moving past, nodding, trying to meet the parents' tear-filled eyes.

He moved closer. The procession was slow. There were three people ahead of him in the line for Chamon's father, and he tried to see how Emanuel was reacting to all of the people passing by.

Hand on heart. Nikola was now face-to-face with Chamon's father. He thought of the walnut baklava Emanuel had always given him when they were younger.

"Nikola," Emanuel whispered, taking ahold of him. It wasn't a tight hug, but it felt like the entire church was about to come crashing down on top of Nikola.

"I know you did what you could to save him," Emanuel continued, letting go. There was a moment of silence. And then he howled. Chamon's father's anguish filled the church—everything came to a standstill. Everything froze—time froze in an eternal chasm, and would crack beyond repair. At rock bottom. From the end of life.

And Nikola thought: I'll never get out of this. I'll never be able to move again.

During the wake in the function room at the church, Yusuf came over to Nikola. He smelled like gum and had a gold chain and cross around his neck. They hugged. "Isak wants to talk to us later," he said.

"What about?"

"We'll find out then."

"Your chain, is that Chamon's?" Nikola pointed to the cross.

Yusuf kissed it. "Yeah, he gave it to me at the hospital, just before you arrived. He wanted me to have it."

They met an hour later, in the back room of Steakhouse Bar. Isak was sitting down: it looked like he didn't have the energy to stand. Yusuf, Bello, and the others were hanging around him. They were all still wearing suits. There were ten or twelve of them there, and it was four in the afternoon. It was the first time Nikola had ever seen Isak, or any of them, for that matter, in anything but sweatpants.

Subdued small talk between the boys. One of Mr. One's guys, Jacub, told Nikola that he was the one Isak had ordered to go to the hospital to watch over Chamon, but that he had been stuck in traffic. Nikola didn't know what to say to that.

Everyone was waiting for Isak's sign, for him to hush them or start talking. But nothing happened. Yusuf shifted his weight. Bello glanced over at Mr. One. Eventually, they understood—he was waiting for them to fall silent on their own. Isak demanded dignity, respect for the situation.

"Whores," Isak said.

Someone's phone beeped. The guy quickly pulled it out and switched it to silent.

"We can't let those little whores scare us. Who do they think they are? We'll fuck their mothers in the eye. We'll do their sisters up the ass. They'll know what we've done."

Quieter than quiet now, not even the kitchen staff could be heard.

"I'm completely devastated. Chamon was like a little brother to me. And you couldn't find a better one. You get me?"

They all nodded slowly.

"But if they think they can break us by taking out the people we love, they're wrong. I've worked hard to build up what we've got. Blood, sweat, and tears. Nothing comes for free. It's taken us over ten years. You know? But, that whole time, it's always been about principles. That if someone hits us, we have to hit back ten times harder. And that means everyone has to be in. Everyone."

The boys nodded. Everyone looked deadly serious. Nikola wondered if Isak knew who the killers were. The boss's eyes flashed at him.

"So now I'm wondering: Who's volunteering? Who's going to help me find out who these bastards are?"

Nikola saw Emanuel Hanna's tear-filled eyes before him. Could still hear his desperate cry. One of the explosion headaches had started to pulse behind his forehead, lightning flashes in his mind. He thought of George Samuel and the electrician's certificate that was within reach, so close, how proud Linda and Teddy were.

He felt Isak's eyes burning. The boss lowered his chin and seemed to be staring straight through him. Nikola himself barely knew what he was doing. It was as though Isak's eyes were pulling at his body.

He raised a hand. There was a full-blown storm raging in his head now.

"I'll do it."

Isak breathed out through his nose. Nodded slowly.

Nikola said: "Chamon's blood was my blood. I'll find whoever was behind this. I swear."

PART II

MARCH–APRIL

15

They hadn't been able to keep their hands off one another, even in the elevator. They had tumbled into the hallway, knocking Emelie's coats from the hooks as they rushed past, and staggered on toward the bedroom. Their clothes were off before they even landed on the bed. As Teddy entered her, she had bitten his lip so hard that it started to bleed. The whole thing was over in a few minutes.

That was more than a month ago now, and it was as though something had exploded. Despite Teddy's "No, I don't believe in the two of us" line, they had grabbed one another the minute the door had started to swing shut. Emelie still didn't know what had made him change his mind.

Half an hour after they got to her apartment that night, they had done it again. This time, they had taken it slow, their fingers and lips exploring one another—she had felt Teddy following her breathing, panting, rhythm. They had kissed, nuzzled, explored their way forward, as though it were the first time for both of them. Or maybe it was the feeling that had been smoldering since that night in a Palma hotel room, more than a year earlier. She didn't know and, in the moment, she didn't care. Teddy had kissed her back, right down to the base of her spine, moving across her buttocks. His hands had embraced her, his entire body surrounding her. He had stroked her hair, his tongue grazing her breasts. She had clung to him, felt how wet she was. Then he was beneath her,

his big body like a wiry bed of muscles. "Come on," she had whispered, taking ahold of his dick.

There had been something about the way he looked at her, like
he was really seeing her, like he could see *into* her. It was as though
all he wanted was to be a part of her, without holding anything
back. And maybe that had scared her, even as she lay there—the
fact that she couldn't picture a life with Teddy. It was impossible to
imagine him at her place on an ordinary Friday night, cooking in
the kitchen and with a friend over to visit. She couldn't even fanta-
size about him going to meet her parents in Jönköping. He was so
far removed from her ideal. He was so far removed from her world.

But, in the moment, she had ignored it—that night, a month
ago, she had brushed away those thoughts and looked at him instead.
Picked up speed. Felt him inside her. She had glowed. Looked deep
into Teddy's eyes.

She was at the office today, but her thoughts wouldn't give her any
peace. That night with Teddy was a bright point, but her mind
was overflowing with unpleasant images. Katja's lifeless body and
slashed T-shirt. The blood on the floor. The writing on the wall.
The images popped up whenever she ate, whenever she tried to
work. They were there when she tried to sleep and they came back
again later, in her nightmares. They had even been there when she
tried to watch something on Netflix.

Emelie's appetite had been worse than the stick insect she'd had
as a pet one summer as a child. Her periods were irregular. She was
averaging fewer than four hours' sleep a night, despite popping
melatonin pills like they were mints. She knew she could get ahold
of something stronger—not just sleeping pills but proper sedatives.
She had done it before, but she didn't want to go down that road
this time. She had to resist it.

The police had interviewed her: once at the scene, in Katja and
Adam's apartment, and twice at the police station. "Did you hear
anything in the stairwell?" "Did you see anyone outside?" "Was

Katja alive when you got there?" "Do you know why Katja didn't want to go to the police interview?"

Emelie had replied no to everything, unfortunately. She wished she could have given them something, but she knew far too little.

"Why exactly do you suspect her partner?" she had wanted to know.

The policeman conducting the interview looked at her like she had just asked whether he was unfaithful. "The preliminary investigation is confidential, as you well know. I can't tell you anything."

Chief Inspector Nina Ley had called her up in tears—yes, a police officer who cried. Emelie hadn't known how to take it. When their call ended, she had spent two hours sitting at her desk without moving an inch. Could she have prevented this? Was it because she pushed Katja to go to the police and testify?

A few days later, Anneli rang through to her. "You've got a call."

"Who is it?"

"I have no idea. He won't say his name."

Emelie held the receiver to her ear. At first, she heard someone yelling. Then a scraping sound, followed by agitated voices.

"Hello, who is this? I can't hear you."

She heard a voice, a man, amid the noise. "It's me. You have to help me."

"Who is this?"

The same voice, heated: "Adam, Katja's partner. They want to arrest me." He was short of breath. She could hear noise in the background. "The cops. They've been hunting me ever since what happened to Katja. I need you, Emelie. You have to talk to them."

Emelie didn't know what to say.

"They're going to find me. Sooner or later," he continued.

"Why haven't you called them yet, or gone in voluntarily?"

"I'm telling you. They'll arrest me, they'll try to convict me of this. I'm completely crushed. Katja's been murdered, for God's sake. I haven't slept since it happened."

"Did you have anything to do with it?"

Adam's voice sounded almost calm now. "I loved Katja, but love leads to strange things sometimes. You have to help me, Emelie. You're the only lawyer I trust, because Katja trusted you. You have to save me."

"I can't," she said. "I can't be your lawyer. I'm sorry. There could be a conflict of interest. I was Katja's counsel and now you're a suspect. It isn't allowed."

There was a crackling sound over the line. "Is it because I work in the erotic industry?"

"No, I've just told you why. I have certain ethical rules to abide by. I have to follow them."

Emelie heard other voices in the background. Then the call ended.

It was the first time she had worked out in a month. She hoped it would help make the pictures in her head disappear.

Right-left. Hook-uppercut-elbow. Her blows struck the pads Jossan was holding up. Bam, bam, bam.

It was incredible that she had even managed to get Josephine to come along. Her friend was always going on about the latest exercise classes: barre, streamed fitness programs, PT training in Takkei, kripalu yoga, hot yoga, air yoga, dark yoga, made-up yoga. Though maybe that was just it: fighting sports were hot right now. Or, as Jossan put it: "Kayla Itsines says that it's part of the HIIT trend, and that's enough for me." She held the pads at head height, moved around the blue rubber floor. Emelie followed her—chin to her chest. Eyes on the pads. Breathing through her nose. Back leg moving first every time.

When she and Josephine swapped positions, her arms were shaking with exertion. The drops of sweat were clouding her vision. She was breathing loudly. "You might not have worked out for ages, but you've got a punch like Manny Pacquiao, you know that, right?" Jossan said as she pulled on the boxing gloves.

They got going again. Jossan looked like a kitten snatching at a ball of wool. This was relaxation for Emelie—but it did nothing to get rid of the images. Katja's wide eyes, like they were staring at something on the ceiling. WHORE on the wall. The carving knife on the floor.

"Wait," she panted. Jossan's arms were hanging heavily. "I have to stop," Emelie said. "This doesn't feel right."

Jossan's face was red. She just nodded. Josephine's strength might not have been in the force of her punch or the size of her cultural capital, but somehow she always understood.

Emelie was freezing as she waited for the bus. She had thought the police would get somewhere after she, Jan, and Teddy found the backpack on the roof opposite Katja and Adam's apartment. But she hadn't heard a thing from Nina Ley and her team since they interviewed her—Emelie assumed that meant they still hadn't arrested Adam Tagrin.

She had also assumed that she and Teddy would continue to see one another after their night at her place. His scent had hung around all weekend, on her body and on her sheets. But he never got in touch, and she didn't either. Playing games felt unnecessary with Teddy: they knew one another too well. Though maybe that was precisely why she hadn't called him—it was too big, too serious, too impossible.

Her phone beeped, and she scanned through the email that had just arrived.

40 YEARS OF LEIJON

Dear alumnus,

Leijon Legal Services is celebrating 40 years with pomp and circumstance. As an alumnus, you are hereby invited to celebrate with us on Midsummer's Eve. Expect mingling, lunch and Midsummer tradition.

Yours faithfully,

Josephine Söderlund, Alumni relations.

So, Emelie thought, Jossan was even advancing in the old firm's social circles. She was responsible for the alumni now, which could be important. Many of the firm's former employees had moved on as corporate lawyers, several of them now general counsel, which meant they became important clients for the firm—in need of Leijon's expertise. And though Emelie would never be a particularly significant buyer of legal advice around corporate transfers or the art of setting up extremely complicated company structures in order to avoid tax, she was an alumnus. But having the party on Midsummer's Eve? They were crazy, those corporate types. She knew she should probably go to make Jossan happy, but it wasn't worth it. Emelie would RSVP no.

It really did bother her that the police hadn't been in touch—Emelie had been counsel for Katja, after all. She wanted to know more about what was happening with the investigation into her murder. She pulled out her phone and called Nina Ley.

The chief inspector's reply was surprising. "Come to the main entrance on Polhemsgatan tomorrow, before lunch, and we can talk. Wait for me outside."

The motorbikes clustered along the pavement outside—it was a well-known fact: cops were inclined toward vehicles of the two-wheeled variety. Biker men, men who felt like men, who played the role of men. Emelie doubted that many of the female officers she knew had driven here on a Triumph Thunderbird XL. She wondered what Nina meant by asking her to wait by the main entrance. When she had come here with Katja, Emelie had just reported to reception.

The cold felt biting today. She caught sight of her reflection in the large glass panels that formed the main entrance: she needed a haircut. Her current style was nondescript, an attempt at a side parting that looked more like she was trying to hide her face behind her long hair.

Nina Ley's movements were abrupt when she opened one of

the tall glass doors and stepped outside. Nothing like the calm—or at least seemingly balanced—vibes she had given off during the interview with Katja. "I thought we could have a chat," she said, pointing up toward Kronobergsparken.

Emelie's fingers and toes felt like they had been in the deep freeze. "Not in your office?"

One of Nina's eyebrows twitched. "No, we thought our security was tight on this case, no one should even have known that Katja was being interviewed, but then what happened happened. I can't rule out a leak, which means I can't really trust my own team. I'd rather do this outside."

They walked up the gravel path between the bare trees and bushes.

"You want to know why Adam Tagrin is a suspect, and what we're doing about it?" Nina said once they were well inside the park.

"I was Katja's counsel, so I feel I have a certain right to know, yes."

Nina laughed shrilly. "I'm a bad, disloyal officer."

"Don't say that."

"During my fifteen years in the force, I've never seen anything like this. And I'm not sure I'm doing the right thing by getting you even more involved, but somehow I have to try. Besides, you and your boyfriend have already shown yourselves to be competent."

"Teddy isn't my boyfriend."

"It's like this. Adam Tagrin has been lying low for over a month now, he desperately doesn't want to be interviewed by us, so we're considering him a suspect."

"But does anything point to that? Other than him not wanting to come in voluntarily?"

Nina's nose was red with cold. "It tends to be a good reason to suspect someone, don't you agree?"

"People might have other reasons for lying low."

"Do you know of any reason? Something he's told you?"

Emelie suddenly wondered whether Nina knew that Adam had called her after the murder, but it seemed unlikely; she must just mean whether Adam had said anything before the event.

"No," she said, trying to recall what Adam had actually said during their short phone conversation. "But why do you really suspect him? You must have something?"

"Yes, of course we do. Katja was killed by two stab wounds. One penetrated her lung, the other damaged her stomach. She died within a few minutes, on the floor where you found her. The murder weapon was the carving knife you saw lying next to her. We found her blood on the knife and we've compared the width and depth of the wounds, so we're ninety-nine percent sure. The stab wounds are deep, meaning they were made with force, and the kitchen knife didn't have a hand guard, so the perpetrator's own hand may well have slipped forward as they stabbed. That's quite common."

Emelie started to realize where Nina was heading.

"We have a witness who let Adam stay over for the first few nights," the detective continued. "And this witness claims that Adam had wounds on his palms, the kind made by a knife. Scars he doesn't want us to see. So, what do you think, does that count as reasonable grounds for suspicion?"

They continued to the highest point of the park. Below them, on the other side, the paddling pool was empty.

"I suppose so," said Emelie. "But couldn't you have told me that over the phone?"

"Maybe, though I just committed misconduct by giving you confidential information. If you find out anything about Adam, or if he gets in touch with you, you have to let me know."

"I'm under no obligation to do that."

"But you do have morals?"

Emelie didn't reply.

"There was one more thing."

"What?"

"I'm happy for you and your friend to continue trying to work out why Katja was killed."

"The Police Authority wants to hire us as private investigators, is that what you're saying?"

"No." Nina shoved her hands into her coat pockets. "The Police Authority doesn't have anything to do with what I'm saying right now. And you wouldn't have any special authority. I'm speaking as myself, Nina Ley. And you can do what you like with what I've just told you."

"You have doubts that Adam is the right person?"

"Not really, but there's more to this case, there's a background, a history, you know that."

Emelie was no longer freezing. She felt remarkably warm.

Nina said: "Help me, Emelie. Please. Help me."

16

They were high as cumulus clouds, both of them, sitting side by side on the sofa. The computer was open on the coffee table, they had just watched two documentaries on STV Dox. *McFusk & Co* and *OJ: Trial of the Century,* though Z had spent most of the time playing with his new phone. It was the first evening in a while that they had spent chilling at home.

More than four weeks had passed, though in a way it felt like everything had happened at once. The day after they gave Billie and her gang ketamine at Dusky, she had called Roksana. "Shit, yesterday was great. Can you and Z come to Kaboom tonight? Pleeeease?" That was new: Billie had never begged Roksana to go to a club with her before—it was usually the other way around.

After an hour in Kaboom, everyone seemed to know what they had. People were begging them, crowding around them, following them like Beliebers, like they were Beyoncé and "her own little Z guy" without security guards, as Z had joked. Rumor had spread faster than Roksana thought possible. People wanted her to give them some, to try it, to buy—they wanted *a lot* of it, to experience the K high immediately. Roksana and Z had partied like they were at Gagnef and Coachella simultaneously. It was insane.

Over the days that followed, seven invites to various illegal clubs had come buzzing in on Roksana's phone—Billie had even called *Roksana* to ask whether she, *Billie,* could tag along to some of them. By midweek, friends and friends' friends and Billie's friends' friends' friends had started calling to ask which clubs *Roksana* would be going to at the weekend. Everything was upside down.

She and Z had made seventy thousand kronor in under four hours. By only two thirty in the morning on that first Saturday. They had plenty of time left to party.

During the next week, twice as many invites had come in, plus a thick paper invitation to an art event: *The Substance of the Void.* Roksana had never even heard of it, but apparently it was an artist's collective that aimed to "tear down all the power structures." She didn't know why they wrote in English when all the artists had stereotypical Swedish names, but she had asked Z if he wanted to tag along all the same.

They were living like kings—which, as Z pointed out, was actually a gendered expression, it should have been living like presidents or something equally neutral, but still. They had gone to the Paradiset supermarket by Bysistorget and bought three thousand kronors' worth of organic raw food. Roksana had bought three pairs of patent vegan leather Doc Martens in different colors, a nylon Prada backpack and a new MacBook Air. She had even made a down payment of thirty thousand kronor to a girl who had promised to take the university aptitude exam in her name and get a score of at least 1.9—if she managed it, Roksana would pay her another thirty thousand. Z had gotten himself a couple of new My Little Pony tattoos before flying to Berlin to go to Bergheim, coming out so late the next morning that he missed his plane home. Roksana's Instagram account had swelled from 234 followers to 12,000 in just six days, and no matter what she uploaded, the likes came flooding in.

Z had come back from Berlin with a pair of Fairphones for them: "The police might be listening in on someone who calls us." He looked shrewd. "Plus, these phones don't contain any minerals from conflict zones, and the workers aren't screwed over." It was the first time the thought had even crossed Roksana's mind: What would happen if the police found out they were dealing? How serious a crime was it, really? But, at the same time: How would they find out? The risk was minimal. Party on.

During the third week of February, the cute guy from Dusky had gotten in touch. He really wanted to see her, he said—but Roksana didn't have time. She had been invited to a real VIP party: DJ Ora Flesh's birthday bash. Billie's jaw had dropped when Roksana told her. "Ora Flesh invited you to her twenty-third birthday party? *You're* friends with *her*? Seriously?"

Roksana had laughed. "No, but I think she bought off me once."

The last week in February had arrived with invitations to more than twenty events. Roksana managed to make it to four of them, two a night on both Friday and Saturday. She and Z had sold K like it was candy before donating almost all of the money to Save the Children, UNHCR, and the Feminist Initiative, going to an art show, each buying a diamond nose ring, and taking a couple of trips of their own.

Roksana loved the rush like a capitalist loves money: it was simple and uncomplicated. She even forgot to call her dad on his birthday.

By early March, they had brought in more than six hundred thousand kronor, but they had already burned through two-thirds of it. Still, it had been worth it. Easily.

Now they were on the sofa, taking it easy. Everything had been fantastic lately. There was just one problem, and it was a big one. Far too big.

They had nothing left to sell. The ketamine was gone. It was *finito*—the bags were empty.

"I think it's pretty lousy toward our friends that we don't have any more. They're expecting it from us," Z said. It was the first time they had discussed it without being on a dance floor or with an apartment full of guests.

Roksana could only agree. "Still," she said. "I guess we just have to be grateful. It's been insane."

Z pursed his lips—did the whole unhappy look. "But what are we going to do now?"

Roksana unfolded a bag of green. "Go back to what we used to do. I've missed, like, a million seminars at Södertörn. I think I've got an exam next week."

They half-watched another documentary, sat in silence, continued to relax.

Roksana's phone beeped practically every other minute: SMS, Facebook, Insta, Snapchat, and more. People wanted to know which party she would be at next weekend, if she wanted to go to Burning Man, to art shows, if she could swing by with some of the good stuff, just a quickie, please.

Roksana said: "I think we're going to have a sweet term anyway."

Z said nothing; he wasn't even watching the film anymore.

After a while, he got up and went out into the hallway. "I'm going to buy breakfast. You want anything particular? Oatmeal? If we're going back to our pure, normal lives?"

Roksana stayed on the sofa, laughing to herself. She felt like the film on-screen was being shown in double vision. She thought back to the weekend before last—when they were still in full swing. At seven in the morning, she had been waiting for a ride out on Råsundavägen. She could have just taken the bus, but what the hell—she and Z had brought in record amounts of money.

It was a gray and gloomy morning, and she had seen someone coming toward her. A pusher? She glimpsed the guy's dark eyes, though maybe they weren't actually that dark. He had also been wearing a puffa jacket, but it was a completely different cut to hers—super puffy, black, new—and he was radiating something. Oozing something that none of her other friends even came close to.

"Ey, woman," he had said.

"What do you want?" she replied, realizing that her voice sounded strangely shrill.

"You new around here, or what?"

"What d'you mean?"

"You usually here?"

"No, not really."

"What's your name, then?"

"Roksana." She had taken a step back. "I don't want to buy anything."

"Did I ask if you wanted to?" The guy had taken a step toward her. "I'm not a pusher. But they're saying *you're* pushing."

Roksana could feel his presence: he was far too close to her personal space. She had wanted to get away, but she couldn't make herself move.

"Who says that?" was all she managed.

The guy hadn't bothered to reply. Instead, he moved even closer, like he wanted to whisper something in her ear.

"You pushing for Chamon?"

Roksana had shaken her head. "I don't know who that is."

The guy didn't even seem to notice that she had replied. "'Cuz if you were working for Chamon, you should know that he's done. We've taken over. You need a re-up anytime, or help with anything, you just call. And most of all, you hear any talk about Chamon, I want you to call me immediately. He was like a *baradar* to me, you know?"

"You speak Farsi?"

"No, but I think you do."

"How do you know that?"

"I've got an ear for languages, *wallah*," he said. "And you've got an almost inaudible deviation in your vowel sounds."

Roksana had stared at him—was this guy for real?

He held out a note. "I'll pay well for anything you know or hear about my brother, my *baradar*. So call me if you hear anything."

Roksana had taken the scrap of paper. She squinted down at it in the morning light. There was a phone number and a name: Nikola.

The buzzer rang. Had Z gone out without his keys? The door should still be open, Roksana hadn't locked it after he left. She heard the buzzer again. Z was probably just messing with her: maybe this was his way of joking, saying that if he went out to get breakfast, she could at least open the door. But she had a bad feeling all the same: Z didn't usually do that kind of thing.

She got up, went out into the hallway, and opened the door.

It was Z. But there was another guy beside him. He wasn't someone she knew—he looked like he was of Somali origin, with a hood covering his head and a pair of Beats headphones around his neck. He was almost as broad as the doorway. "Hi?" Roksana said.

The man dragged Z into the hallway and slammed the door shut behind them. He seemed to be limping on his right leg. "Where's the stuff?"

The bad feeling now became a really crappy feeling. Roksana took a step back, annoyed that this guy had just barged in. But at the same time, she realized something else: they'd never discussed this, her and Z—who did the ketamine they had found actually belong to?

"I don't know what you're talking about," she said. She was infinitely glad that they had thrown out the boxes and bags they found everything in.

"Just take it easy," Z tried to say. But the guy was already on his way into the living room. The computer was still open on the coffee table. The intruder spoke clearly now: "You know what I'm talking about. There was a guy who lived here before you, but the cops got him. Those losers didn't find his stash, so there were a few kilos left here, hidden away. And then the apartment was leased to you. I came here once, looking for it, but I couldn't find shit. And my foot got so fucked-up that I had to take off. My boss thought maybe the guy had screwed him over, that he'd sold it to someone else. But he hadn't, it was all still here. Meaning it's actually you two who've screwed him over."

Roksana felt cold.

"So either you give me his stuff now," the guy continued, "or you'll have serious problems, you get me?"

"But I don't know what stuff you mean. You can look around. There's nothing here."

Z nodded.

The guy cocked his head, a vein pulsing in his forehead. "Do I look like some kind of junkie, or what?"

"No, no, we just don't know what stuff you're talking about," said Roksana, but she could hear that her voice didn't sound entirely convincing.

"You seem to be having trouble understanding me. We *know* you've been selling our shit. I don't like hurting girls, but your friend, on the other hand . . ."

Z didn't have time to react or pull back before the guy grabbed his hand.

"Let me go," he moaned.

Roksana tried to grab ahold of the intruder's arm. "Please, stop."

The guy bent Z's fingers.

By the time Roksana worked out what was happening, it was too late, even though she seemed to be watching it unfold in slow motion. The index and middle fingers on Z's left hand were bent back, unnaturally. Eventually, there was a clicking sound, and Z screamed.

The guy dropped Z's hand. He closed his eyes—as though he couldn't bring himself to look at what he had just done.

Z whimpered, shouted, cried. Two of his fingers were flopping limply. They were broken.

"You cry like a whore," said the guy. "But you've screwed over the wrong guy."

TELEPHONE CONVERSATION 10

To: Hugo Pederson
From: Göran Blixt (boss)
Date: 6 November 2005
Time: 13:46

GÖRAN: Hugo, are you at the office?

HUGO: No, I'm just out for lunch.

GÖRAN: Do you think this is the public sector or something?

HUGO: Ha ha, I wasn't planning on *eating* out, I'm just grabbing something for the office.

GÖRAN: That's better. I just wanted to let you know, we're pulling out of the Danfoss deal. I'll give the same instructions to everyone else now.

HUGO: What, why?

GÖRAN: KKR doesn't want us in as a major shareholder, so they've been buying A shares like idiots. We could fight them, like we did with Scania, but this time my judgment is that it's just not worth it. The price has already gone up 4 percent, so we're not doing a bad deal, it's just a long way off what we had planned.

HUGO: I'm wondering if that's the right call. We should wait a few days.

GÖRAN: Once you've made up your mind there's no reason to wait, but of course we'll offload the shares quietly, so the price doesn't drop.

HUGO: But the timing'll be better in a week. I'm convinced the Fed's going to lower interest rates. That'll get the market moving again.

GÖRAN: No, we can't wait for macro measures. We'll start selling today. See you at the office.

HUGO: Okay.

GÖRAN: Oh, Hugo, buy me some lunch, too. But be back here in ten minutes.

TELEPHONE CONVERSATION 11

To: Pierre Danielsson (co-suspect)
From: Hugo Pederson
Date: 6 November 2005
Time: 13:48

HUGO: Hey, call me on the burner.

PIERRE: What's going on?

HUGO: Let's do it on the burners.

TELEPHONE CONVERSATION 12

To: Hugo Pederson

From: Pierre Danielsson (co-suspect)

Date: 6 November 2005

Time: 13:49

PIERRE: So what's going on?

HUGO: We're calling off the Danish deal.

PIERRE: What're you saying? Why?

HUGO: Göran doesn't want to be involved anymore, I don't know why but think it's because KKR doesn't want us in. I've got to dash now.

PIERRE: Hang on. You need to control this. You've been buying these shares yourself, so if you start panic selling now, there's a damn good chance someone's going to notice. I need you to take it easy.

HUGO: But we have to sell now, otherwise we're looking at crazy losses.

PIERRE: I don't care. If you're in the game, you've got to take it up the ass sometimes. Now take it easy, you hear me?

HUGO: I'll try. Maybe we can short it at the same time? But I've got to go now. Ciao.

TELEPHONE CONVERSATION 13

To: Jesper Ringblad (stockbroker, Nordea)

From: Hugo Pederson

Date: 6 November 2005

Time: 13:50

HUGO: Hey, Jeppe. I want to sell Danfoss.

JESPER: Already? It's at 118. You've dropped almost five percent. I think it could recover next week.

HUGO: Yeah, but I'm telling you to sell. The whole lot. In blocks. Extremely important that it's in blocks, even more important than before.

JESPER: You're the boss. What limit?

HUGO: If you can shift them for 117, I'm happy. But I'll go down to 116. Everything has to go.

JESPER: Okay . . . hold on . . . I think I can offload them right now, hold on . . . (inaudible)

(*Note: Jesper Ringblad can be heard talking about the Danfoss B shares with someone in the background.*)

JESPER: I'm back. You're in luck, I've just sold them all in one lump. But it's a loss of almost two million kronor.

HUGO: You're a star, my man. A star.

JESPER: You almost sound happy?

HUGO: I'm so happy, I could suck you off right now.

TELEPHONE CONVERSATION 14
To: Hugo Pederson
From: Louise Pederson (wife)
Date: 6 November 2005
Time: 20:35

LOUISE: Hi, do you know how late you'll be working today?

HUGO: Hey, Mousey. I have no idea, things're pretty busy right now.

LOUISE: It was so nice when we went out to eat a few weeks ago. Can we try doing that again soon? Maybe on Thursday or Friday?

HUGO: Nah, no can do.

LOUISE: Why not?

HUGO: We're so busy right now.

LOUISE: But you can sneak off for two hours, can't you? I can book a table and everything, somewhere near you. You don't even have to drink, I can drink your wine . . .

HUGO: I have to go now.

LOUISE: No, wait. I spoke to Premiform.

HUGO: Who?

LOUISE: The interior architects, you know.

HUGO: We're having interior architects?

LOUISE: Yeees, of course. You have to. Anyway, they've put in all the orders now, but I swapped the limestone for the little bathroom for Kolmård marble. I think it could be really nice. I saw that the Oberlands have it at their place.

HUGO: How much extra is that?

LOUISE: I'm not really sure, but what I wanted to say was that I've also decided we should redo the floor. I want to get rid of the radiators. They're so ugly. So now Premiform are drawing underfloor heating into all the rooms.

HUGO: Mousey . . .

LOUISE: It'll be fantastic.

HUGO: I mean . . .

LOUISE: What?

HUGO: Ahh, nothing. See you later, if you're still awake. Otherwise, see you tomorrow. Kisses.

TELEPHONE CONVERSATION 15

To: Carl Trolle (friend)
From: Hugo Pederson
Date: 6 November 2005
Time: 21:58

HUGO: Hey, man.

CARL: Hey hey, how's it going?

HUGO: Ah, so-so.

CARL: What? What's the problem?

HUGO: Ah, you know, sometimes you just feel a bit off.

CARL: I've got a tennis slot at lunch tomorrow, want to come and play?

HUGO: I don't have time.

CARL: But you do have time for whining?

HUGO: Nah, but you know what it's like.

CARL: You're still coming on Saturday, though?

HUGO: We'll see. Do you never feel like you've lost all your energy?

CARL: What?

HUGO: I mean, like you can't cope. Like you're thinking about just dropping everything and running away?

CARL: Strip club in London, or what?

HUGO: I don't mean it like that. I've been working tons lately, and I know that I'm in one of the country's best places, but it's like that's not enough. Everyone always wants more, no one respects that I just need to be on my own sometimes. Louise is the worst. She thinks I should be delivering more and more every month, but sometimes there might be a lull, you know? Sometimes you just have to take a breather and consolidate everything, your finances, relationships. Not everything has to be so intense all the time. My head's burning, sometimes it feels like I'm going to boil over, or explode somehow.

CARL: Uhhh?

HUGO: Do you know what I mean? Do you never feel trapped like that?

CARL: No, not really.

HUGO: Plus, I've been having trouble sleeping at night.

CARL: You're just worked up, keeping at it the way you are. You're probably thinking about your deals.

HUGO: You bet.

CARL: Maybe thinking about them too much?

HUGO: Impossible. All I really want is to be filthy rich.

CARL: That's what everyone wants.

HUGO: Sure, but it's like I want it more. Not even so I can buy a load of crap, consume and all that. I just want to be rich. I want to own a lot. Full stop.

CARL: Mmm. So you're not coming tomorrow? Me and Gustaf. If you two double up, we'll have ourselves a match.

HUGO: I don't think I have time, sorry.

CARL: Okay, but listen, I have to go now. Speak later.

HUGO: Yeah, okay.

17

"I like it when chicks pretend to come," said Dejan. They were in his car, on the way to meet a middleman. "Like, they want me to feel like a man, no matter what they're feeling. You know?"

"Nah."

"You getting any these days?"

For once, Teddy could have answered the question that Dejan asked at least once a week. But he kept quiet. He didn't know why he had followed Emelie up to her apartment that night after they went out to eat, even less why they hadn't spoken since. At the same time, the image of her on top of him was practically tattooed on the inside of his eyelids. There had been something about her there, in bed; it was like she had lowered her defenses for a moment and let him in, like she had been willing to meet him for a short period of time. But he still hadn't had the nerve to get in touch—plus, it felt like Emelie's request that they work together had collapsed after Katja's murder.

They climbed out of Dejan's car. Necks craned, heads turned. Södermalm—this was somewhere a Model X stuck out more than a Formula 1 car on a cycle path. The exchange office was fifty feet down the road. Dejan's various construction firms meant that he had hordes of carpenters, cement guys, prefab people, electricians, and HVAC guys all waiting to be paid. The setup he used was classic: Dejan's firms were invoiced by companies that had been set up by the launderers, often recruitment agencies on paper. They paid these invoices and could therefore deduct the costs—including VAT. The launderers' companies then passed the money out into the world: there was no art to withdrawing or depositing large sums of cash in Turkey or Hong Kong, for example—the checks there were nonexistent. The money was sent back to the exchange offices scattered around Stockholm, and was paid out, in cash, to the tradesmen. It was a system in which everyone involved gained.

Teddy was with him today for the same reason as at the car garage: so Dejan didn't appear alone. Everyone had to be able to show that they could put some force behind their words, that they had backup. He thought about what Isa at the employment service would have said if she'd had to write his job application. *Teddy has plenty of previous experience working as a gorilla.*

The man who came toward them from the exchange bureau had probably already split the cash into two envelopes, one for Dejan and one for his people—and he also had someone waiting in the background. Teddy's counterpart was sitting in an X6 parked just over the road, he was sure of it.

He thought back to the past few weeks. He'd spent his nights lying awake, seeing things. Mats Emanuelsson's kidnapping redux— being arrested, sentenced to prison. He imagined he was back in the cell in Håga prison, where the corrupt police officer, Sundén, doing the network's dirty work, had kept him prisoner last year. A blurry face: Sundén's accomplice, who had never been caught. A demon in Teddy's head. He heard noises, explosions, over and over again: the blast that had echoed through the darkness as someone shot Sundén. That crap had started up again. Katja's murder had brought it all back.

Maybe Emelie had decided to give up when her client was murdered; maybe she didn't want to follow through. But Teddy had no such plans—he had spent the past month trying to find out as much as he could about Adam Tagrin. He had to be able to find the guy.

After a week or so, he had met Loke Odensson over a mead, as Loke called the beer they drank. They had talked about the old days, when they were both in the slammer, and about Loke's family life. Loke had written a summary, which he handed over.

"Thanks for taking the time," said Teddy. "You write like a FBI agent or something, do you know that?"

Loke had twisted his fingers in his plaited beard. "*An,* my darling, it's *an* FBI agent. Eff bee eye, you understand? And I hate those fuckers."

Adam Tagrin was forty-two, born in Belarus, and had come to Sweden with his mother during the eighties. He had grown up in Skogås, just outside of Stockholm, and he'd had a number of dealings with social services and the police during the early nineties. Suspicions of alcohol addiction, neglect, abuse. On one occasion, fifteen-year-old Adam had been forced to spend the night on a cold porch after his stepfather threw him out. On another, it was reported that the stepfather had tried to force sixteen-year-old Adam and his friend to act in a pornographic film. Adam himself had no prior convictions, aside from a couple of traffic violations and one instance of violent resistance when he got into trouble with a couple of guards in a metro station. He didn't seem to have any physical ailments. Thirteen years ago, he had become a father, to Oliver, but had never lived with the boy's mother. These days, he spent his time editing porn films, running websites, and, every now and then, organizing so-called shows—Loke had been unable to find out exactly what that involved.

Teddy had staked out the apartment on Gösta Ekmans väg for several days to see if Adam would show up, but no one had set foot in there, not even the police. He had tried to get ahold of the man's mother and stepfather, but they had apparently moved to Thailand ten years earlier. He had spoken to Adam's old friends from Skogås, but none of them had any idea where he was these days. Then his thoughts had turned to Adam's business: K Tagrin Import AB had an office in Farsta Strand. He decided to head out there.

———

A man with glossy gray hair and a pierced eyebrow had opened the office door and studied Teddy with curiosity. He was wearing a Houdini fleece and what looked like walking pants, with side pockets and reinforced knees. Teddy had wondered whether he had accidentally come to a gathering for the Outdoor Association.

"Can I help you, sir?" The old man's mountain style ended at his feet: he was wearing Crocs and tube socks.

"I'm looking for Adam Tagrin," Teddy had said. There was no reason not to tell the truth.

"He's not here, I'm afraid," the man had replied, moving to close the door.

Teddy jammed his foot in the gap. "I don't want to hurt him. I know the police suspect him of what happened, because I'm involved, too."

The man seemed even more curious then. "*Ach soo*. What did you say your name was?" He had a lisp.

"Teddy. And you?"

"Jesús, strictly speaking, but the majority don't seem to think that name suits what we do, so they call me John. Come in, we can talk."

The office was small and smelled of dust and stale coffee. In the room they entered, there were two desks covered in computers and screens. The curtains were closed. John had sat down at one of the desks, rolled back in his chair, and sneezed: he seemed to have a bad cold. "Do you want lunch? I just ordered some pizza."

Teddy had peered at one of the computer screens in front of Jesús aka John: two men and a woman were having sex, she had both of their members inside her.

John followed his gaze. "We do the cutting here, you see. Can't have too much talking, you need to get straight down to it, but everyone has to follow the script."

"I'll skip lunch, but do you have time to talk?" Teddy had asked.

"Okay, while I wait for lunch."

Teddy sat down. "How long have you and Adam been working together?"

"About three years. I was doing instruction videos before this. You know, for installing AC and that kind of thing."

"Did you know Adam before?"

"No."

"Have you met Katja?"

"It's sick, what happened. Katja was a really good girl."

"Has she been here, to the office?"

"Yes, she met Adam here sometimes."

"Did she know what Adam did?"

"What do you mean?"

"That you edit and distribute this kind of film?"

"Of course she knew. Adam's not exactly a secretive person, let's put it like that. He told me they were going traveling, for example. He even kept a packed suitcase here for a while."

Teddy wanted to understand. Whether Adam had been off balance lately, whether he had been angry at Katja for any reason. If he had told John anything that sounded unusual. If he was using drugs.

"Have you heard from Adam since?" Teddy had eventually asked.

"I'm not stupid, you know? I'm aware that the police are looking for him. I don't want to get mixed up in that. I just want Adam to come back to work and stop all this so we can pay the bills. I heard he stayed at a friend's place for a few nights, but that guy's already been interviewed by the police." John had spun around in his chair and sneezed again. "And I don't think he did what they're saying, to Katja." His eyebrow ring glittered faintly in the glow of the desk lamp. "He could be a bit rough with her sometimes, that's true, but it was 'cause he loved her."

Teddy had waited for some further explanation, but John seemed almost absent, his gaze unfocused. The buzzer had rung.

John got up and Teddy heard him talking to someone in the hall-way before he returned with a pizza box.

He cut the pizza into six equal slices. "All right, time for you to go. I need to eat in peace," he had said.

"Just one last question. In what way was Adam rough with Katja?"

John had tipped the salad that came with the pizza onto one slice and shoved the whole thing into his mouth.

"You know," he had said. "Some women just do that to a man. They bring out the worst in them."

18

Sometimes, it felt like a year had passed. Sometimes, it was like everything with Chamon had happened only yesterday. The papers had written about the shooting two days later, but then there had been a triple murder in Malmö and that had taken over the headlines.

Nikola was sleeping like shit. Popping pills and smoking joints just so he felt calm enough to lie down in bed. The sun never rose: he was living in a world of shadowy rage. He didn't have the energy to work out. When he went to buy food, he glanced over his shoulder every other minute, kept thinking he had seen the guys from the hospital. He listened to old music that Linda had given him a long time ago: REM—"Everybody Hurts"; Eric Clapton—"Tears in Heaven."

I don't belong in heaven, either, he thought. Not yet, anyway.

A path through the night. He had to find a path.

But he wasn't planning to take it alone.

Yusuf and Bello rang him from time to time, checking how things were going. Above all, they helped him with what needed to happen. One single word flew through his mind: "revenge."

The day after Isak decided they should get started, he and Yusuf had gone straight to Karolinska Hospital. They took the same route those bastards must have taken, with the difference that they kept looking upward. They immediately spotted the cameras in the entrance and along the hallways—thank God for the surveillance society. Nikola and Yusuf had drifted over to the information desk on the ground floor. Tried to talk to the guard. She had short hair, a nose ring, and a tattoo of Little My on her neck—but she refused to even discuss it with them. According to Yusuf: the guardwoman must be a massive dike. Nikola had asked her to call her manager. After a while, a thin man had come sauntering down the hallway: uniform, long hair, and crooked teeth. According to Yusuf: the hair-guard must be a massive poof.

The hair-guard had shaken his head and looked sad when they asked him the same question. They wanted to see the surveillance tapes from the day Chamon was killed. The guy had looked so distressed that Nicko thought he was about to start screaming—it was a joke, this *kahbo* had never even met Chamon, so what did he have to be upset about?

"I'm sorry, it's against the rules. And it's the police investigating everything," the guard had said, adding: "Not you."

They had waited outside the hospital all day, clocking the guy's movements: when he ate lunch, what time he finished, which parking lot he used. They followed him and identified which car he drove—a worn-out old Fiat with rusty rims. The next day, they had broken into his car, and Yusuf had lain down on the backseat with a carbon fiber knife. Nikola had positioned himself fifty feet away and tried to see into the car. When the guard climbed in later that day, he had watched Yusuf rise up in the backseat like some kind of motherfucking zombie, balaclava covering his face, put the knife to the guy's throat, and explain that they would follow him everywhere if he didn't help. Thirty minutes later, the guard had uploaded fourteen films to a Dropbox account Nikola had just opened. Fourteen cameras. Fourteen angles. Fourteen different clips of the killers in sunglasses.

Nikola, Yusuf, and Bello had picked out the clearest sections of film. They were from the camera by the elevators. For roughly seven seconds, the two men had stood still and waited, the eye of the camera staring straight at them from one side, maybe five feet away. The bastard with what looked like a scorpion tattoo on his neck was clearest, though the image still wasn't perfect: when they tried to zoom in, it was pixellated. Still: it was enough.

Every night for the past few weeks, Nikola, Yusuf, and Bello had gone to Gravediggers, O'Learys, Croc's, Telgias, and every other dive bar in Södertälje. Showed the men from the film to bouncers, doormen, bartenders, and certain customers. "You recognize any of these guys?" The majority knew what it was about. Chamon's murder wasn't exactly a secret in Södertälje.

They had talked to people they knew, to people who knew people they knew. They showed the film around. Paused it right as the murdering bastards stepped into the elevator, when the guy with the tattoo was clearest. Asked the same question over and over again.

Everyone wanted to help. Everyone hoped for favors from Mr. One in return. Since they all wanted to do their bit for the big man, there was no trusting anyone.

Still, no one had recognized the killers.

A week ago, it had been time to report back. Yusuf had talked about needing to lie low for a while. When he came out onto the street from his apartment, a beat-up Toyota had driven by with its windows wound down and automatic weapons in its passengers' outstretched hands. A drive-by, in broad daylight: this was the new Sweden. Yusuf had thrown himself inside—but still: south Stockholm really was transforming into the Wild West. And Murray and his cop friends were doing nada about it. Or rather: society was doing nothing—the brothers were crazy, but they were crazy for a reason.

Lunchtime. Isak was eating noisette. Wearing huge black headphones—all you could hear was the faint sound of the music.

Bello had been playing with his fingers like some nervous schoolkid waiting to see the principal.

Isak: shaved head, stomach that pushed up against the table even though he had moved the chair back. The Syriac eagle tattooed on his forearm. Though, it wasn't really an eagle, Chamon had once explained to Nikola; it was a torch, a sun, with wings. "It's meant to be red, for all the blood that's been spilled. We've been persecuted for centuries." Chamon's voice had been serious. But it was all just crap, Nikola thought. Chamon's family had fled from repression in one place to experience violence in another. It was fundamentally fucked-up.

The boss had wiped his mouth and picked up his glass of cola. He hadn't touched it while he ate. Now he downed its contents in one go.

He burped. Picked at his teeth.

"So," he had said. "What's going on?"

Nikola had summarized what little they had found out. Bello nodded every now and then. Nikola said: "But we don't get how they could've known Chamon was meeting you and Yusuf at the gym, how they could've known *where* you were meeting, or how they could've known which ward he was on."

"I have no idea," Isak had replied, pushing back his chair even farther. "But I think they were out for me."

"So why did they go to the hospital?"

"That's a damn good question, maybe they wanted to send some pussy signal to me. But they can forget about me bending over."

"We even went out west and showed people pictures of the bastards. No one knows who they are."

"I'm so upset, you know? I think about Chamon every day. And I'm always so depressed at this time of year as it is. Everything's so gray. Plus, it's almost always this time of year in Sweden."

Isak had been cooler than when he gave his speech after the funeral. Maybe it was the weeks that had passed, or maybe it was just what it took to be who he was—keeping your cool even though they were trying to grind you down, even though they had managed to clip one of your own. Maybe that was how you had to act—if you wanted to be top dog.

Isak had said: "Keep checking in with Chamon's crowd, the people he sold stuff to at the illegal clubs and all that. It might all be something to do with someone there."

Nikola had already been asking around at those huge clubs, trying to find out if anyone knew anything about the murder. He thought back to one of the pushers he talked to a while back, at some party in an industrial estate. He had immediately recognized the way her vowel sounds were almost sucked when she talked, the way his grandfather often mentioned. She spoke perfect Swedish— but he had been able to hear that someone must have taught her Farsi, too. Roksana was her name—and for some reason, he remembered her especially well.

Back to the now. Boxer shorts. Stale taste in his mouth. Pain in his feet—he didn't know why.

Someone rang the buzzer. Nikola pulled on a T-shirt and went to answer. Before he unlocked the door, he checked the spy hole. He had made a habit of doing it even before the whole Chamon incident—yet another aftereffect of the explosion.

But the person out in the stairwell wasn't dangerous. It was his mother, holding two bags of food.

"It stinks in here, Nicko. I'll do some cleaning," was the first thing she said.

Nikola didn't have the energy. He turned around and started to make his way back to bed. The clock on the microwave showed ten thirty. His mom took off her shoes—completely pointless, since the floor was definitely filthier than the street outside. "You have to stop turning your phone off, Nicko, I want to be able to call you, see how you're doing."

Nikola sat down on the bed, his head bowed.

"I know it's not easy, love, but I think you should start working again."

Nikola turned on his phone. He had a missed call from Bello.

"Did you just come here to nag?" he asked. "Or did you want something?"

"I came here to nag," she said with a smirk.

She went out into the kitchen. Nikola heard her open the fridge and start loading the food into it. He knew there was nothing in there other than a couple of bottles of Coca-Cola and a pack of butter, which could probably crawl by this point. She started to make breakfast.

"Do you just lie around here all day, doing nothing?"

She had no idea, and it was best that way. Nikola had gone to two more raves last night, plus three clubs, trying to get ahold of people who had pushed for Chamon, who might know something. He wanted to track down the girl, too. Roksana. But she seemed to have done some kind of Stockholm delete on herself.

"Hello, Nicko? Anyone home?"

Nikola put down his sandwich, hadn't even taken a bite of it. "Sorry. I'm just tired. I'm not sleeping well."

"I understand that. But let's agree to this: if I clean up here and cook you plenty of good food that you can freeze, you'll at least give George Samuel a call and ask if you can work part-time again?"

Nikola didn't know what to say. He didn't have time for work. The only job he could do right now was try to find those whores.

The next day, he found himself standing outside Södertälje police station. A door in a gray building. Half a story down. Concrete walls, plastic floors, and visitor chairs in pale wood worn shiny from use. Simon Murray had called him in for another interview.

Reception was full of people, like always: the majority were probably there to sort out their passports, but others were there to report stolen cars or break-ins and other crap like that.

After five minutes, that pussy Murray appeared with a colleague in tow. The same black boots, the same sporty rubber watch on his wrist, but a grumpier expression. He didn't say hello. "Let's take it easy today." Nikola knew why he hadn't come alone: Murray wasn't planning to let Nikola degrade him with saliva again.

Instead of an interview room, Murray took him up to a hallway. There were police officers everywhere, standing around and chatting. The walls were covered in old police posters that looked like they were from the eighties. Outside their little offices, some of the detectives had stuck up notes. *Keep calm and stop the hooligans. I love my job . . . during lunch and coffee breaks.* They were trying to be funny.

Murray's room looked like it belonged to someone on amphetamines. He had a bookcase full of books, newspapers, and, above all, folders along one wall. Next to that were piles of jam-packed case files. The rest of the floor was covered in papers, some in plastic folders and others loose, probably all preliminary investigations. In the midst of the chaos was a framed picture of a kid, a boy with blond curly hair who looked about four. Nikola had never realized that Murray might have kids.

"Sit," said Murray.

"Where?"

Murray moved a stack of papers, and a chair appeared. His colleague leaned against one wall with his arms crossed.

The officer started asking his questions, roughly the same ones as last time. Where did the first shooting take place? What did the shooters from the hospital look like? What were they wearing? Which weapons did you see? Nikola replied taciturnly, mostly that he couldn't remember or didn't know. And it was true; he had the images from the surveillance cameras at the hospital, but in his own mind he couldn't see any faces, couldn't hear any chatter. Still: maybe Nikola could get something out of this. *He* was going to interview the cops just as much as they were him.

"Did your technicians find anything? DNA, fingerprints, fibers?"

"Have you done any checks on the cell towers?"

"Have you found out which car they arrived in?"

"What's your main line of inquiry?"

Murray shook his head. "I can't divulge any of that."

"But don't you have a duty to inform the general public?"

The atmosphere was about as far from comfortable as it could be—though maybe that wasn't so strange. Nikola almost regretted spitting in the racist bastard's face.

"*The general public*—you almost sound like you've got an education," said Murray. "It's not often you find that in people from your domain."

Nikola's reply came as quick as an uppercut to the jaw. "Or yours."

Murray smiled, but there wasn't an ounce of fondness on his face.

"I think we'll stop there for today. We're not getting anywhere. You're behaving just like last time. But there's something you should know." He paused. "We've arrested an acquaintance of yours. He'll be remanded in custody tomorrow."

"Who?"

"His name's Isak. It's usually enough just to give his first name."

Nikola couldn't find his way out. He followed Murray like a *kelb* on a lead. They didn't say a word to one another.

Reception was still full. His head was spinning: Mr. One arrested. For what? Did it have something to do with the murder? Murray and his bastard colleague had refused to say.

He opened the door and went out onto the street. The sky was as gray as the concrete.

"Nikola."

He turned around. It was Emanuel Hanna, Chamon's father. He looked ten years older than he had when Nikola saw him at the funeral. They hugged. Still: Nikola couldn't bring himself to look him in the eye.

"How are you?"

"No one should have to go through what Ranya and I are going through."

"I know."

His shoulders looked stooped.

"But what are you doing here?" Nikola asked.

Emanuel held up a paper bag. "I came to collect Chamon's belongings. His wallet, watch, cell phones."

Nikola thought back to the questions he had asked Murray, questions the cop had refused to answer: technicians, car tracing, cell towers.

Cell towers.

"Emanuel, this might sound strange," said Nikola, "but could I borrow Chamon's phones? Just for a few days."

Emanuel held out the bag. "Nikola, there's almost nothing I would refuse you."

19

Emelie was thinking about lying down on the floor in her office and taking a nap. She had slept like crap again last night, which probably wasn't so surprising: Nina had called to say that they had finally arrested Adam Tagrin.

Now she was waiting for Teddy. She had finally decided to break the strange stalemate between them. They needed to talk now that Tagrin was in police custody.

The strange feeling from last night still lingered in her body. She had lain down on the edge of the bed and breathed—she didn't want her face half-buried in a pillow. She needed space and room. But when she needed to think, the opposite was true—a strange truth: the way she lay in bed affected how she thought.

Marcus was working in his room, like usual. The door was open, and Emelie could hear him tapping away at the keyboard. Two of the old fogies—as Emelie and Marcus had secretly started calling the other lawyers—were drinking coffee in the kitchen. She really did have nothing against them—they were all competent lawyers who did their jobs, but they weren't exactly in their prime, weren't top of the line. "How do you know that?" Marcus had asked as he and Emelie were discussing them one lunch. "I mean, there aren't any rankings like there are for corporate lawyers." But

Emelie knew. It was nothing to do with their shrewdness; it was to do with their lack of energy.

Teddy would be here soon.

She had met Oliver, Adam's son, the day before. He had called her and asked to meet.

The boy lived with a foster family in Bredäng, but he had wanted to meet in the square. She spotted him from a distance. His stride was determined, but his body language seemed uncertain overall. He kept glancing around, as though he were worried about being seen by someone, and it had looked as though he was keeping to the walls of the buildings as he approached. He couldn't be much older than twelve or thirteen, but it was obvious whose son he was—he had small teeth, almost like he hadn't lost all of his milk teeth yet. Unlike Emelie, he had been properly dressed for the weather, with a down coat, hat, and gloves.

Why do I never learn, Emelie had wondered. She had been shivering in the cold.

She held out a hand. "Oliver?"

The boy had looked down at the ground and taken off one glove.

"Do you want to go to a café or something? Or would you rather speak here?"

The boy had sighed. "We can talk here."

People were streaming out of the metro station. A train from the north must have just arrived.

"Do your parents know we're meeting?"

"They're not my parents. I just live with them. And I've told them I want to meet you. They don't think I should be doing this. They think it's enough that the police have asked me about Dad."

"I see. So why did you want to meet?"

"You were going to help Katja, so I thought maybe you could help Dad now that the police have him."

"In what way?"

"He didn't do what they're saying. He didn't kill Katja. I know it. They can't send him to prison."

"But he must have a lawyer by now. He has someone to help him."

"Yeah, but are they any good? Can you tell me that? Does he have a good lawyer? Is he going to get out?"

Oliver's mouth and eyes had shifted, as though he had forgotten which expression went with which word. Emelie knew the lawyer who had been appointed to Adam Tagrin: she was one of the best.

"I'm afraid I can't help your dad," she had explained. "There are certain rules, and they say that I can't be his lawyer. That's just how it is. I'm sorry."

Oliver didn't seem to have understood. Emelie had tried to explain again.

"So, I was Katja's lawyer, and now your dad is suspected of having done this to her. It means I can't be his lawyer, because it would be like playing for different teams at the same time."

She didn't know how good an analogy it was, but it seemed like the boy had finally gotten it. He pulled up the hood of his coat and quickly turned around and walked away.

"Call me if you have any questions," Emelie had shouted after him.

She was talking to the back of his head.

Teddy came into her office. She took a step forward. He took a step forward. He looked tired. He could have that: she was more tired.

They stood opposite one another. Shook hands. Like people who didn't know one another, who shrunk back from the other's touch.

"How are you?"

"Okay," Emelie lied. "You?"

"I'm okay."

They sat down. Teddy glanced around like he had never been to her office before.

"You wanted to meet," he said.

"You too," Emelie replied. She had realized when they agreed to meet that he had things he wanted to tell her.

"But you most of all," he said.

Emelie couldn't help but smile. She played with the pen on the desk in front of her. "Yeah, maybe," she said. "They've arrested Adam. So the whole thing might be over now."

She briefly went through what she had found out about the cuts on Adam's hands.

Teddy said: "I hear what you're saying. I've done everything I can to find out who Adam Tagrin is and where he's been over the past few weeks, and I haven't found anything that rules out him killing Katja. But none of it explains the bag on the roof. It could hardly have been Adam's, could it?"

"I don't think so."

"Do you remember what you said to me last time I was here? Just after Katja got in touch with you?"

"Not really."

"You said that we'd never found who was really behind all this. We gave up halfway. And that there was something more to this. So if we're going to get those pigs, we have to keep going. We can't stop now."

"But what happened to Katja might have nothing to do with the network."

"It has everything to do with it."

Emelie knew he was right.

"So what do you want us to do?"

Teddy cleared his throat: "There's only one person who can help us."

Nina Ley spat her pouch of snus tobacco onto the ground. It looked like a reindeer dropping—Emelie remembered getting up early as a child and seeing the small lumps on the lawn. Once, she had pulled on a pair of winter gloves and gathered them all in a bucket. Her mother had been furious, but her father had just laughed: "Maybe we should hire you as a poo hunter?"

"You wanted to meet," Nina said once they reached the top of Kronobergsparken—the same place as last time.

"What is Adam Tagrin saying?"

"He denies any wrongdoing. Otherwise, I can't give you much, you know that."

"Have you analyzed the bag we found on the roof?"

"No, not yet, there's a backlog at forensics. Why?"

"I'm just wondering. It doesn't fit."

"You wanted to meet just so you could ask me that?"

"No."

Emelie thought of Mats Emanuelsson, who was probably living under a different name in another northern European country, with a different personal ID number and possibly even a different appearance. His children, Benjamin and Lillan, were no longer in Sweden, either. Teddy had apparently tried to talk to Cecilia, his ex, but she had said that she didn't know where Mats was, and that even if she did, she wouldn't have told him.

Emelie said, "Now that you have Adam Tagrin, I wanted to know if you still needed our help."

Nina pushed a new pouch of snus beneath her lip. "I do."

"In that case, we need to talk to Mats Emanuelsson."

Nina studied Emelie, adjusting the tobacco with her tongue as she did so.

"I'm afraid that's impossible. His identity is protected, covered by the witness protection program."

"Nina, you want to solve this as much as I do. I'm not just talking about Katja's murder here, but everything you've been investigating this past year. You don't seem to have had much success so far, I have to be honest."

"That's true. But we're slowly moving forward."

"Then there's only one way. We only have one demand for helping you."

"And what's that?"

"I've already told you. That you make sure we can meet Mats Emanuelsson."

20

It could have been a sweet evening. Under Bron was about to make the switch to Trädgården—the indoor club was shedding its skin to become the outdoor space, in other words. UB was held in an old building beneath the Skanstull Bridge, a building that might have been one of Stockholm's most beautiful if they hadn't decided to build the capital's biggest bridge right over the top of it. The club opened its doors in September every year, closing again in spring when TG took over. Right now, people were allowed to move between the two spaces, indoors and out, like drifting beads of mercury. The focus was on dance music, with resident DJs and international guest artists.

It could have been an insanely social evening. Billie and her entourage were there, as was the cute guy and tons of other people who had loved Roksana over the past few weeks. Z was there—and he seemed to be doing well, despite the fact that two of his fingers were in plaster.

Billie didn't know anything about what happened. She was going on about a new art project she had started, which involved sneaking around at night spraying vaginas onto various public sculptures and statues.

"I call it guerrilla pussification. The genital organs of people like us, the people society defines as women, have to become part of the public sphere."

Z laughed like an idiot and offered Billie a hit—the very last one. He must have had a small bag left in his pocket. Roksana didn't know what Z was thinking; everything seemed to be business as usual with him—despite the broken fingers, threats, and chaos.

After they went to the hospital to get Z's hand seen to, they had gone to eat lunch at a café in Akalla. There was a cold band of rain hanging over the center, more like a wet fog than raindrops. It found its way to Roksana even when she stuck too close to the buildings, beneath their overhanging roofs. Some things just got through to you, no matter how much you tried to run.

There was a picture of an icon hanging behind the till. Roksana had ordered cardamom buns and cappuccinos with regular milk for both of them. If Billie could have seen her then, she would probably have tried to have Roksana carted away to be detoxed: white flour, sugar, and lactose, more dangerous than dirty heroin.

"This bun's so good it's like a party in my mouth," Z had said. It seemed like he had already put his recent trip to the hospital behind him.

"What are we going to do, Z?"

Z had enjoyed a few more bites. "We'll have to try talking to them, reasoning with them. Work out what they really want from us."

And so they had tried. The psychos had agreed to meet at the Star Inn in Haninge.

Z and Roksana had arrived at the hotel room first. Three floors up. The curtains were already drawn. She wondered whether reception usually prepped their rooms for this kind of meeting.

After a while, the door had opened, and the same guy who had come to their apartment stepped into the room, followed by another man. The first was wearing the same clothes as before. Hoodie and similar Adidas sweatpants to the ones Billie usually wore. The other guy looked roughly the same age, wearing similar clothes, though he was heavier and his hoodie was leather and said

Gucci in small golden letters on the chest. Good taste didn't exactly seem to be these gangsters' strong point. Still: he was the calmer of the two. It was clear who was in charge.

The leader had shaken their hands and then pulled out the desk chair to sit down. The first guy stayed by the door with his arms crossed. Roksana had thought about how he hadn't been able to look when he broke Z's fingers. Suddenly she became aware of how claustrophobically small the room was, that their only escape route had just been blocked.

No one had said a word.

Z was pressed up against the window—stiff as an ice pop, the hand with the broken fingers hanging by one leg. Roksana was still sitting on the bed. The room's air-conditioning was loud. The bed was uncomfortable, far too soft. It had felt like she was sinking into the floor. She had waited for Z to say something.

The leader had nodded to him. "How's the hand?"

"It'll take a few weeks," Z had replied, holding it up to them.

"It's good you wanted to dialogue," the man had said, as though Z's broken fingers had nothing to do with them. Roksana thought: Dialogue's a noun, fatty, not a verb. Though maybe it was a verb, it suddenly struck her—just like break, abuse. Snap.

"It would've been good if we could have talked before you snapped my friend's fingers," she said.

The fat leader had leaned forward in his chair. "We're always willing to talk, but we're not clowns. And now we're here. We came because you wanted to *dialogue*. So, tell me: What do you want to talk about?"

It sounded as though Z had let out a squeak. Then Roksana heard him try to speak. "We're willing to pay you something, but we don't have much money, so you can't be hoping for some huge sum."

The leader had leaned back. Mouth closed, his jaw still moving—maybe he was working a piece of chewing gum or snus in there. "At first, I thought the kid who rented the place before you had sold my shit to someone else, 'cause my friend here couldn't find a thing. Believe me, I was a cunt hair away from paying someone in prison to cut that bitch down. But I was wrong. You're the ones who sold it. And for that, I want a million."

Roksana's brain had imploded; she could barely breathe.

A million—they would never be able to come up with that much. She had wanted to jump up and leave right then, but it was impossible.

"But what we found would never have made that much, it was just a couple of ounces," Z tried.

The leader hadn't said a word. Just waited. Z had gone on, trying to explain things from his and Roksana's point of view, how they had just tried a few milligrams and given some to a couple of friends. How there hadn't been much at all—in their opinion.

The leader's mouth was moving, but no sound came out: he was chewing or sucking whatever he had in there.

"I think you can understand," he had said, without acknowledging a word of Z's half-true argument, "that I need my money. One million. So don't even start talking about amounts. I know how much the guy who lived there had. And it makes no difference: you two are fucked because you screwed me over."

Roksana had tried to swallow. It felt like someone was trying to force ten cardamom buns down her throat. Z had been on the bed by that point, his head in his hands.

"But it's impossible," she eventually managed to say.

The leader had gotten up. "You've gotta find a way, it's that simple. You can always keep selling the way you have so far. Then we'll get what we need in the end. But don't try to fuck me over again. I'll be really annoyed then. And I'm much more hot-livered than my brother here."

It's hotheaded, not hot-livered, fatty, Roksana had thought to herself. In despair.

It was only one thirty when Roksana caught the night bus heading home. Her taxi-riding days were over. People had been approaching her and Z at least once every fifteen minutes, wondering if they had anything to sell, and eventually, it had all been too much. But Z was still out there, and Billie hadn't noticed that anything was wrong. "Babe, tell me something," she had said. "Why are the floors in unisex toilets always so wet? I'm all for gender-neutral bathrooms, but they've been disgusting since all the cis men started going in. So, I'm wondering: Is the floor wet because the men can't wash their hands without soaking the place, because the toilets break and leak, or because they can't aim when they piss?"

Roksana had genuinely tried to smile. An old Patti Smith song was playing in the background; she recognized it because Billie used to play it all the time.

"I always carry gloves with me these days. The toilets at university are gross, too, even though lawyers are such clean people," Billie had continued, pulling out a small bag of plastic gloves. "So I don't have to touch anything."

It was warm at the back of the bus. Roksana didn't understand how Z could be so calm about everything. They needed help from someone, but she seemed to be the only one who cared. She pulled out her phone and a scrap of paper with a number on it. Called the only person she could think of who might be able to help get them out of this mess.

"Yes."

"Is that Nikola?"

"Yeah, who's this?"

"Hi, Nikola, it's me, Roksana."

"Who?"

"Roksana, we met outside that club a few weeks ago. Do you remember? You asked about your friend."

"Yeah, I remember you. What do you want?"

"Can you talk on this phone?"

"Yeah."

"Some people are blackmailing me."

"Okay."

"I need your advice."

"You know who they are?" Nikola asked.

"No, not really. I don't have any names."

"You need to keep on top of what's going on better."

"What do you mean?"

"Listen, I can't help you. I've got my own stuff to take care of, you know?"

"Please, could we at least meet and talk?"

It sounded like he sighed. "This world has rules, you do know that, right?"

"What world?"

"The world you've gotten yourself into. Simple rules. And one is that you always have to take care of your own shit. I think you get that. Plus, I don't even know you."

Roksana leaned forward; it felt as though someone was pulling her toward the floor.

"No, we don't know one another," she tried one last time. "But there are other simple rules, too."

"What are you talking about?"

"You help a friend who's gotten themselves in the shit."

The next day, Roksana watched as he climbed out of a car that looked both expensive and incredibly bad for the environment. He wasn't the one driving. The way he walked—his upper body swinging forward and back with each step—was the same as it had been outside the rave. He winked when he sat down in front of her. The car tore off.

"Okay," he said.

The restaurant was called Palm Village Thai Wok, and it was close to Kista. Roksana had cycled over. It was housed in a yellow wooden building, but she had sat down on one of the benches outside. She had never eaten there before, but she had assumed that Nikola wouldn't want to talk inside, with all the other diners' pricked ears. He seemed the type.

"How are you?" she asked. She wanted to create as normal a mood as possible, despite it being a shady situation—she genuinely was surprised he had even agreed to meet. They *weren't* friends. They had met once, for five minutes, while she was waiting for a cab.

On Sollentunavägen, the cars roared past. The two beech trees by the entrance to the restaurant cast shade onto the bench where they were sitting, despite being almost bare.

For a moment, Roksana thought he was about to get up and leave when she asked: "You want anything to eat?"

Instead, to her surprise, he nodded.

They went inside. There weren't actually all that many seats in the restaurant—the residential area's very own little low-price takeaway. You ordered, paid, and were given the food at the same time, over a long counter behind which the kitchen was completely visible. The Asian woman who took their order had her mouth open the entire time, showing her gums, and she was completely expressionless, as though they weren't even there.

Roksana asked: "Do you have any vegetarian options?"

"You can have everything," the woman said in halting Swedish.

Roksana didn't understand.

"You can have every dish, one to fifty-seven, without meat or fish." She said the words "meat" and "fish" in English.

Roksana ordered the same as Nikola, only without chicken. It seemed simpler that way.

Nikola used his knife and fork to eat. It was fascinating: he cut every piece of chicken into three, then scooped rice onto his fork and carefully speared the chicken with the very tip of it, all without spilling a single grain of rice.

"So what's going on?"

Roksana put down her chopsticks. "Well, it's like this, my friend and I, we have a lot of friends who like to party, and you asked me whether I was selling for your friend Chamon, but I wasn't."

"Mm-hm."

"And, you know, people just want to be happy and dance, but sometimes they want to take stuff, too. Though you know that—you've been to all those clubs and raves."

"Nope."

"You've never been in?"

"Nope."

"But you came up to me outside one?"

"I don't go to raves. Who do you think I am? I just wanted to talk to the people hanging around there."

"You should try it."

"This wasn't what you wanted to talk about. You said there was someone blackmailing you."

Roksana looked straight at him. His eyes were pale brown and round, but at the same time they seemed pitch-black. Like he only saw darkness.

She had to explain: how, by chance, they had found the Special K; how they had started selling it to their friends at parties and raves; how the drugs had run out and Z had been hurt; what had been said at the hotel; how they had been idiots and not saved a single krona.

"Is he your guy?" Nikola asked once she was finished.

"No, but we live together."

"You live together, but he's not your guy?"

"Exactly."

Nikola raised an eyebrow.

Roksana immediately decided not to react to that—she needed this idiot's help.

"You've got the contacts," he said. "So why don't you just keep going, try to get the money together?"

"We don't have anything to sell."

"You can make your own."

"How?"

"Buy ketamine from the pharmacy and dry the crap."

"But we don't have a recipe. It's a narcotic. We won't be able to buy any."

"Okay, then try an online pharmacy or something, what the hell do I know. Anyway, you need to think differently. You can't just go around moaning. You did actually screw those guys out of their stash. You have to give them that. Big picture."

Nikola pushed the last few grains of rice onto his fork and lifted it to his mouth.

"I've gotta go now. I've got other stuff to do."

Roksana called Z as she was cycling home. The pedals felt incredibly heavy, but Z sounded happy.

"Did you meet that gangster you were talking about?"

"Yeah, but he's not going to help." She briefly recapped what Nikola had said.

Z's voice bounced down the line. "But that's a fantastic idea," he said. "We try to get ahold of the ingredients and we dry up a new powder."

"How, though?" Roksana groaned.

"Wait, let me check."

For a few seconds, all she could hear was the clicking of the keys on Z's computer, then his voice was back on the line. *"Keta-minol vet,"* he said. "It's for animals, but you can extract ketamine from it. It's perfect."

21

Teddy and Emelie were walking side by side through the arrivals hall at Gardermoen Airport, shoes squeaking on the floor. They hadn't sat together on the plane. The color of Emelie's face was more like printer paper than skin. Nina Ley had arranged everything much more quickly than they expected: they would be meeting Mats Emanuelsson today.

"How are you?" Teddy asked as they passed through the barriers for the airport train.

"Do you really want to know?"

"Yes."

"Because you haven't been especially interested these past few weeks," she said.

"Neither have you. But now I want to know how you're doing. You don't have to answer."

They stepped onto the platform. Emelie had been given an address by Nina, a hotel in an area of Oslo known as Tjuvholmen—Thief Islet. The hotel went by the unoriginal name of the Thief.

When the train pulled in a few minutes later, Emelie still hadn't answered his question. An automated voice barked out something about which station they should get off at, but Teddy didn't manage to catch it—Norwegian had never been his strong point, never mind with blocked ears.

They sat down in the first car, Emelie bolt upright in her seat.

"I'm trying to run a law firm, but then all this crap happens. It's dragging me down," she said.

Her shoulders were hunched and her neck tense, one hand constantly drumming against the fabric of the seat.

"I know what you mean." He sighed.

"Why are people such bastards?"

"You're the one who chose to work in criminal law."

"Yeah, maybe you're right. I shouldn't have anything to do with people who'll never change," she said. "Maybe I should just work with people who fit in, like me."

The train pulled into Oslo Central Station. The buildings surrounding it looked ultramodern: tall, slim, clad in mirrored glass. One had a completely irregular white facade on which each window was like a shard of broken mirror. There was no doubt about the intended message, any foreigner arriving here would immediately understand: things were going well for Norway—or at least they *were* when the building went up.

They left the train. Central Station was huge. The Norwegians had an "s"-theme, Teddy thought to himself: salad bars, Starbucks, sushi joints, 7-Eleven. And then a small security booth. They got into a taxi and gave the address to the driver.

To the left, out by the water, was an enormous building with a footbridge connecting it to the quay. "That's the opera house," Emelie said, pointing.

The building looked like a huge, white Formula 1 car had driven into the fjord, leaving only the top poking up above the surface. It seemed popular. Teddy could see people strolling about on its roof, which was made up of various ramps.

Tjuvholmen consisted of newly built residential blocks on a cape in the middle of Oslo. "Most expensive homes in Norway," their driver said in broken Norwegian. Tjuvholmen: super modern, ultra luxe. Metal railings, wooden panels, enormous balconies with views across the fjord. The streets were full of Teslas, and

Anytec boats bobbed hull to hull with Axopars in its canal, despite the cool weather.

Emelie informed the hotel reception desk that they had arrived. They didn't know what would happen next, but the receptionist asked them to wait. Teddy could see that Emelie was studying a painting behind the desk; it looked like someone had spun a round canvas and randomly splashed as much paint onto it as they could.

"That's a Damien Hirst," Emelie said.

"What?"

"That painting over there. He's one of the world's most famous contemporary artists. Those don't come cheap."

"And how do you know that? Have you developed an interest in painting lately?"

"No, but Magnus Hassel had some Hirsts. You know what it was like at Leijon."

Teddy wondered how Mats Emanuelsson was these days. Whether he ever got to see his children, what his life was like. Teddy had served eight years in prison for what he did to Mats, but it was like Mats himself had also been forced into some kind of prison. Seven years—that was how long he had stayed underground, first on his own, then with the help of the police. Teddy wondered how much longer it would go on.

The receptionist waved them over. "I've just had a message. Apparently you should go down to the garage."

Mats looked different. He might have had some plastic surgery, possibly his nose, or around his eyes. Above all, he had shaved off his beard, grown his hair long enough to wear in a ponytail, and he had put on weight—he was chubby now, most visibly beneath the chin.

Teddy and Emelie climbed into the Passat and sat down on either side of Mats. Neither of them had seen him in around a year and a half.

In a way, Mats looked younger, more like he had when Teddy

met him for the first time just over ten years earlier. Maybe it was the absence of a beard, or that his skin was smoother as a result of the fat filling out his wrinkles. Or maybe it was something else, possibly the plastic surgeries. Then it struck Teddy that Mats was probably wearing makeup—that this was his life now: having to change his appearance every day, become someone other than himself.

They hugged.

"It's great to see you both," Mats said in a cheerful voice. The driver, who had frisked them both before they climbed into the car, started the engine and pulled out of the parking garage.

"Couldn't we have met inside the hotel? That place seemed pretty nice."

Mats laughed. "The money from the Swedish state doesn't cover that kind of thing, and if I didn't have a bit of my own money stashed away, I probably wouldn't have even been able to meet you here. But, believe me: hotels are like vanilla soft scoop. I've stayed in so many in my time. They look all welcoming and inviting, but after a few licks you get bored." Mats's face changed here, and he became serious. "All joking aside, we decided that the hotel wasn't safe."

Emelie and Teddy nodded. She said: "We're just happy that you and the police agreed we could meet, hotel room or not. How are you?"

"Back to the usual, I suppose. I lived like this for several years on my own, though things were simpler then, because they thought I was dead. Now they know I'm alive." Mats chuckled again. "If this can be called living."

"How's Benjamin?" Emelie asked. Benjamin Emanuelsson: her old client from the murder case.

"He's okay, considering," said Mats. "He's studying graphic design at university abroad."

"Glad to hear it, do you get to see him much?"

"Yes, we live in the same country. And Lillan is eighteen now, so she's about to move down there, too. As long as my ex isn't too upset about it. But I did wonder when someone would have more questions for me."

"Haven't the police interviewed you?"

"Yes, a Detective Inspector Ley, but they don't seem to be getting anywhere."

Teddy and Emelie began asking their questions. Whether Mats had ever heard of a girl called Katja. What he knew about Peder Hult—the man who had invited Mats to the event at the manor house roughly ten years earlier, when he had found the computer and the films of the abuse. What he knew about the other men at the event.

Mats spoke slowly as he tried to answer their questions. He told them the names he could remember: Peder Hult, again; Fredrik O. Johansson; Gunnar Svensson; a few more. "But," he said. "I've spent over ten years trying to repress the spark that started this hell." A lot of what he had to tell them was no more than fragments, shards of memories.

It still had to be worth something.

"What about Adam Tagrin?" Teddy asked. "Does that name sound familiar?"

"Tagrin?"

Teddy bent down to search for a picture of Adam in his bag.

There was a cracking sound. Glass shattering.

Emelie screamed. The car swerved. There were shards of glass all over them.

The side window was broken.

It was then that Teddy noticed the driver: his head was lolling forward. There was blood running down the inside of the window. Something had hit him.

Teddy threw himself forward as he glanced outside: a black Golf five yards away from them, its side window wound down. Teddy was lying across the driver, clutching at the wheel. The car lurched. He attempted to shove the driver's body to one side as he held on to the wheel and tried to swing his legs around to the pedals. He had to keep the car going straight. Staying low as he did it.

Emelie screamed, "Get down, Teddy!"

Gunfire. Teddy saw the muzzle flash from the wound-down window of the Golf. Figures dressed in dark colors inside. The sound of a mini Uzi: he was almost certain. All around them, cars were sounding their horns. He didn't know where to drive. He saw five-story brick buildings. Pedestrians, pale green buses. Water to the right. He floored the accelerator. It felt as though the car was about to rear up. The driver's limp body bumped into him. The Golf was still driving alongside them, both cars going against the traffic.

Horns were sounding. The scraping din of metal on metal—two cars bumping into one another. The bastard Golf was trying to drive them off the road; Teddy was going to be forced into the fjord if he didn't do something soon.

His vision narrowed to a tunnel: he saw the street as one long line, a light farther ahead. He couldn't think of anything else now, shouldn't. Just drive. He turned the wheel to the left. Thudded into the car alongside.

He heard police sirens. He heard the engine revving.

He heard the panic bubbling in his mind.

He could see the white silhouette of the Oslo Opera House up ahead.

The Golf was in front now, and it swerved toward him. Blocking off all escape routes. He had nowhere to go, only the water. And the opera house on its man-made island.

The man in the passenger seat of the Golf had raised his weapon again. Teddy gave everything he had. Turned the wheel sharply to the right. Drove straight onto the footbridge leading to the opera house. Like some kind of *Fast and Furious* madman.

He didn't brake between the quay and the opera house. He sounded the horn. People saw him coming, heard the horn—they threw themselves to the sides. The footbridge was wide enough for a car. Teddy drove like a crazy person. Like a man who had allowed the panic to take over. But he continued. A glance in the rearview mirror: he almost cried out. The bastard Golf hadn't stopped. It was on the bridge behind him.

He slammed his foot onto the accelerator. Emelie screamed: "What are you doing, Teddy?"

Up the sloping ramp leading to the roof of the opera house. It was bumpy: a highway to heaven. Ten yards to the top—then he braked, put the car into reverse, turned sharply. Accelerated again: up the next ramp, the roof of the glass section. Past the last protruding section of roof.

It was insane. All he could see ahead of him now was sea and sky. They were twenty yards up.

Emelie screamed.

Teddy yelled.

He saw the Golf coming up the ramp behind him. The men with their weapons drawn.

He floored the accelerator—drove out over the edge.

Like a bird.

Three seconds in the air: a moment of calm. Peace. Just the whistle of the wind through the broken windows.

Then they slammed into the downward sloping building and continued toward the water.

Good suspension on this thing, Teddy managed to think before the airbags deployed and the car slammed to a halt.

He glanced back. "Emelie?"

She was stuck to the backseat like chewing gum. "You're crazy," she said.

Then he glanced at Mats.

His seat belt had held, too.

Teddy took a closer look.

Mats's head was sitting at an unnatural angle.

There was a hole in his forehead.

On the inside of the window behind him: blood.

TELEPHONE CONVERSATION 16

To: Hugo Pederson
From: Pierre Danielsson (co-suspect)
Date: 1 December 2005
Time: 09:03

PIERRE: 'Sup, man, things are happening. It's kickoff.

HUGO: What?

PIERRE: Call me on the burner.

HUGO: I get a boner when you talk like that.

PIERRE: Good for you. You're almost a rich man. Call me.

TELEPHONE CONVERSATION 17

To: Pierre Danielsson (co-suspect)
From: Hugo Pederson
Date: 1 December 2005
Time: 09:05

HUGO: Have I ever told you you're like a bathtub with the faucets left running?

PIERRE: Huh?

HUGO: Make like that bathtub, and spill.

PIERRE: Okay. It's as simple as anything. Clean and neat, basically nothing can go wrong. Husqvarna's going to make a profit warning. They'll downgrade the value of their plant in China by more than 200 million as a result of losing official permits and pollution killing a few villagers around the factory, that kind of thing, and they'll warn about lower profits in their North American division over the next year, meaning lower earnings pretax. Little Husqvarna is going to crash at least seven percent.

HUGO: Sounds like it'll crash, but you can't know how much.

PIERRE: I'm going to short the bastards anyway. But that's not it, listen to this. Icahn is also preparing to short them, so maybe he's heard the same thing as us. Once it gets out, it'll lose a few percent just because of the bad news.

HUGO: Ah shit, when's the press statement, then?

PIERRE: In two hours, when the Dow Jones opens.

HUGO: Christ, then we need to rush. Why didn't you call me sooner?

PIERRE: Just found out. But this is what I'm thinking: a two-step thing. Short it now, then the press statement will be given, it'll recover a bit ahead of the report, and we short again. Then, when it crashes a second time, we're set.

HUGO: I feel like I don't have time to talk to you. Need to call my bitch right now.

TELEPHONE CONVERSATION 18
To: Jesper Ringblad (stockbroker Nordea)
From: Hugo Pederson
Date: 1 December 2005
Time: 10:04

HUGO: Hello, hello. It's me.

JESPER: Maestro Pederson?

HUGO: Precisely. And now I want you to listen damn closely now. We're going to short Husqvarna B.

JESPER: Short?

HUGO: Exactly.

JESPER: We haven't done that before.

HUGO: So what?

JESPER: I'm obliged to inform you of the risks of short selling. It involves selling shares you don't own. In other words, you'd be borrowing Husqvarna B shares and selling them on the market. You would then have to buy back all the shares at a later date. If the shares go down in value, everything's fine and dandy, but if they go up . . .

HUGO: Yeah, yeah, I know what shorting is. We don't have time to chat. You need to get to work. I want one mill.

JESPER: You want to borrow a million Husqvarna B and sell direct? Hugo, are you really sure? You know there's no limit to your losses if it doesn't work out how you want? The shares could rise like crazy, and then your risk would be endless.

HUGO: Stop lecturing and get to work instead. Make me filthy rich.

JESPER: Of course. But I'm obliged to inform you of all this and to make certain checks. How can you be so sure about Husqvarna?

HUGO: I've been checking the fluctuations for that share, and it's gone up too much. I think it's going to fall. You know me, I'm a telepathic stock genius. I'm usually right.

JESPER: I know, ha ha. Okay. I'll start hunting blocks, like usual, right?

HUGO: Right, but there's one more thing.

JESPER: What?

HUGO: You've got an hour and fifty-five minutes. It needs to be done by twelve.

TELEPHONE CONVERSATIONS 19–25 (SUMMARY)

To/From: Pierre Danielsson (co-suspect) and a number of other stockbrokers and bankers in Sweden, Switzerland, and England (named in relevant appendix)

From/To: Hugo Pederson

Date: 1–7 December 2005

Summary: Hugo Pederson calls a number of brokers and bank employees in Sweden and other European countries and instructs them to short sell shares of Swedish Husqvarna B on his behalf. In total, they sell 3.4 million Husqvarna B shares. Icahn Enterprises gives a press release at the New York Stock Exchange at 12:00 the same day, detailing their view of Husqvarna B. The share price of Husqvarna AB subsequently falls by 8 percent. Through his short selling, Hugo Pederson makes upward of nine million kronor.

TELEPHONE CONVERSATION 26

To: Hugo Pederson

From: Louise Pederson (wife)

Date: 12 December 2005

Time: 16:45

LOUISE: Hi, baby, where are you?

HUGO: Just passed the bridge. It's enormous.

LOUISE: Have you told the hotel you'll be checking in late?

HUGO: No, they'll just have to deal with it. Le Royal's the best hotel in town, according to Calle, do you think they can't handle a late guest?

LOUISE: Yes, I'm sure they can. Good for you. Where are you having dinner?

HUGO: Probably just room service. I'll be tired, I've been in the car all day.

LOUISE: Of course. And you'll be home tomorrow evening?

HUGO: Looks that way, Mousey. Quick in and out.

LOUISE: And you'll have three million kronor with you?

HUGO: Yes, baby. I'll have three mill, as we say in my world. But it's going to disappear pretty quickly, you know that. Stacek needs paying for the renovation. And I've ordered a new car.

LOUISE: I know. We should also pay for a place on the Magnussons waiting list.

HUGO: What are you talking about?

LOUISE: You know, I've told you. I had lunch with Isabelle last week, and all she talked about was how you have to put the kids on the waiting list for Magnussons now if you want them to have a chance of getting in.

HUGO: But we don't have any kids.

LOUISE: I want at least four.

HUGO: Oh?

LOUISE: Four kids is classy.

HUGO: Okay, but how much does this school waiting list cost?

LOUISE: They want a hundred thousand to reserve a place.

HUGO: A hundred grand? They're insane. A hundred thousand for a place for a child that doesn't even exist. I thought we lived in a social democracy, I thought schooling was supposed to be free. This isn't the U.S., is it?

LOUISE: But our kids shouldn't have to go to some local authority school.

HUGO: No, but surely the state gives Magnussons money? They can't live on private fees alone?

LOUISE: I don't think so, but we're talking about a place in the line here.

HUGO: Okay, okay. Go for it then. Sign up.

LOUISE: Wonderful. But, baby?

HUGO: Yeah?

LOUISE: Is there any risk of you being stopped somewhere? I mean when you're on your way back with all the money?

HUGO: No, no. It's all cool. EU citizens don't have any problems, Schengen and all that. I'll be coming back down here in a few weeks to pick up more money. Don't worry, Mousey. Don't worry.

LOUISE: Okay, that's good. But listen, there was one more thing.

HUGO: What?

LOUISE: Now that everything looks so nice at home, I'd like some art on the walls. I mean real art, not those boring lithographs my mom buys in Skåne. I was at Bukowskis' Christmas Contemporary with Fredrika yesterday, and they had so many nice pieces.

HUGO: Contemporary, that's all that modern crap, right?

LOUISE: Hugo, you don't know what you're talking about. I mean photo art. Really good stuff. I actually put in a bid on an amazing picture by a nature photographer called Nick Brandt, a majestic lion in the dust on the Savannah. Black-and-white, six point five feet by five. It's huge, I think it'll look great above the sofa.

HUGO: How high was your bid?

LOUISE: All you care about is money. I thought you'd be happy that I'm looking after our home.

HUGO: It's great, Mousey, really, I appreciate it, but I'm just wondering how much the photograph might cost.

LOUISE: I don't think we're used to the price of art, that was what Fredrika said, anyway. She said that if you want nice things, you have to pay for them, that's just how it is.

HUGO: So?

LOUISE: It could also be an investment. It might go up in value.

HUGO: What did they want for it?

LOUISE: No more than the new car.

HUGO: That's not saying much.

LOUISE: Enough now. It'll really look great in our living room. We can talk about it when you get home.

TELEPHONE CONVERSATION 27

To: Unknown
From: Hugo Pederson
Date: 14 December 2005
Time: 16:48

HUGO: Hello, my name is Hugo, I'd like to inquire about a work you're selling in your current Christmas special.

UNKNOWN: Of course, which work did you have in mind?

HUGO: I don't know what it's called, but it's a nature photograph, pretty big, by Nick Brandt.

UNKNOWN: Aha. I know the one. It's called *Lioness Against Rock*.

HUGO: That must be it. What's the reserve price?

UNKNOWN: One moment . . . let me just see . . . the reserve is 50,000 euros, or 470,000 kronor.

HUGO: Aha, they don't come cheap, these photographs.

UNKNOWN: That depends on your point of view, but it's a fantastic piece in my opinion, incredibly suggestive, with a clarity and a level of detail that's almost impossible when it comes to wild animals.

HUGO: Now I'd like to know whether you take cash.

UNKNOWN: Cash?

HUGO: Exactly.

UNKNOWN: Mmm, normally we take payment via bank transfer.

HUGO: But I'd like to pay cash. And we're interested in several other works, too. So I think we might count as VIP customers.

UNKNOWN: I understand. In that case, I think it would be best if you came in. I'm sure we can come to an agreement.

TELEPHONE CONVERSATIONS 28–48

To/From: Pierre Danielsson (co-suspect) and a number of other stockbrokers and bankers in Sweden, Switzerland, and England (named in relevant appendix)
From/To: Hugo Pederson
Date: 13–18 January 2006
Summary: Hugo Pederson makes a number of calls with co-suspect Pierre Danielsson and other individuals, as detailed above. Price-sensitive events occur with regard to a number of positions Pederson has taken in Swedish shares, resulting in capital gains for Pederson of c. 24,000,000 kronor. In these transactions, Pederson allows his share portfolio and even his property to be used as collateral. As such, he achieves powerful so-called leverage.

TELEPHONE CONVERSATION 49

To: Hugo Pederson
From: Pierre Danielsson (co-suspect)
Date: 21 January 2006
Time: 11:36

PIERRE: 'Sup, 'sup.

HUGO: How you doing?

PIERRE: I'm like the king of some medium-size European country. No, like the king of Bahrain or somewhere. Unlimited happiness and power.

HUGO: You got something in the works?

PIERRE: Not exactly, but I've been in touch with someone who'd like to deal with us.

HUGO: Deal how? What does he have to sell and what does he want to buy?

PIERRE: Information. He's on a couple of boards, even listed companies, and he's in several important circles.

HUGO: So what does he stand to gain by helping us?

PIERRE: Well, if you look at what you and I have been doing over the past few months, I think it's clear. He thinks we seem hungry, and he doesn't want all his eggs stuck in the same basket, if you catch my drift.

HUGO: You idiot, did you give him details?

PIERRE: No, no, of course not. But he called me and we met for lunch at Prinsen yesterday, and he seems to have worked out most of it himself. It was actually pretty scary. I mean, if he can work it out, other people could, too.

HUGO: That sounds bad, but I don't think we need to worry. We'll just talk to this guy and I'll spread the buying and selling between so many different brokers that no individual deals seem unusual.

PIERRE: I don't know, but he wants to meet you, in any case. Feel like it?

HUGO: Can't hurt. What's his name?

PIERRE: We'll get into that when we meet.

HUGO: Okay. Ask if he can do Monday. Same place you met.

PIERRE: Okay. Bye.

22

Nikola had been given Chamon's phones by his poor father—sadly, they were worthless without the pass codes. Neither Bello nor Yusuf had any idea what combination of numbers his friend used. The whole idea seemed to be on the verge of dying. Whoever was behind the murder of his best friend would walk free. The days passed. They had already found out what Mr. One was being held in custody for: financial stuff, mostly. Without Isak's leadership, Nikola felt weak.

George Samuel had called to pay his condolences for a second time. "You were so close, Nikola, aren't you going to come back to work? So you can become a qualified electrician after all?" The old man was right—Nikola should have dropped everything to do with Chamon by now. Returned to his normal, quiet life. Done something to distract himself. But, at the same time: Chamon didn't deserve that. Emanuel Hanna didn't deserve that. Nikola would have to work harder instead, think better. Track down whoever was guilty.

He had to get into Chamon's phones. The cops always managed it, those pros—they analyzed people's phones. But, on the other hand: the cops clearly hadn't managed to get in to Chamon's, otherwise they wouldn't have handed the phones back so quickly. Nikola had heard about it before: when Apple and Android introduced six-digit pass codes, the phones became virtually uncrackable. So he tried every combination he could think of. Chamon's birthday, his parents' birthdays, the entry code for his friend's door. Nothing worked. Then he remembered someone who might be able to help him—Loke Odensson, Teddy's friend from the slammer.

Loke: when Nikola met him for the first time a few years earlier, he had made up his mind in a split second—the man was a half-shady, utterly nerdy, real-life loser. A middle-aged Swede who looked like he listened to hard rock and played *League of Legends* all night. But Nikola knew differently now. Loke Odensson had helped him before: he wasn't just a death metaller. He was also an excellent cell phone cracker.

Loke agreed to meet him in Kungsholmen. *Dragon's Lair,* the sign above the door read in elaborate script. It was some kind of shop or gaming joint: not video games, poker, or Jack Vegas, but *Lord of the Rings*–type stuff—like Monopoly but with fantasy figures. There were small, painted metal figurines everywhere, on miniature landscapes in glass cases. Two-inch-high knights attacking a red dragon with outspread wings. A whole army of orc-like fighters in dirty chain mail, lined up opposite as many long-haired figures with pointy ears and bows and arrows that no one but a child could have painted: no one with full-size fingers would have been able to paint the feathers on the arrows so well.

Nikola had Chamon's two phones in his pocket.

There wasn't a single woman inside the shop, and yet Nikola found himself thinking about Roksana, the girl he had eaten lunch with the other day. He couldn't quite explain it, but he felt slightly guilty at not having helped her deal with the losers who were trying to blackmail her into paying them. Still: he had to focus on his own problems now; that was just how it was.

Down in the basement, countless wars were being fought. Everywhere: slightly overweight guys in backward caps and black T-shirts with the same kind of script on them. They were chill. All as white as Extra gum. There were a number of large tables covered with the same kind of fantasy landscapes Nikola had seen upstairs, only bigger. The men had set out even more painted figurines. The room smelled of spray paint and sweat. He didn't care what they were up to; it was so lame that he didn't even have the energy to check.

Loke was hunched over the table farthest away. His beard was plaited and he had at least seven earrings in each ear. In one hand, he was holding five white dice, and in the other a folding ruler. He didn't react when Nikola paused mere inches away from him.

"What do you need?"

Loke looked up. Smiled. "Hi there, little shrimp, good to see you here. I need sixes. These Deathwatch soldiers need to move that way, you see?"

Nikola didn't see. But he knew what Loke was like. He had even heard him call Teddy *little darling*.

"Let me try," Nikola said.

He cast the five dice onto the table. Each one showed a six.

"Little sweetie, I almost love you more than your uncle," Loke shouted.

A few days later, Loke called Nikola.

"Hi, sweetie."

"Hi, Loke."

"They've started making things more difficult for us."

"Who?"

"The phone manufacturers. They've started using six-digit codes. No wonder the police couldn't do it. They're practically impossible to crack."

Nikola bit his nail.

Loke continued: "Unless your name is Loke Odensson, that is. Anything's possible then."

"So you managed to unlock them?"

"Yep, both. Not that there was anything interesting on them. They were practically unused."

"Doesn't surprise me. Chamon changed his phones pretty often."

"You guys all do that."

"Not me."

"Nah, maybe not you, cutie. But your friends."

"Can I have the phones?"

"Of course."

An hour later, a taxi pulled up on Nikola's street and the driver handed over a bag. Nikola sat down at the kitchen table and studied the first phone. An old iPhone 4—considering how often Chamon changed his phone, he probably didn't want any expensive handsets. It no longer needed a pass code—Loke must have disabled it. Nikola scrolled through the phone: no names or numbers saved, no apps other than the usual. He saw a couple of meaningless SMS messages that seemed to be to Chamon's parents, plus a number of calls made to numbers he didn't recognize—probably other pay-as-you-go phones. Nikola pulled out the second phone. It was the same story: very few functions or apps, almost no calls or messages. But this one had the Find iPhone app installed. That wasn't like Chamon. Nikola felt a bad feeling creeping up on him. He opened the app. The feeling intensified.

The number saved in the app wasn't Chamon's. It was a number that had clearly been able to track where Chamon's phone was.

A small bell started ringing at the back of his mind. He knew something, though he couldn't quite work out what. He recapped everything for himself: Chamon had been in one of many wards in the hospital, and yet the killers had found him insanely quickly. Chamon was as careful as a principal with his phones. He never left any footprints or allowed anyone to know where he was, yet someone had been able to follow him through the Find iPhone app on his phone.

Was it possible? Could the killers have somehow connected to the app? Used it to track which ward Chamon was on?

Nikola checked the phone number that was linked to the app.

He didn't recognize it, but he pulled out his own phone, made sure his number was hidden, and dialed it.

The ring signal sounded like it had been amplified.

"Uh, hello?" said a voice on the other end.

Nikola breathed in.

He knew who it belonged to. The listless tone. The sluggishness.

The lightning appeared without warning—his head felt like it was about to implode. He practically collapsed. He couldn't think of anything to say. He ended the call.

That voice.

23

Morning in Norway. Emelie felt like vomiting when she woke up.

She and Teddy had been carted off by the police the minute the paramedics determined that they weren't injured. To begin with, she had protested loudly: surely they weren't suspected of anything; they were the victims of the crime here. They were witnesses, the injured party: that assessment couldn't be any different in Norway than it was in Sweden. The female officer had still asked, politely and cutely—everything Norwegian sounded cute to Emelie—whether she had anything against staying a few more days.

"Yes, I want to get back to Sweden as soon as possible," she had said.

"Well, I'm afraid we need to keep you here for now—we have the right to hold witnesses for up to twelve hours. And, as I'm sure you understand, we have a number of questions we'd like to ask you."

Emelie had been put into a cell.

Everything was so similar to Sweden, and yet it was all so different. The cells were the exact same size, but the color of the epoxy walls was lighter. The bench that had served as her bed for the night was concrete. They were wooden in Sweden, but the PVC mattress was the same. The only real difference was that instead of a normal window, this room had a skylight eight feet up—she couldn't see anything but white sky. The policewoman had seen Emelie look up at it as she locked her in. "That window was mandated by the European Commission for the Prevention of Torture. We didn't have anything like that before." Norway wasn't five years behind Sweden, like everyone said. It was *ten* years behind.

She had spent most of the night thinking about Teddy and her father, making odd comparisons. Teddy had saved her life through his driving, and yet he was just like her father. A man who would never change, who was drawn to a bad life. Or maybe it was the bad life that was drawn to him. Her father had always cared about her, looked after her when she was younger, and yet he had drunk away so many days and opportunities to be happy. What did that really mean? How could a person have so many contradictory sides?

She heard a beep, and her cell door clicked. Here in Norway, everything was electronic. The door opened—she assumed it was time for an interview. The Norwegian police hadn't questioned her in anywhere near as much detail as she had expected. Emelie remained where she was on the bed.

"Time to go home now," said a voice she recognized. She looked up. It was Nina Ley.

She was wearing a football shirt with *Fly Emirates* across the chest, and she was chewing gum. She was holding Emelie's bag in one hand. Nina looked sadder than ever.

"What are you doing here?" Emelie asked.

"I wanted to make sure you got home safely," said Nina. "How are you, by the way? It must have been awful."

Emelie stood up. "I'm okay, but how are Mats and the driver?"

"Alive, but both in critical condition, Mats was in the operating room all night, now he's on a respirator in Oslo University Hospital. The bullet penetrated his forehead at a slight angle and exited an inch above his ear."

A flicker of hope appeared in Emelie.

Nina said: "You should be pleased you brought Teddy with you. He's a real Ayrton Senna, he is."

"Where is he?"

"He went home with a colleague of mine a few hours ago."

They spoke more on the way to the airport. Emelie could feel her irritation levels rising.

"Unfortunately, our Norwegian colleagues haven't managed to arrest anyone yet, but we're working closely with them."

"At the very least, one thing should be clear to you now," said Emelie. "This isn't just about Adam Tagrin. There are others involved."

Nina laughed, sudden and shrill. "You know that I know. Why else do you think I let you meet Mats? But my problem—and I know that *you* know this—is that I haven't been able to trust my own damn organization."

"Will you let me go through your files?"

Nina continued to chew her gum. "I can't go that far, I'm afraid."

Emelie felt her cheeks turn hot. She raised her voice.

"What are you doing, exactly? You've been sitting on the films that Mats gave you for over a year, but all you've managed to do is identify Katja. You're completely incompetent."

Nina's mouth was a small circle. Perhaps she had swallowed her gum.

Three and a half hours later, Emelie pulled her front door shut behind her. She was thinking about calling Teddy; they really needed to talk about what had happened in Oslo.

She sat down in the kitchen. The sun was glittering in the windows on the other side of the courtyard. It was three thirty in the afternoon. She had hung a picture on her kitchen wall: Mom and Dad on a beach in Mykonos. The picture was over thirty years old, taken only a few weeks after her parents first met, when they decided to travel to Greece together. Her father was tanned and wearing a vest. His shoulders were relaxed, one foot partly buried in the sand, and he had an arm around her mother's waist. Mom didn't just look young, she also looked happy: her eyes were beaming at the camera like she was proud. Emelie took a closer look at her mother's eyes: did anything in them suggest what was to come? Had her father already had an unhealthy interest in beer and cocktails while they were on the island?

I'll never be able to love the way Mom seems to love Dad, Emelie thought. She could feel tenderness, compassion, and she could get turned on—but loving someone? She wasn't sure she knew what that meant. She wondered whether she even had the ability.

She should pay her parents a visit—it was months since she had last seen them. She pulled out her phone and called Marcus.

"What happened in Norway? You know you had a police interview and a detention hearing you were supposed to attend this morning?" he said. "You should be glad you've got me."

Emelie explained as carefully as she could. "And I'm not really okay, by the way. This whole thing's awful." She glanced up at the picture on the wall as she spoke. "So I'm thinking about going to see my parents for a few days. Could you hold the fort at the office? Check my schedule, cancel all my meetings, visits, and interviews?"

"Holding the fort is all I do all day," said Marcus.

An hour later, Emelie was standing in a rental car garage with an overnight bag in her hand. It was often difficult to get to Jönköping by train, and maintenance work meant she would have had to change in Nässjö. In any case, the tickets for the last departure of the day were sold out. She was renting a car instead. It would take longer, but she could, at least, be by herself, and she would arrive today. That was important: right now, all she wanted was to get away from everything as quickly as possible.

She squeezed the key she had just picked up from Europcar. One hundred feet away, a car flashed: it was hers, a Seat Ibiza, small and cute.

She was alone in the garage, and she stood still for a moment, gathering herself. She had at least three and a half hours of driving ahead of her, but she felt like stepping on the accelerator and doing the journey in half that time.

Suddenly she heard a sound. Someone was approaching. Emelie moved toward her car, but for some reason she paused before she reached it. The footsteps behind her fell silent. What was going on?

She thought back to the parking garage beneath the hotel in Oslo, where they had climbed into the car with Mats.

She took a few more steps, thought she heard the same sound behind her again, but it stopped the minute she paused. Was there someone else in the garage, only moving when she moved? Someone who didn't want to be heard?

She could hear her own breathing, and it struck her that whoever had attacked them in Oslo wouldn't stop at Mats. She should have talked to Nina about that, tried to get a better understanding of the threat.

She turned around, but the garage was empty behind her. All she could see were the rows of cars.

Her heart was racing. She was alone down here, completely defenseless.

Maybe she was just paranoid, but she felt she should have stopped all this a long time ago. She regretted even taking on Katja's case, even more so going to see Mats. She pulled out her phone and called Nina, but there was no answer.

Another sound behind her—it wasn't her imagination, she was sure of that now. She spun around, but she still couldn't see anything but cars. She looked down at the phone she was clutching in her hand.

She called Teddy.

He answered before she even heard it ringing.

"Teddy, I think someone's following me," she said quietly.

"Where are you?"

She explained.

"Go back up to reception," he said. "I'm coming as quickly as I can. And don't hang up. I want to hear that you're there."

She pressed the phone to her ear, turned around and started walking back toward the elevators.

She couldn't hear the footsteps anymore, but her heart was still racing, like she had just done three workout classes in a row.

A clicking sound: the lights in the garage went out.

She heard herself drawing in air through her nostrils.

"What happened?"

"It just went dark in here," she whispered.

"Do you know where the exit is?"

"I think so."

It wasn't completely dark; she could make out an emergency exit sign glowing in the distance. She walked toward it, feeling sick.

Steps, could she hear footsteps behind her? She didn't know. She just wanted to get out. Away from the darkness. She sped up. The emergency exit—it was just what she needed, in more ways than one.

She was jogging now.

Quicker.

Then: *BANG*. Something struck her head. She cried out. Saw stars.

She dropped her phone.

Maybe she fell.

The room was bright. The paper on the bed rustled. On one wall, there was a poster of a human head in cross section. The throat, the neck, the nose. The mouth, the upper section of the spine, the brain. Each part looked like a labyrinth. Emelie was lying down.

Teddy was sitting next to her. "Good, you're awake."

The headache was like a bass drum in her head. She tried to sit up.

A middle-aged woman in a white doctor's coat placed a hand on her shoulder. "Just stay lying down."

"What happened?"

Teddy answered: "I found you on the floor in the garage. Think you must have run into a pillar."

The woman held out a hand. "My name is Fatima Eriksson, I'm the doctor on call. We've been struggling to get through to you, but I don't think you were entirely unconscious. Do you remember anything since you fell?"

Emelie shook her head.

The doctor held up a mirror. Emelie studied her own face: her lank hair—she hadn't showered since Oslo—the bags beneath her eyes, the dry lips, the white tape on her forehead.

"Or maybe someone knocked me down. They turned the lights out."

Teddy looked needlessly happy. "Nope, there was a power cut right across that part of town. No one turned off the lights in the garage. And I'm pretty sure it was the pillar you ran into, because there was a fleck of blood at roughly your height."

Dr. Eriksson also looked provocatively happy. "It's good, at least, that you're yourself again. It's not a particularly big wound, it'll heal nicely, didn't even need stitches. I think it was mostly a stress reaction. And everything else is fine, too."

Emelie sat up. "Everything else?"

"Your baby, it wasn't harmed," said the doctor. "I should congratulate you."

24

There they stood. The moon was playing hide-and-seek between the clouds, and the six-foot fence towered up in front of them. *"Ketaminol vet,"* Z whispered with a wink. Their bikes were leaning against a couple of trees roughly one hundred yards away.

They snickered—it was the first time Roksana had felt hopeful since those madmen broke Z's fingers. On the other side of the fence was the goods entrance for the AniCura Veterinary Clinic where one of Billie's girlfriends had worked as a trainee six months ago. The girlfriend was a sweet girl who only really smoked on special occasions, but Z had added cannabis to the sticky chocolate cake they had eaten for dessert when she came over one evening— his chocolate cakes were always perfect, smooth as caramel in the middle. After just a few bites, the girl had started talking freely about how much she loved golden retrievers and gray horses, and about all the various animal medicines. After her second slice, she had told them the code to get into the clinic.

Ketaminol vet was the shit.

Roksana looked down at her feet—her new Eytys sneakers were covered by the loose blue shoe covers Z had decided they should wear. "Either that or you'll have to chuck the shoes in the garbage afterward, and I'm guessing you're not gonna want to do that? I don't want them to be able to find any shoe prints or dirt that could lead them to us."

Again: a question mark flashed up in her mind. What were they doing? What would happen if they were arrested?

The fence was easy enough to climb. The goods entrance was smaller than Roksana had expected, with no loading bay, no double doors. Z pulled on a pair of workman's gloves and punched in the code. The door was heavy.

They came into a hallway that smelled of concrete and horse dung. They opened another door and the lights came on automatically as they stepped inside. They moved forward: a hallway, a kitchen, a staff room, two offices. Posters advertising sterile dressings for horses, deworming tablets for dogs, animal toothpaste. Roksana wondered what flavor it was.

The storeroom lit up automatically as they stepped inside. It was small: white shelves from floor to ceiling, full of boxes. They closed the door and Roksana held her breath; for some reason, she felt like they had to be quiet. As though someone might be on their way down the corridor, even though it was the middle of the night. She pressed her ear to the door.

"What are you doing?" Z whispered.

"Listening to make sure there's no one outside."

"The clinic's closed. There's no one here."

The corridor was silent on the other side of the door. Roksana turned to Z. "Then why are you whispering?"

They grinned at one another and started studying the contents of the shelves. Osphos, Eryseng Parvo, and so on. Weird names for weird medicines. She didn't understand the order they were in, but maybe the medicines were organized by animal or by the type of condition they were supposed to treat.

"Oh, come on," Z hissed after five minutes of searching. "It should be here. That's what the cake girl said."

Right then, Roksana spotted the cabinet. It was at one end of the room, glossy white plastic and no bigger than a small fridge. The girl had mentioned something about the controlled drugs being locked away.

Ten minutes later, Z's forehead was glistening, and he was furious. Roksana had never seen him like that before. He was trying to break open the cabinet with the bolt cutters they had brought with them. To begin with, he had tried cutting the lock, but it was impossible to get a good grip—the cutters kept slipping every time. Next, he had attempted to shove the cutters into the gap between the door and the cabinet, using them like a crowbar. The fabric beneath his arms had turned damp.

"Let me try," Roksana said.

"I don't think you'll be able to force it open," said Z. "I mean, if I can't."

Roksana took the bolt cutters and opened them slightly—then she drove them into the side of the cabinet as hard as she could. It made a small hole in the steel. She repeated the maneuver. It hurt her shoulders, but the hole grew bigger. Now she could push the cutters far enough in to start cutting.

Five minutes later, they had twenty-two vials of *Ketaminol vet, 100 mg* in their bag.

Then Roksana heard something. No hallucinations. No fantasies. It was real this time. A noise. She put her ear to the door again. It was clear now: there was someone humming out there. A song without any words. She even recognized the tune. It was "Live Tomorrow" by Laleh.

"What should we do?" Z whispered. His eyes were as big as vinyls.

Roksana lay down on the floor—it was virtually spotless. She couldn't see a single fleck of dust. She squinted through the crack beneath the door, out into the corridor. The humming sounded clearer now, it had moved closer. A man. She turned her head so that it was parallel with the floor. Then she saw them: the soles of a pair of shoes and wheels of some kind. Followed, a few seconds later, by a mop moving forward and back across the floor.

The cleaner—it had to be the cleaner. And he was coming closer with every second.

Z got down beside her and tried to see out. "Shit, shit, shit," Roksana heard him whisper with every breath—it didn't even seem like he was thinking it himself.

They waited. The cleaner's shoes swam and multiplied before her eyes.

She thought back to the patch that an optician had decided she should wear over her eye as a child, to stop her from seeing double. "It might itch a bit to begin with, but you'll get used to it," the optician had said. But even on the way home, it had started to itch more than the mosquito bite she had gotten at soccer practice, more than the eczema she had behind her knees sometimes, and more than the knitted sweater she had been sent by Aunt Etty. Still, her mother had said that she couldn't take it off. The next day, at school, everyone had looked at her like she was some kind of alien. The girl with one eye. Her desk mate had turned away from her, the girls she usually jump-roped with had gone to a different part of the playground. Even her best friend had asked whether she had to wear that horrible bit of skin over her eye. That afternoon, she had torn off the patch and shoved it into her pocket, and everything had immediately returned to normal. Life had resumed. Her desk mate had whispered secrets as soon as the teacher turned her back, the girls had wanted her back at the rope. At four that afternoon, Roksana had stood by the window of the classroom, peeping out. She needed to spot her mother before her mother saw her—and when Roksana saw her over by the gates, she had done it. She had pulled the patch out of her pocket, unfolded it, and run a stick of glue back and forth across it. Then she had pasted it back over her eye, as though it had been there all day. Roksana had done the same thing the next day. Went to school with her eye covered, taken it off the minute she got into the classroom, pasted it back on before she went home. It became some kind of game, managing to put it on every afternoon before she was picked up. The glue chapped her skin, turned it red and made her eyebrow fall out, but Mom had never noticed a thing. Six weeks later, they had gone back to the hospital. They had tested Roksana's vision, and when the doctor gave her verdict, there had been something knowing in her eye. "No improvement at all, nothing actually." Roksana had glanced at her mother. The doctor had said: "The patch doesn't seem to be helping, so I think we should try glasses instead."

The light in the storeroom went out, and Roksana felt Z jump beside her. "What's going on?" he whispered.

But she understood, and he should have, too. They had been lying still for too long, and the motion sensors controlling the lights no longer thought they were there. The darkness was now like a warm blanket around them. Z's almost inaudible panting sounded as though it were coming from a stranger. She thought about the girl who had promised to take the aptitude exam for her: Imagine if she blabbed to someone? And how would it feel later, if the girl passed the exam and Roksana used the result to get onto the psychology course?

The cleaner was nowhere to be seen; maybe he was mopping another room now.

Roksana got up. The lights came back on. She grabbed the backpack.

"We're making a run for it," she whispered, opening the door before Z had time to protest.

They rushed out. Down the hallway.

They had made it halfway out when they heard someone shout.

The cleaner had spotted them. He appeared in the hallway behind them. Shouted again.

They sped up. The backpack thudded against Roksana's ass.

The cleaner yelled. Roksana could practically hear her father's voice.

Z was quicker than she was, and he tore open the door to the goods entrance. The cleaner's Crocs slapped against the floor behind them.

Shiiit.

They ran down the next hallway.

Out the back door.

The cleaner was fifteen feet behind them now.

Roksana was panting. They rushed toward the fence. Threw themselves at it, clambered over.

She rushed, sprinted, pounded concrete like Usain Bolt. The buildings around her had transformed into fuzzy, dark gray bodies.

She didn't look back. She ran as though she were in a tunnel.

Eventually she stopped. Z was a few meters ahead of her. She glanced back. The cleaner shouted something inaudible 150 feet behind. She could taste blood in her mouth.

Dawn was creeping across the sky behind the clinic as they climbed onto their bikes.

"Did you take something in there?"

Roksana didn't understand. She barely had the energy to pedal, much less talk. "Only what I've got in the bag."

"But did you take something? Like, did you pop something?"

"Nah."

"Because you were running like a horse on fucking dope." Z laughed.

Roksana breathed in the night air, pedaled: she was still wearing the protective shoe covers. "Horses with blue foot covers always run fast."

She raised her face to the sky: laughed loudly. Kept laughing. She laughed like she had never laughed before.

When they got home, they took the bikes into the apartment. Everyone knew that it took less time to lose a bike in Stockholm than it did to say the words "insurance claim." Plus, both of their rides were new—bought with the ketamine money. Roksana took off her new shoes and her backpack, heard her phone beep. An email: *Test Result University and Higher Education Council.*

Shit, the results of the aptitude test had arrived. She opened the email. *Click this link for your test result.* She clicked, typed in her personal ID number and password, and then logged in to the results page.

1.9.

She read it again.

One point fucking nine.

It was fantastic—it had worked. Or, at least, she was 90 percent sure: there was actually a slight risk that she would need 2.0 to get onto the psychology course. But still: this gave her a real chance. And yet, deep down, she could make out a faint musty smell—it was all a lie.

Z leaned his bike against the wall.

Roksana wrapped her arms around his neck. "I got 1.9 on the aptitude test."

"I didn't even know you'd taken it. That means we've got two things to celebrate. Congrats."

She wondered whether to tell him what had actually happened. But maybe it was just as well she kept it to herself.

Later: they were dressed like total *Breaking Bad* clones. Aprons, sunglasses, masks. Z had Googled like crazy for instructions on what to do. They closed the blinds and started opening the boxes: the bottles of animal medicine they had grabbed. Each bottle: they unscrewed the lid, tore off the security plastic, poured the liquid into a glass carafe—to minimize the risk of spilling anything.

They were going to extract the ket.

They spent the majority of the time laughing hysterically—but they were focused all the same. Using the stove, they boiled water in two pans and then placed a roasting pan directly on top of those. They waited until the steam had heated it up. Z grabbed a pipette that he had bought from the pharmacy and squirted two drops of water onto the roasting pan: it immediately turned to steam, giving off a hiss. "Right," he said, turning down the heat. "It's hot enough now." Roksana slowly poured the liquid from the carafe until the roasting pan was covered. Z's hands were constantly on the dials, making adjustments—Roksana didn't think he really knew what he was doing, but both of them were aware that the liquid couldn't start to boil. After a moment, thin columns of smoke started to rise from the roasting pan, like living spirits reaching up to the extractor fan. They didn't say anything, just laughed and stared at the horse medicine that slowly turned to steam, evaporated.

After twenty minutes, they were left with a thin, crystalline mass on the pan.

Roksana used a knife to break up the layer. It sounded awful. The crystals were brittle. A monotonous scraping sound filled the kitchen. It squeaked. The same movement of the wrist over and over again. She glanced at Z. He had taken off his mask.

"What are you doing?"

"No matter how this ends, I'm planning to experiment with my own psyche while we do it. Z versus the K-cloud."

Roksana laughed so hard that she thought she would die in a coughing fit.

After a total of three hours' work, they had seven bags: a gram of powder in each. It had worked. And yet, it was the biggest disappointment since the American presidential election. Roksana pulled off her mask. "That's no more than five grand."

Z frowned like she had never seen him frown before; Z, the eternal optimist.

"Shit," he said. "We need so much more than this."

They were going to have to find another 995,000 kronor for the madmen.

25

After the doctor broke the news of Emelie's pregnancy, Teddy and Emelie didn't speak for several minutes. They just climbed into a taxi, heading back to her place, in silence. It was like neither of them could speak. Each of them probably had far too many thoughts to put in order. Or at least that was what Teddy was trying, and failing, to do.

When the car pulled onto Rörstrandsgatan where Emelie lived, she turned to him. The tape on her forehead seemed like it was glowing.

"The baby's yours," she said.

Teddy thought he saw the taxi driver jump. Exactly what kind of conversation was going on in his car?

Teddy tried to lower his voice when he replied, "Are you sure?"

Emelie nodded and then looked away, out of the window.

"We need to talk," he said.

"Yeah," Emelie replied. "But not today. I need to get some rest. And to think."

The world: surreal. Life upside down. He was going to be a dad. He couldn't stop that thought from swirling around his head. Emelie was pregnant, with a baby she claimed was his. *They* were going to have *a baby*.

He was thirty-six years old and it had never even occurred to him that it might one day happen. It was something that happened to other people; Dejan sometimes joked about all the illegitimate children he must have, Loke had a kid. But for him—Teddy Maksumic, who had spent half his adult life in prison—it had never been part of the plan.

Children.

It was a contradiction in itself. And yet the only thing he could think was this: his child couldn't be born into a world in which the predators ruled.

The days passed. He called Emelie several times a day. Nine times out of ten, she rejected his call. "But the baby in your belly is mine. And we're at war with *them*," Teddy told her when she eventually answered.

"*You* might be at war. I still haven't decided about the fetus."

"Are you getting any help? Do you feel safe, considering everything that's happened?"

"I've done the best I can."

Before Teddy had time to say anything, she hung up.

Perhaps he should have kept researching Adam Tagrin, but at the same time: Adam was the police's problem now that he was in custody. There was so much else to deal with: Teddy's job now was trying to track down the people Mats had mentioned in Oslo. Twelve names, that was what Teddy had to go on: Peder Hult, Fredrik O. Johansson, Gunnar Svensson, and so on. Mats probably could have given them more details about the men, but he was still in a coma in a Norwegian hospital.

Teddy drove around town. He wanted to keep moving—and he experienced Stockholm with new eyes. Filtered vision: child-tinted glasses. He saw parks, pushchairs, mothers with big bellies. He saw sandboxes, swings, discount offers on car seats. He was no longer living at home—the attack in Oslo had been clear enough. He kept moving, slept like crap. Chewed gum and loaded up on snus.

He wanted to understand what had happened when they met Mats, but according to the Norwegian papers, the police still hadn't made any progress in their investigation. In any case, it was clear that there must be leaks within the force, and that the network's reach was far greater than he had ever realized. He hoped Emelie was being careful.

He had to do something, and he had twelve names on his list—twelve names Mats had mentioned. After a few days' research and help from Loke, he had found out that five of the men were dead. One of a heart attack. One in a boating accident. One of cancer. One had been killed by a robber in Brazil. And one had driven into the side of a mountain in Falkenberg.

One had moved to Switzerland.

One had simply disappeared.

But no Peder Hult matching Mats's description seemed to exist.

Still, the other five were living and registered to addresses in the Stockholm area.

He called their secretaries and receptionists. None of the men had public telephone numbers. The women asked what it was regarding, Teddy answered evasively, and they replied that the men may be in touch. *May*. He called their wives and employees. All he wanted was their private telephone numbers. Some people were helpful—gave him the number for the men's work, numbers he had already tried ten times.

Teddy asked Loke for help again. "I just need a few phone numbers. It can't be too hard."

Loke said: "Cutie pie, I'm helping your nephew with something I can't talk about right now, but I should be able to find you a phone number."

Teddy didn't want to wait too long. He continued his research on his own.

He drank Red Bull and took Ritalin to keep going. He studied the city anew. Put it through an X-ray. Viewed it with a criminal's eyes. He saw the hookers hanging around on Malmskillnadsgatan, outside the apartment brothels. He noticed the hash sellers trading more or less out in the open in Husby. He saw the coat pockets on the hordes of young kids in Alby torg: weighed down with knives, knuckle-dusters, and guns. The papers wrote about murders and violence, and everyone pretended to be upset, but if it had been white, inner-city kids shooting one another, the prime minister would have declared a state of emergency and sent in the army. There was a difference.

He drove past his old school: Lina Grundskola. The trees were still bare, and the playground looked more like a gravel pit. They still hadn't tidied up after winter. The same buildings as when he had been a pupil, but they had repainted them, a darker shade. Or maybe it was just his memory playing tricks on him. Maybe the buildings had seemed lighter when he was a child purely because he had seen the world in a different light then. Everything that came later seemed to be part of his dark penance. And he had thought that he had atoned for his crimes when, right after being released from prison, he had rescued another person who had been kidnapped. Teddy had been recruited by Leijon to help on that case, which was how he had met Emelie for the first time.

Leijon, he thought again—maybe they could help.

Teddy was in reception.

The receptionist recognized him. Once, when he had still worked at the firm, she had asked whether he wanted to grab a glass of wine one evening. Teddy had politely turned her down, but it was a stroke of luck that she was working today.

"Magnus doesn't actually take visitors, but he might make an exception for you," she said with a smile. "It might take a while."

Teddy sat down in the uncomfortable designer chair to wait. He thought back to the first time he had sat here, when Emelie came out to get him. The small, round table still had a pile of boring business magazines on it, but unlike before, there were also a number of iPads on the table. Anyone could have taken one, but Teddy knew the caliber of clients the firm had—to them, an iPad was worth less than they earned in a minute.

An hour later, he was sitting in Magnus Hassel's office.

"Teddy, I don't know what you want, but you've got ten minutes, then I have to rush off," the partner who had once recruited him said.

The walls were covered with crazy paintings like always, and the low bookshelves held the same cryptic artwork as before: a human skull flecked with oil paint, a bird's skeleton and a tennis ball in a bell jar, something that probably represented a greenish vagina made from plastic and marble. There were also three small photos, all seemingly taken at least a hundred years ago, depicting young boys. In each of them: a boy around ten, with dark hair and an uncertain smile. Teddy squinted and read the text beneath them. Stalin. Bin Laden. Hitler.

Magnus could see him thinking. "What do you think of my latest find?"

Teddy thought he was supposed to be in a hurry, but Magnus still pointed to the photographs. "Three deplorable men as children. I think it's an interesting question, when does evil emerge. Because no child is evil, are they? And yet at some point, the child's innocence transforms into conscious evil."

Teddy's chair creaked.

"Anyway," said Magnus, "I'm doing you a favor by seeing you now, I hope you understand. You know what I thought of what you and Emelie were up to, but I still like you, Teddy, for some reason I do. You did a good job when you were here. So tell me what you need."

Teddy's chair creaked even more as he leaned forward.

"I'm here because I've been trying to get in touch with a number of individuals, and I don't know anyone who can get through to people like them. Other than you."

"Aha, and why do you need to speak to them, if I may ask?"

Teddy didn't reply. Instead, he said: "I have their names and I know who they are, but I need a way in. I need a good chat with each of them." He reeled off the five names.

"Is this to do with Mats Emanuelsson?" Magnus sighed.

Teddy leaned back. For some reason, the chair didn't make a sound this time. How could Magnus have known?

Magnus got up and put on his jacket. He carefully pulled down each sleeve so that only a quarter inch or so was peeping out from beneath the arm of his jacket. "You know I'm bound by confidentiality. So even if I did know these people, I wouldn't be able to help you. That's just how it is in my world. Anyway, I have to rush off now."

Teddy got to his feet. Magnus gestured for him to leave.

Teddy said: "Don't try to brush me off. I know you can help me."

"I have to go. I've told you."

Teddy was blocking the doorway. "I've worked for you—you know that I know things about how you run your business, right? Do you see what I mean?"

Magnus's cuff links glittered in the light from the window.

"I think I understand," he said. "Let's talk further."

26

Mr. One had been in custody for more than a month now, suspected of all kinds of crap: tax fraud, serious accountancy fraud, the usual drug offenses—it was a classic. If they couldn't get you for the real crimes, they followed the money. Isak wasn't allowed to talk to or see anyone but relatives. The Swedish system wasn't as open as some people thought—but it was naive all the same. Because the truth was this: right now, Nikola was standing in front of the metal door outside the custodial prison in Huddinge, pressing a button beneath a sign that read *Central Guard*. He heard a tinny voice over the speaker and saw the round black eye of the surveillance camera staring at him.

"Yeah, hi."

He didn't know what he was supposed to say. He had been held in custody himself, but had never visited anyone on his own. Was he supposed to say his name and who he was visiting? Or did they already know he had booked a time?

"Rimon Nimrod, I'm here to visit my uncle."

"And who's that?"

"He's called Isak . . ."

"Aha, got it. Wait a moment."

The metal door clicked, and Nikola took ahold of the handle with both hands and pulled. It was crazy heavy.

The elevator doors were also made from brushed metal. He

pressed the up button and waited. From a loudspeaker, the tinny voice barked: "Don't touch anything. We control the elevator from here."

Like he said: naive. Isak's lawyer had called Nikola a week earlier and asked him to apply for a visit. The lawyer had come up with a way it could work—according to him, they weren't all that sharp within the Prison Service. And so Isak had filled in his visit form and named his nephew, Rimon Nimrod. Nikola had signed the form, sent it back, and borrowed Rimon's ID. The kid was four years younger, but if Nikola styled his hair the same way, they actually looked pretty similar.

In a few minutes' time, he would be able to sit down with Isak and go through what he had found on Chamon's phone. And who had answered when he called.

But he wasn't inside yet.

The main guardroom was on the fourth floor. He thought of Kerim Celalî—the guy he had become friends with through the bars when they had exercise hour at the same time. Kerim must have had a wizard of a lawyer, because he had apparently only been given three years. Given that he had been in custody for so long beforehand, and a year and a half had since passed, he should be out by now. Maybe Nikola should get in touch—Kerim was a cool boss.

A small drawer shot out; the guard on the other side glared at Nikola and asked for his ID.

The moment of truth: exactly how thorough was the Prison Service? This was when it would all be put to the test. Nikola couldn't quite see the person behind the Plexiglas; it was too reflective. Instead, he saw his own mirror image staring back at him. He didn't look normal in his new Rimon style, but it was actually something else making him look like a different person: the deep shadows beneath his eyes—deep as Chamon's grave.

The speaker crackled. He waited. They were probably checking his ID. A memory. They were only sixteen, but Chamon had already had a beard that could compete with any IS fighter. He had let it grow for two weeks and then they had borrowed his cousin's stroller. "You reckon people'll think I'm a homo now? 'Cause Swedes and poofs are the only ones who bother with paternity leave, right?" On the way to the shop, they had stopped an old man and tested it out: "How old d'you think I am?" They had carefully stuffed the stroller, and if you only gave it a quick glimpse, it did look like there might be a baby tucked up inside. The old man didn't seem to have anything against their guessing game, and he had scanned Chamon from head to toe. The beard, the stroller, the chinos—Nikola had never seen Chamon in anything but sweatpants before—the neatly combed hair, and, most convincing of all: the bottle. They had filled a bottle with juice and put it in the stroller's cup holder. All they were missing was a kid—but Chamon's cousin had refused to let them borrow her four-month-old baby, no matter how much Chamon begged.

Nikola had waited outside. It was only ten in the morning—a plausible time for a man on paternity leave to be stocking up on beer before a family dinner at the weekend. He had tried to peer in through the window. He could see Chamon strolling about inside, with the stroller and a basket in his hand, completely at ease. His friend and a few members of AA had been the only ones waiting when the shop opened. If you were on paternity-homo leave, surely there was no reason to stress? Eventually, Chamon had gone over to the cashier and hauled a couple of six-packs onto the conveyor belt. Nikola had had a pretty clear view of it, the exit was closest to the windows, and he saw the cashier, who didn't look old enough to have grown hair on his balls yet, say something to Chamon. Nikola had spotted the small notices by the registers: *If you're under 25, please show us your ID.* Chamon seemed to reply, Nikola had tried to work out what was going on. Chamon had shaken his head. The cashier gestured. Then Chamon had taken the cans off the conveyor belt. Shit. Balls. It hadn't worked. They had wanted to see his ID.

Chamon had pushed the stroller slowly ahead of him, its wheels squeaking.

"I was watching through the window," Nikola said once they met fifty yards away from the shop. Chamon's face had been dogged.

"We should've had a real baby, I told you."

"Can you be bothered trying the shop in Lunagallerian? Might have better luck there?"

"Just having a stroller's not enough to buy four six-packs." Chamon had bared his teeth, then bent down and started rifling beneath the stroller. He had pulled out two bottles of Absolut Vodka. "But it's enough to nick some spirits."

If Nikola leaned forward now and used his hands to cast shadows on the Plexiglas, he would probably be able to see in—but it would also be a really weird thing to do. Maybe they were just checking that there were empty visitation rooms on the computer. Maybe they were calling the police right now, asking them to come and arrest him for fraudulent use of ID, or whatever it was called.

"Okay," the guard said over the speakers. "You can't take any cell phones or other electronic equipment in with you, so put it all in one of the lockers over there. Then you just need to open the door here. I'll buzz you in."

The door opened and Isak was led into the room. Mr. One was wearing prison-issue plastic slippers and a green tracksuit; he looked homeless.

"Rimon," Isak said loudly. Nikola saw that the boss was trying to hide a smile.

Once the door closed, he roared with laughter for at least a minute. "Nikola, you sure your dad's really your dad?"

"All I know about my dad is that he was a cunt."

"Lots of them are. But you must have a bit of *Mëdyad* in you, I can see it now. You don't just speak our language, you're a real brother."

They sat down on opposite sides of the table. Nikola wanted to ask how Isak was doing, how the boss handled the boredom, the food and being allowed out for only an hour a day. But the boss didn't want to make small talk.

"We've got an hour," he said. "And lots to get through."

Isak started reeling off information. Nikola had brought a pencil and some paper. He had assumed they would spend the hour talking about the hunt for Chamon's killer—he now knew exactly who could have tracked Chamon's movements through the app—but Isak had other plans. Nikola wrote as quickly as he could: *Iztvan owes three thousand a month, Homan owes five thousand a month,* and so on. He didn't need to know exactly what it was about, Isak said: Yusuf, Bello, and the others would take care of everything. *Tanning salon in Ronna needs a new director, the company running the restaurant on Badhusgatan needs to declare bankruptcy,* etc. Why didn't Isak just call his lawyer or speak to Yusuf directly to go through all this? Nikola had *never* said he was getting back into the Life just because he wanted revenge for his friend's death.

Isak read his mind. "This stuff's too hot for my lawyer, even though you can trust him. I can't do it over the phone, either; the pigs listen in on all my calls out of here, I'm sure. And it's a bad idea for Yusuf to appear too close to me. So it was pretty sweet that you could come. Really."

Still: Nikola needed to go through his business. He knew something. They had already been sitting here for thirty minutes.

Mr. One continued. A building in Norsberg needed to be bought, one of his cars had to be serviced—though it was leased and registered to Babso, of course—a few contracts for consultancy services needed to be re-signed. Then there were the even more important things. Someone needed to set fire to a Mazda with the registration number MFR490, often parked on Lammholmsbacken in Skärholmen. "It belongs to one of the pigs that've been fucking with me in here." And then the most important part of all:

someone had to move his boxes of explosives from a basement on Sjöbergsgatan.

They had five minutes left. "How's it going finding those bastards?" Isak finally asked.

"I found out someone was following Chamon's movements through a tracking app on one of his phones. It was linked to a different number."

"Oh shit. Who?"

Nikola was burning. "Yusuf," he said.

Isak was silent. Nikola wondered what he was thinking. Yusuf had been the boss's right-hand man for at least eight years. They had grown up together, Mr. One was a few years older. If Nikola and Chamon were like brothers, Isak and Yusuf were like twins.

"I didn't want to believe it," said Isak.

"You thought he was involved?"

"I didn't want to say anything, but yeah."

"Why?"

"Because right before those bastards came to the MMA club and started shooting, Yusuf really needed a shit, he was nervous as anything, and he was saying all this weird stuff. I didn't think much of it at the time, but it makes sense now. He knew they were coming."

"But why?"

"No idea."

The door opened and a guard peered in. "Time's up."

Isak got to his feet and walked toward the door. As he passed Nikola, he leaned in, a quick movement. A quiet whisper that the guard couldn't hear.

"Finish that whore."

27

If Emelie's calculations were correct, she was somewhere around the ninth week, and she knew that people didn't normally tell anyone before the twelfth. But surely that only applied to outsiders? Didn't her mother and father have a right to know? Maybe it was her duty to tell them. The problem was that she still didn't know if she was actually going to keep the baby, and even if she did, it wasn't like her parents were the type to hold her hand; they were usually preoccupied with their own concerns. She had canceled her trip to see them.

Besides, she wasn't living a particularly stable life right now. She had called Nina, who promised to help out. A couple of handymen had come over to Emelie's place. "We're from witness protection," they said, though they would have looked more at home on some TV DIY show. They fitted bars over her door, installed a security system, and gave her a personal alarm—a small fob with built-in GPS and a button she could press if anything happened. It would send an alert straight to the police.

But Emelie still didn't feel secure—Nina herself had admitted that there were problems within her organization.

A few days after she had been to the hospital, she went to the maternity clinic. The operator she had spoken to over the phone didn't seem to think she was in much of a rush—"You can come in in a few weeks"—but Emelie wanted to see a midwife as soon as possible. She took a taxi straight there and prayed that someone would have canceled their appointment.

The clinic was in Gamla stan, and the minute Emelie stepped through the low door, she felt the atmosphere change. It wasn't as though the street was hectic: the alley was narrow, dark, and calm, like most of the other gloomy, winding streets in the oldest part of Stockholm. But inside the clinic, everything was moving even more slowly, more deliberately—it was as though no one wanted to bother anyone else, as though some vital, solemn lecture was taking place in one of the rooms, and no one wanted to interrupt.

The midwife's name was Inga, and she asked how Emelie was doing. She spoke calmly and quietly; she even typed silently. "Do you or the baby's father have any illnesses or take any medication?"

Emelie knew about herself—*nowadays,* she wasn't taking anything. But Teddy? "As far as I'm concerned, the answer is no, but I'll have to get back to you about the father."

Inga continued to talk about the risks of smoking and alcohol, about how Emelie might not be able to work as hard as she was used to; how the nausea she had felt would, in all likelihood, pass as she approached the end of her first trimester.

Emelie realized she should have brought Teddy with her, for the child's sake if for nothing else, so that Inga could carry out her thorough checks. But, all the same: it had nothing to do with him. Emelie was the one with the baby in her belly; she was the one shouldering all of the responsibility just now. She was the one who had to make the decision.

Inga took her blood pressure and asked for a urine sample. She weighed Emelie and took blood samples from her arm. "Your blood type and whether you're Rh positive or negative," Inga explained. "It can also show us whether you're immune to rubella and whether you have syphilis, chlamydia, or HIV."

To begin with, Emelie didn't know how she could have let it happen. Her periods had been irregular for several years, and for some reason that meant she hadn't bothered to take the pill or demand that men wore condoms. She and Teddy had had unprotected sex, in other words. Chlamydia was something she could live with, but what about the others? She knew nothing about Teddy's sexual history or health.

"How soon do you get the results from the blood test?"

"It usually takes a few days."

After forty minutes, they were done. Emelie could feel her hands shaking. "Well, thanks," she said, trying to sound calm.

Inga paused in the doorway. "There's something fantastic happening in your body right now, and you're welcome to call if there's anything you'd like to ask."

Emelie nodded.

"And if the father wants to come in and discuss anything, that's fine, too."

"I don't think so," said Emelie.

"Are you in contact with him?"

"This might sound strange," Emelie said, grabbing her bag from the floor, "but I don't actually know."

Now she was at the office, trying to work. It was eight in the evening. She felt safer here than she did at home.

Teddy had been trying to call her all day, but she had ignored him every time. Somehow, she had to pretend that everything was normal. She had a main hearing in an assault case at the end of the week. Her client was a nineteen-year-old kid who, according to the prosecutor, had participated in the aggravated assault of another boy on the platform at Hallunda metro station. The images from the surveillance cameras were fuzzy, but you could clearly make out a figure in a red hoodie in the vicinity of the victim at the start of the assault. It looked like the figure had knocked the victim to the ground. Things were less clear after that—there were at least five other people moving around the injured party, but it was impossible to tell what the figure in the red hoodie was doing. Fifteen minutes later, the police had arrested five boys by the Thai kiosk outside the station. Emelie's client was one of them, and he had been wearing a bright red hoodie. They had interviewed him on three occasions, but all he had repeated was: "I'm not the person in the film. I wasn't on the platform. I met my friends later, when they were getting noodles." The injured party had gone through a lineup, during which he had pointed out Emelie's client with 90 percent certainty. The problem was that apart from Emelie's client, only one other figure in the lineup was from a non-Nordic country. Emelie knew what she thought of that kind of evidence—it belonged in the gutter.

Despite that, almost all she could think about was Katja and the shooting in Oslo.

Then Nina Ley called.

"I've changed my mind," she said. "You can look through what we've got against Adam. Off the record."

"Have your suspicions been strengthened?"

"You can read everything for yourself. If you come here, you can read through the investigation," said Nina. "But I can't say they've been weakened."

Emelie read what they had. The crime scene report, the analysis of Katja's phone, forensic statements relating to her injuries and likely cause of death. Two stab wounds to the abdomen, caused by a sharp object, and so on. Photographs and a brief statement regarding the wound on Adam's hand. Analysis reports into the blood found at the scene. Analyses of the carving knife. Analyses of the backpack on the roof. It was still the only question mark: they had found neither fingerprints nor DNA on it. Who had been on the roof opposite? Maybe the backpack actually had nothing to do with the murder.

Emelie glanced at the time on her computer: it was quarter to ten. There was something she was missing here. Something the police had missed, which she should be able to see. There had to be a pattern of some kind. Or maybe she was overestimating herself, thinking of crime novels and thrillers, where the hero always came up with something no one else had seen, where intuition was key and feelings led the way. But Emelie knew what reality was like: intuition came from hard work. From commanding the material.

She closed the lid of her computer. Placed her hands on her belly. She wasn't showing yet, but she could still feel the difference. She was going to be a mother. A parent. Or was she?

Suddenly it came to her: she couldn't remember any mention of Katja's parents in the investigation.

She went through everything again. Katja's father was dead, but she had a mother.

Emelie was going to try to get ahold of her tomorrow.

Haninge Centrum looked like any other shopping center from the past fifteen years. The same pale flooring, the same white walls, the same illuminated walkways between shops and the same open-plan, indoor squares full of cafés, juice bars, and cell phone stands. It was remarkable: in an age of choice, everything was the same.

As she scanned the people sitting inside Wayne's Coffee, she immediately worked out which one must be Gunnel—a lone woman in her fifties, with such bad posture that it was hard to see how she had even managed to get there. Emelie wondered why Katja's mother hadn't wanted to meet at her house, or at Emelie's office, but maybe that was her business.

Gunnel had a cup of tea in front of her. She was hunched over it as though she was about to fall, not looking up once. Her long blond hair seemed lank and greasy, but she had tried to hold it back with two pink clips—the color felt almost perverse.

The tables around her were all busy, but everyone seemed pre-occupied with their own concerns, and the majority seemed to be speaking different languages—Emelie assumed that their ability to eavesdrop on her conversation with Gunnel was probably quite limited. This should be a safe place to talk.

"So you were Katja's lawyer?" Gunnel asked.

"Yes, but we only managed to meet twice. When did you last see her?"

"She was such a good girl, deep down. This is so hard."

Emelie had steeled herself for a difficult conversation. "I can't even imagine what you must be going through right now," she said.

"No one can," Gunnel replied.

Emelie was clutching her coffee cup, but the minute the liquid beneath the thick layer of foamed milk touched her lips, she realized she didn't feel like drinking it. She placed the cup back on the table. Gunnel hadn't answered her question.

"So when did you last see Katja?"

Gunnel slurped her tea. "Why are you asking that?"

"I'm trying to understand what happened, and that means I need to gather as much information about Katja as I can."

Gunnel hunched so far over her cup that her nose was practically touching it. "I see."

"So, when did you last see her?"

"I called her a few months ago to warn her about that Adam. But she didn't listen. I hope they send him down for life."

"I'm sorry, I don't want to be inquisitive, but it would be great if you could answer my question. You might have seen or heard something important. WHEN did you last see Katja?"

Gunnel straightened up, sitting upright in her chair. "I haven't seen my daughter in five years, not since she turned eighteen. So, there you have it." She pushed back her chair. "And the reason has nothing to do with you."

"No, I know. But maybe you want to tell me anyway?"

Gunnel got up. "Katja accused me of all kinds of crap ten years ago. It was always someone else's fault that things ended up the way they did."

The thought struck Emelie hard, like a punch to the face: neither when Katja talked to her nor when she was being interviewed by the police had she said anything about *how* she had made contact with the first man. But now she remembered Katja's words from the police interview: as though in passing, she had mentioned that she met him through someone she trusted.

Someone she trusted. Then. When she was thirteen.

Emelie tried to speak as softly as she could. "Did Katja think something was your fault? Is that what you mean?"

Gunnel's voice no longer sounded sad. It was burning. "She was quick to get things into her head, Katja. She had far too big an imagination."

"Did she get something into her head about what she went through when she was thirteen?"

"God knows what she thought."

Emelie's mind was racing: the conversation with Katja in her office, the interview with Nina Ley. The questions that had been asked, what Katja had answered, what she hadn't answered. How she had reacted.

She had reacted strongly. Physically. Cried. Shaken.

Emelie could hardly look at Gunnel any longer. But she had to ask: "Gunnel, did you have any idea of what was going on with Katja?"

28

"Roksana *joonam*," Dad said as he opened the door. "How are you? You look tired."

Roksana had taken out her nose ring, but she couldn't hide the rest of her appearance—she was beyond exhausted.

"I'm fine," she said anyway.

There was a new pair of guest slippers in the hallway, but Roksana couldn't find the pair she usually wore.

"Where are my slippers, Baba?"

"I don't know, you'll have to ask your mother."

Her father was wearing sweatpants today. They looked like a pair of Billie's yoga pants, but Roksana knew they were from Iran. The two of them sat down in the kitchen. Her mother hugged her, then returned to her cooking.

"Here," her father said, holding out a bowl of pralines.

Does anyone *really* like pralines, Roksana thought to herself, taking the one that looked least disgusting. *"Merci."* It contained some kind of strawberry cream that was far too sweet.

She knew she would have to put on a more cheerful face— she was here to give them good news, after all, to tell them something that would make them happy. But there was just one thought whirling around her mind: How were she and Z going to scrape together the money? Their only chance would be if they could start making it themselves, but at one hundred times the scale they had managed with what they stole from the vet. How would that work? They would need to raid twenty clinics to get their hands on even a tenth of what those madmen wanted.

They had looked up a number of animal hospitals and storage facilities anyway, but the security at each of them was far too tight—they were hardly break-in specialists, after all, and they didn't want to get caught. Z had put out some feelers on Darknet, to see if there was anyone who wanted to sell Ketalar or similar, but the only people who got in touch were recovered junkies with half a bottle that they no longer wanted in their bathroom cabinets.

She made an effort. "I've got some good news to tell you."

Her mother turned around. Dad stopped chewing on his chocolate.

"I'm going to get into the psychology program," she said, drawing out the next sentence for a few seconds. "Because *I* got really high grades on the aptitude test."

Twenty minutes later, the celebrations had finally calmed down. Her father had responded by uncorking a bottle of champagne and eating the rest of the chocolates; her mother had sent messages to Caspar and their relatives in Tehran. Her father had hugged her, laughing with joy. He had even put on some of his old tapes: Dariush at full volume. Her mother had pulled Roksana from her seat and danced her around the kitchen. And now the replies had started coming in: Dad's sister and her children wanted to Skype.

They sat down in front of the computer. Five minutes later, they could see one another. On-screen: Aunt Etty and Roksana's cousins, Leila and Val. She hadn't seen them since last summer, when they came to Sweden.

Etty seemed to have had yet another nose job—she was starting to look more and more like Michael Jackson—but Leila and Val looked like normal. Both wearing jeans and T-shirts, Leila slightly paler than Val.

"My darlings," Etty shouted.

Dad didn't even ask how they were; he couldn't hold back: the words just tumbled out of his mouth. "Roksana is going to be a psychologist. She got the highest, best, and finest score on the entrance exam for university, which means she can study wherever she likes."

That wasn't quite right, but Etty was beside herself with happiness. Leila mostly grinned, Val simply nodded—ice cool, like usual. Then Dad and Etty started talking about other things. Dad's aches and pains, Aunt Etty's renovations and trips to Paris.

"You have to see what we've done," Etty said after ten minutes of chatter. The image started to move. Roksana didn't know whether Etty was holding her phone or a laptop computer, but now they were being treated to a tour of her house. The living room and all of its rugs. The bathroom and its golden taps. And then the newly built rooms, of course. Etty's bedroom. Leila's bedroom. Val's music room.

The camera swept past two guitars and a keyboard. But Roksana had spotted something else. On the wall, on a hook: something black. Round.

"What a nice room," said Roksana.

"Yes, isn't it," Etty practically screeched. Val and Leila were no longer even part of the conversation.

"And look at this," said Etty, moving the camera over to the window. "The view."

The object on the wall became clearer. Etty moved forward.

It was a helmet.

A riding helmet.

On the way home from her mother and father's house, she called her aunt's number again over Skype. Etty wanted to chat, but Roksana asked to speak to her cousin.

"Val," she said. "Can you help me?"

————

Four days later, it was all settled. Roksana was on her way. She wasn't really in all that much of a hurry, not now that she had started the journey. The plane wouldn't be leaving for two and a half hours. Still, the only instruction her father had given her was: "Leave plenty of time for checking in, Roksana *joonam*. They're crazy with their bureaucracy."

On the whole, both he and her mother had been thrilled when she told them she had booked the trip. "But I noticed that you didn't get along *so* well when we called them on Skype," Mom had said, her feelers as long as ever. Roksana knew she would have to come up with an explanation, so she told them the truth—almost. "But I met them when they were here. And then I called Val, and we really clicked."

"Welcome to the Arlanda Express," the automated man's voice said. "The cheapest and most environmentally friendly way to travel between Stockholm city and Arlanda Airport." When Billie had found out that Roksana was flying to Tehran, a skeptical note had appeared in her voice. "You're *flying*?"

"How else would I get there?"

"You shouldn't fly. Think of the environment."

"You went to Los Angeles last autumn."

"Yeah, but there's a difference. I had to be there."

Exactly why Billie *had* to be at the Moonfaze Feminist Film Festival was beyond Roksana, but she kept quiet.

The old man next to her smelled of sweat, and the cabin was cold. This plane seemed shabbier than the one she had taken on the first leg of her journey, to Istanbul. But she had also paid less than 3,200 kronor for the flights, so she couldn't complain. It was surprisingly cheap.

She tried to read—she had bought two Susan Faludi books at Arlanda. One was *Stiffed:* a classic, according to Billie. The other was her latest: *In the Darkroom.*

The words merged together on the page. Roksana's eyes were tired; she was seeing double. It was the same old thing. Her left eye was weaker than the right, an unusual visual defect, her optician had said. Plus four on the right side, minus two on the left—and the patch over her eye hadn't made the least bit of difference.

She thought about why everything had turned out like it had. It had been niggling at her—not just the ketamine and the fact that everyone had wanted to pay for her and Z's stuff, but the rest of it, too. She couldn't put it into words, other than to say that the feeling had been very nice. But now she didn't know what they were going to do. The crazies needed their money. This trip had to deliver what she was hoping for.

The pointed, snow-covered mountains surrounding Tehran glittered in the sunlight. The city looked like an enormous, deformed butterfly from the air: the center with its shopping streets and museums a feeble body in the middle. Imam Khomeini International Airport, on the other hand, looked small, but it felt far from petite when Roksana left the plane. There was another, bigger airport—Mehrabad—but Imam Khomeini was the biggest for international flights, according to her father.

Huge banners of Ayatollah Ali Khamenei hung across the gate where Roksana's plane pulled in. Her mother had told her: "They don't recognize dual citizenship, Roksana, so your Swedish passport will be worthless there. Legally, I mean."

"But I'm not an Iranian citizen."

"You are. They follow the paternal line, and since your father is an Iranian, they consider you one, too. You'll have to get an Iranian passport."

There were, if possible, even more people in this airport than there had been in Istanbul, and almost all of them reminded her of Dad, Etty, Val, and Leila. For some reason, none of them resembled her mother. Maybe it was the way she moved that made her unique: her mother was always slightly irregular, bouncy somehow, like she was drunk or had a splinter in her foot—when, in actual fact, she always knew exactly where she was going.

Roksana clutched her new passport in her hand, concentrating on not allowing her eyes to wander, which happened easily in such situations.

Everything went much more smoothly than she had expected; her bag even appeared first on the luggage belt. All around her, there were uniformed guards with automatic rifles in their hands—soldiers. As Roksana started to drag her bag toward the exit, one of them peeled away from the group and began moving in her direction. She sped up: he couldn't be after her, could he?

The soldier's gun bounced against him. Roksana was only a few yards from the barriers now. He was following her, that much was clear.

"*Khahar,*" he shouted.

Roksana turned around. Met the young man's tense eyes. He gestured to his head. Roksana glared at him. A moment later, she understood: she had forgotten her headscarf. She wasn't allowed outside without it. As luck would have it, it was already around her neck, and she pulled it up over the back of her head like she knew Leila usually did. Her mother had given it to her at Arlanda, and it was actually pretty nice—a bit crazy, yellow with orange flowers.

She knew which exit she was supposed to take, and the first thing that struck her as she left the airport was the view: the city laid out in front of her was completely surrounded by the magical mountains she had seen from the air. They looked even more powerful now than they had from above, like something out of a Disney film. She took a deep breath and got another surprise—it was difficult to breathe here. The air was thick with exhaust fumes, stinging her nose and filling her lungs with dirt.

She spotted Val standing next to an enormous SUV.

"Welcome to Tehran, *soedi,*" he said.

Roksana smiled. "Swede"—she had never been called that before.

29

Dejan looked like one of those guys with an unhealthy interest in the military. He was wearing camo pants, a camo top, and a camo-colored cap with the words *Savage Arms* on the front and *The Definition of Accuracy* on the back. "Bought it at the shooting range when I was in Vegas last autumn," he claimed.

"I thought you hated the Americans after what they did to us in Serbia."

Dejan lowered the pistol. The pungent smell of gunpowder was thick in the air. "Eh, it's a complicated world. Your enemy's enemy is also your friend. The U.S. has constantly been at war, sometimes they made mistakes, they attacked us, Vietnam was insane, what do I know. In the majority of cases, though, they've been on the right side. What d'you think would've happened if they hadn't joined in the First or Second World Wars? The Ustaše would've slaughtered us like they slaughtered the Jews."

Dejan's outburst was surprisingly audible through the ear protectors: they contained some kind of electronic amplifiers that filtered out the gunshots but increased the volume of human voices. Dejan's dog, the Mauler, was locked in the back of the Tesla outside—there were no headphones that could help him.

Teddy wondered how Dejan could have become a member here: there had to be more entries in his criminal record than there were bullet casings on the floor outside the booth. Maybe this club had a special book for people like his friend, who probably sponsored them in cash.

Dejan heckled himself. "I'll admit it, I'm a serious gun nut. I've got seven pistols and two rifles in the cabinet back home. You want to try my Colt 1911? It's got a great kick on it, you know. Or do you want to keep using that cop piece?"

The shooting range was blasted into the rock face in Sollentuna, and it went by the nickname Bunker Mountain. From the outside, incognito: just a metal door in the rock, but to Teddy, the walk from the damp entrance was like a crescendo. The modest, rusty door led to a narrow entrance with old pipes on the ceiling, which then led to an antechamber with slightly higher ceilings, carpets, and soundproof glass dividing it from the shooting range, and ultimately to the shooting range itself—the climax. The ceilings inside had to be at least twenty feet high, surrounded by granite, blasted right in the heart of the ancient Swedish rock.

Dejan was over the moon that Teddy had agreed to go with him. He talked nonstop about pistol types, calibers, recoil management— whatever that was—body position, and focus.

"I sometimes whisper calming words to myself. Things like cunt, fag, whore, you know," said Dejan. "Makes me harmonious inside, so my hands stop shaking."

He really was sick in the head. When they were just fourteen, he used to creep around in the woods behind Ronna, shooting crows with an air rifle. But today, Teddy was here with one thought in his mind.

"Did you end up doing a deal with those guys with the beards?"

BAM-BAM-BAM.

"Not so good. I jump when I fire."

Teddy repeated his question. "Did you buy that ID card business?"

BAM-BAM-BAM.

The casings were flying. The gunpowder stung his nose.

Dejan put down the pistol on the green felt-clad table.

"Nah, nah. Not from those terrorists."

"Couldn't they lower the price?"

"You know that wasn't the problem. You want to try the Colt now?"

Teddy had to get Dejan's attention. He picked up the pistol.

The Colt was heavy, but somehow it felt comfortable and natural when his fingers curled around the butt. He took off the safety catch and raised his arm in front of him. The front sight was supposed to be perfectly aligned with the rear one. He breathed in. Lowered his arm again; it was too heavy. Took three deep breaths. In his mind, he could see only one thing. Emelie's stomach. He hadn't seen what it looked like now, whether it had started to grow, but he imagined it bulging all the same. Then he thought about the child inside it—not that he pictured a face or a body, he just felt a presence, as though there was a child standing in front of him, waiting to hold his hand. As though Nikola was two again. Then a new thought: someone was pulling at the baby. Someone wanted to hurt his child. A shadow was trying to take Teddy's child away from him.

He raised his arm. Took aim at the shadow.

BAM-BAM-BAM.

The three shots had virtually fired themselves. Dejan went over to collect the target.

"Shit, man. Bull's-eye." He held it up—each of the three holes was within the black area. "Maybe I should call you Pia Hansen?"

Teddy put down the gun. "Call me whatever you want. If you'll help me with something."

"What?"

"There are some old men I want to talk to me. And I want them to understand the gravity of the conversation."

Dejan's face lit up.

The old men were still trying to pretend that he didn't exist, but Teddy had played his trump cards, his two jokers: Dejan and

Magnus Hassel. Back when he worked for the hotshot lawyer, Teddy had used methods that wouldn't stand up to even the slightest scrutiny. Magnus had understood that immediately. He'd had no other choice but to help.

Hassel had called the numbers that Loke had helped Teddy get ahold of. When they realized who they were talking to, the men's tone changed. *No problem, good to talk to you. When would you like to meet?*

Magnus had been instructed to follow the same script with all five men: he told them that he wanted to meet to talk about a confidential matter. Ideally at their homes, if possible—not at his office, where people might talk if they were seen together.

All five had said yes.

The first person they visited was Fredrik O. Johansson. He was fifty-seven, lived in Djursholm, and was the majority owner of an investment company called Pecuniarapid AB. He also sat on the board of a number of other companies. Fredrik—or Fred O. as Loke had seen he was called by his friends on Facebook—came from humble origins in the north of Sweden, but had said in the only interview he had ever given that "with a little luck, you can damn well get anywhere. Just look at Jesus."

Fredrik O. opened the door for Teddy, Dejan, and the Mauler. His hair was dyed black, probably naturally gray, and he had a triple chin. The house wasn't just the size of a smaller Arab Emirate, it also faced out onto the water. Dejan whispered something about being able to buy half of Södertälje for the price of the plot alone.

"Which of you is Magnus Hassel?" the man asked the minute he closed the door behind them.

The Mauler's tongue was lolling from his mouth.

"We haven't been entirely honest with you," said Teddy. "I'm the one who wants to talk to you, and neither of us is Hassel."

"Aha," Fredrik sighed. "Then I shall have to ask you to leave. You've come here under false pretenses. We may as well meet in my office, or with my lawyer."

Teddy didn't move.

"No, we'll be staying for a while," he said, with what had to be the coolest voice in northern Europe. "We just need a few minutes."

Fredrik O. Johansson glanced at Dejan. His chins trembled. "Okay, let's talk. But you should know that I have alarm systems and surveillance cameras installed. My cleaner will also be arriving any minute now. So don't think you can get up to any funny business with me. They have keys and are aware of our security routines."

Teddy resisted the urge to glance at Dejan. This guy could easily have been one of their kidnapping victims back when they did that kind of thing.

They sat down in a long, cool room the size of a tennis court. It was full of art and huge potted plants. On a small table by one of the windows, there was a silver candlestick with three arms that snaked around one another to form what looked like a knot. The walls were covered in classical depictions of Swedish winter landscapes that Teddy did actually recognize. He seemed to think that one of the artists was called Anders Zorn.

"Do you know a Peder Hult?" he asked.

"No, I don't recognize that name. And, before we talk, I would like to know exactly what this is about."

"You'll understand soon enough," said Teddy. "Do you know a Mats Emanuelsson?"

Fred O.'s eyes darted back and forth.

"I, err, do actually recognize that name, yes," he said. "But I can't place it. Give me something else."

"Roughly ten, eleven years ago?"

"I'm trying to remember."

"At a country estate, with some others, perhaps?"

"Where? Which people?"

"Among them Peder Hult. Mats gave a short speech, gave you tax advice and so on."

Fredrik's face was tense. "Ahh, of course. I know who he was, he went on to commit suicide?"

Teddy didn't answer that question. "Do you remember when you met Mats?"

"Not particularly well. But I do vaguely remember his talk. I never actually moved any money with him. Something I'm damned glad about today, given that not even the best legal firms seem to have staff who can keep quiet."

"Where was the estate?"

"I think it was in Södermanland, but I got a taxi there. Damned lavish if you ask me."

"What was the name?"

"I wouldn't know it if someone said it to me. At least, I don't remember a name. This was ten years ago, as you said."

"What did the house look like?"

"Big, grand, nineteenth century, I would guess. Wood panels, yellowish. I don't remember any more than that. It was rather dark when I arrived. Why do you want to know all this? I haven't done anything wrong."

"Maybe not. But some of the others who were there have," said Teddy. "Who organized the event?"

"I don't want to say."

Fredrik O. Johansson twisted his wedding band on his finger.

"Why not?"

"Because I'm not an idiot. That advice, and there were plenty who did listen to it, was about tax optimization. Nothing wrong with that if you ask me, but if anyone starts digging into it, they'll decide that people have done plenty wrong, just like you said. And why should I contribute to entirely honorable people being drawn into that? Why should I be responsible for people being accused of all kinds of old crap for which the statute of limitations should have long since passed?"

Never rat. Teddy couldn't blame him—clearly that was a golden rule at every level of society. But there were limits—for everyone.

He pulled out a chair. Now his face was inches away from Fred O.'s sweaty mug.

"Look, Fredrik. I don't care about your money laundering or your tax evasion. This is about rape, human trafficking. And murder."

Fredrik O. Johansson looked like someone had just told him that he had lost all his money. When he next spoke, his chins were so still that they looked like porcelain.

"Murder? That sounds worrying, to say the least. But if that's the case, why aren't the police looking into it?"

"You don't get to ask questions."

"But you have to understand that I'm surprised. It was so long ago, but what I remember is that the person who arranged the advice meeting, who invited us there, was called Gabriel Sveréus. That much I can say."

Teddy made sure his face remained as still as the chins in front of him. But he had studied Fred's eye movements. Gabriel Sveréus was one of the names Mats had given them in Oslo—he was also the man who had died of cancer.

That afternoon, he and Dejan met the man living on Narvavägen, Gunnar Svensson. His apartment was big and heavily furnished. Above the open fireplace, Teddy noticed the same candlestick that he had seen at Fredrik O. Johansson's house: silver, three arms, a knot. He tried the same tactics as with Fred O., but they didn't work half as well. This guy remembered nothing, he said. No Peder Hult. No Mats Emanuelsson. No Gabriel Sveréus. The man couldn't even remember being at an estate in Södermanland. Eventually, Teddy asked whether the idiot could remember what he had eaten for breakfast that morning.

"Sandwich," he replied. Then: "No, actually, it might have been a fried egg."

Sly bastard.

Men three, four, and five gave the same empty results. They managed to get in without any problems, since Magnus had booked the meetings, but that was as far as they got. The men didn't want to remember a thing.

The Magnus Hassel opening hadn't yielded what Teddy had been hoping for. He wondered if Hassel had forewarned them somehow.

Outside, nature was starting to come to life. Blue and white anemones were brightening the edge of the road in the colors of Finland, even though dusk had started to fall.

"What do you think?" Teddy and Dejan were in the Tesla, heading home.

"It's over ten years ago. Understandable if they don't remember. What's this even about, anyway?"

"Think you already know."

"I heard you mentioning Mats Emanuelsson. Teddy, I've told you to drop all that."

Teddy tried to look straight ahead. A tunnel of headlights. The world was becoming blurry along the edges of the road now. "I'll drop it, but not until it's ready to be dropped."

"Okay. I'm not going to dick you about. You know which of the guys we met today was lying, right?"

Teddy turned to Dejan. "Do you?"

Dejan was holding the wheel loosely. "You were trying to look in their eyes, I could see it. Everyone thinks you can tell who's lying from their eyes. Especially the cops. Whenever they were interviewing me, I would always find a spot on the wall and stare at it—they thought I was telling the truth then. Idiots."

Teddy wondered whether Dejan could see that he had blushed in the dim light.

Dejan said: "Judges think they can tell who's lying, too. 'His story does not bear the stamp of credibility,' they say, those clowns. They've got no clue. But you know what the research says, right?"

"The research? What do you know about that?"

"More than you think, anyway. All the research that's been done into who can detect a lie points to the same group of people."

"Who?"

"The group you used to belong to. That I still belong to. We see. Because we know."

The edges of Dejan's mouth had curled upward. He looked unashamedly pleased with himself.

"So who was lying?"

Dejan continued to smile; he drew out his answer. "The first loser, he was lying. Fredrik O. Johansson. He wasn't telling the truth."

"How do you know?"

"I can't say exactly what it was that screamed liar, but it was like his hands and his voice weren't on the same page. He started speaking more gently when you pressed him, did you notice that? And he moved his hands less. With a lot of people, their voice goes up when they lie. And almost everyone moves their hands less. But, like I said, you can never know with that stuff. I'm just going with my gut. It takes one to know one, and I am who I am."

Teddy raised his hand to the touch screen and pressed "Controls." Then he pointed to the *Ludicrous* button.

"Dejan, drive back to Djursholm as fast as you can," he said. "I want another chat with Fredrik O. Johansson. Old style."

The car leaped forward.

Dejan was practically screaming. "Teddy, I love it when you talk like that. You're back."

TELEPHONE CONVERSATION 50

To: Louise Pederson (wife)
From: Hugo Pederson
Date: 22 February 2006
Time: 22:43

HUGO: Mousey, I'm going to be late, have to work tonight I'm afraid.

LOUISE: But you said this morning that you were pretty much done with that project?

HUGO: I know, but some new stuff came up. Sorry.

LOUISE: How are you doing, really?

HUGO: What do you mean?

LOUISE: I was thinking about it yesterday. You've aged so quickly. Hugo, have you even noticed the hair on your temples, it's like salt and pepper? You look ten years older than you actually are, did you know that? I don't think it's good for you to work the way you do.

HUGO: You don't complain when it means we can renovate.

LOUISE: Maybe not. But I think you should think about it. And come home now. I don't have anything against doing some kinky stuff with you tonight, then you can go back to the office afterward if you need to.

HUGO: Baby, I don't have time.

LOUISE: You always say that. Do you know when we last had sex?

HUGO: Stop now.

LOUISE: Do you, though?

HUGO: Some time in autumn?

LOUISE: No, it was in August. Six months ago. I'm thirty-one and my husband doesn't want to sleep with me, how do you think that feels?

HUGO: Enough now, Louise, you know how busy I've been at work, and you know things've been going well precisely because I work hard. So if you're going to moan about us not fucking enough, it's because you don't want to.

LOUISE: When you come home wasted at four in the morning wanting anal, yeah. I tend to be asleep then, in case you were too drunk to realize.

HUGO: Are you really going to bring that up again now? It was a mistake, like I told you, I was drunk.

LOUISE: Mmm.

HUGO: Anyway, listen, I found out a few hours ago that the photograph has arrived. They can send it by courier from their depot tomorrow, or you can go and pick it up yourself. They'll help you get it into the car.

LOUISE: Will it fit? It's pretty big.

HUGO: Yes, if you fold down the backseat. I love our new car.

LOUISE: It cost twice as much as the picture, and you tell me that I'm the one spending unnecessarily.

HUGO: Jesus, it's a Porsche Cayenne, it's a fantastic car.

LOUISE: Okay, okay, but listen, can't you come home for a while anyway?

HUGO: Mousey, definitely tomorrow, but not tonight. I really don't have time. But listen, I've been thinking of something. Do you think we should buy a summer house somewhere?

LOUISE: What about Strömsund? We've talked about building one there.

HUGO: I'm so sick of my dad. I can't cope with him anymore.

LOUISE: Has something happened?

HUGO: Not exactly. Listen, I have to get back to work. Kisses.

LOUISE: Kisses. Bye.

TELEPHONE CONVERSATION 51
To: Hugo Pederson
From: Göran Blixt (boss)
Date: 26 February 2006
Time: 12:30

GÖRAN: It's me. Are you in the office?

HUGO: No, I'm at lunch.

GÖRAN: Aha, who with?

HUGO: Uhh, my wife.

GÖRAN: Nice, lunch is a good time of day to show the missus a bit of appreciation. Where are you?

HUGO: You're not planning on swinging by to disturb us? Ha ha.

GÖRAN: Ha ha, no, like I said. You have to show the wife respect. But I do want a chat with you once you're back. I've found out that Svenska Dagbladet's been sniffing around our Danfoss bid. I don't know what they think they're going to find, but I don't like it. Once they get their teeth into something, they twist and turn it so that people think it looks suspicious. And when the press wakes up, that means the Financial Supervisory Authority wakes up, never mind the other authorities. We can't have that, can we?

HUGO: No, of course not. I agree.

GÖRAN: Good, now I know we're on the same page. And I haven't been unclear?

HUGO: No, I understand, if anyone gets in touch with any questions, we need good answers.

GÖRAN: Exactly, and we need to go through all this with Danielsson Lind, but that's not all. I'm assuming you haven't done anything on your own.

HUGO: No, no, we aren't allowed.

GÖRAN: Exactly, you're aware of our insider trading rules.

HUGO: Yeah, of course.

GÖRAN: Good, because just between us, it should be very clear that if the hacks find anything that doesn't look right, anything to do with you, you'll get the boot immediately. No discussions, no damn disagreements over severance, about how I should have known or about there being problems with my leadership. Right?

HUGO: No, no, why is this even an issue?

GÖRAN: I'm not saying it is an issue. I'm just saying that *if* that happens, I want you to have signed the relevant contracts. Do you understand?

HUGO: I understand.

SMS MESSAGES
To/from: Unknown
From/to: Hugo Pederson

26 FEB

In: Hi, Hugo, thanks for lunch today. Would like to work with you and Pierre. We'll be in touch.

Out: Thanks to you, very interesting chat earlier. Let's speak when we have something in the works. /Hugo

1 MARCH

In: We have something in the works.

Out: Interesting. Want to meet for lunch? Same place as before?

In: Happy to meet but not a good idea to be seen together. Have booked a room with my lawyer, the one I mentioned. Today, 12:00?

Out: Good, perfect. See you there.

2 MARCH

Out: Thanks for yesterday. I have more information for you. Will send by encrypted mail. Regards to your lawyer. Nice guy!

In: We'll get to work tomorrow before lunch. Important that not everyone goes at once. You can't start before 15:00 tomorrow.

TELEPHONE CONVERSATION 52

To: Pierre Danielsson (co-suspect)
From: Hugo Pederson
Date: 2 March 2006
Time: 15:34

HUGO: Hey, hey.

PIERRE: Hey, how's it going?

HUGO: Incredibly well. I met our friend at his lawyer's office yesterday.

PIERRE: Interesting.

HUGO: Very, I think he's a nice guy. Big art collector, too. Told me he collects Zorn, for example. You know Anders Zorn?

PIERRE: Of course I do. Those paintings don't come cheap.

HUGO: Apparently he hangs the best ones in his fernery, as he calls it, where only certain guests get to go.

PIERRE: Okay, get to the point.

HUGO: I just wanted to say that the ball is rolling, I'll be able to send you more information, but we can't do business before 3 p.m. tomorrow.

PIERRE: Understood. Listen, though, there's something else. I'm guessing you're finding the logistics as tricky as I am.

HUGO: Yeah, it's pretty tough. Taking bags to and from Switzerland or the Isle of Man, just to bring the money back home.

PIERRE: I think I've found a solution.

HUGO: What?

PIERRE: A guy called Mats Emanuelsson. Apparently he helps out with exactly the kind of thing you and I need.

HUGO: Sounds great.

PIERRE: But I don't know much about him. Maybe it's not safe getting help from an outsider?

HUGO: Let's think about it.

TELEPHONE CONVERSATION 53

To: Carl Trolle (friend)
From: Hugo Pederson
Date: 14 March 2006
Time: 01:34

HUGO: 'Sup, man. Were you sleeping?

CARL: Ehh, couldn't sleep. Just been twisting and turning like a hot dog.

HUGO: Fredrika's not home?

CARL: Nah, she's out with the girls, Pauline and the others.

HUGO: Late.

CARL: She's always out late.

HUGO: So what time does she get up in the mornings?

CARL: I leave before she even wakes up.

HUGO: Calle . . .

CARL: Yeah?

HUGO: I'm not doing so well.

CARL: What d'you mean?

HUGO: I'm sleeping like shit.

CARL: Welcome to the club.

HUGO: But it's not just that. I've been having attacks of some kind. Like, my breathing gets faster, I feel like I can't cope, start sweating, just want to scream, have such crappy thoughts, like everything's worthless. Like I'm worthless.

CARL: Um, hello, things are going insanely well for you right now. New car, looking at places in the country, everything.

HUGO: I know, I know, but this is something else. I don't know what it is. I've been trying to go to bed later and later, so I'll be really tired, but I still can't sleep. Then there are all these images in my head, like I'm locked in with a pack of dogs and can't get out. And then I just want to scream. Louise is lying next to me the whole time, completely oblivious.

CARL: You never did like dogs.

HUGO: Maybe that's it.

CARL: Can't you talk to Louise about this?

HUGO: No, what do you think?

CARL: You working out enough? Maybe you should start some kind of fighting sport, heard that Foffe loves Thai boxing.

HUGO: Yeah, maybe. I don't know.

CARL: Listen, I can hear the key in the lock. Fredrika's home. Can we talk tomorrow?

HUGO: Okay, speak later.

30

The exclusive private pool suite at Sturebadet Spa: booked. The Turkish Baths, they called it. Bello snorted. "Why would they want to call anything Turkish? Don't they know what animals they are? What they did to our people, us Armenians?"

"I know," said Nikola. "But the place is perfect. And everything's prepared."

He and Bello were waiting in the lounge, both wearing the spa's thick white dressing gowns and complimentary slippers. They had booked the place through Bello's cousin's friend's former employee—a semi-alcoholic guy who now lived in a trailer by Slagsta Marina. The guy had paid for the entire booking in cash—Nikola didn't want a money trail that could be followed back to him. He had canceled the spa's own therapists and paid extra to bring in his own people: a couple of Thai women who didn't speak a word of Swedish but who worked at a massage studio on Nygatan. Maybe that would satisfy Yusuf: a happy ending. The guy probably enjoyed a hand job more than the real thing.

Because *he* was involved in what had happened. He had betrayed his own brother. Let him down. *Yusuf*—who had given Chamon work for several years. *Yusuf*—who was supposed to be helping Nikola find the bastards, when in actual fact he was one of them.

The women in reception had stared at Nikola and Bello as they checked in: sunglasses and caps pulled low on their heads. They

weren't used to people from the 'burbs in this part of town. Naive,
gullible, weak Stockholm: how could they think they could treat
someone the way they had treated him without there being consequences? A father who was allowed to leave his wife and child—
a society that valued that particular freedom over the family. A
school that crammed twenty-five overenergetic boys and seven
shy, quiet girls into the same class, with a teacher who had broken down after the first term and never returned. A city that let its
social worker hags, school welfare officers, asshole principals, and
local-pussy-police harass him and the boys throughout their child-
hoods. That had condemned them before they even stole their first
bags of candy from the supermarket. That had sent out a clear
message when they were ten years old and their parents were laid
off from Scania, given long-term sick leave, forced into early retirement or taxed to oblivion the minute they tried to run their own
business: you don't belong in this society. You won't be given a job
anywhere, but you can't run your own business, either. Plenty was
written afterward, when the same people's kids started shooting
one another in gang disputes and downward spirals of revenge. But
once you had decided to get out, wind down, go legit, the police
authorities didn't even arrest those who had killed. Everyone let
them down. No one stepped up. This country closed all roads but
one: the one Nikola was now on.

But he was being careful all the same. The guy had checked
that there weren't any surveillance cameras in reception itself, and
Nikola had sent a fourteen-year-old kid through the rest of Sture-
gallerian two hours earlier, to spray over the four cameras there.
Nikola didn't want to be caught on film—he was smarter than those
bastards.

Yusuf had sounded surprised when Nikola called him. Guarded,
almost: he had replied primarily with monosyllabic sounds from
the very back of his throat. As though he didn't care. But Nikola
could hear it: the cunt was happy. The cunt thought he had got-

ten away with helping those whores. The cunt thought that the cunt could fuck Nikola in the ass, like a real, genuine, 1,000 percent cunt.

"I've tried calling you a hundred times. I even went over to your place, tried to get ahold of your mom, everything," said Yusuf. "Where you been?"

"Uhh, I've been lying low, was knocked out with some shitty flu," Nikola lied. He knew that Yusuf had been looking for him, but he had deliberately kept his head down. He didn't know how he would react if he was forced to see Yusuf unexpectedly. "But I'm back on my feet and we need to chat now that Mr. One's inside. I was thinking we could meet someplace nice."

"Ahh, sweet," said Yusuf. "I need to talk to you, too."

"Good, 'cause I was thinking we should go someplace where no one's listening and all that."

"Sure. Sweet."

"You ever tried Sturebadet? The Östermalmers' fave spa."

"Uhh. Nah."

"They have their own suite, insanely luxe, never been there myself but Bello's bro had a bachelor party there."

The place really was perfecto: there was no way Yusuf could suspect a thing—not in the middle of town, not at the swankiest of addresses.

"Sweet," Yusuf said again.

If the cunt said the word "sweet" once more, Nikola wouldn't just do what he had planned. He would cut off his dick, too, and shove it in his ear.

"Meet you there, then? I'll tell Bello. And I'll send you the exact time on Wickr."

"Sure. Sweet."

It was agreed: they were going to meet. And the cunt's dick had to come off.

———

Bello looked shaky. It wasn't just that his leg was trembling like Grandpa's hand when he poured tea—there was something about his lips, too, like they were moving the entire time, even though he wasn't saying anything.

The sofas were long and comfortable, the room meant for larger parties than theirs. Like Nikola said: bachelor and bachelorette parties, corporate events, group activities for Svenssons who thought they needed peace and quiet. The music was soft and low, some kind of Indian melody, pan pipes and synth drums.

"Bro," said Nikola. "What happens happens. Just take it easy."

"Can we go over everything again?" Bello looked strange in the dressing gown, which was two sizes too big. He actually reminded Nikola of Linda in it.

Nikola took a sip of his cola. He had instructed the Thai women for later: they would serve cocktails and stuff, but Nikola's and Bello's would be alcohol-free.

"Okay, it's like this. The women come in first and do some massages and cleansing rituals for an hour and a half. After that, we've got the place to ourselves for two hours. Yusuf'll be more wasted than us, but we'll have to drink beers in the sauna so he doesn't get suspicious. And the good thing is he'll be as naked as we are, so we'll know he doesn't have anything on him."

"Then?"

"Then, when the timing's right, we do what we said."

His friend's leg was shaking worse than a massage belt on turbo. "Okay, bro," said Bello. "And Isak's completely cool with this?"

"Yeah, for God's sake. It's his order."

"Shit, man, Yusuf was practically like a father to me a few years back."

"To Chamon, too, but look how that turned out. You call me Bible Man, don't you?"

"What d'you mean?"

"Do you read the Bible?"

"Nah, not really. Even though the old lady wants me to."

"Doesn't matter. An eye for an eye, a tooth for a tooth. You know that, surely?"

Bello understood what he meant.

Yusuf was late. Nikola's stomach was full of butterflies. He wished he could be as calm as Chamon always was—oozing Prozac, chilling like a man. But with a stressed-out Bello on the sofa and a couple of Thai masseuses arriving at any minute, plus the spa's own staff, who had already been up twice to check whether everything was "to their contentment"—what kind of word was "contentment," anyway—Nikola wasn't even half as chill as he would like to be. He got up, did a loop of the room to check the place out.

The changing room was on the other side of the lounge, and he counted twenty lockers, all made of some expensive-looking wood. On the shelves beneath the mirrors, there were various complimentary products: hair gel, cotton swabs, skin lotion. The actual pool was in the next room. Nikola wondered how old the place really was. Tall columns with flourishes at the top, all clad in marble; more flourishes on the panels along the walls; a forty-foot pool with a complex mosaic pattern in the middle—honestly, they *could* be somewhere in Turkey three hundred years ago. Kind of. There were showers on the other side of the pool room, an anteroom with tiled walls and two saunas. The showers were the only thing to depart from the antique feeling: their long pipes shone like they had only been installed today.

Nikola heard a voice he recognized from the lounge. It was Yusuf—the cunt had arrived.

"Bro," he said to him as they hugged. "We've got the entire pool to ourselves."

Yusuf smiled. "Crazy nice. When're the chicks arriving?"

Nikola and Bello sat on the benches in the changing room while they waited for Yusuf to change: watching him like he was an inmate at Guantánamo. Checking to make sure nothing caught the light, listening to make sure nothing jingled.

"Sweet dressing gowns they've got here." Yusuf smiled once he was done.

They sat down in the lounge. Bello handed them drinks from a little bar, prepped just like Nikola had ordered. They talked about Isak's arrest, how they thought the boss's trial would pan out. They talked through all the different things they were doing for the boss: the tanning salon in Ronna, the restaurant on Badhusgatan, the explosives Mr. One always wanted topped up, people who needed to pay and guys who needed paying. The pigs' Operation Secure and Operation Phoenix. They discussed Chamon's murder. Who could *really* be behind it?

After twenty minutes, there was a knock at the door, and the masseuses came in.

"*Dachri,* I thought you would've found some Romanians or Bulgarians," said Yusuf.

"Nah, doesn't work in a place like this. You know that."

The music in the background was like waves crashing onto a beach.

The hamam ritual was nice. The girls must have taken some kind of class, or maybe it was just in their genes. First, the boys showered: Bello wanted to keep his swimming trunks on, for some weird reason. Yusuf roared with laughter at that. "Bro, is it 'cause your *dachri*'s nothing to boast about?" The room steamed up. Nikola turned the heat a little higher. He touched the glistening pipes. One of them was hot: he pulled back his hand. On the other, tiny droplets of water were condensing: it was cold.

They lay down on the massage beds. After thirty minutes' massage, it seemed like Yusuf had fallen asleep. If it hadn't been for the masseuses, Nikola would have gone for him there and then. They drank their cocktails. Yusuf was going on about his plans to go over to fraud full-time, rather than blackmail. So much more cash, but only half the risk. Next, they were told to stand by the edge of the pool with small towels wrapped around their hips. The marble floor was remarkably warm. The masseuses pulled on exfoliating gloves and started scrubbing their bodies. After a few minutes, they rinsed off the cream. Then it was time for some kind of clay. Feet, legs, stomach, and back. The clay hardened quickly, arms, hands, neck: it changed color and became more grayish. It gave Nikola a bad feeling, like it would be impossible for him to break free from it, like someone was trapping him in wet cement.

"That's fine, it's enough for me," he said, starting to rinse himself off. As the clay ran away in the shower, it looked black again.

The Thai masseuses left. Yusuf started moaning again, going on about how he had expected something other than forty-year-old Thai women with chubby hands. But he was in a good mood all the same, wanted to go into the sauna, talk plans, drink beer.

"What d'you guys do with all your cash?" he wanted to know.

Nikola gave an evasive answer. "I'm a simple man, I don't earn much." It was also true.

Yusuf said: "I've got a guy who drives down to Denmark in a rental every other weekend, there and back in one day, no problems. I stash all mine there."

"How d'you know you can trust your guy, though?"

"They have to be scared of you. That way they won't screw you over."

Nikola was now just waiting for them to climb into the pool. That was when it would happen. But Yusuf wanted to warm up first.

The sauna was big. The thermometer on the wall showed eighty degrees. Bello's leg had started shaking again—balls, he needed to hide it. Yusuf was sweating like a pig wrapped in plastic wrap. He was still wearing the gold cross and chain he had gotten from Chamon—what a traitor. The towel was still wrapped around his hips. A beer in his hand. The sweat had started to glisten on his chest. Pool soon. Nikola closed his eyes.

He thought back to the first time he and Teddy had gone to the adventure pool in Södertälje. His school class had taken swimming lessons every Tuesday, but since Nikola realized that almost everyone but him could already swim, it was embarrassing. Time after time, he made his excuses: he wasn't feeling well, he had eczema, he'd forgotten his swimming trunks. In the end, he hadn't gone to more than two lessons in the pool; he still couldn't swim. But he hadn't told Teddy any of this when they climbed into the pool that day. He stuck to the edges, tried to move his legs the way he had seen his friends do in swimming lessons. But the whole time, beneath the surface, he had been clinging to the edge of the pool. Teddy swam alongside him, playfully splashing him with water. Asking if they should jump in from the edge. Nikola had tried to reply, tried to laugh, but he had been terrified of getting water in his mouth. He was scared of the surface, which felt like it was closing in on top of him. There was no power in his legs. His body had sunk, he had tried to grab the edge more tightly, to pull himself forward—but he couldn't. The water dragged him down. The depths cried out for his body. He was going to drown. But then Teddy had grabbed him: "Come on, hang on to my back for a while." His uncle had swum over to a shallower section. Then he stood up and held Nikola beneath his stomach. "Your strokes look good, show me again." Nikola had kicked his legs. After twenty minutes, they left the pool. They had gone back there every weekend for the next six weeks. The same routine every time: Teddy holding him beneath his stomach and asking him to do his nice strokes. Little by little, his uncle had let go, until he was no longer holding Nikola, until Nikola could move three feet through the water, push off from the edge and make it six feet on his own. Until he really was swimming. And not once had Teddy said anything. Not a word about Nikola not being able to swim. Not a word about Teddy needing to teach him how to kick. Nothing. He had just acted.

A creaking sound. Was that the door to the sauna opening?

Maybe the Sturebadet staff were back again, despite Nikola having told them they wanted to be left alone. Maybe it was Bello or Yusuf needing to go and cool down. But the steps sounded harder than someone walking barefoot. Nikola dragged himself back to reality.

A guy in sweatpants and a T-shirt: clothes that had no place in a sauna. Clothes that definitely didn't belong to the staff from Sturebadet. He recognized the man: Fadi—one of Yusuf's guys.

Fuck.

It was a setup. Yusuf must have seen through their plan from the very beginning.

Fadi stepped inside. Even Bello understood now: his eyes were wide, like he had seen a ghost. Fadi: a big guy, everyone knew he was Yusuf's muscle. He was holding two switchblades, and he handed one to Yusuf.

FUCK.

Fadi was in front of Nikola now.

F-U-C-K.

This wasn't what was supposed to happen.

Nikola had time to get up. Fadi's hand moved quickly, but the motion was too obvious. Nikola clocked the direction, parried the stab. Full contact—the pain shot up his arm like lightning. But he hadn't been stabbed; they had just bumped arms. And Nikola could be quick, too. He brought his knee up to Fadi's dick. The guy bent double. Screamed.

From the corner of one eye, Nikola could see Bello trying to fend off Yusuf. Both men were naked.

Nikola shouted, kicked at that Fadi bastard again. This time, he was too slow. He didn't see the stab, just felt it in his thigh. It burned, as though Fadi had shoved a firecracker into his flesh and set it off. His leg gave way. He dropped to the floor. This was some *Eastern Promises* shit, for real. He saw his own blood. Heard his own cry, it almost sounded distant, as though it belonged to someone else. He opened the door to the sauna, crawled out into the pool room and toward the exit. Fadi came after him. He heard Bello shouting inside the sauna.

Fadi kicked him in the stomach, a full-on soccer player's kick. Nikola couldn't breathe. He twisted, gasping for air. Rolled around. The edge of the pool was five feet away. The marble shone.

Fadi took aim again, but Nikola grabbed his leg—the guy fell. Nikola launched himself at him. Tried to land blows like an MMA fighter, but the pain in his thigh put the brakes on him. Behind them, the door opened—Yusuf came out with the shitty knife in his hand. What had he done to Bello back in the sauna?

Nikola tried to get up, his leg shaking. Yusuf swung at him. Nikola twisted his body, moving his side around the stabbing motion. Yusuf tried again. Missed.

Suddenly he felt Fadi's arms around his waist—shit, he couldn't let himself be held down—that would be it.

Yusuf pulled back his arm to stab again, but he was too obvious about where he was going. Nikola risked everything, tore himself away. The knife hit flesh—but not his.

Yusuf looked shocked, his eyes wide. Fadi looked even more confused: enormous eyes—the knife was in *his* stomach, not Nikola's. Yusuf had stabbed his own boy.

Fadi gurgled, blood running from his mouth. The knife was still in his stomach.

Yusuf shouted: *"Dachri."* His head turned from his hitman, who was sinking to the floor, to Nikola, whose guard was raised. The pain in Nikola's leg was tearing at him, and all he wanted was to drop down, lie still. Rest. But he forced himself to stay in position.

Facing Yusuf.

One second.

Yusuf had accidentally cut down his own bro.

Five seconds.

Maybe Nikola was alone now. Maybe Bello was lying dead in the sauna. He felt like his leg was about to give way beneath him.

Ten seconds. Two pairs of eyes locked on to one another. Two terrified naked men who had both thought things would end differently.

Nikola moved first. Swung at Yusuf. Tried to be like a cobra, full force. He hit air. Yusuf threw himself to the floor instead: toward the knife sticking out of Fadi. Nikola was stupid for not thinking of it. Yusuf yelled, grabbed ahold of the knife. Both men fell. Rolled around on the marble floor by the pool. Trails of blood following them like they were carcasses in a slaughterhouse. They wrestled, fighting for the damn knife. Nikola wouldn't be able to keep going much longer. His wound was tearing at him. He didn't know how much blood he had lost. If he didn't come out on top now, he was dead.

Yusuf launched himself at Nikola with the knife in his hand. Nikola ended up on his back; he grabbed Yusuf's arm, tried to force it back. His strength was running out. Yusuf's teeth were bared, not far from Nikola's face. The tip of the knife moved closer: it was like a blurry gray dot just an inch away from his eye.

He wasn't going to make it. It would dig its way into his brain through his eye. He pushed back. Tried. Sweated. Heard his own strained breathing. Saw images pass by: Mom, Teddy.

Then the pressure disappeared.

Yusuf rolled away. Blood was bubbling from his mouth. Bello was standing behind him with Fadi's knife in his hand. He had driven it into the back of Yusuf's neck.

Yusuf's mouth was moving. It looked like he was trying to speak. There was something calm about him, something that had stopped fighting.

"Nicko," he gurgled, without finishing. His eyes rolled back.

The man on the marble floor in front of them was no longer living.

Nikola bent down and took Chamon's gold chain and cross from him. "You shouldn't have those," he said quietly to himself. He staggered to his feet. "Bello," he said. "Thanks."

———

Fifteen minutes later: Bello had called a cousin and asked him to drive over like crazy in his car. The guy should arrive in another fifteen. Nikola was still reeling from how lucky they were that Yusuf had given Bello only a bit of a kicking in the sauna, rather than stabbing him.

They had found an emergency exit in the lounge and managed to pry the door open. It could work: the exit led to a stairwell that Bello had followed all the way down to a door onto Grev Turegatan. But the bodies—what were they going to do with those? And what about Nikola's wound?

Bello wound towels tightly around Nikola's thigh until the bleeding stopped.

In each of the lockers, there was a large frotté towel and a dressing gown like the ones they had been wearing. They wrapped them around the bodies like funeral shrouds and then they dragged them behind the sofas in the lounge. Jesus, they were heavy. Nikola whimpered.

Bello rinsed off the sauna with a hose that he managed to find, and then did the same in the pool room. Carefully: walls, floor. Walls, floor again. Nikola lay down on the floor in the changing room with his leg raised on a bench. He glanced into the pool room. The majority of the blood had run away down the drain, but not all of it. Shit: the water in the pool had turned pale pink from the blood which had run into it. SH-IT.

They couldn't leave any trace of what had happened.

So crazy. It was all so fucked-up. All they had been planning was to waterboard Yusuf and make him talk, but now they were stuck with two dead bodies.

Bello's phone rang. His cousin was waiting for them down on the street.

"Park your car as close to the metal doors on Grev Turegatan as you can, opposite Grodan. Leave the keys on the seat," Bello instructed him. "It's best if you aren't in the car yourself. You don't want to get caught up in this."

It was time.

Bello tried to drag the first body into the stairwell, but it was too heavy for him on his own. Nikola got up, swayed. Tested his leg to see if it would hold.

"Bello, I dunno if I can do this."

"You can't drop now. Just think of your uncle or something. You grab that end, I'll grab the top."

Nikola took as deep a breath as he could, stopped the pain from taking over.

They carried the first body down to the street. The car was parked five feet from the door. Bello's cousin was nowhere to be seen. They folded down the backseats and shoved the body inside.

Nikola could feel the shitty lightning approaching. He had to lean against the handrail in the stairwell. Bello said: "What do we do about the pool? You can tell it's got blood in it."

Nikola staggered back into the lounge. He blinked. Spotted the bottles of spirits on the bar. Saw a couple of bottles of wine.

"I've got an idea," he panted.

He staggered over to the bar. Grabbed two bottles of red wine. Shuffled back into the pool room and smashed both bottles on the floor. The red wine gave the pool water even more color.

Bello was behind him.

"You're smart, bro."

31

Josephine had forced her to meet for a drink in town. Emelie didn't feel like going, but Jossan was stubborn and had also agreed to pick her up.

"Hello, Pippa," Jossan said, practically stumbling in through Emelie's front door. For some reason, she practically always tripped through doorways—a bit like Kramer in *Seinfeld*—something which Emelie couldn't usually stop herself from laughing at. But not now. Not tonight.

They hugged. "I wanted to give you a bit of a cuddle after all the strange stuff you've been through lately. I do technically have an STA to be working on, but it'll have to get finished tomorrow."

"Can't we just stay in? It's ten o'clock—there's no way you can be your sharpest self right now, either."

"Nope, we're going out. And don't say that. You know what working at Leijon is like. You were in my shoes less than two years ago."

"But my heels were never as high as yours."

"Ha ha, you're a funny one, Emelie."

They sat down at a table in Ling Long, and Emelie went over to the bar to order. Her fingers played with the personal alarm in her bag—this had to stop soon. Over the past few days, she had felt the panic creeping up on her increasingly often: the minute she heard a loud noise or saw someone move quickly. Those shots in Oslo had punched holes in her safety zone.

She thought about Katja's mother. Though she hadn't found out exactly what Gunnel had done, Emelie was sure: she didn't deserve to be called a mother. Emelie wondered how the line preventing a parent from betraying their own child could be so flimsy, whether the human instinct to protect your own offspring was really so weak. It couldn't be—it was also about choice. Gunnel could have made different decisions. There were always alternatives. Emelie still didn't feel ready to be a mother herself—she couldn't see herself in the role. Even less see the child's father as a dad. She had looked up the regulations: she could do what she wanted until the eighteenth week, but from the thirteenth week of pregnancy, abortions became more complicated—requiring a so-called two-step abortion. She knew what she wanted to do: the world was too cruel, motherhood too uncertain a task. She also knew she couldn't keep ignoring Teddy. She should call him and let him know.

Then she thought about how Marcus was trying to keep her legal practice afloat while she was a mentally absent boss. A few more weeks and she would have to be on top of everything again, otherwise the entire firm risked collapse. At the same time, she didn't know how she would manage it. She was spending most of her time with the Katja material: writing her own summaries, making lists. Marking, underlining, making notes. Questions that hadn't been asked, analyses that hadn't been completed, samples that hadn't been taken, boxes that hadn't been studied, and so on. She didn't feel quite as unwell as she had earlier during her pregnancy, but she still wasn't sleeping properly. She drank all kinds of coffee, ate apples, and wolfed down mixed candy like it was amphetamine. She desperately wanted some real pills—but resisted. She didn't even scroll through the illegal pharmacy sites online.

The police had received the forensic reports from the murder scene. The National Forensic Center's DNA analysis adhered to the usual scale: *Degree of likelihood:* + 4. According to the attached explanation, that meant that it was *more than a million times more likely that the DNA comes from the person in question than from anyone else (1,000,000 ≤ V).* Adam's and Katja's blood had been found on the floor close to where her body was discovered—and Adam had a knife wound on his right hand. It was unshakable.

But still.

She bought a nonalcoholic drink for herself and a G&T for Jossan.

"Are you coming to the firm's fortieth anniversary party, by the way?" Josephine asked as Emelie sat down.

"I haven't decided yet," Emelie lied. "I got the invite."

"I'm organizing it, so it'd be cool if you came. Leijon always wants to show off its elite, you know?"

"*Natürlich,* so why do they kick out the best?"

Jossan winked at her. "You know why you couldn't stay. And no matter how much I think you did the right thing by taking on that case, you also made a mistake, from the firm's point of view."

Emelie couldn't argue with that.

Jossan started chatting away about something else.

"I've started taking holistic magnesium," she said. "It's good for the muscles, nerves, protein synthesis, the immune system, and your sex life. It makes you have more friends, too. It's clinically proven."

Emelie cackled. "I'll take three pills now."

They talked careers, old colleagues. Apparently Magnus Hassel wasn't happy with the year's dividends to the partners at Leijon. Anders Henriksson had met a twenty-two-year-old girl at his gym whose body was more than 40 percent silicone. Eva Rudolfson's son wrote crappy headlines for the tabloids and petitions on social media. It felt good to hear ordinary legal gossip for a change, to avoid thinking about Katja or the shooting in Oslo.

Jossan might have noticed that Emelie asked the bartender for the "same again" when they ordered for a second time—though just by looking at her drink, you couldn't tell that it was non-alcoholic. Maybe she should just talk to Josephine, tell her everything. Katja's murder, the attack on Mats, the network, and, above all, the child growing in her belly. Who the father was. Or maybe she should see a psychologist, because she was going to need to release the pressure sometime soon—she could feel it. There was only one problem: she didn't know how to talk. It had never been her thing—while all of her girlfriends wanted nothing more than to talk things over, to psychologize, play hobby therapist with one another, Emelie usually chose different topics. It wasn't that she didn't reflect on herself, it was just that she could never find the right words.

Or maybe she should drop it all. Drop the murder. Drop the fact that at least ten men had abused Katja and others without ever being arrested or brought to justice. Drop any possible leads from Mats Emanuelsson. Everything would go back to normal. No concerns. No anxiety. No fear.

Jossan elbowed her. "Listen, Emelie, I just want you to know that whatever it is that's bothering you, I'm here. If you want to talk about it."

Emelie slowly swirled her straw in her drink. Josephine was her best friend.

"Oh, look," her friend suddenly said, in a completely different tone. She pointed toward the entrance. "Your old bosses."

Emelie turned around. Magnus Hassel and a couple of other partners from Leijon had just stepped inside. She turned her face to the wall and hoped they wouldn't see her.

"They're going into the restaurant," said Jossan.

"Good, I really don't have the energy to talk to them."

Josephine went off to the restroom.

A few days earlier, Oliver had called the office and asked to speak to Emelie. When she phoned him back, he had begged her to meet him again. She eventually agreed, initially because she thought she wanted to stop his nagging—but in truth, it was mostly because she was curious. She wanted to know more about Katja and Adam. In line with Swedish regulations, he was still being held in custody—there was no upper limit to how long someone could be denied their freedom before trial.

"Nice to have you *visiting* us," Anneli had joked when she went into the office. She had nodded in the direction of the visitor's chairs. "There's someone waiting for you." Oliver was more than an hour and a half early. Emelie had been planning to go through some mail before he arrived, but she realized she may as well speak to him right away; she wouldn't be able to relax with him waiting outside. She had gone over to him and held out a hand. "Hi, Oliver, welcome."

He got up. Avoided looking her in the eye. Avoided shaking her hand.

They went into her room. Oliver seemed slimmer than when they had last met, maybe that was why he didn't shake her hand—he simply didn't have the muscles, the strength. "Dad's lawyer is no good," he said.

Emelie had tried to catch his eye. "In what sense?"

"I'm never allowed to talk to Dad. I've called the police and the prison a thousand times, but they just say I have to take it up with his lawyer. But the lawyer doesn't care about me."

"I understand," Emelie had said. She recognized that tactic, even if she did feel sorry for Adam's son. Family members and relatives often thought that the lawyer was *their* representative, too—something that could lead to even the best of lawyers being overwhelmed by calls.

"I'm sorry," she had said. "But it's not my place to get involved. Your dad will have to bring it up with his lawyer himself. She isn't *your* lawyer. And Adam isn't *my* client. I think you understand."

"Please, there must be something you can do?"

"Have you spoken to your father at all?"

"Once, a few weeks ago. There was a guard listening in on our conversation."

Emelie hadn't been able to hold back her curiosity. "What did he say?"

For the first time, Oliver had looked up. "He wants to get out."

She turned away. She couldn't ask any more questions like this to a thirteen-year-old boy; it was unethical. They had spoken for a few more minutes, Emelie still trying to convince Oliver that she was the wrong person to talk to. Eventually, she had said: "Okay, I can help you write a letter to your dad's lawyer. That's all."

They had jotted down a few lines on her computer. She printed out the letter and he signed it. "But I can't send it in one of my firm's envelopes," Emelie said. "You'll have to post it yourself."

Oliver's hand had been shaking as he took the letter from her.

Why wasn't Josephine coming back? Emelie feared the worst—that she had taken a detour through the restaurant to speak to her bosses. Then she saw something even more challenging: Magnus Hassel was coming toward *her*. She really didn't have the energy to talk to him right now, particularly not without Josephine. She turned away again, praying he would pass her by, but five seconds later she felt a hand on her back.

Magnus was wearing a coat that was buttoned up to his chin and he was carrying a leather briefcase. "Nice to bump into you," he said, sounding genuinely happy. "Are you here on your own?"

Somehow, it felt like he was standing too close. "No," she said. "I'm here with Josephine."

Magnus was standing unnaturally still, the way only drunk people do when they're trying to look sober. "You're brave, you know that, don't you?"

Emelie wondered what he meant. Did he know something about the shooting in Oslo? Or did he mean something else? That she was digging around, doing research, trying to work out what had happened to Katja—was he aware of that? Or did he mean that she was sitting here, drinking, even though she was pregnant—could he know about that?

"What do you mean?" she asked.

Magnus placed an arm around her shoulder. "I mean that you're brave, leaving us to do your own thing. Not many would take that leap."

Emelie breathed out. "But I didn't exactly choose to leave. You and Anders fired me, as you might remember."

"That wasn't quite what happened, Emelie. But it's all history now. I like you, always have." He squeezed her shoulder.

Emelie didn't want to hear any more.

"Can I buy you a drink?" he asked.

Emelie *really* didn't want to hear any more. She glanced over toward the restaurant and the restrooms, urging Josephine to reappear and save her.

"What about a martini?" Magnus insisted.

Emelie felt like a marble sculpture as she sat there. She couldn't say a word.

"Come on," said Magnus.

Emelie swirled the ice in her otherwise empty glass.

"Or maybe you want to follow me somewhere else?"

She glanced toward the exit and the restrooms.

"Jesus, why're you so tense?"

She should get up and leave, but it was like the hand on her shoulder weighed ten tons.

"Leave her be."

Emelie turned around. It was Anders Henriksson.

"She doesn't need to be dealing with clingy old men like you," Anders said, trying to make it sound like a joke. "What a state you're in."

Magnus was swaying almost imperceptibly. He seemed to be holding his bag tight. Emelie seized the opportunity. "Good night, then," she said, nodding first to Anders and then to Magnus. She walked toward the curtain-covered exit. She would have to explain to Jossan tomorrow.

In the light of the bar, she could make out the shapes of Magnus and Anders. Anders in a loose suit. Magnus in his coat, clutching his briefcase.

She pushed the curtain to one side. Her head was spinning.

Coat *and* briefcase. Magnus had brought his *briefcase* over to her.

Just like that, something clicked in Emelie's mind. A thought had appeared, and she was going to have to look into it. Katja's killer—the answer might be much simpler than they thought. Much more difficult, too.

32

Roksana had been in Tehran for four days now, but it felt more like four months. She had never experienced anything like it. It wasn't that Etty, Val, and Leila weren't treating her like a member of the family, because they really were. Etty had even insisted that she go over to her grandmother's place, in the building next door, at least twice a day, and complained that she was using the wrong air-conditioning setting as though Roksana were her own daughter. Nor was it that Velenjak wasn't an insanely nice area, full of huge parks, handsome houses, and relatively relaxed girls with chic, pushed-back shawls and pants as tight as workout leggings. It was something else—a sense of belonging, of having a base, of living an uncomplicated life with people who accepted her as she was—who didn't demand top grades or prestigious jobs or yell for ketamine the whole time. But within that feeling, there was also a hint of something else. Imagine if this was how life could have been—imagine if Mom and Dad had never had to run, never had to emigrate?

Still, Roksana had a job to do here: something she had to get done. Nothing lasted forever. She would be going back to Stockholm soon.

Val and his friend Jahan drove her around town. Along the wide highways, past the huge Khomeini Mausoleum and the grand mosques, through the melting pot of Tehran's lower districts, by the small children selling chewing gum and flowers, and alongside the crazy murals—there was one in particular that caught Roksana's eye: the Statue of Liberty depicted as a naked skeleton. Everything going on in the United States right now was crazy—but the strange portrait still gave her the creeps.

The air became cleaner as they rose toward Tehran's more northerly parts—"the good neighborhoods," as her father had described them, where the lush trees stooped over the streets, leaning in like they consciously wanted to provide shade for the yellow taxis, the Porsches, and the death-defying Vespa drivers.

On her first day, Dad's cousins and Roksana's second cousins had come to visit. The next day, her father's aunt had come over. They all wanted to know when Mom, Dad, and Caspar would be coming to Iran. They ate chunks of watermelon and enjoyed a long dinner around the dark dining table in the middle of the house. Her aunt Etty had talked about working in Paris in her youth—"at night, I took the Champs-Elysées by storm"—and laughed so loudly that there had to be a risk of the neighbors calling the morality police, thinking she was drunk. "Yes, you have to promise us, Roksana, take us out in Stockholm one night when we come to visit. Your father says you party even more than Val."

The houses were large, surrounded by walls and gates, but they had pools out back. In certain areas, the buildings rose up into the air, practically skyscrapers reaching the mountaintops—the view down must be astounding. There were cranes everywhere. Val smiled: "That's how we make our money. The prices have tripled in just seven years. Lots of places in town have grown by seventy, eighty percent; they're taking shape now, taking character, like a child growing up."

Roksana knew the background. Val and Leila's father, Omid, had previously worked for the town planning office, but had started to buy up land through his former colleagues during the nineties. The money, however, came from her aunt's side of the family. Omid had died two years ago, but Etty continued to look after the property empire he had built up. Roksana couldn't quite work out exactly what Val and Leila did.

"I help Mom," Val claimed, but Roksana hadn't seen him do anything but eat, play his electric guitar, cruise aimlessly in his absurdly large Range Rover, and sleep half the day away while she had been there. And ride—that was what Val loved doing most. Horse riding up in the mountains. It was the reason Roksana had come, after all—she had spotted his riding helmet and an idea had taken hold.

She had wondered how she should explain the details to him, but Val had sounded positive over Skype.

That evening, they were going to a party at Jahan's. There was no telling what the guy's crib usually looked like, because the apartment had been transformed for the party—a remake deluxe. He had hung huge drapes that created the feeling of rooms within rooms. In one area, there was an illuminated bar; in another, a DJ booth. Stroboscopes, disco balls, and spotlights hung from the ceiling. Roksana couldn't see a single woman wearing a head scarf, and she even saw two guys who were topless—they had more tattoos on their chests than Billie and Z had combined. A few girls and guys were running around in swimwear, spraying water pistols at the warm guests. In the bar room, there was a thick rug and a circle of people passing a bong between themselves. *Shahs of Sunset* was playing on a laptop. Behind a curtain, a girl in a tiny shirt was making out with a guy with a mustache.

The bartender poured mojitos, but Roksana didn't see him adding any alcohol. When she raised the glass to her lips, however, she could barely manage a sip—the cocktail was so strong. Val laughed. "They premixed everything, no bottles of booze visible."

An hour and a half later, Roksana sat down on the huge rug. Her clothes were soaked. This party: she was trying and failing to work out how she would describe it to Z when she got home. All she knew was that she was filled with an energy she had never felt before, either with or without the Special K in her body. She didn't recognize a single tune from the dance floor, hadn't drunk more than two cocktails, hadn't seen either Val or Leila in a while—but it didn't matter. The night felt like it was practically tailor-made for her.

"How's it going?"

Roksana turned around. It was Val. He sat down beside her, holding a modest shisha pipe in one hand.

"Great party," Roksana said.

Val fiddled with the water pipe. "Yeah, it's good. Jahan made an effort for once."

Roksana smiled. Val took a long drag on the pipe. She could smell it now: sweet, floral, but also something else. "Are you smoking weed?"

"Yeah, what else?"

Music was spilling out of the room with the dance floor.

"I don't know, I was just thinking that if the police came . . ."

"They won't, not to a private party like this. And if they do, we'll end up in a cell for a day or two, it's happened to plenty of people before. You won't miss your flight, don't worry."

Val passed the pipe to a guy sitting next to him. "People are under a lot of pressure here, so you've got to find a way to emigrate, even if it's only spiritually."

Emigrate, Roksana thought—she wondered whether Val also wanted to leave.

Two days later, she and Val were sitting beneath a pergola at the ranch. It was the hottest day since she had arrived. Everything had to go without a hitch now—this was what she had come for. Val had guaranteed that the amounts were large here, that there were several kilos in the cool room.

A guy with a mustache and a hat kept glancing over at them at regular intervals. "He'll be here soon," he said. "Busy day."

Val hadn't asked what Roksana wanted the medication for, but he had set up the meeting. They were waiting for one of Tehran's premiere horse breeders, a man who also happened to be Aunt Etty's former neighbor's brother's best friend. Mr. Isaawi.

The brick stable building was low, and Roksana could see magnificent horses being led in and out of it. Their hooves kicked up dust. There were openings in the wall in a few places, and she could see horses peering out of them, taking in the view.

"I rent a space here, along with over four hundred others," Val explained. "Those of us who are better off love riding, and that means you need your own animal."

A bright white horse peered out of the opening closest to them. It turned its head and stared at her. It was beautiful, strong. She thought about her grandmother.

Roksana had visited her that morning. Whenever she had been over to her grandmother's house before, her grandmother had either been in bed or sitting in front of the TV. The carer was usually cleaning or cooking, not that Roksana understood why she bothered with that kind of thing all the time; whenever Roksana had seen her grandmother at the dining table, she had never eaten more than a few bites, and her house was hardly dirty. But the carer hadn't been there that morning, and her grandmother had been sitting on a bench in the garden behind the house. She was elegantly dressed, her blouse embroidered with gold and the moccasins on her feet featuring an emblem that looked like it belonged to some royal house.

"Roksana *joonam*," she had said, sounding exactly like Dad. She patted the bench beside her. "Sit down."

Roksana had done as she was told. "How are you today, Grandmother?"

"I am as I deserve to be. Too old, but I still like living. I understand you will be going back to Sweden soon?"

"Yes, the day after tomorrow."

Whenever Etty had forced her to go over there before, her grandmother had barely said a word, just taken Roksana's hand and squeezed it. But she had been different today. She talked about when she, Grandfather, Etty, and Dad had moved into the house forty years earlier. "Your father wasn't like Val. He was always studying." Then she had pointed to the flower bed and the purple flowers closest to them. "Look at those. I planted those over twenty-five years ago, and they still come every year. Do you know what they are?"

"Crocuses?"

Her grandmother had laughed. "Yes, but what type of crocus?"

"Crocus *crocus*?"

That had made Grandmother laugh even more. "You're funny. You must have inherited your sense of humor from your mother. It's saffron, Roksana *joonam*. It has grown in our country since the beginning of time. Do you like saffron?"

"I love saffron."

"Good, then you haven't been completely Europeanized. How is your dear father?"

"He's well, I think. But he's bored."

"I know. And does he tell you that you have to get an education?"

Her grandmother's short hair was still dark in places. In some respects, she looked younger than her own son, but her eyes were very similar to his. Deep, watchful.

"Yes, and I'm going to."

"Good, good."

Her grandmother had turned to the crocuses again. The sun was shining between the cypress trees onto the grass.

"You can be whatever you want to be. He could, too."

"Yeah, but maybe not in Sweden."

"That isn't what I mean. Do you know what your father studied to become first?"

"An engineer."

"No, no, that was later. Your father wanted to play music, he studied musicology. He played throughout his childhood. Guitar, sitar, drums, piano, everything. And he got into the School of Performing Arts and Music, only seven out of the thousands of applicants managed that. He even got to play with the big stars a few times, Googoosh and Vigen. He was brilliant, your dear father, a prodigy."

Roksana hadn't known what to say. "But there was a small problem," her grandmother had continued. "He didn't tell his father, your grandfather, that he was studying music. Your grandfather thought he had already started his engineering degree."

Her grandmother had leaned back, as though she was studying the sky.

Roksana turned to her. "What happened?"

"What had to happen. Like always. We can't escape who we are. When your grandfather found out, it came to an end."

Roksana had tried to see her grandmother's eyes, but they were up among the clouds, lost in another time.

"Welcome to my ranch," said a tanned man in his fifties. He was wearing a cap and sunglasses.

Val and Roksana got up. Her head scarf itched in the heat. Val introduced her, and they shook hands with Mr. Isaawi.

"Would you like a tour?"

They started walking along the edge of the stables. Roksana wondered how much Val had told him about what she really wanted. "The Persian Arab and Caspian horses are one of the foundations of our civilization," Mr. Isaawi explained in a slow, clear voice that suggested that this might be the most important piece of information they would ever hear.

Roksana wasn't listening; she was just thinking about how she could bring up what she needed to bring up. She must be crazy—why hadn't she discussed the deal in detail with Val beforehand? She didn't even know if she, a woman, was allowed to speak to the man.

"The horses give us wings. Persia was the first place on earth where horses were tamed, Khayyam mentions more than forty-one different types of horse in *Nowruznameh*," Mr. Isaawi said, continuing to drop names of famous owners and breeders. Roksana was sweating. She wished she were wearing sunglasses, too.

After fifteen minutes, they returned to the pergola and sat down. The guy with the mustache served them iced tea and small cookies. "So," said Mr. Isaawi, grabbing two cookies. "You wanted to talk business." He glanced at Val.

Roksana took a deep breath. "I want to buy some Ketalar from you."

The ranch owner raised an eyebrow but then waved a finger for her to keep talking.

Roksana spoke quickly, trying to summarize what she needed.

"We call it ebastine here," Mr. Isaawi said after a moment. "We use it to tranquilize the animals. That's no problem. I have plenty, kilos. What do you need it for, if I may ask?"

Roksana didn't know if the guy realized she wanted to send it abroad. She tried to smile. "I need it for horses."

Mr. Isaawi smiled. "That sounds good. That was all I needed to know."

Mr. Isaawi was a super nice guy. Possibly the coolest on earth.

In the Range Rover on the way back to Velenjak, Val laughed.

"I thought you were going to sweat to death up there. Why didn't you say anything?"

"I did."

"Yeah, but only after he gave a speech more boring than the ones my mom always gives."

Roksana said, "There are just two things I don't know now, and that's how I'm going to pay for it, and how I'm going to get it all back to Sweden."

"It won't cost much. I can lend you the money," said Val.

Roksana couldn't help but laugh. "I swear I'll pay you back. But how do I get them out of the country?"

Val stopped at a red light. "Listen, they've lifted the sanctions, but we're still experts at smuggling things *into* the country. You're wanting to smuggle something *out,* and that's never been a problem. Never."

33

Almost two weeks had passed—that was two weeks too many. Still, Teddy had been working day and night. He and Dejan had gone back to Fredrik O. Johansson's house immediately, but it was too late. The man was no longer home. Teddy waited outside all night, but Fred O. never came back. The next morning, he had phoned Loke and asked him to help bug Johansson's place in Djursholm. Loke—the world's most loyal computer nerd—had delivered, and not just with his time: he had also lent Teddy money for the equipment they needed to buy. Three hours later, however, he had dealt the plans a blow. "This villa's tricky. They've got tons of alarms, surveillance cameras, and sensors. I don't actually know how I'll manage to get anything in," he said.

"I thought you were a magician?"

"Yes, darling, you might think that, but I'm just an average hacker with plenty of self-confidence and far too much to do right now."

"What about the guy's phone? Can we tap that?"

"Yes, if he uses it indoors, I can probably set up something to catch the signal, but not if he's outside. We'll lose him then. The plus side is that you'll be able to see his texts, too."

Teddy had spent every day in a different rental car, waiting outside the house. A plastic bottle to pee in, a phone linked to the bugging, and three PowerBars for lunch. He thanked his friends again—Dejan had paid for the car rental.

In a way, it was a calm, mostly restful job. It could have suited him, if it weren't for the fact that it *wasn't* a job—no one was paying him like they had when he was doing roughly the same thing for Leijon, and besides: something else was driving him now. Worry was clawing at his body. Eating him up from the inside. For Emelie's sake. And for her tenant's: their child.

Fredrik O. Johansson moved around less than Teddy had expected. His various companies seemed to look after themselves. Fred might have been on a number of boards, but Loke had told him they didn't meet more than twice a month. Emelie would have been useful there, she knew all about companies and groups—but right now, their unspoken agreement seemed to be that they would each work on their own. What he didn't know was what she was planning to do about the baby.

Every now and then, the old bastard went to the Grand Hôtel gym in central Stockholm, occasionally cycling to DJTK—Djursholm's tennis club—with a racket bag over his shoulder. Twice, he ate lunch at a restaurant after working out, and on four occasions Teddy saw him taking a hunting dog for a walk along the water's edge. The rest of the time, the dog seemed to be walked by some kind of assistant who took it out for regular shit and piss breaks.

He heard the old man making calls and saw him send messages to his sons and to the supervisor of the estate he owned in Skåne; he called the other board members and the CEO of his parent company. He spoke to the construction workers fitting a new pool at his house, to friends about an annual tennis tournament; messaged his wife every other day—she seemed to spend most of her time traveling around various big cities, looking at pieds-à-terre to buy. He made calls to his lawyer about the angry neighbors of his estate in Skåne and about his will; he talked to his personal trainer about starting to work out at home rather than the hotel gym. Teddy tried to filter, sort, understand. It was an information overload. Who were these people Fred was speaking to? Often, he had no idea, even less whether it was relevant to what he wanted to know. He started to doubt that Fredrik O. Johansson had even lied, despite how certain Dejan had been.

"You need to smoke him out," Dejan said when Teddy raised it with him.

"How?"

"Give him a bit of a scare. He'll show his true colors then."

Teddy spent the whole day in the car thinking. He almost drifted off. He shouldn't tilt the seat so far back. He popped caffeine tablets and drank even more energy drinks. He thought about swapping the Ritalin for real amphetamine—he needed to be at his very best.

Then he hit the number on his phone and called Fred O.

Fredrik sounded groggy.

Teddy masked his voice as best he could. "Good afternoon. My name is Daniel Olofsson and I'm calling from the police."

The old man sounded wide-awake now. "And what do you want from me?"

"We would like you to come in for an interview."

"What is this regarding?"

"A murder investigation."

"Now, I don't know what you're talking about."

"No, no, I understand that. But you'll have a chance to speak. We just want to talk to you. You aren't suspected of anything."

"I don't know anything about any murder. I don't think I want to come in for an interview."

Teddy made a real effort now. He wanted to sound authoritative. "By law, we have the power to bring you in if you refuse."

"I'd like to talk to my lawyer about this."

"Please do. But there's just one more thing."

"What?"

"The case we want to discuss with you involves the murder of a young girl, but as far as you are concerned, it relates to your possible interaction with the girl during the mid-2000s."

Teddy counted heartbeats, boom—Fredrik O. Johansson waited a nanosecond too long to reply—boom, boom.

"Aha, well I still have no idea what you're talking about," the old man eventually said.

Time passed. The seat was uncomfortable. His back felt stiff, the muscles in his legs rigid. A false tooth was niggling at him, the problem that had flared up while he was in prison troubling him again. The air in the car was stuffy. It smelled of desperation. The heat enveloped him like a suffocating pillow.

Fredrik O. Johansson continued to make his usual calls, to send his usual messages. Teddy tried to determine whether his voice sounded any different—whether he was stressed now.

Then an SMS appeared on his screen: the man was sending messages to a number Teddy had never seen before.

A policeman just called me to go in for an interview.

The unknown number replied:

What for?

It's crazy, it was about that girl in Hägersten. But they shouldn't be able to see any connection?

Do they suspect you of something?

No, apparently not. Do I have the right to take you to an interview like that?

Yes, you can take a lawyer even if you aren't a suspect. But the question is whether I'm the best person for the job, I don't work with crimes in that way.

OK, think about it. We probably need to tidy up. Just to be on the safe side.

Teddy sat bolt upright. His mind was racing. He knew what he wanted to do—he wanted to drag the old bastard outside, give him a once-over, burn down his house. But he couldn't do that now. He *couldn't*. He had to keep his cool.

He didn't have to wait long—after fifteen minutes, the garage door opened, and Fredrik O. Johansson drove out in his new Range Rover. Teddy followed him.

Just under an hour later, after taking a detour to Norrmalmstorg to pick up a man that Teddy didn't recognize, Johansson turned onto a small side road outside of Sparreholm in Södermanland. Dejan was helping out: he was slightly behind—his car was too conspicuous. He and Teddy had still taken it in turns sitting behind the guy, Teddy in his rental car, Dejan in his Model X. This journey was definitely a departure from Fredrik O. Johansson's usual—it must have something to do with his recent SMS conversation. And the side road was enough for Teddy: he checked Google Maps. There was only one place they could be heading to along that road: Hallenbro Storgården was the name of the estate.

He and Dejan killed their engines. It was half a mile away: the estate which, in all likelihood, was the same place Mats Emanuelsson had visited and to which Katja had been taken as a thirteen-year-old. Where a number of men had raped her and other young girls. Teddy opened his car door. The air was cool and fresh. The half light felt calming. He walked over to Dejan, who had parked behind him. The window wound down without a sound—apparently it wasn't only the engine that was silent in a Tesla. Dejan handed him a backpack.

"Wait for me here," Teddy said. "I'm just going to check out the house. If I'm not back in forty-five minutes, you'll have to come and find me."

It took him five minutes to jog along the edge of the road. He could make out the house from a distance. As he approached, he realized how big it was. There was a fence surrounding it, but he had a pair of bolt cutters in his bag. One of the many reasons Dejan was a good friend.

He thought of Emelie. She must be somewhere around twelve weeks now. Teddy hadn't told anyone, but had feigned curiosity with Linda. Asked how far developed a fetus would be at various stages, how the mother usually felt, when people typically told others, how late an abortion was allowed. Linda didn't seem to remember a thing from her own pregnancy. She had given him her best tips: "There's this thing called Google, you ever heard of it?"

A huge lawn spread out in front of Teddy, and beyond that he could see the rectangular house with the tiled roof that was probably still yellowish, just as Mats had described it. Teddy thought back to the latest he had heard about Mats—he was alive, but still hadn't woken for more than a few moments.

Teddy could either walk straight across the lawn—the darkness might provide enough cover to prevent anyone from seeing him—or he would have to try to find some other way of getting closer to the house. Then he thought: Exactly what is it I want to achieve right now? He had found the house, and it was definitely connected to the man who called himself Peder Hult. He had even found Fredrik O. Johansson, who was also linked to the network. Wasn't that enough? Shouldn't he just call that police officer, Nina Ley, and ask her to show up with her team? Though, on the other hand: the cops hadn't managed to get anywhere in more than a year, and now he couldn't even trust them. Not even Emelie seemed trustworthy right now. Plus, he was here. Just a hundred yards from that hellhole of a house.

He started walking straight across the lawn.

The windows in the house were dark.

Dogs. Those old men were dogs.

He did a lap of the house. It took him five minutes. If there was anyone inside, they would have trouble seeing him in the darkness. The building was a rectangle. He spotted three entrances: a main door with a wide stone staircase, balustrades, and enormous pots containing small trees; a side entrance, which probably led straight into the kitchen; and a basement entrance, which seemed to be half a level down, belowground. Each of them was locked. He couldn't see anyone through any of the windows, but he knew there should be at least two men in there somewhere.

He rifled through the backpack Dejan had given him. He was Najdan "Teddy" Maksumic: before prison, he had been a made man. A multi-criminal. A hooligan in every sense. By the age of seventeen, he, Dejan, and a few other kids were already raiding houses in the more upscale areas of Södertälje, sometimes even going as far as Mälarhöjden. Break-ins were easy: people didn't have particularly sophisticated alarm systems back then, and if they did have alarms, then Dejan would usually manage to find the power supply in advance and knock out that crap. For the most part, they had made their way in through basement doors—they were always less solid than the main door, and if anyone was asleep inside, they wouldn't hear the noise from so far away. They grabbed watches and tennis rackets, sometimes even golf clubs. Jewelry and cash. On several occasions, they had stolen car keys, once finding the keys for a Mercedes Benz 500 SL, V8 engine, which had barely done 1,200 miles. The car had been parked outside the house, and Teddy could still remember the way its rims had glistened like freshly polished silver, despite the darkness of the night. Teddy and Dejan didn't have driving licenses at the time, but they had managed to drive the car all the way to the former Yugoslavia that summer—the war wasn't entirely over there yet, but that just made things more exciting. They sold the Merc for more than four hundred thousand in cash, and spent two weeks in Belgrade partying like drug barons.

After just three minutes, Teddy had managed to break open the basement door with the crowbar Dejan had thrown into the backpack. Dejan would have been so proud to see him at work—"the old Teddy," he would have said. "Cracking doors the way I crack eggs into the frying pan."

Teddy stepped down into what looked like a DIY pub. A huge bar stretched across the room. Red drapes, sofas, and armchairs along the walls. Dark paintings that seemed to depict animals copulating. A crystal chandelier hanging from the ceiling. He moved past the bar. Beyond it was a hallway containing several doors. The light was on. Teddy listened for any noise.

He cautiously opened a door. A well-lit room: it looked like a mocked-up bedroom. The only genuine thing in it was the large bed in the middle of the floor. He opened another door. This room was tiled, but it wasn't a bathroom—there was some kind of swing hanging from the ceiling. He opened a cabinet on one of the walls: it was full of leather straps, whips, masks, packs of condoms, dildos, pillboxes, lace underwear, small metal batons that seemed to contain batteries, handcuffs, tubes of various lotions, ball gags, and all kinds of other crap. I'm definitely in the right place, Teddy thought—they're dogs.

Right then, he heard a sound from the third room. He focused: it could be Fred O. and his passenger.

Teddy stepped back into the hallway and opened the third door. This room looked more like an office, with a desk and a sofa.

Fredrik O. Johansson was leaning over the desk, tipping something into a Samsonite suitcase—papers, contracts, possibly DVDs. The old man was evidently *cleaning up.*

"That's enough now," Teddy said.

Fredrik looked up. Uncomprehending. Surprised.

Then he recognized Teddy. They were standing fifteen feet apart, in the half light, but it was perfectly clear. The old bastard looked like he had just seen John Lennon or Olof Palme walk through the door.

"You shouldn't be here," Fredrik said in a strangely bright voice.

Teddy could feel the blood raging through his veins. *The old Teddy* really was back: he was Bruce Wayne about to become the Dark Knight; Bruce Banner about to transform into the Hulk. He wanted to beat the man in front of him to a pulp. Wanted to tear off his dick and shove it down his throat. He never wanted to hear his squeaky voice again.

He hissed: "You just keep calm and stop whatever you're doing. It's over, Fredrik."

He wasn't going to let Fredrik the monster Johansson go, not under any circumstances. But, at the same time, he wondered what he was doing. He really should have called the police a long time ago, or at least called in Dejan. Plus, he thought he could hear sounds from out in the hallway—was that Fredrik O. Johansson's passenger?

Fredrik slowly stepped forward, pulling the suitcase behind him. He was like a new man coming toward Teddy: he was no longer a terrified, busted, shameful old man. Fred O. was growling, his fists clenched, his body tense. He attacked like an animal. They tumbled into the hallway.

Teddy lashed out. He felt Fredrik O. Johansson's nose break.

At the same time, he saw something else from the corner of one eye: the passenger was coming down the hallway toward them—another middle-aged man.

Teddy had to knock Fredrik out right now. He was landing blows like a machine. Blood splattered. Teeth flew. Fredrik cried out in pain.

Teddy waited for the passenger to launch himself at him, but he just grabbed the Samsonite case. Teddy tried to get up, but Fredrik O. Johansson wouldn't give in: the man had twisted, wrapping his legs around Teddy's waist, and was pushing him backward—like some kind of UFC fighter. The other man vanished with the bag. Teddy rolled over. This time, it was Fredrik who was first to his feet. But he was no longer punching or kicking—he was running. And he was much quicker than he looked.

Down the corridor, through the bar, up the short staircase, out through the door.

The grass was damp with dew. Fredrik was a few feet ahead of Teddy, running like a hundred-meter sprinter.

Teddy couldn't even see the other guy, the one who had disappeared with the suitcase—but there was no damn way he was going to let Fredrik O. Johansson escape.

Teddy was panting, gaining on the man. Ten feet away.

Five now.

He threw himself at him, American football–style. This time, he wasn't going to let go.

The man struggled. Teddy crawled on top of him, got him in a leg lock. Just held on. Gripped. The seconds passed.

Fredrik pulled and tore at him. Teddy continued to hold him back.

The minutes passed. Fredrik was flapping like a fish on a hook. Teddy could feel himself getting weaker, but the man had to be even worse. Teddy tried to pull out his phone to call Dejan.

"What do you want?" Fredrik hissed.

Teddy didn't reply.

The ring signal sounded weird, like the coverage was poor. His call failed.

More time passed. He had to try calling Dejan again, but that was no easy task while he held on to Johansson. His sweat was turning cold on his body. The man was twitching like a fish on a dock, thrashing back and forth—Teddy didn't know where he was getting the energy from.

Then he saw blue lights over by the gate. The cops had arrived surprisingly quickly, given that they were in the middle of nowhere and Teddy hadn't called them. He must have set off some kind of alarm when he broke in, or maybe the man who ran off with the suitcase had called them. Or Dejan.

It wasn't a police car, he saw now: it was a motorbike. Its blue light went out, and a headlight came on instead. The motorbike rolled slowly toward the main building. The gravel crunched beneath its tires. After a few seconds, it turned and started moving over the grass toward them. The beam of the headlight hit Teddy in the face, blinding him, but he could hear the puttering of the engine as it approached.

The motorbike stopped ten or so feet away, and the light went out. The officer started walking toward them, heavy gear rattling.

Teddy slowly loosened his grip on Fredrik O. Johansson's body. He heard the man groan and he breathed in the cool air—finally. Teddy never thought he would be happy to see a police officer, but now he relaxed slightly. The officer was standing in front of them, still not saying anything, and the visor of his helmet was still down. Teddy wondered whether he and Fredrick would be asked to lie down or hold their hands above their heads.

"Arrest this man!" Teddy said loudly, gesturing toward Fredrik.

The officer turned from him to Fredrik O. The grass was wet. Teddy thought he could hear the rattle of handcuffs, and he looked up at the biker cop again. His dark visor reminded him of a blank TV screen. But it wasn't handcuffs the officer was holding—it was a pistol.

A gun? That was probably good—Fredrik O. Johansson had to understand how serious this was. But Teddy wondered why the cop still hadn't said anything.

Then he heard a shot.

Teddy felt something warm and wet. His ears were ringing.

What the hell had just happened?

Teddy turned to Fredrik. At first, he didn't understand. Then he understood all too well: Fredrik O. Johansson's face was gone. The cop had shot him in the face.

Teddy raised his head. He was staring straight down the barrel of the officer's gun.

"What the hell are you doing?" he panted.

The black eye of the pistol stared straight back at him. The cop still hadn't said a word. If he even was a cop. There was nothing Teddy could do. His only hope was that he would think Fredrik O. Johansson was enough.

Was he about to die?

Was it all over?

Suddenly: *SWOOSH*. A rushing electronic sound.

The gun was no longer there—and neither was the officer.

The Tesla had appeared in front of Teddy. The passenger side door opened.

"Get in!" Dejan shouted.

Teddy crawled into the passenger seat.

Dejan pulled the door shut. It took Teddy a few seconds to process what had just happened. Dejan had driven straight onto the grass and at the officer, who must have thrown himself to one side. His friend had, in all likelihood, just saved him from a bullet to the head. No one had heard Dejan's electric car coming—because the Tesla Model X was as quiet as death. And death comes quickly with *Ludicrous Speed*.

Teddy turned around, saw the cop disappearing into the darkness on his motorbike. Lying on the grass was the cooling body of one of Sweden's most successful investors.

AFTONBLADET
ONE OF SWEDEN'S
WEALTHIEST MEN MURDERED
Well-known figure in financial circles

A financier considered one of Sweden's wealthiest men has been found with a bullet wound to the head on an estate in Söderman-

land. Parts of the estate were gutted by fire and police are appealing for witnesses.

The financier established his investment company in the mid-1990s and followed a strategy of imitating well-known American investor Warren Buffet. "I only go in on things I understand," he claimed in an interview eight years ago.

The strategy proved very effective, enabling the financier to count himself among Sweden's wealthiest individuals for a number of years.

Police were called to a large fire at an estate in Södermanland in late April. Upon arriving at the scene, officers made the macabre discovery of the financier's body outside the building, with bullet wounds to the head.

"The evidence suggests a deliberate killing," says the preliminary investigation leader. "But we can't rule out suicide."

According to Aftonbladet sources, the police investigation is slowly moving forward. The strongest lead to date is a car seen in the vicinity of the crime scene.

"He had no enemies, as far as I know, and I definitely don't think he would have killed himself, he wasn't the type," says one of the financier's friends. "It's all so sad and awful. He was a good person."

Police are appealing for witnesses.

"The surveillance cameras from the fire-torn building may also provide evidence," says the preliminary investigation leader. "We're looking into everything."

PART III

MAY–JUNE

MAY–JUNE

34

The motion of the plane was making Nikola feel sick. He didn't say anything to Bello, but the truth was that he hadn't flown all that many times before. Once with Mom and Grandpa, when they went to Belgrade to visit relatives and to look at the house where Grandpa grew up, but Grandpa had spent that whole journey reading to him from *Harry Potter,* so he had barely noticed them taking off. Another time, he and Mom had flown to Mallorca, but he had fallen asleep with Jay Z and Rihanna in his ears after just a few minutes: *Know that we'll still have each other / You can stand under my umbrella.*

They were on the way home: he and Bello. They had to get back to Little Sweden, even if they should maybe have stayed longer.

They had been in Dubai for a month. They'd needed to cool down. Above all, the situation back home had needed to cool down, by many degrees. The speculation was worse than when Isak had made Nermin Avdic disappear nine years earlier. Nikola was only twelve at the time, but he remembered the chatter. The guesswork. The fear that had spread like a virus through the boys in Södertälje. How they had started to arm themselves. Now: Chamon was massacred, and Yusuf and Fadi were missing.

He and Bello had taken the bodies to Bello's uncle's construction site, wrapped them in black plastic bags and dumped them into the concrete slab his uncle was busy pouring. The last thing they saw was the section of bag that must have been covering Yusuf's face, possibly his nose, sink beneath the gritty mass of concrete, bubbling like the lava in *Revenge of the Sith*. Nikola could just imagine it: Yusuf reborn as an evil Sith Lord.

Bello's uncle didn't ask any questions, but he hadn't let any of his men see what they were up to, either. "We keep the garbage disposal in the family," he said, baring his yellow teeth.

Nikola had been close to screaming. He didn't know how things could have ended up this way. Just three months earlier, he was close to becoming a qualified electrician with George Samuel, heading toward a crazy good future. Now they had *killed* a man. He had chosen a completely different path—and the sick thing was that when he announced that he wanted to get revenge for Chamon, he hadn't even considered where it might lead him. Now he knew.

Now: he knew.

"Bello," he had said. "D'you think we did the right thing?"

"What?"

"I mean, we wanted to make Yusuf talk because he helped the guys who killed Chamon, and it ended with us cutting him down. But that's not going to bring Chamon back, you know?"

"Nah."

"Sometimes it feels like we've just added more shittiness to the world. I mean, maybe we're the bastards in all this. Maybe we're the bad guys."

Bello had been standing with his hands in his pockets, staring at the hardening concrete. "We're not bad guys," he said quietly, as though he had carefully considered every word. "But we're not good, either."

"What are we, then?"

Bello's gaze was distant. "We are who we are," he said. "That's it."

Dubai: the world's biggest asshole, camouflaged as a tourist trap. *Shopping capital of the world,* a plastic beach resort full of child-friendly pools shaped like bananas . . . but if you dug down two feet into the sand on the beach, you hit the concrete bottom. Nikola thought back to the black bag containing Yusuf's body, how the concrete mix had swallowed it up like it never existed. He wondered: how many Bangladeshi slave laborers were buried beneath the beaches of Dubai?

The first few weeks had been relatively good. Nikola's thigh wound had healed nicely. Isak had given them work through his lawyer in Sweden. They were meant to visit a bank with such a long name that he'd had to spell it out seven times just so that Nikola wouldn't forget. He and Bello had picked up two Rimowa bags with combination locks.

"Sweeeet," Bello had blurted out as he weighed the bags in his hand.

Nikola hailed a taxi. "It's probably cash. 'Cause these just need to be moved to another bank, you know, the chain needs to be broken so no one can see where the money's gone. If anyone tracks this dough, the trail will end at the last bank. Do you know what Isak said when I saw him inside?"

"Nah."

"It's only the C-league players and the Hells Angels who try to launder money through Swedish banks and exchanges. Down here, people launder money more often than they wash their own dicks. No one cares."

Bello had exploded at that, laughing so loudly that two police officers outside the bank started to approach them. Then he had caught his breath. "Aha. How much of this do we get, then?"

"I don't know yet, but he's coughing up for our hotel."

They had checked into a four-star hotel with views out onto the seven-star hotels. Mövenpick Heights Hotel—honestly: Mövenpick as in the ice cream with chunks of cookie dough that his mom always ate when she watched TV shows. The hotel logo was everywhere: on the soaps, the pillows, the towels, even on the toilet paper. On their first day there, Nikola had asked room service to call a doctor to examine the wound on his leg. Nothing vital had been damaged, even if the doctor did wonder who the botchers who had patched him up were. The botchers in question were Bello and Bello's uncle.

Dubai didn't smell the way Nikola had expected a hot country to smell. The air there was dry but also metallic. The artificial park beneath the hotel was kept alive with enough water for an entire town, and the air-conditioning whirred like an extractor fan twenty-four/seven. There were huge SUVs everywhere, all matte paintwork and with rims bigger than a tractor's. The Nigerian cleaners in the hotel bore signs of torture on their hands: burn marks and extracted nails. Every day, one of them left a small flower in the vase in Nikola's room—he had tried to thank them once, but the maid had just shaken her head: they weren't allowed to talk to the guests.

Bello loved the whores the porter could arrange at any time of day. "The Ukrainians here are better than in Ukraine," he had said.

Nikola hadn't felt like it. "How do you know?"

Bello had guffawed. "One of them told me."

They spent their days chatting by the pool, drinking beer in the roof bar, or walking mile after mile through the shopping centers. Nikola was still trying to work out how involved Yusuf had been in Chamon's murder, but Bello just said: "It must've been some internal thing, maybe Chamon came onto his woman. Everyone's so fucked-up these days. The smallest thing and that's it."

Once a week, they had gone to pick up bags from a bank, hailed a cab and dropped them off at another one, where an account had also been opened in their names. Bello had bought himself a Louis Vuitton backpack and a pair of sneakers from Prada, then his share of the money ran out. Nikola had been thinking about a hoodie from YSL, but he changed his mind when he saw the graphic on the back: it looked like a G clef. Chamon's words had flashed through his mind: his mother had thought he was musical.

He thought back to the conversation he'd had with Roksana before the spa, before Dubai. He hadn't helped her. A real man probably would have stepped up—Chamon almost definitely would have. Nikola didn't even know the woman, but still: he should give her a call when they got home. Check how she was doing, or something.

It seemed like Bello was doing other jobs while they were there. Maybe they were for Isak, maybe for other guys back home, but he had dragged Nikola along to meetings with Germans and Dutchmen. Nikola knew what they were about: guns, flak vests, grenades. His friend was wheeling and dealing. Playing the big businessman. Bouncing figures about like a math teacher.

"Seems like you're buying up half of NATO," Nikola had joked after one of the meetings. He and Bello were in a hotel bar down by the water—tourists were allowed to smoke and drink alcohol there until twelve. Some of the guys around them were wearing flip-flops and shorts, others jackets and loafers.

Bello had waved his hand to order another drink.

"NATO barely exists anymore, you know that. But people back home need stuff, it's basically high chaparral in the hood. And Mr. One is building up his supplies."

"Guessed as much. He always wants more explosives."

"I know."

"Do you think there's gonna be a war now, once Yusuf's family works out that he's dead?"

"How would they know that he's dead?"

Bello had spoken to the waiter in Arabic, ordered a glass of champagne, and then he turned to Nikola. "*Habibi*, I don't think it can get much worse than it is right now."

The sun had been setting over the water. The palms, the silhou-ette of the famous hotel, the red clouds: Nikola felt like the Dubai tourist board had draped a huge Instagram filter over the entire sky. The world wasn't that beautiful in reality.

———

Nikola had received the Snapchat message from Jacub, one of the boys back home, after three weeks and four days: it was only on-screen for five seconds, but he didn't need to see it for any longer. *Completely insane: Mr. 1 got out today, they're not gonna prosecute. You two have to come home. He needs help.*

They landed at Arlanda at twelve thirty at night. The May air felt good. The guy who had sent the message was waiting for them in the arrivals hall. Just over an hour later, they were at his place, having everything explained to them. The apartment was full of empty cans of Monster, tubs of bodybuilding protein, and bottles of vitamins.

Jacub was some steroid-pumped, Instagram-filtered fitness guru. Nikola had met him only once before, after Chamon's funeral, but he knew who he was: Isak's man along the red metro line to Bredäng.

Jacub's phone buzzed. He looked up at them. "He's here."

Nikola noticed both Jacub and Bello stiffen.

A minute later, Isak stepped into the room. He looked more tired than he had when Nikola saw him in prison—probably because he had spent the past few days partying hard.

"Boys," he said, moving over to Nikola and Bello. Nikola tried to see how Bello acted. Bello was probably doing the same. Eventually, Nikola stepped forward. Hugged Isak.

"Congrats," said Nikola. "It's incredible."

Bello hugged the boss, too. "*Yani*, totally crazy, insane."

Isak slowly sat down. The sofa creaked. "Yeah, yeah. It's not that strange. My lawyer's the best in town, always has been. I admitted the drug stuff, should've been given three months for that, but since I'd already been in custody for close to two, that meant I'd served my time, with conditional release taken into account. But it was actually for the financial charges that my lawyer came up with the really good stuff. I voluntarily submitted everything to the Tax Authority, which meant they gave me some penalties, but that also stops them from bringing any further charges against me. You understand?"

Isak went on like he himself was a lawyer. Nikola didn't understand a word of it, but he and Bello continued to congratulate Isak all the same.

"I hope you had a good time in Dubai, that the hotel was chill. But you're back now, and we've got work to do. Plenty of people thought I was down for the count, but you know what my dad used to say?"

"No."

"'It's when they think you're down that they're weak. They lower their defenses.' So now's the time to go after them. We've gotta go all in. We need to expand." Slowly—Isak spoke slowly. "ID fraud's the new thing. There's so much cash in it you have no idea. Then there's domain hijacking and the recycling centers—copper, metals, and environmental waste. You're gonna be rich, boys. You do what I say, just follow my word. You get me?"

Nikola wasn't sure whether he understood. He had been prepared to continue the hunt for whoever clipped Chamon—the hate was still burning in him for that, and Yusuf had only been the *instigator* or *coconspirator,* as they said in legalese. But this: being a runner for Mr. One—stepping back in time?

"What about those bastards? The ones who got to Chamon, what do we do about them?"

Mr. One got up. Rubbed his cheek with the back of his hand, scratched his stubble. "We've sent our message. Two of the cunts are missing. No one knows what happened, but everyone knows what it's about. That's enough. Now we have to drop what happened to Chamon, focus on other stuff. It's time to turn the page."

Nikola looked down. He stared at the packets of Star Nutrition Gainer Pro and Mutant Creakong that were lying everywhere. He should say something. He should.

"What you can do, Nikola, is have a chat with Magdalena. You know who that is?"

"Nope."

"Yusuf's girl, she's been calling me like a whore every fucking day since I got out."

Nikola was waiting for her in the middle of Stortorget. There weren't many people about: it was only quarter to nine in the morning, and none of the shops were even open yet. The new town hall and courthouse rose up behind him, Saint Ragnhild's Church to the left and the old town hall, cafés and other crap in front. The sky was as blue as a Smurf and the air felt nice. Compared to Dubai, it was sheer paradise—but the situation was still fucked-up. There was nothing smart about Isak sending him, of all people, to talk to Yusuf's widow.

Magdalena's heels clicked over the paving stones. Her head was bowed, knees bending with every step like she wasn't used to her shoes. Her long, dark hair was parted in the middle, but it looked matted and uncombed, and he could see a tattoo behind her ear: a dolphin.

They were standing in the middle of the square now. Södertälje had started to wake up: there were more people moving around them. Apparently she knew that Nikola spoke her language, because her first words were in Syriac. "Why didn't Isak come himself?"

"He's busy with other stuff. But he sends his regards and knows you must feel terrible."

"Where's Yussi?"

"We can't talk about that, sadly. But Isak still wanted me to let you know that if you need anything, we'll fix it. Anything."

"Where is Yusuf?" Magdalena repeated.

"Like I said, we can't talk about that."

"Isak knows where he is."

Nikola didn't reply. He could feel the lightning starting to invade his skull.

"I want to know where my husband is."

Nikola massaged his temples. "You know what happened to Chamon?"

"I know. And I'm sure this is linked somehow. Yussi was so scared."

"Did he know something was going to happen?"

"Yeah, ever since they killed Chamon. But I want you to tell me what happened."

"I can't say anything. Because I don't know."

Magdalena started to sob. "I can feel it, that he's not alive anymore."

Nikola almost felt a pang of compassion, of sorrow. Yusuf had gotten what he deserved: First, he had betrayed Chamon. Then he had tried to kill Nikola and Bello, but Magdalena was her own person; she had just hooked up with the wrong guy. "Hey, now," he said, reaching out for her.

"Don't touch me," she shouted, staggering back. "I want to know where my husband is," she shouted, in Swedish now. "You, *Nikola*, you have to tell me," she was yelling—roaring, like a wounded animal, like a mother clutching her dead child.

Nikola glanced around. People were turning to look at them. A couple of men seemed to be weighing whether to come over and ask what was going on.

He tried to calm her down. Hold her arms. Hush her. She was crying. Shouting. He wanted to lead her away, but the first lightning bolts had struck in his head. He practically collapsed.

"I want to know where Yusuf is," she repeated.

People all around them had stopped what they were doing and were openly watching them. Waiting to see what would happen.

"I want to see Isak. *Isak Nimrod!*" she yelled, so loudly that Mr. One's name could probably be heard all the way to Ronna.

"I want to know who killed my husband!"

Nikola staggered away without turning around. Crazy headache: his vision had gone white.

People were staring.

"I want to know who killed Yusuf!"

He had to shut off. Stop listening. But it had affected him. He also wanted to know more—he wanted to know who, other than Yusuf, had been behind Chamon's murder. Yusuf hadn't ordered the whole thing, he was sure of it.

His head was about to be blown to pieces.

He wasn't planning to drop it like Mr. One had told him. He had to continue his hunt. He had to find whoever was responsible.

35

Emelie was on one of the new machines at the gym, trying to work out. Josephine had talked her into going.

Almost a month had passed since they went out for drinks. In a way, Emelie felt calmer now: she knew who had killed Katja. The police knew now, too: she had been the one to tell them. The idea had come to her as she left the bar after Magnus Hassel's strange approach. All the same, the past few weeks had also been the worst of her life: she still couldn't decide what to do about the baby growing in her belly.

She had been surprised by Magnus's behavior. It was undignified, and she almost felt sad on his behalf—it just wasn't what she had expected from him. He must have been heading home when he approached her with his drunken proposition. He hadn't realized he would be stopping off at the restaurant, in any case, because he wouldn't have had both his coat and briefcase with him otherwise. The coat could possibly be explained, people did sometimes keep those on, but not the case—there was no reason to have that with him if he was planning to stay.

That was when Emelie had had another, bigger thought: someone planning to leave somewhere takes their bag with them, while someone planning to return may well leave it behind. She transferred that thought to Katja's murder: the backpack they had found on the roof was a sign. Whoever was up there must have been planning to go back; since the bag was still there, it figured that they must have been disturbed, or that something unexpected had happened. Something that wasn't planned. It could be a murder. It could be something else.

Adam didn't fit as the perpetrator. The backpack on the roof had never fit him. Besides, you didn't kill someone you wanted to protect, that felt like a golden rule. He was the wrong person from an emotional perspective—he lacked the emotional motive. And that was when the past few weeks' unprocessed, incoherent thoughts suddenly became clear. Adam's son, Oliver. Thirteen years old. When she met him for the first time outside Bredäng metro station, he had begged her to help his father. It was a cool, March day, and Oliver had been wearing gloves. Emelie could picture them clearly: dirty, torn, winter gloves that were far too thick for the weather. He had taken them off when they shook hands: on the palm of one hand, he'd had a large bandage. She hadn't thought much of it at the time, but now she knew what it meant. When they met for the second time, in her office, when she helped him write a letter, the bandage was gone—instead, he'd had a pale red scar. It perplexed her that she hadn't thought of it at the time. Jan had also analyzed the backpack on the roof: it was too small to fit a grown man, but it would have been perfect on Oliver. Still—it could all be nothing but a coincidence.

The minute Emelie got home from her night out, she had pulled out the pictures of the backpack from the preliminary investigation. She had logged on to Facebook and brought up Oliver's page. There were a number of pictures of him there. She knew what she was looking for without even daring to formulate the thought—she didn't want it to be right.

But it was: in several pictures, Oliver was wearing a backpack. *The* backpack. It didn't just fit him, it *was* his.

Middle of the night: Emelie called Nina Ley, even though she still didn't quite understand how it all hung together.

———

Nina had called her back a day or two later. "We're going to release Adam Tagrin," she said glumly. "He's no longer a suspect. His son's going to be placed in a young offenders' institute. We have reasonable grounds to suspect him of Katja's murder. He confessed in an interview."

Emelie had wanted to cry. "What did he say?"

Nina kept it brief. "He said that he was the one on the roof, looking down at the apartment. Your backpack theory was right: it is his. And when we searched his house, we found the keys for the padlock on the hatch."

"But what has he said about the actual crime?"

"There's a background."

Emelie had heard her taking a deep breath. "In what sense?"

"There's always a background. The background's important."

"What is it, then?"

"Katja and Adam didn't want us to interview her again. She was going to refuse. They also knew there was a certain level of threat, so their plan was to leave Sweden, just run away from everything. Oliver overheard them talking and realized all of this."

"What happened?"

"They were planning to leave the country without him, and he had trouble accepting that, he didn't want to lose his father. In his world, it was Katja's fault that his father was going to leave him. In his world, it was her whoring that risked taking his dad away from him. So, he ran up to the roof, where he apparently hung out quite often. But when Katja came home alone that afternoon, he went down to talk to her. He wanted to try to convince her that she and his dad should change their minds."

"And then?"

"Well, Oliver wasn't exactly clear here, but according to him they were just talking to begin with. He wanted Katja to leave his father in peace. They started arguing, and after a while Oliver became, in his own words, 'so crazy with fear' that he started waving the carving knife around. We haven't managed to work out exactly what happened next, but he did, at least, stab her. I think it was some kind of blind rage."

"And no one noticed the wounds on his hands afterward?"

"You saw them yourself, but you didn't think anything of it at the time, right? Oliver is just a child. He's not even criminally liable. We never interrogated him like that."

Emelie had felt the tears welling up in her again.

Nina continued: "When Adam got home a few minutes later, he immediately worked out what his son had done and tried to disarm Oliver. That was when Adam cut his hand, the so-called disarming wound, and it's also how his blood ended up in the living room. We found Oliver's blood there, too, but our technicians confused it with Adam's. It's easily done with such close relatives. After that, they both fled the scene as quickly as possible."

The line had gone silent. There was one question remaining, but Emelie already knew the answer—because the answer was just plain humanity. She laid it out herself: "And Adam didn't call the police or say anything in your interviews because he didn't want you to arrest his son."

"Exactly."

"It's awful."

Nina's voice had been composed. "Murder is always awful. But this is what rage and fear does to people. We see them everywhere these days. Rage and fear."

The next day, Nina Ley had called her again. She sounded even more serious than she had during their last call. "Something else has happened."

Emelie didn't have the energy for any more difficult news, but she was curious all the same.

"Your friend Teddy," Nina said, "is suspected of murder and aggravated arson."

Emelie had been in her office at the time. She had closed the door as she clutched the phone to her ear. The bright sunlight was accentuating the dirty windows, glittering in the filth. Everything was on the verge of falling apart.

"What are you talking about?"

"Someone has been murdered and a large building has burned down, and everything points to Teddy. We have a warrant out for his arrest. He's been charged in absentia."

"What points to Teddy?"

"I'm afraid I can't give you any more details this time—you know one another and I'm bound by preliminary investigation confidentiality. But I have to ask: Do you know where he is?"

Emelie had felt like she was about to run out of air, like the oxygen around her had vanished. For a brief second, she had weighed up ending the call. She needed to gather her thoughts. She had to understand. Teddy was supposed to have killed a person and burned down a house. The father of her unborn child. The man she thought she knew.

"I have no idea where he is," she eventually said. "I've been trying to call him since I worked out everything with Oliver, but he isn't answering."

After the call, she had gone back to her own apartment, locked the security gate from the inside, taken the key into the bedroom with her, and clutched the personal alarm fob in her hand—she wondered whether it still worked. She had to talk to Teddy. About everything. She slumped down onto the bed. It was too soft, she thought, instinctively bringing her hands to her belly. It was growing, and a trained eye could probably tell exactly what was going on in there. She had been wearing loose, baggy blouses over the past couple of days, but in just a few weeks' time, there would be no more hiding it. In a few weeks, she would be out of time for making her *decision*. She felt like she should, at least, tell her mother. And above all: she *had* to get ahold of Teddy.

She had called and sent texts to the numbers he had been using recently. She had written a letter and sent it to his apartment. She

had even gone out to Alby to knock on his door—thinking about
the bomb that Nikola had gotten caught up in there. Was this
Teddy's way of saying that she had burned her bridges by ignoring
so many of his calls over the past few weeks? It made no difference.
Emelie had called his father and sister, but they hadn't heard from
him in a long time, and they didn't have any numbers but the ones
she already had. Then she had called the only one of his friends
she knew well—Loke Odensson—but even he had no idea what
Teddy was up to or where he was. She should talk to Nikola, she
thought, but when she finally managed to get ahold of him, he
hadn't been willing to talk, for some reason. "I'm in Dubai," he had
said. "And I have no idea what Teddy's number is. We don't talk
anymore."

She had moved in with Josephine on Norr Mälarstrand—she could
no longer handle living on her own, and she didn't trust anyone but
Jossan. Even though she didn't know exactly what had happened
on the estate, she instinctively felt that there was something off
about the whole thing. She had tried to manage a few things for
work, calling Teddy at regular intervals. She had even sent Marcus
to two court hearings on her behalf—she didn't feel safe going in
herself.

"Don't forget your tie," she had said to him, half-joking, half-
serious. Even though Emelie herself didn't have even a fifth of the
interest in clothes that someone like Jossan had, it was important
to make the right impression in court. In many respects, a lawyer's job was to play a part; the different actors in the courtroom
each played out certain roles. The prosecutor prosecuted, the
judge judged, the lawyer defended. It made no difference what you
yourself thought or felt: the positions were fixed, and your duties
stemmed from that. That was why clothing was so important—
defense lawyers had to dress the part. In many European countries,
they wore capes, and that would probably have been easier in Sweden, too—making it even clearer for everyone involved that you

weren't there as an individual but to carry out your predetermined task.

Marcus had handled it well. At one of the hearings, the client, an old junkie, had failed to show up, meaning the trial was adjourned. At another, he had handled the drunk driving and illegal driving charges so well that the trial had ended with a court-imposed care order—which was unusual. The old fellow was thrilled to have avoided prison, and Marcus had probably found himself a client for life.

The media was still speculating about what had happened out at Hallenbro Storgården. Emelie knew more than most: it had to be the estate that Mats Emanuelsson and Katja had talked about—meaning there was a definite link to Teddy. After a few minutes of trawling the gossip pages online, the link had become even clearer: the murdered financier, as the papers were calling him, was Fredrik O. Johansson—one of the names Mats had managed to mention in Oslo. Emelie became obsessed, trying to find out everything she could about the man. His businesses, his family, his friends. Yet it hadn't brought her any closer to what had actually happened out at the estate.

In the background, another question was constantly on her mind, niggling away at her. What was she going to do about the baby?

The story of Katja and Adam's son was so sad. A child who didn't want to be abandoned by his father; a man who wanted to protect his girl. If Katja and Adam had been planning to leave Sweden to avoid testifying, why couldn't they just have taken Oliver with them? Why couldn't his son go, too?

A child was a commitment.

Emelie carefully grabbed the metal handle and tried to lift it straight up. The machine was for shoulder, thigh, and core exercises, but Jossan had given her a considerably more detailed analysis of what the machine could do. Next to Emelie, a middle-aged man in a blue sports top, pale tights, and a hat was doing sit-ups. He looked like he was about to hit the ski run, even though they were indoors. Josephine was at the other side of the room, taking long, rhythmic strokes on the rowing machine. Emelie was wearing the baggiest clothes she could find—ordered online and delivered direct to her door.

Anneli had called from the office yesterday and said that Adam Tagrin had turned up. Emelie had immediately climbed into a cab and gone in.

Adam looked like a cross between a living ghost and a psych case. The truth was that she had never seen a person look so confused. It was understandable, given what had happened. Emelie was surprised he had even managed to make it there.

"Sit down," she had said.

She thought back to when he and Katja had come in a few months earlier.

Adam placed his hands in his lap, but Emelie had been able to see that they were shaking.

"I'm so sorry," she had said quietly. "It's awful. I can't imagine what you must be going through."

Adam's body rocked back and forth. "Do you know what Katja used to say?"

"No."

"She used to say that there were two mistakes you could make on the way to the truth. Not going the whole way or not starting at all." He stopped rocking. "She wanted to do the right thing. But she was a broken woman. Trust didn't come easy to her. And Oliver . . ."

Emelie had barely been able to listen.

"Oliver," Adam said again. "He only trusted one person in this world, and that was me. And I betrayed him."

He had bent down and buried his face in his hands. He sat like that for a moment, and Emelie had realized there was nothing she could say to comfort him.

Once he was sitting upright again, his voice had been different, containing a hint of anger. "But there's one thing I haven't even told the police. I don't trust them."

"What?"

"I know you've been involved in this mess for a while. Katja trusted you, so I trust you. Is that right of me?"

"Katja was my client."

"I'll tell you. It's about why Katja didn't want to go to the police interviews, why we were planning to run away from it all. It's like this. The night before the interview, someone came over to the apartment. I wasn't home at the time, but Katja told me afterward. Some middle-aged man who wanted to come in, but Katja refused, so they talked in the doorway instead. His message was clear enough, in any case. He said that if she continued to spread lies to the police, there would be consequences."

"Did she know who he was?"

"No."

"So that was when the two of you started talking about disappearing?"

"Yes. Or more like it was the final straw."

"Why didn't she say anything to the police?"

"She didn't dare."

"I understand. But she didn't say anything to me, either."

"She did, indirectly. She asked you to come over, she wanted to tell you we were leaving. But by then it was too late." Adam's voice had cracked. "We spent the whole night getting ready to run. Those were the discussions Oliver overheard."

The gym could be an energizing place if you felt stable. The man doing sit-ups next to her seemed relaxed. The equipment was fresh, despite the hundreds of people who must sweat over it every day.

Emelie hoped that Jossan would want to go home after their session, so that they could walk together. She didn't want to be out on the streets on her own. It was insane that she didn't dare live in her own home, but that was how it was.

She loved her apartment on Rörstrandsgatan. The tiny thing had cost a fortune when she bought it a few years earlier, seventy-seven thousand kronor per square foot. Her parents had wondered whether she had come down with something. Their own house was 1,720 square feet, with a garage, ground source heating, and views out onto Lake Vättern, but they would never have been able to sell it for anything close to what Emelie had paid for Rörstrandsgatan. Since then, prices in Stockholm had risen by at least 40 percent, so she would be a millionaire if she sold today. She was up to her eyes in debt with the mortgage, of course, 85 percent, and even if she paid off ten thousand a month—something she definitely couldn't afford to do on the income she brought in from her firm—she wouldn't finish paying it off for almost twenty years. And now there was talk of interest rates rising: the Trump effect. It wasn't enough that the old man seemed crazy—he was threatening to ruin Emelie's finances, too. The property market in Stockholm was psychotic. Over the past twenty years, prices had increased tenfold, while protected tenancies had been hunted like crazy; they were practically an endangered species these days. She didn't understand the logic behind it: how were young people ever meant to find a place of their own if it cost three million just for somewhere to sleep?

Then she thought about her own job again. She doubted her firm would survive if she didn't get back to working like normal soon, giving it some momentum. Suddenly it struck her: the firm wouldn't survive if she went on maternity leave. Marcus couldn't run it on his own: he wasn't bringing in any new business.

Interest rates possibly going up.

A company that might collapse.

A father who would probably be sentenced to life in prison.

A mother who couldn't live at home.

She pulled out her phone and did some Googling. Checked that

Josephine was far enough away. Then she called Ultragyn's abortion clinic.

"Hi, could I book an appointment?"

The man doing sit-ups glanced over to her.

"It's regarding an unwanted pregnancy," she said.

36

The things had arrived at the post office just over a week after she flew home. *Home?* She felt confused, different from how she had felt before she left. "Home" had become a strange word. She knew her way around Stockholm; it was where her parents were, her brother, Z, Billie, and all her other friends. It was where her memories were, linked to people and places. But *home?* Did she feel at home? In Tehran, things had felt different. Everything was new to her there, the wide streets flanked with umbrella pines, the way people touched one another and laughed, the smell of exhaust fumes, the mass of the Alborz Mountains looming up as though Tehran were some kind of hidden treasure to be shielded from the eye of the world. Somehow, all that was hers, it belonged to her. They had demanded she travel on an Iranian passport—and she really could understand why.

Plus: when she got home, there had been bad news waiting for her on the mat in the hallway. A score of 1.9 on the aptitude test hadn't been enough to get into the psychology program at Stockholm University. She had known it would take a high score, but it had never, as far as she knew, required more than a 1.9. Maybe this was her punishment for cheating. Money in the ocean. Morals down the drain. She didn't know how she was going to explain it to her parents. But right now, she and Z had bigger problems.

They had been jittery as they scanned the area outside the post office in Akalla Centrum to make sure there weren't any police waiting for them. Z had suggested they give the collection card to a beggar or homeless person and ask them to collect the parcel; it was undeniably safer that way. "But that feels immoral," Roksana said. She was willing to pick up the crap herself.

The delivery was much heavier than they were expecting: eight parcels in total, each as big as a moving box. Roksana couldn't manage to lift even one of them on her own. The question was how risky it would be for her to stand around guarding the boxes in the square while Z dragged them home one by one. It would take hours, and if someone she knew came by and asked what was in them, she wouldn't know what to say.

"I won't be able to carry one of these more than a few feet at a time, either," Z said. "I'm already sweating like an athlete on dope. This natural, organic deodorant that Billie made me buy is useless. I'm just going to stick to Axe in the future."

She called Caspar, but he texted her to say that he was in a lecture. She called Billie, who said that she didn't think they needed to use a car just because they had a few boxes to move, that everyone had to make an effort to reduce their carbon footprint. She had just started an action group with some of the other students in her law program, to study the legislation around diesel cars.

"Oh, come on," Roksana groaned. "If I promise to start using a menstrual cup?"

Billie was silent—she had been going on about this for months now: "It's partly because it's good for the environment—do you know how many tampons the average woman uses in her lifetime? It's also because it doesn't dry out the mucus membrane, and because tampons are just some invention thought up by men to con women out of money. But the most important thing is"— and Billie had practically started shouting with excitement at that point—"that it enables you get to know your pussy. And that's something those of us involved in guerrilla pussification really value. They don't want us to know our own bodies. Our bodies are taboo, forbidden by the patriarchy. But we're going to change that."

When Billie next spoke, her voice sounded happy. "Okay, then," she said. "You can borrow the car if you'll try a menstrual cup. But remember: smooth driving reduces emissions. Smooth driving saves Mother Earth."

They were planning to prepare everything at home, just like before, but after only one round it was clear that their kitchen wasn't made for producing industrial quantities of mindfuck. Roksana felt so light-headed that she had to go out onto the balcony every fifteen minutes to get some fresh air. They were going to have to find another solution—the crazies had demanded their money again a few days ago. Roksana and Z didn't know how much time they had, but she knew they needed to get the money together. How were they going to manage this?

Palm Village Thai Wok: Roksana's new favorite restaurant, where she often cycled to order food for her and Z, and where she had once met Nikola. The owner was a Swedish guy married to a supercute woman named Sunee. She was from Thailand and she seemed to be about twenty years younger than him. In truth, it was Sunee who ran the place, and Roksana had started exchanging a few words with her whenever she went in, mostly to help Sunee with her broken Swedish. In any case: Sunee had nothing against letting Roksana and Z use the basement space—it was empty anyway.

"What you do there?" she had asked when, for the third time, Roksana tried to explain that they were just going to be producing healthy flour.

"We're just making and packaging flour. You know flour, the thing you use to make bread." She used her hands to butter an imaginary slice of bread. "But it's healthy flour, it doesn't actually contain any cereals. You know, so you don't get as fat." She gestured again, showing what happened to your stomach if you ate cereals.

"I talk to Lelle," Sunee said, calling her husband, Lennart. They spoke for a moment in Thai—Roksana hadn't known that Lelle spoke Sunee's language, but it explained why her Swedish was so patchy.

After a few minutes, she turned to Roksana. "It fine. Thousand kronor month."

That was dirt cheap.

Z bought four blowtorches with tripods, gas cylinders, metal sheets, and water baths. He got ahold of two fans to keep the heat down and another to remove the steam—plus a large white box he claimed was an air purifier. "We don't want Sunee's customers tripping on K. Not unless they're paying for it, anyway," he said with a snort. Roksana laughed with him—she felt like they were back on track.

They bought gloves, white overalls and masks, pipettes, glass measuring jugs, cylinders, and other lab equipment. They got zip-lock bags, labels, and milligram scales. She also ordered a menstrual cup online.

Once they had all the equipment lined up, once the burners were linked up and Z had set up the extractor fan, he went out to fetch one last box.

"Tadaa!" he shouted as he cut it open. It was a speaker. "Saved the most important thing till last. This is Bose's best. Now we can get going."

Two days after Sunee gave them the key, they started production. At ten times the scale this time. This was the real shit: she and Z looked like serious Walter White clones, like nuclear technicians. They reduced liters of Ketalar. They listened to Axel Boman, Kornél Kovács, and stuff Z himself had produced and recorded. They burned themselves on the hot metal, had coughing fits from the smoke that rose up as the liquid turned to steam, and burst out laughing when Z, on the third day, started to complain about hair loss. "It's either the K smoke or that natural, organic shampoo Billie sold me." They listened to Linda Pira and First Aid Kit, they drank coffee and smoked smokes, they talked about Billie's different hair colors, house parties in Tehran, and the insane fact that the Sweden Democrats were polling 20 percent according to the latest reports—despite a leading representative of theirs, some idiot with the exact same name as all the others, saying that there should be regulations on the number of globalists and tree huggers within the media—meaning Jews and members of the Greens. They worked late into the night. Sweating. Dancing around their bags of K. Shouting along with one of Linda Pira's songs. They set up a computer and watched the sixth season of *Girls* over and over again—even Z said it was the best thing he'd ever seen, and he usually dissed Roksana's suggestions. Their legs ached from standing up all day, so Z went to Ikea and bought bar stools on wheels. They pushed one another around and pretended they were go-karting. The Ketalar bubbled like lava. They listened to Tove Lo, Asaf Avidan & the Mojos. Roksana's menstrual cup fit like a glove—it was the world's best invention. They smiled at Sunee and ordered noodles with tofu, extra cashew nuts, and thick, strong sauce.

After four days, their first batch was ready. More than six hundred grams of Kit Kat, packed, weighed, and measured into pouches with a gram in each. They opened the doors and left the lab. It was five in the morning. The May sun was rising like a volcano over by the road.

"Sunlight, here we come," Roksana yelled.

The amounts and the speed they were cooking it: if they sold the whole lot, they might be able to claw together enough money for the psychos—they had a real chance of making it. The very next night, they went to Transmission#3; they went to Ghost Town

Sessions the night after that. They sold the ket for more than fifty thousand kronor. The old crowd was flocking around them again: club organizers, old friends, new friends, friends of friends. Above all: buyers. It was like nothing had happened, like they had never been away. To begin with, Roksana barely had time to go onto the dance floor. But during the last hour, once people had already been on their K trips, twice and even three times, she danced like she would never run out of energy.

Billie wanted to know where they had been lately, and when they gave a vague answer, she started roaring with laughter. "You two always said you would just be friends."

"And we still are just friends, nothing else," Roksana replied.

The next weekend, they set out with new bags, to new illegal clubs, to old and *new* customers. They lowered the price to one hundred kronor a hit, three hundred for a bag. People gathered around them in crowds like they were some kind of Håkan Hellström show. They off-loaded sixty thousand kronors' worth of Kit Kat. Concentrated horse tranquilizer was a sweet product. The rumors about them, the cheap new party makers, spread like a Kardashian post over Snapchat, WhatsApp, and Kik Messenger. They paid off two hundred thousand of the psychos' money.

A few days later, the Boss called.

"It's taking too long."

"But we've paid off two hundred thousand."

"I don't care. I want the rest of our money. You've got three weeks. Understand?"

"Okay, okay, but that's almost impossible."

"Three weeks."

Click.

She went over to her parents' place. They had seen each other only once since she got back from Tehran, the week before the goods arrived—back when she still had time. Her mother had practically started crying when she pulled out the silver cutlery from Etty and the slippers Roksana had bought, and then she had questioned her for more than two hours. Her father had been more cautious, but she could see the eagerness in his movements; he was curious, too, and glad she had gone.

Today, only her father was home. He was sitting in front of the TV, watching some French documentary about ISIS. They hugged. He smelled like he always did, was dressed like he always was. When she sat down next to him, he turned off the TV.

"Roksana *joonam*, I get so depressed watching things like this."

"Then why do you watch them?"

"I can't help it. It's like when you drive past an accident on the highway. It makes you feel sick but you still can't help looking, reading, following what they're doing down there."

Her father leaned back on the sofa. He looked so small, like he was about to drown among all the cushions. "How could the world have ended up like this? When your mother and I were young, it felt like things could only get better."

Roksana had to say it now—she had no choice, no matter how hard it felt. She had to ask her untruthful question. "Dad," she said in a serious voice. "I don't know how much longer I can live with Z. It's not working out. I need to find somewhere else."

"I'm sorry to hear that."

"I've been frantically looking for a place that doesn't cost too much, but when I eventually find one, I'm going to need to move fast." It felt shitty having to lie to him, of all people, but she had no choice. "So, I was wondering if you could increase the mortgage on the house, so I could borrow some money from you?"

"Can't you just live here for a few months? Until something else turns up, something you can rent rather than buy?"

"But, Baba, I should still buy something. I don't think it would be good for Mom and I if I moved in. We'd get on one another's nerves. It wouldn't be good for you two. It's better if I have the money ready."

Her father tipped back his head. "You're right, *azizam*, you're right. And you'll need your own place when you start your psychology course. It'll be fantastic."

That last part was particularly painful, and she thought of asking him about what her grandmother had said, about how he had wanted to be a musician but been forced onto another course. But now wasn't the moment.

He continued: "Of course you can borrow money from us, the minute you find something. But not now, it seems unnecessary. We'll wait a while."

Roksana broke down inside.

On the bus away from her parents' house, she checked Instagram. One type of post was dominating the American accounts: this year's Coachella festival had just started. Pictures of the geometric tents, of the people who were so pretty and yet so bohemian that they all looked like Gigi Hadid, of spotlit stages full of smoke and pyrotechnic marvels. Another type of image dominated the Swedish accounts: people proudly showing off their bookings for Into the Valley and so on—tickets for that summer's Swedish festivals had just gone on sale.

At the same time, on repeat in her head: she and Z needed to come up with another eight hundred thousand kronor. In three weeks. The sums just didn't add up, even if they were selling well.

On her phone: pictures of wasted Americans dancing in the desert.

And then she had an idea. They had gotten to know plenty of DJs, party planners, and buyers lately. Theoretically, they had a great network of contacts. A handle on the Stockholm party scene.

The thought grew in her mind. Their only chance of getting the money together in so short a period of time was if they organized something themselves. Plus handled all the sales and ticket revenues.

She and Z should organize a club. Their very own mega nightclub.

37

Teddy pressed the button on the intercom. He was expecting a gruff voice on the other end—someone asking who he was and what he wanted—but instead, the door clicked open immediately. He turned to Dejan before he stepped inside. "I'll have my phone on the whole time, no matter what happens," he said.

Dejan grinned beneath the brim of his LA cap. "And if she gives you gas?"

Trendy fashionistas could wear soft black caps. Skaters and trash metal wannabes sometimes wore caps with straight brims and logos, while rich Swedes from Saltsjöbaden and Täby preferred navy blue NY caps. But on Dejan: a cap looked about as natural as a wizard's hat.

Teddy said: "If she gives me gas, you'll have to hold the ropes till I wake up."

The state-run dental clinic in Alby: someone had carved a stylized dick beneath the buttons in the elevator. Teddy's old tooth had started to ache—or rather, the implant that had replaced the tooth he'd had extracted while he was in prison. It would have cost him four months' wages while he was working at Leijon—but the dental work had been covered by some kind of insurance he had by working for the firm. He no longer had private insurance. He had practically nothing now, and the implant crunched like he was chewing gravel every time he ate. It hurt so much that he couldn't sleep, couldn't eat, couldn't even think; so even though he had been on the run for a month now, he knew he had to do something about it. It was urgent.

But his biggest concern was that he didn't dare just go to the dentist like normal, Dejan had to keep watch outside. If the police caught wind of his appointment today, it could all be over.

The dentist had dimples and asked him to lie back in the chair. Her soft Finnish accent and faint smile calmed him somehow. He checked that his phone was still turned on, that he had coverage, and then he opened his mouth as wide as he could. There was a bookmark taped to the light shining down into his mouth: a picture of an angel. Teddy closed his eyes. Let the dentist do her thing. His life was anything but calm right now. He really could do with an angel to watch over him.

Keeping a low profile in relation to the network wasn't easy—their reach was clearly extensive—but the police force was virtually impossible to avoid, at least in the long run. Teddy had plenty of friends who had done stupid things in their youth, illegal activities, who had been wanted. They had often thought that they just needed to stay with their parents for a while, lie low, play computer games at some cousin's place, crash on the sofa at some woman's house, and pretend everything was normal. But that life didn't suit anyone genuine. You got the urge to go out and cruise around with the boys, you wanted to meet women, you wanted to be involved when things happened. The cops had your picture and your description in all their radio cars, you were on their red list. They had you in their nationwide register, they knew who you were friends with, which networks you were a member of. They even knew who taught at the school that your kid, who you saw only every other Friday, attended. Eventually, they would find you.

But Teddy had taken precautions. He wasn't going to make the same mistakes his friends had made fifteen years ago. He had gotten rid of the Volvo and bought a worn-out old Fiat instead, registering it to a friend of Dejan's. He had tinkered with the driver's seat so that it could lie flat—he had been sleeping in the car as best he could, with his long legs drawn in to his chest like a child, parking in different wooded areas outside of the city and setting his alarm to go off several times a night so that he could stretch, keep moving. He never went home. Lived like a traveler. Wore the same T-shirt six days in a row, then washed it and his underwear in the sink in restaurant toilets. He stopped taking showers at Dejan's place and started going to Sydpoolen, a swimming pool in Södertälje, instead. He had watched from a distance as the police raided his friend's place. He had seen them do the same at Linda and Bojan's, and of course at his own apartment, but he didn't dare call them to say it was all bullshit. He hadn't even taken any calls from Emelie—he didn't want to drag her into a bad situation, suspicions of co-conspiracy or anything. He had taken caution to new levels: if he had been careful before the events at the estate, he was paranoid now. He grew a beard, didn't go anywhere without sunglasses, took a detour if he saw someone who might know him. He borrowed cash from Dejan. He didn't work out. He ate badly. He could feel what it was doing to his stomach and had been sleeping badly even before the toothache started torturing him. He became the world's loneliest man.

During the day, he had spent most of his time in various 7-Elevens, using their rental computers. He had gone over what happened out at Hallenbro Storgården again and again. How he had interrupted Fredrik O. Johansson and his nameless passenger, who were clearly trying to empty the place of evidence. How deeds, DVDs, and other material had vanished into the Samsonite case, which, in turn, had vanished with the nameless man. How Teddy *really* wanted to find the contents of that bag—clearly it was something the network didn't want to come out. And then: the cop in the motorbike helmet who had clipped Fredrik O. right in front of him. He couldn't be a real police officer—he had to be a fake.

The big house had burned down—Teddy's theory was that the

passenger must have set it alight, though maybe it was the biker cop. In any case, the police didn't seem to have found much other than the rental car Teddy had arrived in, which they had clearly managed to trace back to him. Maybe he had been caught on the surveillance cameras, too, he didn't know. They should have burned down with the rest of the crap.

He wanted to know who owned Hallenbro Storgården and to find out more about the men he had met and those he hadn't. Above all: he wanted to know more about Fredrik O. Johansson. He had asked Loke if he could hack into the police's internal computer system to find out which officer had been on the scene at the estate, if he was even a real officer. To find who the real killer was.

Loke had gotten back to him a few days later. "Sorry, little man," he had said, wrinkling his nose as he sat down in the passenger seat of the Fiat. "But I couldn't do it. They've got new firewalls and new security programs. I thought I could get in anywhere, but not anymore. Maybe I'm getting old."

"Isn't there a course you can take?" Teddy tried to joke.

"I'm the one who runs them, cutie," Loke had said. "By the way, Emelie Jansson got in touch with me last week. She sounded really keen to get ahold of you."

"I know she's been looking for me. But I don't want to drag her into all this."

"She was fully aware that you're suspected of all this crap. And she *still* wanted to talk to you."

It was true, what he had said—he didn't want to drag Emelie into this. But, in the end, he had called her anyway. They hadn't said much over the phone, and decided instead to meet in the place they had gone for dinner a few months earlier. Teddy had dropped his phone from a bridge as soon as they ended the call. He didn't know whether she was still pregnant; he was just happy that she wanted to see him, despite everything that was going on.

———

Raw Sushi & Grill, a few hours later. Teddy had arrived an hour early and scoped out the area outside. Though he fundamentally trusted her, he had to be sure that she hadn't called the police or that they were tapping her phone.

He had waited until she came through the glass door into the restaurant, and watched her order what looked like a juice. She seemed worried, her eyes darting back and forth. When he stepped inside, it didn't seem like she had recognized him at first, but that was the point. He, on the other hand, couldn't tell whether she was still pregnant; her top was far too loose.

They hugged. And when their heads were at their closest point, he had felt her warm breath in his ear. "I know you didn't do it, Teddy, but what happened?"

Teddy had wanted to hold her there, to whisper back into her ear. But she had pulled away and sat down.

"No," he said. "I didn't do it." Then he had leaned forward and explained, in a low voice. About the men he had visited. How he had tried to put pressure on them and how he had tricked Fred O. He talked about Hallenbro Storgården, where this Fred bloke had gone to tidy up. About the Samsonite case that had been taken away from the house. Once he was finished, it was her turn. She told him that they had released Adam Tagrin and that Oliver had been placed under arrest for Katja's murder while they investigated further.

Then she had said: "Teddy, I'm not going to keep it."

He glanced at her glass of juice; she hadn't taken a single sip. "Why?"

Emelie looked around, possibly to see whether anyone at the tables around them was listening. Then she had crossed her arms, demonstratively. "I wouldn't be able to cope with being a mother right now. And I don't think you and I would make a good parenting team."

It felt like a rock had dropped inside him. A weight dragging him down to the floor, to the ground. "But I think you'd be a fantastic mom," he had said. "And I could be a good dad. I can learn."

It seemed like Emelie was searching for the right words; he had never seen her like that before. Eventually, she said: "Maybe you're right, but I have my doubts."

"I don't think you really have doubts."

"Stop, Teddy. I can't be in a relationship with a man suspected of murder."

"But you know I'm innocent."

"Yeah, but it's not just that. You know who you are. Someone who attracts this kind of crap, someone whose history is just full of trouble. You're trouble, and that doesn't work for me. I've made up my mind. I'm sorry."

Then she had stood up.

The cute dentist pushed back the light. The bookmark angel disappeared from Teddy's field of vision. "Okay, you can rinse out now," she said.

Teddy sat up; he didn't know how long he had been lying there. The plastic cup was standing on what looked like a small, porcelain fountain which, in turn, was part of the equipment around it. He swilled the water around his mouth and spat into the fountain. His cup automatically refilled. He ran his tongue over his new tooth.

"Want to take a spin in my new car?" Dejan asked as they walked away from the dental clinic.

"Nah," said Teddy. "But I'm glad you've got a new one." The Tesla was about as discreet as a Lamborghini.

Dejan laughed, his Adam's apple bobbing up and down like a pinball. "You're in a real shitty sitch, my man. You sure you don't want to leave town? I know people in Palma, Marbella, Belgrade."

"I need to straighten all this stuff out."

"You can follow me to the car, at least?"

"Okay."

They passed huge billboards advertising some TV channel. *Relax with the best crime shows,* it said. Apparently it was relaxing to watch people killing one another. As they approached Dejan's new car—a Porsche Panamera—the door of another one opened. A man climbed out and started striding toward them. It was Mazern, aka Kum.

Kum: the godfather, Teddy's old boss from before he was sent down. Not that he was a godfather in any religious sense of the word. Kum was a myth in the Stockholm region; a ghost to the police, a gangster legend with more than nine lives. He was the mentor and father figure all the guys needed, at least if they lived the Life. The man rumored to have earned more from tobacco, coke, smuggled booze, and money laundering than anyone in Sweden before him. The man who had apparently quit, and now only invested in legit businesses. They shook hands.

"*Mi friend,*" said Kum. "Dejan called me. Is your tooth better?"

"Fine now, I hope."

"A man's got to look after his teeth. They're the first thing a person notices."

"I didn't get any dental care when I was first sent down. You had to be given leave for that."

"It happens. And now you're borrowing from Dejan to pay the dental bills?"

Teddy couldn't tell whether Kum was joking or serious. There were practically no wrinkles on his face: it looked like someone was pulling his skin from both sides. Had the godfather had a face-lift?

"I'll pay him back," said Teddy. There was no denying that his feelings for Kum were complicated.

Kum shook his head. Though he was talking, his face remained still. "You won't pay anything back. I want to remind you that it was me who ordered you to do that kidnapping, even though I had no idea who the kiddie fuckers behind it were. And there's one thing you should know about me, Teddy . . ." Kum paused for effect. "I might have stopped with what I once did—but I'm still a

man. How much of our language do you know, Teddy? *Lojalność,*
do you know what that means?"

"I think so."

"That's how you were when you were convicted: they ground
you down in interviews and you still did your time without ever
mentioning another name. Without saying a thing to the cops.
Lojalność, Teddy. It means loyalty. A good principle to live by. I
place more value on that than most other things in this world. And
you upheld it better than many. So even if we've had our problems,
you and I, I'm here now. I want to help you."

Teddy actually felt himself relax slightly. Some of the tension,
loneliness, fear, it ran right off him. Kum really did want to help.
But at the same time: he had no idea how it would work. He was
wanted for murder by the Swedish state—what could a former *godfather* do about that?

Kum said: "You need to find out whether that cop, Nina Ley,
can be trusted. No matter how much I hate the pigs, she's your best
hope right now."

Kum and Teddy were standing at the top of the Katarina Elevator,
looking down. Teddy had called Nina Ley and said he wanted to
meet.

"You know there's a warrant out for your arrest?" she said. He
couldn't hear any compassion in her voice.

"Yeah, of course I do. But I'm not going to hand myself in voluntarily. I didn't shoot Fredrik O. Johansson, but I do know what
happened out there, and I think you do, too."

"So tell me."

"It's not a good idea over the phone."

"Then we'll have to do it outside of protocol, like I have with
Emelie and all the other stuff. Can we meet outside the station?"

"No," said Teddy. "I'll send you a location. And just you, no one
else. Promise me that."

"I promise. How will I recognize you?"

"I'll message you when you're there."

The walkway between the Katarina Elevator and Mosebacke was roughly 130 feet aboveground. Teddy felt almost dizzy as he peered down at Slussen. Or rather: what was left of Slussen. Directly beneath them were a number of large holes the size of soccer fields. Right in the middle of town: they were busy demolishing the past; the pavements and roads, tunnels and channels were laid bare like wounds. The gray gravel, the yellow diggers, and the brownish-orange planks piled up like some enormous game of pick-up sticks looked like something imported from a war-torn city in the Middle East. The steel reinforcements hung like rusty strands of hair from the torn-up remnants of road. Loose paving stones and lumps of concrete spread out like something from *The Road*. And everywhere: holes. Holes into the underworld, holes between former pavements, holes down to the water that threatened to eat Slussen from beneath. That was what a city changing shape looked like: as though a dusty bomb had dropped, and once they were finished something new would rise up here, impossible to imagine right now. Something without any connection to what once was.

Beyond the planks, on the other side of the holes, Teddy could see Dejan. Teddy had sent the location to Nina: Södermalmstorg, directly in front of Slussen metro station. Right now, Dejan was checking out the scene down there, making sure everything seemed calm.

I'm wearing an LA Dodgers cap, Teddy wrote in his message. He could see Dejan pacing back and forth, like a bear or a tiger in a cage at the concrete zoo. It was ten to six: Teddy would have to go down now. In ten minutes' time, Nina was meant to show up.

"What's your gut feeling?" Kum asked.

Teddy tried to see whether she was anywhere nearby. He could see the flower cart down there, the herring truck. The square was crawling with people, the last throes of rush hour—people jogging down to the metro, carrying heavy bags onto the buses, confused people trying to understand the new walkways that had been set up to cross the building site. And then the cyclists: they streamed by. Few of them were wearing helmets; those airbag collars were clearly popular these days. Teddy had read about them; the inventors claimed that by using advanced sensors, the collar learned the cyclist's patterns of movement and then inflated to become a protective hood if they crashed or fell off.

"My heart says I trust her, because she clearly trusts Emelie," he said to Kum. "But my brain says that she's a cop. And I'm a wanted criminal."

Kum bared his teeth: they were unnaturally white. "A pig's always a pig. And it's in their nature to act like one. But this particular pig seems to have characteristics of other animals. Come on, let's go down."

Dejan was over by the flower stand. Kum was next to Teddy, talking about his businesses as though everything were normal. He owned four asylum shelters outside of Stockholm, and was planning to open as many more. Teddy was getting bored. Maybe Nina wasn't planning to show up at all; maybe she had been delayed or felt compelled to cancel since it would be serious misconduct not to arrest him.

There was a helicopter hovering high in the sky.

Suddenly something happened: Teddy felt it in the air before he even saw it—clearly his gangster senses were still working. He saw four men moving quickly from different directions as three unmarked cars pulled into Södermalmstorg with blue lights in their windows. Inside the metro station, he saw more men positioning themselves in front of the down escalators. Men wearing windbreakers, walking pants, and sneakers: the standard uniform of a plainclothes officer. The cars pulled up with screeching tires.

All around them, everything came to a standstill. The plainclothes officers moved closer, with deliberate movements: they thought they were about to catch a killer.

He still couldn't see Nina Ley, but people began to scatter—what had happened to this town? Four well-built men rushing toward another man, and not a single person stopped to help, no one shouted anything, no one cared.

The only thing Nina had promised was that she would meet him *alone*. He knew she would be being fed information about how they were about to arrest him now. There was no point running—there were too many of them.

Kum said something.

Teddy turned around.

Kum grunted. "Oink, oink. Always oink oink."

Teddy tried to smile, but all he could see was him being arrested more than ten years earlier, in the cottage where they had been keeping Mats Emanuelsson prisoner. Fragments of a memory that he had tried to repress. First the darkness when they cut the power. Then the pinpricks of light from their MP5s before they threw smoke grenades inside and stormed the place. Finally, the pain when the first cop knocked him down—his back and his head, like a forewarning of what was to come.

Then it all kicked off on Södermalmstorg. Teddy would have liked to see Nina Ley's face right now—when she realized that Teddy *hadn't* trusted her. That he had taken the safe approach ahead of the risky one: told her he was wearing a Dodgers cap when in actual fact that was Dejan.

The officers threw themselves at his friend, held him down. Maybe they were cuffing him, it was difficult to see even though they were only fifty feet away.

Dejan didn't put up any resistance: he had been expecting this; it was all part of the plan. Teddy saw his Dodgers cap disappear beneath the mass of plainclothes officers' bodies. Excessively brutal, like always.

"We should probably go," said Kum.

Teddy tore his eyes away. He hoped they wouldn't hurt Dejan too much.

They started to walk in the opposite direction.

TELEPHONE CONVERSATION 54

To: Pierre Danielsson (co-suspect)
From: Hugo Pederson
Date: 23 March 2006
Time: 14:45

HUGO: Hey

PIERRE: 'Sup?

HUGO: I've met him now.

PIERRE: Who?

HUGO: Mats Emanuelsson, the fixer you thought I should talk to.

PIERRE: So how did he seem?

HUGO: Good, really good. We met at a law firm, the same one the old guy uses, and I gave him a brief explanation of what we need his help with. He hasn't had our caliber of client before, more sleazy stuff. I did a bit of research into him, think he's working for the slavic mafia.

PIERRE: Ah, maybe he's not the right person for us, then?

HUGO: No, for God's sake, he knows this stuff. I think he could be a perfect fit.

PIERRE: Does he know who you are?

HUGO: No, that didn't feel necessary. I made up a name, mixed around some letters in my actual name. Guess what I ended up with?

PIERRE: Peder Hugoson?

HUGO: Almost, but that would've been too obvious. I called myself Peder Hult. Think it sounds great.

PIERRE: Ha, ha, yeah, that sounds good.

HUGO: Right? Listen, I'll send you more stuff the encrypted way. I believe in this Mats guy.

TELEPHONE CONVERSATION 55

To: Hugo Pederson

From: Louise Pederson (wife)

Date: 28 March 2006

Time: 12:30

LOUISE: Hey, it's me.

HUGO: I can see that, Mousey. What are you doing?

LOUISE: I had a headache, so I left work.

HUGO: So you're at home now?

LOUISE: Yeah.

HUGO: Are you feeling any better?

LOUISE: No. I want you to come home for dinner tonight. I want to talk to you.

HUGO: Sounds like something's happened. Can't we do it now?

LOUISE: Tonight's better.

HUGO: But I won't be able to make it to dinner, there's no way. Can't we talk now?

LOUISE: Okay, fine. You know I haven't really been happy with how much you've been working and how little time we've spent together this past year. Then there's the whole bed thing, and you know what I think about that. I don't feel like you're listening, I don't feel like you're doing anything to change where we're heading. I'm not happy, Hugo. I need change. And what we're heading toward, it doesn't work.

HUGO: What is it you think we're heading toward?

LOUISE: Stagnation, coolness.

HUGO: Come on, you're exaggerating.

LOUISE: It's how I feel. Hugo, I want us to start going to couples' therapy. And I need some kind of project to give me energy again. Right now, that's not you.

HUGO: Please, Louise.

LOUISE: No, listen, you're the one who wanted to talk now rather than later. Anna and Fredric went to couples' therapy in London, and it's been great for them. You know he started working less afterward?

HUGO: But that's because he changed departments at the bank.

LOUISE: Maybe, but why do you think he changed departments? This is what I want from you, Hugo. If you can't even consider talking things through with me, then I don't see how we can keep going.

HUGO: Are you serious?

LOUISE: I've never been more serious. Also, I've seen an estate in Upplands Väsby that I want us to buy.

HUGO: What are you talking about?

LOUISE: Kalaholm, it's online now. Five hundred acres and a run-down castle building, which needs a thorough but sensitive renovation. It's practically made for me. I think we'd be happier out there, or at least I would.

HUGO: But, but . . .

LOUISE: They want forty million in total, which includes a riding place and three villas, which are being rented out to ordinary people right now. I've talked to Fredrika and she can see the potential in the place; she thinks I'd really be able to transform it. I've already thought through the renovation of the kitchen and the stables, it could be magical.

HUGO: Mousey, forty million is a bit beyond us, at least right now. Maybe in a couple of years?

LOUISE: You could get a loan, couldn't you? Stop worrying so much. It's about our relationship, don't you get that?

HUGO: But a forty-million-kronor estate can hardly determine how we're doing?

LOUISE: It doesn't seem like you're listening.

HUGO: Calm down, I just don't see how the estate would help us.

LOUISE ENDS THE CALL.

HUGO: Hello? Hello? Did you hang up? What the hell?

SMS MESSAGE

To/From: Unknown
From/To: Hugo Pederson
Date: 29 April 2006

Out: Hi, we've got something new in the works. Can you meet at the usual place at 14:00? / Hugo.

In: I'll come. By the way, I understand you have a new consultant, Mats E.

Out: Yeah, he does the job. Lots of good ideas and arrangements. I call him Mr. Money Man.

In: Interesting.

Out: But I'm extremely careful, hidden numbers and encrypted messages from new accounts all the time. I don't think he knows who I actually am. I'm using an alias.

In: Ha ha. Sounds very interesting. We can talk more about him when we meet.

TELEPHONE CONVERSATIONS 56–80 (SUMMARY)

To/From: Pierre Danielsson (co-suspect) and a number of other stockbrokers and bankers in Sweden, Switzerland, and England (named in relevant appendix)
From/To: Hugo Pederson
Date: 3–17 May 2006
Summary: Hugo Pederson has a number of conversations with co-suspect Pierre Danielsson and the above-named brokers and bankers in Sweden and Europe regarding a number of companies. The total capital gain for Pederson from his business transactions is upward of two million euros. Each transaction is documented separately.

TELEPHONE CONVERSATION 81

To: Pierre Danielsson (co-suspect)
From: Hugo Pederson
Date: 17 May 2006
Time: 15:15

HUGO: Teenie weenie Pierre, how're you doing?

PIERRE: I'm all good. That last trip was wild, huh?

HUGO: Yeah, incredible, the sky's the limit, nothing else. I'll be able to buy up Göran and shut him down soon.

PIERRE: Ha ha.

HUGO: But that's not why I called. I saw the guy. He's got a few ideas. I told him how happy we are with Mr. Money Man, and now the guy wants to take him out to meet his friends and business contacts.

PIERRE: Aha.

HUGO: So is that okay with you?

PIERRE: As long as it's all handled nicely, it's okay.

HUGO: Exactly, I just thought it would probably be good for us to be invisible, you know, if we're bringing in others. You got much of a presence online?

PIERRE: Nothing.

HUGO: Good, me neither. I just asked my secretary to take down my picture from the home page. No pictures from nights out or anything, if you go to any events. We need to be careful about that kind of thing.

PIERRE: I already am.

HUGO: Good, then I'll talk to Mr. Money Man and see if he can give a little talk for twenty or so potential clients. Apparently the guy has access to an insanely nice estate in Södermanland, Hallenbro Storgården.

PIERRE: Okay.

HUGO: He wants it to be lavish, so dinner jackets and a good atmosphere. No names. Mats doesn't need to know any names.

PIERRE: Sure, sure, let's do it. Could be cool. I'm wondering if we should take the helicopter up. I bought a Robinson, did I tell you that?

HUGO: Yeah, you haven't talked about anything else lately. What's it like to fly?

PIERRE: Incredible. You have to come.

HUGO: We'll take it up there together. Mats can come along, too; it'll impress him.

TELEPHONE CONVERSATION 82

To: Carl Trolle (friend)
From: Hugo Pederson
Date: 24 May 2006
Time: 01:10

HUGO: Hey, man.

CARL: Come on, it's ten past one in the morning.

HUGO: You don't have to answer when I call.

CARL: But I assume something must've happened.

HUGO: Something's happened.

CARL: What? You managed to leave work early for once?

HUGO: No, I've actually been home for a while, but Louise and I had the worst argument ever. She's gone.

CARL: You're kidding? She just left?

HUGO: Yeah. But you should've heard it, man, she was screaming like a two-year-old.

CARL: Why was she so pissed off?

HUGO: Ahh, she thinks I'm working too much.

CARL: That's it?

HUGO: Nah, it's everything, you know? She was going on and on about how we don't spend time together like normal people, how all I do is work, how I don't want to invest in our relationship. And by our relationship, she means that estate in Upplands Väsby. She goes on about it every single day.

CARL: Can't you just buy the place, then?

HUGO: They want forty million.

CARL: That's not for the poor man.

HUGO: Yeah, but honestly, it's really risky. I told Louise we can't afford it right now, but she went completely crazy and screamed that I've got no idea what she's feeling, and then she started going on about our sex life like always, even though she's the one who doesn't want to do it, though she denies that, too, and then she goes on about how I only want to do it when I'm wasted, that she wants to otherwise, even though that's bullshit, because the only time she wants to do it is ten in the morning on Sundays, and then we have to lie in bed talking about the estate for an hour first, then I have to give her a massage, and then we have to make out for another hour, and it's only sometime around lunch that I actually get to come. I told her that. She could damn well hear it.

CARL: I don't know, Hugo. You have been working a lot lately, she's right about that. And the estate does look nice.

HUGO: But why expose ourselves to that risk right now? We were fine as we are: we just renovated, and if I can have another year, I'll be bringing in tons of money. It's as good for her as it is for me.

CARL: And the sex life thing, that's the same for everyone, but you do go to others, so maybe you don't feel like it when she does.

HUGO: What're you talking about, going to others? I've never cheated on Louise.

CARL: What about the girls in Switzerland?

HUGO: Jesus, they're strippers, it's not the same thing.

CARL: Aha.

HUGO: What is it with you? What are you talking about?

CARL: I'm going to be completely honest with you, Hugo. Things have been happening very quickly for you lately, and I wish you every success, but maybe you should hit pause for a while. Get away for a few weeks, with Louise. So the two of you can talk and spend some time together without any interruptions.

HUGO: You sound just like her. Yeah, things have been moving quickly, you got a problem with that? Is that a little social democrat I can hear? A little Marxist? A jealous whiner?

CARL: Come on, calm down.

HUGO: No, I don't think I will. You've always been a loser, you know that, Carl? Do you remember when you started going on about the scratch cards we got from my dad? You started crying when you didn't win. You sound exactly the same right now, you know that?

CARL: I'm hanging up now.

HUGO: Yeah, you do that, you loser. Loser.

CARL ENDS THE CALL.

HUGO: Fucking loser.

TELEPHONE CONVERSATION 83
To: Pierre Danielsson (co-suspect)
From: Hugo Pederson
Date: 1 June 2006
Time: 14:34

HUGO: I've messed up.

PIERRE: What's happened?

HUGO: I left my laptop in a taxi.

PIERRE: What are you saying? How did that happen?

HUGO: I'm sloppy as hell, I just forgot the bag when I was coming home from the airport.

PIERRE: Have you checked with the taxi company?

HUGO: Yeah, hundreds of times. Such fucking bad luck, Pille. But since we're going to the guy's event with Mats this afternoon, at least I won't need it this evening.

PIERRE: You have a backup, right?

HUGO: Most of it, I hope. But imagine if someone sees the stuff on it.

PIERRE: Yeah, and what's going to happen then, do you think?

HUGO: I don't fucking know.

PIERRE: Let me tell you: they'll see that Hugo Pederson's about to be very successful. That's all.

TELEPHONE CONVERSATION 84
To: Hugo Pederson
From: Jesper Ringblad (stockbroker, Nordea)
Date: 1 June 2006
Time: 14:56

JESPER: Hi, Hugo, I'm sorry to bother you.

HUGO: No worries. You got something in the works?

JESPER: No, that's not why I'm calling. It's actually to let you know that we've got a problem.

HUGO: Spill.

JESPER: We've received information that HMRC, that's the British tax authority, has requested that the Swedish authorities inspect us. We've just found out from unofficial sources, and of course we'll do everything we can to protect our clients.

HUGO: Ah no, do you know why?

JESPER: Nothing certain, but it's to do with alleged Swedish-owned accounts in the Channel Islands.

HUGO: I've got money there.

JESPER: Exactly. That's why you're one of the clients I'm calling right now.

HUGO: When are they starting?

JESPER: We don't know anything for sure, I should say, and in the best of worlds they'll just request written documentation and deeds at a more general level. Another scenario is that they'll request access to our premises and documentation and schedule a number of days when they could turn up. But worst case, they'll be at our doors in two minutes and just force their way in.

HUGO: But you must have some kind of contingency plan?

JESPER: Of course, Hugo, we've made all the necessary preparations, but it's still my duty to inform you. I think you understand the gravity of the situation and why I can't say any more. I'd risk putting myself in a compromising position. That said, you may well want to spend the rest of the day dealing with certain things. Promptly, I might say.

HUGO: Come on, this is incredibly bad timing. I've just lost a computer with a ton of information about those accounts on it.

JESPER: I'm sorry, but that isn't actually my problem. I hope you can sort it out today.

38

The abandoned gravel pit looked like the world's most deserted place, or actually: maybe this was what it was like on the moon. Still, the highway was only a couple of miles away. They could hear its faint droning buzz through Bello's open window, something like a super fat artery pulsing through the forest. Somehow, the pile of gravel looked almost delicate, like it could collapse at any moment. Nikola thought about Frodo and Sam tumbling down a steep gravel slope after scouting out the huge black door into Mordor. Gravel, dust, tumbling rocks.

"Bello, there's something I've always wondered," said Nikola. "You know in *The Lord of the Rings,* how when Frodo and Sam hide beneath Frodo's special cloak, they look like rocks and gravel—they become invisible."

"Yeah?"

"The thing I don't get, do they look like the rocks beneath them, the ones they're lying on top of, or do they look like new stones on top? What I mean is, if someone looks at the cloak, do they see the ground beneath it or a new pile of rocks on top?"

Bello scratched his crotch. "I don't watch that kind of thing."

"You haven't seen *The Lord of the Rings?*"

"Nah, I don't care about films with dwarves and swords. Everyone I know watches *Narcos, Sons of Anarchy,* classic episodes of the *Sopranos.* No one watches stuff filmed in New Zealand or Dubrovnik."

"But they're movies, not TV shows."

"*Scarface, Goodfellas, The Godfather.* And *Straight Outta Compton.* But no knights or wizards."

"You're missing out."

"Maybe, maybe not. I'm just staying true to style."

Nikola laughed and climbed out of the car. He wanted to keep Bello in a good mood. This was sensitive. "You can go now," he said.

"Bro, who exactly are you meeting?"

"Doesn't matter. I don't want you getting drawn into this." Though he didn't know why, Nikola felt nervous—he had been through things that were a hundred times worse over the past few months.

"Okay, whatever." Bello started the engine and drove away. The gravel crunched beneath his tires.

Nikola shivered. It was a cool day and he was wearing only a T-shirt. He thought about his conversation with Roksana. She had told him that she was planning to organize the biggest party, a huge illegal club. He couldn't help it: he liked the idea. And Roksy had asked whether he could help out with the security. Maybe it wasn't such a stupid idea after all.

Then she had started talking about something completely different. "We're going to see a stand-up at the Globe."

"Why?" The only stand-up Nikola knew of was Seinfeld, who his mom watched sometimes.

"Because it'll be funny."

"What's his name?"

"It's not a man. *Her* name is Amy Schumer. She's been here before, and it was so good, like piss-your-pants funny. Billie, my friend, bought the tickets in February—it sold out in a couple of hours, you know. Anyway, one of our friends who was supposed to be coming has dropped out."

Roksana had kept talking about how funny this Schumer was,

and Nikola couldn't stop himself from wondering: Should he ask if he could tag along? She had said that someone else had dropped out—why would she say that if she didn't want Nikola to ask? But, at the same time: a golden rule—the first person to show their hand always risked being screwed over. If you told a girl you liked her and wanted to go home with her, you risked having a no thrown straight back in your face. Or, even worse: a laugh—like a slap to the face.

"Listen," he had said. "What're you doing with that spare ticket? Selling it online or what?"

Roksana had laughed. "You're not so smart, are you?"

Nikola felt his face burning.

She continued: "I've been going on about how good Amy Schumer is for five minutes now, all because I want you to ask if you can come along. Can't you do that?"

The black Volkswagen that pulled into the gravel pit ten minutes later looked dusty. Ordinarily, plainclothes officers drove Saabs or Volvos, but this must be Simon shitty Murray's private car. It was ugly, in any case.

Murray wound down the window. "You don't have a car?"

"Not my own. I got a lift."

"Do you want to talk in here," Murray asked, "or take a walk?"

"We'll talk out here," he said.

Simon Murray smelled faintly of sweat and cigarettes. Nikola hadn't thought that cops smoked—they were all so sporty. Murray had swapped his heart rate monitor for some kind of rubber wristband, which probably did the same thing as the Garmin had, but it was only a third of the size. The pig's boots were dirty and dusty, just like his worn-out old car. Nikola wondered whether he had come here to scope out the place in advance.

"Well, you wanted to meet," Simon said once they had walked a few feet away from the car.

Talking to a cop like this was dangerous, not something he could tell anyone. But Nikola needed answers. "Have you got anywhere with your investigation into my friend's murder?"

"Do you mean Chamon or Yusuf?"

"I mean Chamon. Why do you think someone clipped Yusuf? Have you found something?"

Simon's laugh was gentle. It sounded more like he was blowing air from his mouth.

"Okay, let's say this: if I tell you about the investigation into Chamon, I want something in return."

"What?"

"For you to tell me what you know about Yusuf's disappearance first."

The gray vibes of the gravel pit were reinforced by the rain clouds now rolling in across the sky. Nikola looked up at the piles of rock—he was in deep water now.

"Okay," he said. "For starters, we think another guy's disappeared, too. Fadi's his name."

"We already know that."

"But the big thing is that we think Yusuf was involved in Chamon's murder somehow."

Simon pissing Murray tilted his head, trying to look smart, as though he was thinking deeply or trying to work out whether Nikola was messing with him. "Come on, why would he have done that?"

Nikola played with the phone in his pocket.

"You gave Chamon's phones back to his dad," he said. "But you didn't know Chamon like I did. You might've analyzed his phones, but did you think about the fact that on one of them, Find My iPhone was installed, and that the app was linked to a different number?"

Simon didn't say anything. He just watched Nikola.

"*I knew* Chamon," Nikola continued. "I know he never used his phone like that."

"But that's exactly what he was doing," said Simon.

Nikola didn't understand a thing. "What are you talking about?"

"Maybe you did know your friend, but we've searched both Chamon's and Yusuf's places, and we found other phones that they talked on."

Nikola's head was spinning. His thoughts were bouncing around his skull like Super Mario.

"And both Chamon and Yusuf were scared, let me tell you," Murray continued. "So they'd installed those apps on their phones to keep track of one another. And to find one another if necessary."

Nikola could barely listen. This was crazy—if what Simon Murray was saying was true.

"Have you spoken to Isak?" Murray asked without turning to Nikola.

Nikola didn't reply. Their conversation was over. He needed to think. But Murray continued. "Because I saw the charges against him. I saw the investigation. It was the most robust case I'd seen in years. He would've been given at least three years for the financial crimes alone."

Nikola couldn't help but snap in response. "Lucky you aren't a lawyer, then."

They were standing fifteen feet from the car now.

Murray held out a hand. Nikola didn't take it.

Murray said: "Maybe we'll speak again. And say hello to your boss when you see him. Tell him he'll only get that lucky once. This isn't Mexico—he can't buy us off. Not yet, anyway."

In the car, as they were driving away, Bello was playing Adele at full volume. Nikola was fiddling with his phone again, but he couldn't drop what Murray had said. He was close to screaming, but he had to say something. He tried to overpower the music. "Man, it's incredible, you know."

"What's incredible?"

"That they let Isak go. Everyone said he was screwed, but they dropped the whole thing."

"Agree. Never heard of anything like it. Sometimes you just get lucky, I guess."

Bello clearly didn't want to talk about it, because he turned up the volume. Nikola looked out at the road. They were heading back to Södertälje; they had work to do. His friend floored the accelerator. New deals with Estonia, new security products for small business owners in town, new guys selling good times, new jobs for the identity hijackers. He didn't know how it had happened—but he was involved in most of it now.

Bello turned off at Sätra.

Nikola didn't know what was happening. "Where are you going?"

"I want to show you something," Bello said, turning off onto Björksätravägen.

The water tower was in the middle of the woods. Two hundred and eighteen steps. Nikola had been up there once before, when he was younger. Back then, they had simply cut the padlock on the metal door at the base and climbed to the top to smoke. These days, there didn't even seem to be a lock. The tower had to be at least 150 feet high, and he was out of breath by the time they got to the top. Bello was panting like he always had after PE lessons at school. The roof at the top was circular, clad with black roofing felt. Beneath it was more than two million gallons of water. All Nikola knew was that it was from here that water rushed toward Sätra, Skärholmen, Vårberg, and a ton of other places along the southern half of the red metro line. At the very edge of the ledge, there was some kind of metal framework, possibly an antenna or measurement device. He couldn't handle looking down to the ground; it made him dizzy. Bello kept even farther from the edge.

Nikola wondered what his friend wanted to show him. It felt strange that he hadn't said anything.

He felt a shove and turned around.

Bello was standing three feet away from him, holding a gun, pointing it at Nikola's chest.

"What the hell are you doing, man?" Nikola asked. He could hear the blood pounding in his own ears. "Put that down, Bello, what are you doing?"

"I'm keeping it here till you tell me what the fuck you're up to." He cocked the Sig Sauer.

"Come on, Bello, drop it."

"Tell me what you're up to first."

"Nothing."

"Who'd you meet at the gravel pit?"

"No one important."

"Motherfucker. I'm not stupid, Nicko. I didn't drive so far from the pit that I missed Simon Murray in the car going in the other direction."

The wind was blowing so hard that it whistled in his ears. Nikola was even colder than before.

"Bello, you don't understand . . ."

"Shut it. I'll put a bullet in your brain if you keep talking shit, or you can walk over the edge. I swear," said Bello.

Nikola tried to stand as still as he could and spoke as softly as possible. "Please, Bello, put the gun away."

"Tell me why you're meeting cops."

Nikola could feel the presence of the edge a foot behind him. He felt dizzy even though he wasn't looking down.

"Okay," he said. "I met Murray, I did. But not to squeal. I swear on my grandmother's grave, on my uncle's name. I haven't ratted on anyone."

"My *dachri,* you swear. But you met a pig in secret. Why?"

Nikola realized he was starting to breathe more quickly. He had to make an effort to speak calmly now, to keep the lightning at bay. He said: "I met him because I wanted to swap information. I wanted to know what they've got on Chamon's murder, on everything with Yusuf, so we can move on."

Bello glared at him. "But why're you getting the pig involved?"

"Because we aren't getting anywhere ourselves. And he told me some really shitty stuff."

"Like what?"

Nikola pulled out his phone. He had recorded his chat with the cop—he wanted everything Simon Murray said recorded.

He played the cop's voice.

When it was finished, Bello lowered the gun.

Nikola said: "This whole thing is so messed up. We've been hunting the wrong person. Yusuf and Chamon were using those tracking apps all the time. And it ended with us stabbing an innocent guy. Yusuf was innocent, Bello."

39

Emelie considered herself to be a rational, considerate person. Always had been. In many respects, she thought it was a positive trait. She assessed positives and negatives, analyzed situations before she acted; she could see herself from an outsider's perspective, and she tried to understand the reasons for her actions. She contemplated the world before she took it on. But maybe there was a better word to describe her, and that word was "indecisive." She had trouble making up her mind, drew out decisions rather than taking the leap and moving forward. She often spent far too long weighing different points of view, procrastinating until the opportunity had passed her by. Sometimes, she thought that her tendency to overthink things was her one great incompetence.

She had gone to the gynecology department at Söder Hospital the week before but changed her mind and not taken the pill. An indecisive act, a nondecision. Especially considering her last chance to have an abortion was in week eighteen, this week. After that point, the process required so-called special circumstances, according to the National Board of Health and Welfare's guidelines, and those only applied if, for example, it involved a very young girl who hadn't realized she was pregnant, or if tests had determined that there were severe complications with the baby. Emelie obviously didn't apply. It was now or never.

An abortion at this stage could still take place medically—she could take a pill under supervision at a medical center. She *had* to make a decision.

Emelie had stayed up half the night at Jossan's place, talking things over. She told Jossan she was pregnant. Josephine—her friend who had just gotten lip fillers and whose happy place was Chanel's new Stockholm boutique—was the best conversation partner she knew. The only one, in fact: she hadn't told anyone else, not her colleagues at the office, not Marcus, none of her old friends back in Jönköping. Not her mother and father.

"I have to do it tomorrow at the very latest," Emelie explained. Both she and Jossan had a glass of Sancerre in front of them.

"Because you should at least be able to smell the wine," Josephine had said. But then she asked: "What does the father say?"

"I don't know who the father is," Emelie had lied. They were sitting in Josephine's top spec kitchen.

"Do you remember two years ago, when I was dating a guy who worked at Lindhag Orre?" Jossan had asked.

"Yeah, the one who always wore a Hermès tie?"

"Exactly, and I'm glad you remember the ties, because those were one of the main reasons I thought he was so nice."

"Yeah, the purple one with the little horseshoes on it went so well with his green eyes."

"Precisely. But I never told you he got me pregnant, did I?"

Jossan took a sip of her wine. Outside, darkness was falling, though the night wasn't really closing in. Norr Mälarstrand at the end of May: the sky was a deep shade of blue, but the city lights were glittering on the water in the distance, the traffic creating a soft haze of color.

Emelie grabbed her glass and considered taking a sip. If she was going to have an abortion tomorrow, it made no difference. "No, you never told me that. What happened?"

"I wanted to keep the baby," said Jossan. "But he didn't. We went back and forth about it and couldn't come up with a solution. I was working like an idiot at the time, you know when EQT was selling Sourcefounder? I was sleeping at the office, Anders Henriks-son was, too, believe it or not. We used to brush our teeth next to one another in the bathroom on the ninth floor."

"No way. So what happened with the pregnancy?"

"I got rid of it."

Emelie clutched the glass she still hadn't drunk from. "I'm going to cry, and maybe I'll regret it. But I can't have this baby, either."

"All I can say is that I'll be here for you no matter what you decide." Jossan snorted. "The same way I'm always trying to get you to buy a proper handbag."

There was something comforting in the stupid comparison: Josephine never gave up on her. She was stubborn, and the thought that she would be as stubborn in her support for Emelie as she was about bags felt good. Irrepressible, somehow.

Emelie had been given her own room at the clinic, she had met the midwife, and now, in a small plastic dish on the table in front of her, she had the tablet. Mifegyne: the abortion pill. Josephine was sitting next to her, dressed for the day in workout pants, high-tech sneakers, and a thin white cashmere sweater.

Next to the dish was a plastic cup of water. All Emelie had to do was put the pill on her tongue, take a big sip of water, and swallow it down. Then she would have to stay for another hour, for observation.

She could do this. She sat down on the chair and stared at the pill in front of her. White, round, small. So small. But with such a huge potential impact.

She had tried to get ahold of Adam Tagrin again and was following the legal process against his son as closely as she could. She had met Jan to go through how she could find out more about the person Adam claimed had threatened Katja the night before the second interview was supposed to take place. Jan had been wearing workmen's pants and some kind of fishing or hunting jacket when they met. He didn't look quite right, but then again he rarely did.

"We could try checking the surveillance cameras at the metro station closest to Katja and Adam's apartment—it must be Örnsberg or Axelsberg—but I don't think they keep the films for very long, and it was a while ago now. Plus, we'll never get permission to view that kind of material."

"I have to try."

"We could also look for fingerprints or DNA, but I doubt we'll find anything so long afterward. The stairwell has probably been cleaned."

"Okay."

Jan had fiddled with his jacket. "Apart from that, I don't know."

"I understand."

She had tried to research Hallenbro Storgården. The estate was owned by a company registered in Malta. She had looked it up: Paradise Nordic Estates Ltd. She had requested as many documents as she could from the MFSA—the Malta Financial Services Authority. It was all very sparse: they either couldn't or wouldn't provide her with any documents relating to who was on the company's board. The only noteworthy thing she had spotted was that the company was owned by a holding company registered in Cyprus, Nordic Light Investment Group Ltd. She had read the meager documents forward and back. After a few hours, she had spotted it: on some of the contracts, there was a handful of small letters and numbers at the very bottom of the page. *324SAL*, it said. She had seen that kind of thing before, when she worked at Leijon—she was convinced it was part of a legal firm's documentation system. Many firms used something similar, in order to keep track of which versions and which items were which, and it had been particularly common a few years back. She had Googled like mad, talked to Jossan and some of her old colleagues from Leijon; she even called around a few of the large British and American firms, pretending she was still in the field. Eventually, she had gotten lucky: a British lawyer she had dealt with while she was at Leijon had recognized the code. SAL: it was a Panama-based firm called Suarrez Augustin

Landman. Emelie had skimmed through their home page: it was perfectly clear what they were up to—Mossack Fonseca looked like a kindergarten in comparison.

Teddy had been calling her from different numbers roughly every other day. For the most part, she had rejected his calls, but when she did answer, the first thing he always did was to ask how she was doing and how she felt. She didn't have any answers for him. But he wouldn't make her change her mind; she had made her decision.

Jossan was holding her hand. The bowl where the abortion pill had been was empty. Emelie had put it in her mouth. The midwife was sitting on a chair in one corner of the room. There was plenty to be said about how health care in Sweden had changed over recent years, but at this particular clinic at least, the level of care didn't seem to have gone down—it was high.

The nurse had explained: "The Mifegyne pill has to be taken under supervision, because that's the moment you're carrying out the abortion, so to speak. But it'll be a while before you feel anything."

"How long?"

"It depends. Some women don't feel anything, but if it is painful, just lie down and get some rest, turn off your phone, and try to relax."

She couldn't feel a thing.

Josephine's nails were neat and manicured.

Emelie was sitting on the bed, but she didn't turn off her phone. For some reason, she wanted to keep it on, not that she knew who might call.

40

How did you go about organizing an enormous club in three weeks? How did you arrange Stockholm's sweetest party, something that would crush Summerburst and make Coachella and Burning Man look like end-of-the-year plays—in just three weeks? A party that had to bring in at least eight hundred thousand kronor in profit. There was only one person who could pull off something like that. And that crazy, happy, overenergetic person had a weird, cool name: Z.

Z was a genius. A brilliant madman who wouldn't take no for an answer. An Energizer Bunny with an extra charger pack, a manic upward entrepreneur, a doer with no equal.

Three weeks: they didn't smoke, they skipped the Kit Kat, drank only coffee and vitamin juice with added ginger and açai boost. They slept five hours a night, spent the rest of their time cooking ket and eating Sunee's best noodles as they worked. They bounced names back and forth. The start date was pinned to June 6: Sweden's fuuuucking national day, three days of partying in all. Should the name have something to do with that? National Day? They trawled the Net, talked to Billie, considered smoking a joint just to find inspiration. Eventually, Roksana had come up with a suggestion: "Our Land Club—The Isaawi Experience." Z loved it. Especially the subtitle, an homage to the ranch owner who had sent enough horse tranquilizer to knock out half of Sweden.

But how would they manage to book the big DJs? Even though Roksana had enjoyed her fifteen minutes of drug fame, the agents and managers were still impenetrable; they did their jobs: acted like firewalls for the stars. The people Roksana and Z wanted to book were impossible to get ahold of; the only contact details they could find went straight to representatives and intermediaries.

Despite that, they didn't give in. Roksana ignored the middle-men: she sent a message straight to DJ Ora Flesh—they had prac-tically been friends, after all. The model/DJ seemed like she was about to cream herself when Roksana got in touch; she could see it from the emojis in her reply. They met two days later at Berns, ordered a couple of glasses of cava, chatted about the latest Skril-lex video and about Our Land Club, of course. There was noth-ing wrong with Ora Flesh, even if Roksana had forgotten her real name. She was nice, her finger firmly on the hottest music, the lat-est opinions, and she had a new reaper man tattooed on her neck in a naivist style. Above all, she was hotter than hot, plus she was with that supercool photographer. But it was like there was something missing all the same. She never said anything surprising. Roksana knew which word she was looking for: authenticity—Ora Flesh lacked authenticity. In any case, she was going to ask. "I know you DJs all know one another," Roksana began.

"Yeah, but I know only the best."

"Exactly. I couldn't get some of their private phone numbers, could I? Thought that some of them might want to play at my three-day club."

DJ Ora Flesh looked disappointed: she was probably wonder-ing why Roksana hadn't asked her.

Roksana added: "And obviously I really want you to play, too."

It wasn't easy to get ahold of hyper-famous DJ people: time differences and upside-down routines. Ibiza and LA time. But with Ora Flesh's name on the list, everything was easier. Roksana man-aged to get ahold of six of the biggest names on the electro scene. She set out the deal in plain terms for each of them: "We don't have much money to offer you, it's short notice, and we know you're the biggest name on the scene, but we had another idea." The DJs listened closely. "You'll get a royalty from the tickets, but that's not all, you can also have ten percent of all royalties going forward. From the name, from future clubs, gigs, everything."

They thought she was crazy, and yet two of them accepted her offer all the same, canceling other gigs to be there. Choosing to come to Estocolmo for *The Isaawi Experience*.

"You're the best," Z shouted when he heard the two names she had managed to bag.

Z had found two students from some art school no one had heard of and promised them the world and a gallery contract if they could handle the decor. They thought he was a talent scout for some huge American player, somewhere like the Gagosian Gallery in NYC. He borrowed an industrial building in Haninge where the two budding artists could go wild and show off their work; the guy who owned the building didn't want any rent; he was happy to take twenty grams instead. Their art project caused a stir in the traditional media: both *Expressen* and *Dagens Nyheter* wrote about the three-day party. "What does *The Isaawi Experience* mean?" the journalists mused. "It's to do with my Iranian roots," Z said, glancing at Roksana. They had laughed nonstop for an hour afterward.

Z had also chatted up one of Billie's girls—she worked as a social media consultant for some PR firm and had agreed to set up a private campaign for their party for very little money. Still: it would cost more than they could afford. Z took out an instant loan of two hundred thousand kronor so that they could pay for the web design and the advance fee for the sound system and other equipment. Roksana asked her father for a loan again, but he continued to hold out. Instead, she borrowed from Bank Norwegian and quickloan.se. The interest rates were crazy, but she was counting on being able to pay off the debt in just a few weeks' time. Z set up an Instagram account and a YouTube channel, where he uploaded pictures and films of himself dancing and telling insane in-jokes about various open-air parties in Sweden. The PR consultant optimized their searchability, meaning that their streams were visible to anyone interested in the same music as him, and making them pop up in the top ten whenever anyone searched *club Stockholm* or *summer Stockholm*. DJ Aziz and Sandra Mosh repped them and gave them mentions. By the end of that week, there wasn't a hipster south of Västerbron who didn't know about their club. But best of all: Ora Flesh raised Our Land Club to the heavens with three posts in a row. She had 1.2 million followers—after ten days, the Our Land Club account had more than seventy thousand of its own.

They booked men to build the two stages, which luckily didn't need to be all that big—they weren't exactly having live bands. They arranged for helium canisters and more than two thousand balloons, beer barrels, bars and bar staff, special rubber wristbands for people who had paid entry for all three days. They hired people to look after the entry, lighting, and laser shows. Roksana called Nikola and tried to organize the security.

"I'll be bringing a guy called Bello," he said.

"That's definitely not enough. This isn't some shitty little party. We're going for three days, in a huge space. And you'll get paid."

"I just need to check."

"Who do you have to check with?"

"Can't go into that."

"Are you still coming to Amy Schumer? You don't need to check with anyone about that, do you?"

But what about the venue? Where would they be? Roksana had solved that riddle, too: "Why don't we use the place where Dusky was, in Ulvsunda industrial area?"

Z looked at her with his red, sleep-starved eyes. "You might be the best person I've ever met. Can I call you Edward Snowden?"

They sent in applications for a license to serve alcohol, unsure whether they would be approved—they really were cutting it close.

"We'll do it anyway," Z decided. "We just need to make eight hundred thousand, then the rest doesn't matter."

Eight hundred thousand kronor: easy as pie. Roksana loved that Z was so relaxed, despite the fact that his fingers were still crooked.

The only time Roksana did anything not connected to their planning during those three weeks was when she went to see Amy Schumer at the Globe Arena. And the cool thing was that Nikola went with her. Billie and the others stared at him like he was a chimpanzee at the zoo, but there was also something else in their eyes: worry, possibly even fear. Respect, too. Roksana had brought a guy who was genuinely from the 'burbs, who was authentic.

The Globe was completely packed. Schumer hollered gags from the stage. Roksana laughed so hard that her stomach ached.

Billie was about to fall off her seat. People were crying with laughter all around them. Roksana kept casting side glances at Nikola—he looked stiffer than a Christian Democrat at a leather-bear club.

"Last time she was here, some guy in the audience shouted 'Show us your tits!'" Roksana said.

Nikola turned to her. "What happened then?"

"Amy replied: 'That was cute, but now you're going to be saying that to the people in the parking lot,' and two guards came in and escorted the guy out. Everyone cheered."

Nikola leaned in to Roksana, as though he didn't want anyone around them to hear. "You don't think it was planned?"

Roksana had no idea, and she didn't care. "Don't you like her?"

"She stands up for who she is. I like that."

Roksana changed the topic. "Did you check how many you can get for the Our Land Club security?"

"It's gonna be fine. But this is a onetime thing, me doing this," said Nikola. "Just so you know."

Roksana felt a double warmth in her body. Maybe the club thing would work out. Maybe they would manage to get the money together. Plus: she would get to hang out with Nikola again. For three whole days.

Finally, the day arrived. June 6. The Natio-anal Day, as Z called it. The starting shot. Roksana climbed up onto one of the stages and looked out at the old industrial building. It was insanely impressive. In just a few hours, it would all begin.

More than eight hundred tickets had been bought in advance, for five hundred kronor apiece. But they had huge overheads, too: wages, staging, the sound system. They would need to sell at least double that, plus a serious amount of K, just to break even. Not to mention what they needed to sell to cover their debt with the psychos.

Billie was beaming when she arrived with her six-foot-tall images of various vaginas that she would be setting up as an installation in one of the party rooms—they had promised her that in exchange for all her help. "I'm thinking this could be the breakthrough we've been waiting for in the pussy guerrillas."

Roksana and Z had worked for twenty-two hours of the past twenty-four. Organizing entry, setting up bars, mediating between the two art students who had fallen out over their different views on the symbolic meaning of neon colors in shaman culture.

She called her father.

"How are you, Roksana *joonam*?"

"I'm really good. Z and I have organized a huge party."

"What's that? A party? What party?"

"A music festival, I guess you could call it. We've invited some DJs to play."

"That sounds nice. But are you also finding time for your studies?"

Roksana sighed. "Dad, I've been working on this day and night for the past few weeks."

"On a music festival?"

"Yes, Baba. Organizing it so people can play and listen to *music*. Music, Dad, that's good, isn't it?"

He started talking about Roksana's trip to Tehran again, but she thought that he sounded happy. What about her? Was she happy? Yes, she definitely felt *very* exhilarated and *very* happy—there was just a tiny hint of worry there, too. Would they manage to make enough money? They were putting everything on the line right now.

Their three-day party was finally under way. DJ John Hudson kicked things off on the big stage, with more than five hundred people dancing like they had never done anything else. You could hear the bass line right over in Södermalm. On the small stage, DJ Asian Girl was playing. It was hysterical—she had announced that she was releasing two new songs in honor of the club, and that had gone through Stockholm like lightning. After just a few short hours, anyone who hadn't heard of Our Land Club before, now knew all about it. The line was snaking back practically all the way to Bromma Airport. Song after song, gig after gig. DJ after DJ. Tunes pumped out through the old turbine halls like two hearts pumping blood through the body. The cops came by and wondered what the hell they were doing, but Roksana waved the alcohol license they had been granted at the last minute in their faces—the police smiled then and congratulated her.

They kept going until 3 a.m. the first night: they didn't want to overstep their license. They managed to sell more than three hundred thousand kronor worth of K.

Day two was the same, only better, with even more people. Even more people on a K high. Even more banknotes in the huge Nike bag one of Nikola's guys was watching over.

Day three was a haze. Roksana hadn't slept a wink. She was running around fixing things the whole time, selling Special K—the one thing she regretted was not getting a chance to talk to Nikola. The weather was so warm that people were talking about a tropical night. More than three thousand people turned up that day, and the money was flooding in faster than into the Minecraft inventor's account. The music washed over them, embraced them, took them on a deep journey. People weren't going home. They were drinking energy drinks and getting half an hour's sleep to recharge their batteries behind the closed outlet shops. People were breathing the helium from the balloons, drinking beer, and taking Kit Kat like it was food. They danced until seven thirty in the morning. It was a blast. The club of the century. It wasn't a success—it was a phenomenon.

At eight in the morning, Z pulled the plug on the amplifiers. The DJs staggered down from their booths. The handymen turned up and started taking the stages apart—they had probably slept like normal people last night. There were still people everywhere, both outside and in the two halls.

Roksana, Z, and Nikola were standing by the entrance, breathing the fresh air and chatting. Eyes narrow with tiredness. She weighed the duffel bag in her hands. "I'm glad we took only cash. It'll make things easier for us. Want to guess how much we've got in here?"

Z grinned. "Over two mill, I reckon."

Nikola looked happy, despite the fact he had barely slept for three days. "I'll say three."

Roksana took his hand. Nikola squeezed it back: his palm was warm and dry. Z smiled; Roksana could see from his face that he understood.

"What're you two doing now?" he asked.

She squeezed Nikola's hand harder. He did the same. She whispered to him: "Shall we show our tits to one another?"

Then she saw something she really didn't want to see. Three police cars pulling up on the gravel out front. Nine officers opening the doors and striding toward them.

"Oh shit," Z groaned.

"Run," Nikola hissed.

Roksana ran. She ran with everything she had. Over the gravel. Toward the road. Nikola was beside her, Z somewhere behind them. She was panting. Her feet ached. Her chest burned. She was clutching the bag as tightly as she could. It swung against her side. So long as they hadn't had any plainclothes officers in there to see how much ketamine they had sold . . . Please, God.

She thought about throwing the bag behind a building, but the police officers were too close behind her. She could see them out of the corner of one eye: huge, with their chunky boots and jingling belts.

She thought about her father's voice when she told him she had organized a music festival: somehow, it had contained a note she had never heard before. Some kind of surprised hope. She could hear her grandmother's words: "You can be whatever you want to be. He could, too."

Roksana *had thought* she could do what she wanted—she was an idiot.

She glanced back. Saw the flushed officer's face sneering at her. He shouted: "Stop."

The morning light felt too bright. The sun too warm.

She could see the water's edge up ahead. Huvudsta on the other side.

She wouldn't be able to make it much farther. She needed rest. Sleep.

The police officer threw himself at her.

Roksana stumbled. Tried to break her fall, scraping both knees in the process. Her chin hit the gravel and rocks.

At least five kilos of ket: how many years would that be? Z had once mentioned four years. The officer pulled her hand behind her back. She dropped the bag.

Four years in prison?

"I'm arresting you on suspicion of illegal alcohol sales," the cop panted.

Roksana almost started to laugh, she couldn't believe it was true—so they *weren't* suspected of dealing. What a joke. What a triumph. There was nothing to be afraid of.

She got up; the officer no longer seemed as gruff as she had first thought.

She smiled.

"I'll take that," the officer said, taking the bag of money from her hand.

Roksana started to cry.

She was so tired.

41

The pigs had arrested the person they thought was Teddy but who was, in fact, Dejan. Kum's stomach had quivered with laughter as he and Teddy walked away. "Those idiots," he said. "They'll have to release him within thirty-six hours. Those are the rules."

Teddy hadn't been laughing. "I thought I'd met the world's first honorable cop. But I guess I was wrong."

"I think you need to try Restylane. I can help you with that. And this isn't some homo thing, I swear."

After half a day at the clinic in Östermalm—which, according to Kum, his wife frequented more often than she went to the gym—Teddy had looked like a new man. Mazern tried to explain it, sounding like a nutty professor: "They inject this gel beneath your skin with the thinnest needle I've ever seen, it gives you volume and smooths out fine lines and wrinkles. Then I think we should emphasize your chin and get rid of your nose-to-mouth lines."

"Nose-to-mouth lines?"

"You'll see," Kum had said.

It didn't matter. The doctor had given him a local anesthetic. Teddy's face went numb, disappeared: he wished he could stay in that state. When he looked in the mirror afterward, he didn't just look ten years younger—he didn't look like *himself*. It was another face staring back at him. Fresher, happier. And they had removed all the hair on his head, too. He was as smooth as a baby's bottom. His scalp was glistening—and his beard looked even longer than before.

Kum had opened the door and stepped into the room. "Dejan told me you were living like a *pas* these past few weeks."

"I've been living in a Fiat," said Teddy.

"That's not over yet," Kum had replied. "Just because you look different, you can't go back home or show your face in town like normal. You're still wanted for murder, my man."

"I know."

"But now you look like a cross between a bald Viggo Mortensen and a Ryan Gosling with cancer. It'll make your life easier."

Teddy knew the godfather was right.

Two days later, Dejan had been released.

"They had plenty of questions about you, let me tell you," he said when they met by a clump of trees in Skärholmen. "But I didn't say shit. Kept my mouth shut and breathed through my nose like you're meant to."

"Thanks for all your help."

The Mauler nuzzled Dejan's leg.

"Kum's done a good job on you, I have to say. Did I mention that you look like a mix of a bald Mads Mikkelsen and if Ben Mendelsohn had survived a nuclear war?"

"Hopefully it'll make my life a bit easier."

"But you're still in the shit."

"Yeah, I don't need you to tell me that. They'll arrest me eventually, and I'll be sent down for a murder I didn't commit."

"That's probably true, sadly. Because they'll never believe it if you tell them that the dude out there was shot by a pig. That's not in their worldview."

The Mauler had been running free, sniffing at old trunks. Teddy studied the dark trees. He knew Dejan was right. "So the only way is to find out who the cop at the estate was, if he even was a cop," he said. "Otherwise, I'm screwed."

Dejan's eyelids had drooped. "Yeah, otherwise you're screwed."

The next day, Teddy had stepped into the garage where he had gone with Dejan a few months earlier. The same signs above the entrance ramp: *Car Wash, Reconditioning—Central and South Stockholm*. The same smell of exhaust fumes and cleaning products. Teddy had a plan. It was as crazy as it was simple.

The Arab who ran the place seemed to still be there, though Teddy had barely recognized Abdel Kadir—the man he knew as the Beard Man had shaved it all off. Teddy wanted to know whether his *other* business was still being run out of the garage. The concrete floor, the Ditec signs with pictures of maintenance products, equipment, wax, and polish had, at least, been the same.

Abdel came toward Teddy: rolled-up sleeves and flecks of oil on his hands. Acne scars and an old harelip now visible on his smooth face. "Maestro, how can I help you?"

The guy hadn't been wearing his crocheted cap, and his tattoos were also visible. Teddy had scanned for signs: was he an ordinary mechanic with trendy tattoos, or were the images and words on his powerful forearms authentic? Arabic letters, symbols, a skull. And among those, the usual cursive script: *Mamma tried*.

"We met about six months ago, I was here with Dejan, the little Serb," Teddy had said.

Abdel's face showed even less expression than Teddy's had after his cosmetic treatment a few days earlier. Maybe he didn't recognize Teddy—that was the point, after all—or maybe he was just playing.

"I don't know who you're talking about."

"Yeah, he wanted to buy your other business because you were leaving, you said."

Abdel Kadir looked boyish without his facial hair, but his voice was surprisingly deep. "Aha," he had said. "*That* little Serb. I know who you're talking about now. But I'm not going away anymore. I'm not doing that shit anymore."

"Have you sold the business?"

The man's upper lip looked almost unnaturally bent. "No, no. We're definitely still doing *that* shit."

Teddy had pointed to the curtain in the office. "Good, because I need something special. I need a police ID."

The next day, Loke had faked a phone number from a local police station in northern Sweden and had called to register Teddy's new cop alter ego. They had cooked up a story about his visit being part of a wider investigation with links to Stockholm; Loke had given them case numbers and the names of other police officers. The secretary at police HQ didn't care: as long as the number displayed on the phone came from another station in Sweden, all was cool.

Today, Teddy was here: outside the Swedish Police Force's headquarters—their enormous fortress in Kungsholmen. The protruding roof was shielding him from the sun. This was where Katja and Emelie had come for Katja's interview, he knew that much. He strode through the tall, revolving glass doors and stepped into reception. There were a number of smartly dressed men and women, who he assumed were lawyers or prosecutors, chatting in small groups. They were probably waiting to be taken to interviews or run-throughs of various cases. He could see other people coming and going through the security barriers in the distance: people in jeans and chinos, wearing sneakers or military boots. They were cops: guaranteed.

Teddy walked over to reception. The guard behind the Plexiglas gave him a weary look. Teddy wondered how it must feel to spend every day dreaming of being a real officer but having to sit here keeping watch in a pretend uniform instead. He pushed his fake ID through the gap. "I should be registered."

His heart was racing like a small bird's. He was wanted on a national level—and now he was heading into a building containing more officers than anywhere else in Sweden. The reception guard said something in too broad a southern accent for Teddy to grasp, but he nodded as he did it.

Teddy was buzzed through the security barriers—again a revolving door, this time controlled by the guard. He was inside now. This was insane. He felt the USB stick in his pocket, the one Loke had given him.

He started walking: cops everywhere. Old men with glasses and checked shirts, probably the ones who had investigated Teddy and his friends back in the day. Muscular women with ponytails, in exercise pants, and T-shirts with sports logos. Middle-aged guys with tattoos, beards, and ungainly gaits. Teddy hadn't thought he would still be thinking like this, but the feeling bearing down on him was clear: *I'm in enemy territory. I'm a parachute trooper who's jumped straight into the lion's den.*

Loke had said it was simple: "You just need to go into a room where there's a computer, any will do, and push this USB stick in. I'll look after the rest remotely."

Teddy kept moving, walking with his eyes fixed straight ahead, trying not to glance around, deliberate, as though he knew exactly where he was heading. The stream of pigs around him was never ending; he was like a fish in a school of sharks.

In the distance, he could see a couple of escalators. He took one down and found himself on the lower floor of the new building— the complex was enormous. There was a row of retro police motorbikes on display, and the ceiling had to be at least thirty feet high. To the left was the staff cafeteria, where a hundred or more cops were eating lunch, drinking coffee, and chatting—like they were completely ordinary people. There was no denying it was fascinating. To the right were three Ping-Pong tables, which felt out of place in the grand inner hall, but the cops playing on them seemed enthusiastic. They shouted and cheered between rallies, as though in the park. Teddy felt like wiping the floor with all of them—if you had spent as long inside as he had, you became a pro at table tennis.

Ahead of him was another set of glass doors. He didn't have to open them himself; the policewoman in front held them for him: polite and kind. He went out into the inner courtyard. It was a glorious day, and there were even more people sitting out here, with cups of coffee and bottles of juice in their hands. Teddy walked straight ahead. He thought about all the cops he had met. The ones who had arrested him after the kidnapping of Mats. The ones who had escorted him to court for his remand hearing, the ones who had interrogated him afterward. All the local police, county police, special anti-gang officers who had watched him like hawks over the years. He would guess that he had met more representatives of the police force than any other profession. So why was he taking the risk that one of all these officers might recognize him here? It was easy: if he didn't manage to prove his innocence, he would be sentenced to life in prison for murder. And the evidence had to be here somewhere, on their computer system.

He hoped that his new appearance, his shaved head and smoothed wrinkles, would be enough to camouflage him. And, above all: *no one* expected to see an old criminal wandering about in a police stronghold.

He opened the doors on the other side of the courtyard and stepped into the older building. This part of the station looked different: from the early twentieth century, all corridors and conduits. Walkways and small rooms. There were tall panels on the walls, and lights that looked at least a hundred years old hanging from the ceiling. He walked slowly, making sure that everyone passed him by, that he was always last. He searched for open doors, empty rooms.

He couldn't help but think about what Isa from the employment service would say if she could see him now, how he would try to explain his situation. At some point, all this had just started, and he hadn't been able to stop it. He wondered what the first domino had been, how it had all begun. In the third grade at school, people had been absolutely crazy about erasers. The girls had wanted pink ones that smelled like strawberry, the nerds had wanted big white ones with images from *Star Wars* and *Indiana Jones* on them, and Dejan and Teddy had wanted the ordinary green school erasers—the ones with a red line through the middle—but only so that they could cut them up and use them as ammunition in their slingshots. They used to go up to the teacher at least once a day to say that they had lost theirs, that they needed a new one. But it wasn't enough: they had needed more, many more. One day, while everyone else was outside during recess, Teddy had snuck back into their classroom. Their teacher usually locked the door, but clearly not on that day. He knew where she kept the key to her wheeled cabinet. The sun was shining obliquely through the windows, making the dust glitter in the air. He had never done anything like it before, but he lifted the lid of the desk and took out the key, then used it to unlock the cabinet. There it was, inside: the holy grail. The teacher's unopened box of erasers. *The lost ark*. He had snatched the box and run down the steps. The next evening, his father had called him over. "Najdan, come here." Teddy had gone into the kitchen and found his father standing by the table, as though he were waiting for Teddy to sit down first. But neither had time to sit. Instead, his father had hit him with the back of his hand. White dots filled Teddy's field of vision, and his cheek had stung as though he had burned it. His father was holding the as-yet-unopened box of erasers. "No one who goes by the name Maksumic is a thief." His Serbian was crystal clear. "If I find out you've been stealing again, my hand won't be open." That had been the *first* time. Since then, his father had had to clench his fist on many other occasions. Eventually, many years later, Teddy had even stolen a person. Kidnapped another man. Now he was suspected of murder.

There: an open door. Teddy craned his neck, tried to peer in. He strolled toward it as casually as possible. The room was large, the tables set out in a horseshoe. At the very back, there was a whiteboard and some office equipment. It looked like some kind of seminar had been going on in there, and the participants were taking a break. He stepped inside and pushed the door closed behind him.

The air was stuffy and smelled like people. He went over to the lectern—there was a desktop computer there. He checked the back: a USB port. Loke had shown him what to look for. He pushed the little plastic stick into the slot and turned around to leave.

He tried to keep calm, to keep walking. The stream of cops was still dense. Did they just walk around these buildings all day? Maybe they were doing one of those step-counting challenges.

He opened the glass doors to the inner yard. Slightly fewer coffee drinkers now; lunch must be over. He passed the old motorbikes and the Ping-Pong tables. The escalator was moving slowly, as though it was set to half speed, and he had to force himself not to rush up it.

Teddy thought about his sporadic calls to Emelie. He wondered what she was up to right now.

The walls were covered in old police posters.

For the first time in a long while, he felt a real sense of exhilaration—he had managed to get Loke's trojan into the system. He kept moving forward. Stairs and side passages. Clusters of sofas and enormous potted plants. Huge windows and hundreds of cops.

He could see the security doors ahead of him. Just thirty seconds more, and he would be out. Mission accomplished. It felt unbelievably good.

But then he heard a voice. "Teddy? Teddy Maksumic?"

It couldn't be.

Shit.

He didn't know who had said his name, but someone had recognized him.

Teddy kept walking toward the exit as if he hadn't heard. It shouldn't be possible to recognize him, that was the whole point of all the Restylane treatments. But the police officer was shouting after him now. "Teddy, stop!"

He picked up the pace, didn't turn around, just jogged forward. The doors were about a hundred feet away.

The police officer raised his voice again. Shouting to his colleagues this time. "Stop that man, he's wanted!"

Teddy had broken into a run. He was charging now.

He threw himself forward as police officers all around him hurled themselves at him like American football players.

He avoided them. Zigzagged between them.

The doors were so close now.

Then he tripped, stumbled.

He was chewing police station floor.

The cops threw themselves onto him. Pulled him down to the ground, jammed their wide knees into his back.

The police officer who had recognized him came over and looked down at him. "Cuff him."

Teddy said: "I want my lawyer."

"We can arrange that later." The police officer bent down to help one of his cop colleagues.

"No," Teddy groaned. "I'm not going to open my mouth again before my lawyer's here. And there's one in particular I want."

"Who?"

"Call Emelie Jansson."

42

The Body Academy. It smelled like disinfectant and Dior Homme. The walls were a shade of white you never saw in ordinary apartments, a ghostly glow. The skin therapists—as they called themselves— with their smooth foreheads and Japanese face masks, drifted around like they were floating on clouds.

Mr. One was lying with his face through some kind of hole in the bed. It was necessary, so that the customer could breathe while they had their massage—or, in this case: while they had their back and shoulders waxed.

"Just because you're more ape than human doesn't mean you have to look like one," Isak had shouted when Nikola came in.

Couldn't he have waited twenty minutes to ask me to come in, Nikola thought. This was intrusive. Plus: he had never been so tired in his life. The three-day party had been one of the most fun and exhausting things he had ever done—in fact, he had even felt happy for the first time since Chamon died. But then the cops had stormed the industrial area and arrested Roksana. He had managed to get away, along the water's edge, and had just heard the cops' shouts behind him.

Nikola had called to ask what she was suspected of, whether they were planning to release her, but they just referred to the confidentiality of the preliminary investigation, like the losers that they were. So, really, he had other things on his mind—but if

Mr. One wanted a meeting, you came, regardless of whether the boss was flat out on a massage bed, waiting for a ghost therapist to tear off a coat of fur thicker than a real gorilla's.

"Tell me what's going on," Isak mumbled. Since his face was turned to the floor, Nikola could barely hear what he was saying.

He glanced at the therapist: she was applying the hot wax with some kind of brush.

"You mean the club we were doing security for, or all the rest?"

"I don't give a shit about the club," Isak said without looking up.

The therapist carefully placed strips of papery material onto the thin layer of wax. Nikola's back started to ache from bending down to hear what Isak said.

"Nicko, tell me what you're up to, you and the boys. You looking after everything?"

Nikola wondered what he was getting at.

"You talk to Bello, don't you?"

"I talk to all of you. But I want to hear *you* tell me what you're doing."

Nikola wondered whether Bello had mentioned something about his chat with the cop, but he doubted it. They had agreed to forget that business up on the water tower. Instead, Nikola went through the various tasks and jobs he was doing for Isak: the exchange offices he visited, the sellers he gave jobs, the boxes of explosives they were topping up.

"Okay, and what else?" the boss said once he was done.

Again, Nikola wondered what Bello had told Mr. One.

"Nothing else."

"Mm-hmm. And you're not snooping about in that Chamon stuff anymore?"

Nikola now realized how nice it was to talk to Mr. One without seeing his face. "Nah, I've dropped it, just like you said."

The therapist took hold of one of the strips and tore it off.

"Ay!" A red mark appeared on Isak's back in its place. "Take it easy," he hissed. "Nikola, you see that bag over there?"

There was a small black fanny pack at the end of the bed.

"In the outer pocket, there's a phone. Get rid of it somewhere, in a lake or something. There's so much shit going on right now, we've gotta be extra careful."

Nikola got up and went over to the other end of the massage bed. He heard Isak cry out as the therapist tore away another wax strip. The bag was larger than he had expected, and he started rifling through it. He weighed the phone in his hand.

"Thanks, you can go now." Mr. One's voice sounded shrill, pained. Nikola had never heard him like that before, had never heard him suffer, but somehow it made a part of him feel good.

He met up with Bello: they had work to do. Nikola was like a pack donkey—Mr. One kept loading him up like an animal when all he really needed was to sleep.

He called his mother.

"It's been a while. Have you heard what happened?"

"No."

"They're accusing Teddy of murder."

"What, really?"

"Yeah, it's so awful."

"But you don't believe he did it?"

"I don't know. All I can say is that he seems to be right back at square one. We're so disappointed."

Nikola had heard those words before: throughout his entire childhood. Mom and Grandpa—disappointed in Teddy, unhappy with Teddy, ashamed to have a brother and a son who had done what he'd done and been convicted like he had. But to Nikola, Teddy had only ever been one thing: a hero, even if he had kidnapped a man. Nikola knew he should try to get ahold of him— but things had gone wrong last time they met. As though Teddy had been above Nikola, looking down on him; as though Teddy's choice of life was suddenly better than Nikola's. But now his uncle was prize game—he really should call.

"Listen, love," said his mother. "I know not everything went like we planned."

"What are you talking about?"

"Well, you're refusing to go back to George Samuel, and you're not going to get any grades from college, either, are you?"

"Come on, my best friend was murdered."

"I know, I know it's hard. But listen, Nicko, it's for your own sake. You have to stop doing what you're doing."

He couldn't deal with any more of this. He ended the call.

Bello quickly turned to him. "That your mom?"

"Yes."

"Problems?"

"Yes."

"Is she disappointed?"

"Yes."

"They always are."

"Yeah, I know."

"She thinks you've gone crazy?"

"Yes."

"What's she going to do about it, then?"

"Nothing. She's the one who's gone crazy."

"Aha."

"Can we swing by some water somewhere? I've got something I need to chuck."

"Isak give you a phone?" Bello asked.

"How'd you know that?"

"He switches up a lot, so he usually asks me to chuck his old ones into the telephone graveyard. That's what I call the bottom of the lake by Saltskog. Though he usually wants me to keep the phone for a few days before I dump it—so it's my movements that get tracked by the masts, not his. That way, if everything goes to shit afterward, he can always show that he's been in other places than he actually has, or that the phone has been different places to him. It's his alibi."

Isak: Nikola thought about the boss. He might be the smartest guy he knew.

"The telephone graveyard," Nikola said. "Can you show me exactly where that is?"

43

Emelie was still sitting on the bed. Her cell phone was still beside her. She couldn't feel a thing—though the mental strain of just being here was surprisingly tough.

"How do you feel?" asked the midwife.

"Fine, so far."

"Then I think you can go home in half an hour or so. Would you like us to call you a taxi?"

"No, it's okay."

"I also wanted to tell you about the counseling service that's available, but we can do that before you leave."

The midwife went out, the door closed. Jossan poured a glass of water and gave Emelie a pitying look as she held it out to her. Emelie shook her head.

Jossan said: "Should I call a taxi?"

Emelie shook her head again. "Wait a while."

"It's done now," said Josephine. "You've reached the point of no return. I think that can feel good, in a way."

Before Emelie had time to say anything, her phone started to ring. To begin with, she wasn't going to answer—it didn't feel like the right place to be talking on the phone—but there was something about the number, she recognized it. The Police Authority was trying to get in touch.

"Hi, my name is Elisabeth Carlberg and I'm calling from the National Operations Department."

"What is this regarding?"

"We have a person in custody who has requested you as his public defender."

"Aha. In that case, I'll have to refer you to my deputy. I'm afraid I can't take on any new cases at the moment."

"The suspect said you would say that, but he insisted that we called you."

"What's his name?"

"Najdan Maksumic, but he seems to go by Teddy."

Emelie was close to ending the call there and then. Jossan was watching her with one eyebrow raised, wondering why she was sitting in silence, breathing.

"Hold on . . . ," Emelie said to the officer on the other end of the line. She had to process this information: they had arrested Teddy, and that meant he would likely be convicted of murder. Emelie knew he hadn't done what they claimed, but he would still be locked up, and this time he wouldn't get out alive. He would rot away in there. He would never get the chance to live a normal life, to live a life with anyone else. The thought echoed through her mind—because she also felt that it made *her* life meaningless somehow. Everything she had ever striven for would come to an end, like a deflated balloon that left behind nothing but a limp pile of rubber on the floor. At the same time, every action, every decision she now made was extremely important, every moment so dear. She had to see him. There were certain things she needed to say to Teddy.

She placed a hand on her stomach and then replied to the policewoman. "I'll take the case. You can send the decree straight to me. Where is he being held?"

Josephine got up, and for a brief moment, Emelie thought she was trying to block the exit. "What's going on, Emelie?" Jossan asked, taking her hand instead—the feeling that she was trying to block Emelie's way vanished.

Emelie opened her hand. In it was the abortion pill she had spat out minutes after taking it. "I'm going to keep the baby. And now I have to get to work."

Hanging from the rearview mirror of the taxi, Emelie noticed a small brass disc with Arabic text on it. "Is that a profession of faith?" she asked.

The driver reminded her of Naz in *The Night Of.* "Yes, the Islamic profession of faith. *Shahada,* we call it in Arabic."

"Does it help if you read it to someone who's neither a Muslim nor believes in God?"

The driver glanced at her in the mirror. "I don't know."

It didn't take long to get down to the cells. The visitor's room was cold, all concrete and plastic, and the air smelled of stale sweat. Teddy was covered in bruises, and he looked different. There were red marks on his cheeks, and one of his ears was bandaged.

"You still have your bump," was the first thing he said once the guard closed the door.

"Yes, but we can't talk about that now."

"And you must be in week eighteen," Teddy said, as though he hadn't heard her. "Which means the little one in there should be about six inches now."

Emelie sat down. "You know I'm not really supposed to be your lawyer, not according to the Bar Association rules. It's not appropriate to defend someone whose child you're carrying. It can lead to certain conflicts of interest."

Teddy grinned. "Yeah, I guess it can. But I notice you're here anyway. Is it because I've rejuvenated my face, started going for Restylane treatments?"

"Give me the details now," Emelie replied. Though the situation was so strange, she couldn't help but smile—Teddy really did look weird.

He went over what had happened at Hallenbro Storgården again. Emelie already knew most of it: they had spoken at the restaurant, after all. This time, now that she had her defense cap on, she saw everything in a different light.

"You said there was a witness," she said once he finished. "Your friend Dejan saw what happened."

Teddy twisted in his chair. "Yeah, but you know Dejan. How credible do you think he is? Serious criminal, known by the police as one of the worst in the county for just under two decades."

"But he drove at the person who shot Fredrik O. Johansson and made them jump out of the way?"

"Yeah, and probably saved my life in the process."

They kept talking. Discussed their way forward. Not just about what Teddy was accused of, but about everything to do with Mats Emanuelsson and Katja. The visitor's room was cold. Teddy's remand hearing would take place within four days, and then the evidence against him would become somewhat clearer.

Teddy said: "You have to talk to Loke right away, before the police discover the USB stick with the trojan."

"If it really was a police officer out there, I'm thinking it should be visible on one of their IT systems."

"That was my thought, too."

They sat in silence for a moment.

"How do I find out who was at Katja's place the night before she was killed?" Emelie asked.

"Do you remember what I did when we were working on the kidnapping?"

"Lots of things."

"I knocked on doors."

That night, Emelie got a worse night's sleep than usual, which was saying something. Over the past few months, her sleeping patterns had been more like a number of rest breaks in a row than a full night's sleep, and it wasn't just because of her growing bump. Now it was as though she didn't even *want* to wind down, as though she was consciously forcing her brain to deal with the different trains of thought that were bothering her, even as she came close to dozing off. Or maybe it was because she was sleeping on Josephine's sofa. It was actually pretty comfortable, but the knowledge that her friend was only a few feet away, in her bedroom, was constantly on her mind.

Or maybe it was because the father of her child was facing life in prison.

Or maybe it was just that everything was so messed up right now.

She got up at five, pulled on some clothes, and started walking along Norr Mälarstrand. She was less anxious at that time of day: for some reason, it felt too early to be dangerous. The sun was already glittering on the buildings as though it were the middle of the day. The streets were clean and empty, and the only living beings she saw were the paper delivery people in their bulky green trucks and the birds pecking at the crumbs outside the shuttered restaurants. An early summer morning in Sweden: ordinarily, she thought it was the most beautiful thing on earth.

A few hours later, she found herself in the stairwell of the building where Katja had lived. She doubted Adam would be able to bear living there any longer. It was seven thirty, and she was counting on the neighbors not having left for the day. She rang the bell on the door next to the Tagrins' apartment.

An old man in a threadbare, practically transparent dressing gown opened the door. There was a walking stick leaning against the wall behind him, and the musty smell of old age seeped out from the apartment.

"Hi," Emelie said. "I'm here with the police and I have a few questions for you, if you've got a moment."

The man squinted at her as though he couldn't see very well—he probably couldn't. She could barely hear what he said when he replied in a weak, croaky voice. "Is it about the poor girl there was such a hullabaloo about?"

"Yes, your neighbor."

"Poor girl. I wasn't here that day, I play bridge, you see, I already told one of your team members."

"I understand, but I was wondering if you saw anyone visit her apartment the night *before* she was killed, on January nineteenth."

"January nineteenth?"

"Yes. In the evening."

"That was an important day. Often the last day for submitting the accounts. I worked as an accounting consultant for forty-two years, you know. Pure hell for the back, there weren't any nice padded chairs back when I started there, we stood up and worked for days on end."

"So were you home that evening?"

"I'm always home in the evening. Have been ever since the wife died, that was nine years ago, it was cancer that took her, started off in the large intestine, but it spread."

"I'm sorry. But did you see or hear anyone visiting Katja?"

"See?"

"Yes, or hear."

"I can't see very well, you see, haven't since 2004 when they discovered my cataracts. They tried operating, like they do, but they've come back, and . . ."

"Did you hear anything, then?"

The old man started talking about his hearing loss; it seemed like he could go on forever. Emelie did her best to end the conversation. She knocked on two more doors, but the families living there had neither seen nor heard anything. On the fourth door, there was a large sign above the mailbox: *No goddamn junk mail and no free papers. Got it?*

A huge bearded man with a bare chest opened the door. He was so wide that he filled the entire doorway, and his upper arms quivered like a waterbed. "What do you want?"

"I'm here with the police." Emelie couldn't see the hallway behind him. "I was wondering if you were home on January nineteenth."

The man studied her from top to toe, as though his eyes were a metal detector scanning her for hidden objects. "Like hell you are," he said.

"Pardon?"

"You're not with the police, not with that stomach, I don't believe that for a second."

"You don't think pregnant women can be police officers?"

"No idea, but there's something else about you. You're not a cop, anyway, same way I'm not a long-distance runner."

Emelie put her hands on her hips. "I'd like you to answer a few questions."

The man put his own enormous hands on his hips—the fat on his arms wobbled like huge chunks of meat. "Okay," he said. "I like that you're lying. Shoot."

Emelie asked her questions.

"I was home, and I heard Katja getting upset in the stairwell," he said. "So I looked out through the peephole and managed to catch a handsome man disappearing down the stairs."

Emelie realized she had stopped breathing—she filled her lungs. "Where did he go after that, did you see?"

"All I know is he jumped into a taxi out on the street."

"Do you remember which taxi company it was?"

Emelie started calling around the various taxi companies the minute she left. The huge man hadn't been able to remember the company or the registration number—but there still had to be a chance.

She tried the same story with all of them. Said that as far as she could remember, she had taken one of their taxis from Gösta Ekmans väg that night, and that she had left something behind in the car. Now she wanted to know if the company could see her trip, and who had been driving.

Emelie tried to focus, to concentrate on the conversations. She wanted to sound friendly, to be put through to the right person, to be given all the relevant information. She started with the big companies: Taxi Stockholm, Taxi Kurir, Taxi 020, and so on. She called several times, spoke to different receptionists, all to make sure that they really were following up on her inquiry. Then she tried Uber.

"Yes, we had a ride from that address on the evening of January nineteenth," she was told by the woman in the call center that it had taken forty-five minutes to get through to—the app companies didn't want you to contact them via old-fashioned methods. "But surely you can see that in the app?"

"No, unfortunately I've lost my phone."

"Then all you need to do is re-download the app, log in, and your ride history will be there. You'll be able to see the driver, too."

"Aha, so what was the driver's name?"

The woman's voice sounded cool. "No, I can't give out that kind of information over the phone. The whole idea behind Uber is that our customers manage their data themselves. It's cheaper for everyone that way."

Emelie said: "I'm going to keep calling back until you give me the name. I doubt it'll be cheaper for you to be stuck in a bunch of phone calls with me."

The woman groaned. "Fine, you can have the name."

Emelie jotted it down.

A movement. She paused, ended the call. There it was again. A movement. She placed her hand on her stomach.

The little one was stirring in there. The little one was living.

Her child—Teddy's child. Their child.

She had to track down the driver and find out more.

SMS MESSAGE

To/From: Unknown

From/To: Hugo Pederson

Date: 2 June 2006

In: Hi Hugo, just wanted to thank you for bringing ME to the event at Hallenbro yesterday. Everyone thought his talk was incredibly interesting.

Out: Thanks for a fantastic evening. Both Pierre and I felt honored to be there.

In: Good. Heard you had a tricky time yesterday, by the way. How did that go? HMRC and the Financial Supervision Authority all at once?

Out: Pretty nasty, a lot of people are going to find themselves in trouble. My brokers were damn stressed. But we managed to resolve a lot during the day, even though I lost my computer. Terrible luck for it to disappear on the same day. Thanks for letting me borrow yours, if I hadn't been able to use it there's no way I would've been able to get as much done with ME. Don't think it'll lead to anything unpleasant for me now, in any case.

MEMO

During the summer of 2006, a large number of calls were made, all recorded separately. None of these calls led to business transactions being concluded.

TELEPHONE CONVERSATIONS 85–104 (SUMMARY)

To/From: Pierre Danielsson (co-suspect) and a number of other stockbrokers and bankers in Sweden, Switzerland, and England (named in relevant appendix)

From/To: Hugo Pederson

Date: 12–20 September 2006

Summary: Hugo Pederson has a number of conversations with co-suspect Pierre Danielsson and the above-named brokers and bankers in Sweden and elsewhere in Europe, regarding the planned purchase of shares in a number of companies. The speculative value amounts to more than nineteen million euros (recorded separately). Hugo Pederson has taken out margin loans amounting to at least twelve million euros. According to our calculations, his leverage is greater than his net worth. Should the transactions fail, he risks being struck by losses that could lead to insolvency. More information to follow.

TELEPHONE CONVERSATION 105

To: Hugo Pederson

From: Louise Pederson (wife)

Date: 20 September 2006

Time: 10:45

LOUISE: Hi, it's me.

HUGO: Hi, Mousey . . .

LOUISE: Don't call me Mousey.

HUGO: But you are my Mousey, my pretty little mouse.

LOUISE: Enough now, Hugo. You haven't been home while I've been awake for eight days now. And the estate agent just called, he wants a decision on the estate. Someone else has put in an offer.

HUGO: I can't help it if you go to bed early.

LOUISE: I've asked you to at least come home and eat dinner with me. I have nothing against you going back to work afterward.

HUGO: You have no idea what I've got going on right now. This time, it could be the jackpot, for real. I'm talking really big numbers.

LOUISE: You just don't get it. You say you have to work so that we can afford an estate at some point in time, but if all you do is work then it's even more important that we buy the place now. Otherwise it's a lose-lose situation for me. Look, it's like this, and I'll keep it brief: if we don't buy the estate, it's over between us. I'm not going to be happy without that estate. So you need to come home now and discuss what we're going to bid.

HUGO: I mean, I don't know what to say. I don't have time right now, I've told you. And we can't afford the price the agent is asking.

LOUISE: If you don't have time to come home and make sure we can buy the place, you don't have time for me, full stop. I'm this close to the end of the road with you.

HUGO: Mousey, you're being too hard on me. Can't we talk about this?

LOUISE: I've told you, don't call me Mousey. Just buy the place.

TELEPHONE CONVERSATION 106

To: Carl Trolle (friend)

From: Hugo Pederson

Date: 21 September 2006

Time: 11:32

HUGO: You have to talk to her.

CARL: What are you talking about?

HUGO: Louise. She's completely lost her mind. She's crazy. But if you can just get her to calm down for a few days, it'll all be fine.

CARL: And you're calling me? Do you remember what you said to me last time we spoke?

HUGO: No?

CARL: I think you do. You told me I was a loser.

HUGO: Sorry, Calle. I really didn't mean it, I was having a bad day, I was just really fucking stressed. I really didn't mean anything like that. Can't you talk to her, nicely?

CARL: I think it's too late.

HUGO: Come on now. It'll all be fine, because listen to this: I've bought the estate for her. I put in an offer yesterday, and the sellers accepted it immediately. I arranged everything with the banks this morning, I've got great contacts there. So now I'm mortgaged up to the hilt, double credit risk and all that crap. But I've also got the world's best deal in place, the biggest I've ever done, so it's all going to be fine. I'll be able to pay back whatever's needed, but before that I obviously don't want to say anything to Louise. So if you could just talk to her, make sure she doesn't do anything stupid before I know it's a done deal, I'd be incredibly happy.

CARL: I'm sorry, I can't help you.

HUGO: What if I paid you? Just one call from you to Louise. If we say I'll pay you a hundred grand.

CARL: Money can buy anything?

HUGO: What?

CARL: Money can buy anything?

HUGO: Yeah, that's what I was thinking, is that okay for you?

CARL: You're not right in the head.

TELEPHONE CONVERSATION 107

To: Pierre Danielsson (co-suspect)
From: Hugo Pederson
Date: 22 September 2006
Time: 17:02

HUGO: Hey.

PIERRE: Hi.

HUGO: Something's happened.

PIERRE: You sound worried, don't tell me it's all going to shit. No more dawn raids by the FSA, no more lost computers or someone backing out of the deal.

HUGO: No, nothing to do with any of the banks down there, and nothing to do with the deal, thank God. I've just bought five hundred acres of land in Upplands Väsby for my wife. No, Mats just called me.

PIERRE: Okay?

HUGO: He was really agitated.

PIERRE: Why?

HUGO: When he helped us at that event in Södermanland, you know when I needed to borrow a computer to deal with the Financial Supervision Authority people snooping around? Well, apparently Mats went onto some other computer out there, and he might have copied stuff off it.

PIERRE: What did he do that for?

HUGO: How should I know? I let him work on our stuff by himself. He was alone in one of the rooms there; it's not like I was watching over him. But he said he found some strange films on the computer and that he's been to the police to report them.

PIERRE: Are you kidding me? What kind of films? Was it something to do with our deals?

HUGO: No idea, but I don't think so. I didn't get the impression it was linked to us, but like I said, I don't know. I just wanted to let you know. Maybe the guy knows what it's about.

PIERRE: You'll have to check with him.

SMS MESSAGES

To/From: Unknown
From/To: Hugo Pederson
Date: 22 September 2006

Out: I just got a strange call from ME saying he'd found some weird films on a computer at your event, he must've copied them. I'm guessing it happened when he was helping me with my little audit crisis. I don't know which computer or what the films are. You know?

In: No need for you to worry about that. I'll figure it out.

Out: Perfect.

TELEPHONE CONVERSATION 108

To: Hugo Pederson
From: Unknown
Date: 23 September 2006
Time: 21:45

HUGO: Hello?

UNKNOWN: Hi, it's me.

HUGO: Who's that?

UNKNOWN: Don't you recognize my voice?

HUGO: Yeah, now I do, sorry. Hi.

UNKNOWN: I've got some questions about your consultant.

HUGO: Who do you mean?

UNKNOWN: I think you know who I mean.

HUGO: You mean M.E., Mr. Money Man?

UNKNOWN: Exactly. Do you know where he works?

HUGO: No idea.

UNKNOWN: Where do you normally meet him, then?

HUGO: We don't meet very often.

UNKNOWN: But you must sometimes meet to hand over documents?

HUGO: Yeah, occasionally, but we usually choose different places.

UNKNOWN: Where does he live?

HUGO: I don't know.

UNKNOWN: You could make a bit of effort to answer my questions here.

HUGO: But I have no idea. We don't have that kind of relationship. If you're so curious, you can just Google him yourself. It's not like he's a secret, he's got a normal job too. Why do you want to know all this?

UNKNOWN: I think you know.

HUGO: I don't know that I do.

UNKNOWN: I think you could be a bit more helpful. You've used the meeting room at my office several times, after all. I'd like you to organize a meeting with ME at Odenplan the day after tomorrow, at 9 a.m.

HUGO: What's going to happen then?

UNKNOWN: We'll see. Just arrange it with him.

TELEPHONE CONVERSATION 109
To: Pierre Danielsson (co-suspect)
From: Hugo Pederson
Date: 23 September 2006
Time: 21:47

PIERRE: Hey.

HUGO: Hi. Something shady just happened. The lawyer called me and started asking a ton of questions about Mats.

PIERRE: Hmm, but you answered them, right? We can't get drawn into all that. We've got no idea about those films. It's none of our business.

HUGO: Okay, but it just didn't feel right. Plus, he wanted me to organize a meeting with Mats at Odenplan the day after tomorrow, 9 a.m. What should we do?

PIERRE: We?

HUGO: Come on, you're using Mats' services too. He's your consultant as well.

PIERRE: Yeah, but I'm not his contact person, that's you. And it was you who didn't have a computer of your own, despite all the crap with the Financial Supervision Authority, so we had to borrow the guy's computer.

HUGO: Oh come on, I can't just announce that we have to meet at Odenplan. This really doesn't feel good.

PIERRE: I'm sure it's fine, Hugo. Don't give it another thought, it's really not our problem.

44

The first thing she did when they released her was to call Nikola. Maybe she should have tracked down Z or gone to see her parents, but speaking to Nicko felt like the most natural thing to do.

"You're out already?" he said when he heard her voice. Roksana almost thought he sounded happy. What she was trying to work out was whether he sounded *very* happy. "I'm out," she replied. "And I'm seriously pissed off."

She really was furious. She felt like suing the Police Authority, demanding compensation from the arresting officers, prosecuting the cop who had knocked her to the ground, going to the press and writing a debate piece. *We brought happiness to Stockholm and this is the thanks we get.* "Those fascist bastards," she said.

Nikola agreed. "Plenty of them are racists," he said. "But *fascists*? What do you mean by that?"

Roksana didn't really feel like it was the best moment to get into the concept of fascism, and, if she was perfectly honest, she wasn't entirely sure she knew what it meant. She just knew that the world seemed to be overflowing with idiots right now.

"Listen, Roksy, they let you go after a day," Nikola then said in a calm voice. "You should be happy about that. It looks pretty good if you ask me. They're not accusing you of a ton of worse stuff."

"Maybe not. But they probably still have Z. And they took the whole Nike bag, all our money. Everything. I don't know what we're going to do. I want to see my lawyer today and prepare my counterattack."

"You've got a lawyer already?"

Roksana laughed. It was the first time she had felt even a glimmer of happiness over the past twenty-four hours. "No, I thought maybe you could be my lawyer. Could you?"

"I'd like to see you," he said. "But I've got some stuff I have to straighten out first."

They hung up. The Täby Centrum shopping mall loomed behind her, completely colorless and numb. Roksana really was furious—just like she had told Nikola. Though maybe she wasn't quite *so* angry, because what he had said was right, something Roksana had realized for herself fairly quickly. She was actually more worried than anything. And afraid.

It was quarter past ten in the morning, the day after their legendary club: the police had held her for exactly 25 hours and 44 minutes. Her mobile phone and card holder were in the brown paper bag they had handed her when she was released. She had countless missed calls and more than seventy messages from people thanking her for the experience, praising the organization, the performances, the love that had been in the air.

Oddly enough, she had slept like a rock in her cell, deeper and more soundly than she had in a long time. She hadn't had any nightmares about Z's broken fingers or her parents' disappointed faces when they found out what she was up to. No jolting awake with her breath in her throat and a sense of stress a hundred times worse than ahead of Our Land Club; no weird K sweats with an extreme urge to pee, a shaking body and soaked sheets. The truth was that she couldn't remember having slept so well since they first found the ketamine. But now that she was awake, the anxiety was tangible, like a rat crawling around her body. The police station where they had kept her locked up in the basement looked like some kind of nice-ish travel agency from the outside, or maybe the employment service. But it was far from nice inside, she knew that now.

She got onto the bus that would take her into town, where she would have to change to the metro. It would probably take her more than an hour and a half to get home, but she didn't know any other way. Täby and Akalla were in such different parts of Stockholm: like fire and water, land and air. Though, maybe she was exaggerating; maybe it was just the worry dirtying her thoughts.

She tried to think about what the police knew and what she had actually told them. They had interrogated her for only an hour and a half. Most of their questions had been about whether she and Z had had the proper licenses for their club, how they had kept track of the ticket sales and overheads for the DJs, handymen, door people, and all the others. Roksana had been expecting questions about *the other stuff* at any minute: about the large number of small plastic pouches they must have found in the trash, about the traces of powder on the inside of those bags, about the cash in the duffel they had seized, about all the guys they must have grabbed with backpacks *full* of powder bags. But they never came. Maybe they thought that the cash in the bags was from ticket sales alone.

She worried about her own tracks. After all, she and Z had shifted kilos of the mindfuck in larger bags. But, at the same time: she had put safety first. Billie's advice about always keeping a pair of latex gloves in your bag in case you had to use a disgusting shared toilet had proved useful in more than one way—Roksana hadn't touched the ketamine at Our Land Club even once without a pair of those transparent plastic gloves on her hands. Not because she thought there were particles of piss on them, but because it felt right. Intuitively.

Still: despite the gentle interrogation and despite the fact that they didn't seem to have anything on her as far as the drugs were concerned, anxiety was creaking away inside her like a big, rusty machine. The cops had still taken the money. Money meant for the psychos.

What were they going to do now?

She tried to call Z, but he didn't answer.

She called Billie.

"Have they let you out? So cool that you were remanded, so fucking authentic," she yelled, and Roksana immediately wondered if Billie had even less of a grasp of reality than Joshua Pfefferman in *Transparent*. Roksana *hadn't* been remanded, just held. And it *hadn't* been a particularly authentic experience.

She lay down on the bed. Didn't even take off her clothes, just curled up her legs. Fetal position. Her roller blind was down. The apartment felt lonely without Z. She tried calling him again. "This number cannot be reached right now," said a robotic woman's voice, without an ounce of compassion or sympathy.

She tried to listen to music, but couldn't find the right cables for Z's complicated stereo equipment. She thought about calling her dad but didn't have the energy right now. She had no appetite, but she was *freaking starving* all the same—all she had eaten in her cell was a bit of cold rice. The yellow slop they had called curry smelled like dishwater; she hadn't even tried it. Still, she couldn't be bothered to get up to see what they had in the fridge.

Suddenly her phone started to ring. A number she didn't recognize. Maybe Z had been released.

"What are you playing at?" It was the leader of the psychos. A conversation she really didn't want to have. "I've tried calling you twenty times," he hissed. "Who the fuck do you think I am? Some telephone salesman, or what?"

"I'm sorry," Roksana began. "But I was locked up for twenty-four hours. We'd just got your money together, but then something happened, the cops came."

It sounded as though the leader was blowing his nose over the line. "Little girl, you seem to think this is some kind of negotiation." He paused; now it sounded like he was drawing back the mucus in his throat, swallowing several times, really savoring it. "But it's actually very simple. You know what we want. And you've had three weeks. I want my money now. That's it."

"Please, we do kind of have the money, I just can't get at it. So far, we've always paid you the minute we get any money. But the police took everything we had yesterday, it was completely crazy, so right now we can't pay a single krona. Can't we put the deadline back a few weeks?"

The leader seemed to have an inexhaustible amount of mucus in his throat, and he continued to swallow it as though it were dessert. "I heard what happened. You organized a party, over several days."

"Then you know, it was an insane success. We got your money. But they confiscated everything."

"So how're you planning to fix this? How am I gonna get my cash?"

Roksana had no answer to that. "I don't know," she said carefully.

"You don't know?"

"We had it."

"You've said that a hundred times now," said the leader. Then he shouted: "But you haven't said WHEN I'M GONNA GET PAID."

She was on the verge of tears now. Nothing she could say would calm him down. She was out of ideas.

He said: "You'll have to come up with something real fucking clever. It's that simple. I'm a generous man. You can have two more weeks, just 'cause I think midsummer seems like a good time to get paid. There's something nice about it, y'know? Celebrating the summer with cash. But that means I want interest, so we'll put it back up to a million. Since I've had to wait like an idiot. And if you don't pay up then, you can forget about your friend. It'll be worse than a few bent fingers." The leader suddenly sounded different, almost as though he were sad.

Right then, Roksana's phone beeped, and she saw that someone had sent her an MMS from an unknown number.

She opened the picture message. It was a photograph of her father.

The leader continued: "I'll personally see to it that the old bastard in that picture ends up at the bottom of a lake."

Roksana was on the verge of hanging up. The picture must have been taken recently, outside her parents' house. The leaves on the trees in the background were pale green.

"Understood?"

Roksana couldn't make a single sound. She swallowed and swallowed.

"You understand, or what?"

A croaking, gurgling sound. "Yeah," she tried to say.

"All right then, now you know," he said. "Two weeks. One million. Simple math."

Roksana slumped back onto her bed. The phone was like a dead weight on the pillow next to her. She and Z genuinely didn't have a kronor. It wasn't just something she had said. Plus, they owed money to everyone who had worked for Our Land Club. It wasn't just talk now: this time, the psychos were serious. Her stomach ached. It had been hard enough pulling off eight hundred thousand before they came up with the idea of the club. But now: *one million—in two weeks.*

ONE MILLION. TWO WEEKS.

She and Z would never be able to cook up that much K themselves, and having enough time to sell the crap was out of the question—even if Nikola helped out. Maybe she should just run— fly to Tehran, stay with Etty, Val, and Leila until the leader and his boys died in some gang dispute or until they retired as old men. But what would they do to Dad then? Shit, shit, shit.

How could things have ended up like this? She and Z: they had just found a bit of ketamine hidden in a closet—that was all. They hadn't robbed anyone; they hadn't stolen a thing: it was in *their* apartment. She couldn't understand how it could have gotten this far. Why hadn't she hit pause: tried a little herself and then saved the rest of the powder until the psychos turned up? Something inside her had forced her further. Upward. Toward a worthless top.

She twisted back and forth, stared out the window. The sky was still blue: two weeks until midsummer. The lightest time of the year. The darkest time of her life. She had to get herself a life, for real. It had been stupid to ask someone to take the aptitude test for her. She should have taken it herself—but right now, she wasn't in top form.

Maybe it was the crowds of people who had suddenly started appreciating her. Billie, who had wanted to hang out with *her;* the invitations, the art shows, all the friends who had loved her, acknowledged her. Though at the same time, she thought, it was something else. The danger. It was the danger that had tempted her: the feeling of doing something as far removed from her parents' expectations as she could get. The tingle of banking on top marks, a prestigious university education, and being their good, clever girl while also being the K queen par excellence. Stockholm's fucking top dog number one.

But she hadn't fooled anyone—other than herself.

And now they were going to go after Baba. She couldn't even bring herself to think about that.

45

The courtroom on Polhemsgatan. A lame irony—he had been arrested less than two hundred feet away, aboveground, in the police station itself. Sometimes, he imagined he could hear the footsteps of all the police officers above him. Pig steps. Pig land. Piggy honor—for some stupid reason, he had trusted Nina Ley.

It was a Sunday in early June, and the prosecutor seemed to think there was some kind of rush to have him remanded in custody. They could have just waited until Monday to hold this hearing otherwise. Instead, with it taking place at a weekend, they had to use these special premises. The district court was closed and deserted.

The room was belowground, and Teddy had been led there through the hallways beneath Police HQ, straight from his cell. Fifty feet of earth, rock, and concrete above him, it felt like someone had forced him to bench-press four hundred pounds and then left the bar lying across his chest.

When Emelie walked into the small waiting room, he thought that her bump seemed even bigger than when she had come to see him in his cell. They hugged as best they could. He felt her belly push against him like a soft pillow.

"How are you?"

"I'm okay." Emelie sat down on the only chair. "Almost halfway now. I have to take iron pills, but otherwise everything's fine. But we don't have time to talk about it now, sadly. I just got the remand order from the prosecutor, right outside."

"You're kidding."

Emelie waved the stack of papers held together with a paper clip, size XL. "Nope, it's always the same. The defense never gets any time to prepare ahead of remand hearings. Maybe you've forgotten?"

The hearing was due to begin in ten minutes' time. Emelie removed the enormous paper clip and spread out some of the sheets in front of her. Teddy leaned forward and tried to read at the same pace.

> We request that Najdan "Teddy" Maksumic is remanded in custody on suspicion of the murder of Fredrik O. Johansson at Hallenbro Storgården, Malmköping, in May.
>
> – There is a risk that the accused, through the destruction of evidence or other means, may attempt to obstruct the investigation.
>
> – For the specified crime, the prescribed sentence is no fewer than two years' imprisonment, and no reasonable grounds to deny custody have been established.
>
> – It is of particular importance that the accused is detained pending further investigation of the crime.

Teddy remembered enough to know that it wasn't the reasons given for remand that mattered—if you were accused of murder, the court would virtually always keep you locked up. What he wanted to know was *why* they suspected him. He had been at the scene when Fredrik O. Johansson was shot, but the only people who knew that were Dejan and the killer. Where had the information that he was linked to the murder come from, other than the fact that a car he had rented was found in the vicinity?

They scanned through the papers: pictures of the burned-out mansion, a mediocre crime scene investigation from the lawn outside, a partial analysis of the bullet that had penetrated the old man's skull, an examination of the various tire tracks on the gravel and in the grass, a report about the rental car Teddy had driven to the scene. But no interviews with anyone. And, as yet, no analyses of the forensic evidence had been finalized—though Teddy knew they would likely find his DNA inside the house. Then he saw what he had suspected all along: images from surveillance cameras that had survived the fire. Though the stills from the camera were grainy, they were clear enough: they showed Teddy himself making his way inside through the basement door.

He still found it strange that the police had managed to arrive at the scene so quickly.

The guards led him into the courtroom. His handcuffs rattled quietly. On the other side of the Plexiglas, he could see five people who might be journalists, plus Dejan—it felt good to have him here. The judge was sitting behind the bar, looking like she should have retired ten years ago, next to a notary with a neat red beard. The prosecutor was a woman in her midthirties, and she was wearing a gray dress with a pink scarf tied nonchalantly around her neck. A quick thought flashed through Teddy's mind: Was she sitting so far away because she thought he might launch himself across the room and strangle her with that bastard scarf?

In truth, the person he most felt like strangling was Nina Ley, who was sitting beside her. He wondered what she was doing there. In all likelihood, she was assisting the prosecution; it wasn't entirely unheard of for prosecutors to have a cop by their side during hearings. What surprised him was that it was Nina Ley, of all people. Especially considering she was also the lead investigator. But maybe that wasn't so strange, either: she had been trying to find Hallenbro Storgården and the people linked to it ever since Mats Emanuelsson first handed in the films. And now a murder had taken place there. A rat, that was what she was. A traitor.

The two guards sat down behind Teddy. The room was completely silent—murder cases were always shrouded in a certain atmosphere. Emelie placed her bag on the table and took out a pen and pad. She was holding the remand order in one hand. It already looked well-thumbed, as though she had been reading it for months. The paper clip came loose and fell to the table with a clink. Ten minutes: that was how long they had had to go through the documents—it was a joke, but that was clearly how it worked. Apparently the rule of law was a relative concept.

The prosecutor cleared her throat and read the exact same words as in the order. The judge asked for Teddy's position.

Emelie spoke slowly and clearly. "Teddy Maksumic denies the crime; he disputes that there are even reasonable grounds for suspicion. He disputes the special grounds for remand. He demands immediate release. No objection to closed doors."

"Very well," the judge said in a croaky voice. "Then we shall close the doors, and I would ask all spectators to leave the room."

Dejan and the reporters got up and left.

"Well," the judge said, her hair bobbing like she was on a trampoline. "The prosecutor may begin."

He didn't feel any claustrophobia. The last time he found himself in a place like this, he'd had serious anxiety: he had promised himself, there and then, that he would never return to a cell. Facing a long prison sentence. But that wasn't how he felt today.

The cell walls seemed to be sloping gently inward, falling in on him. But he had been here before. He wouldn't panic this time. He wouldn't shout and cry. No, something else had crept into him now, a new feeling for him. Something he didn't recognize from his own personality, something that meant he felt alien to himself. He didn't know what it was.

He had been remanded into custody, of course. It made no difference how good Emelie was. At custody hearings, the evidence was never studied the way it was during the main trial—a simple statement from the prosecutor was all it took for the judge to rule that there were reasonable grounds for suspicion or probable cause for the crime. A custody hearing wasn't a trial: it didn't require anything to be backed up with evidence.

Teddy thought back to all the times he had lain in a cell like this, thinking about the same thing he was now: his mother. In the cozy children's corner of the library, all sofas and cushions, curled up in his lap. *The Brothers Lionheart* in his hands. "There are things you have to do, even if they are dangerous. Otherwise you aren't human, just a piece of dirt." His mother had looked serious. "My golden boy, do you know what that means?" Teddy had shaken his head. Six or seven years old. "What things do you have to do, *Mamma?*" She had kissed him on the cheek, even though Teddy didn't like it when she did that in front of others. "You have to be kind, Teddy. Sometimes you have to be kind, even if it's hard."

Teddy stared at the metal door. He had done it before the hearing, too, back when he was officially just being held. He listened for noises: the shuffle of slippers in the hallway outside. He pressed his ear to the door. Tried to hear whether there was anyone breathing out there. He ate his food as if he were tasting it for poison. First, he poked at it, searching for crushed tablets or strange liquids. Then he took small bites, one at a time, his taste buds trying to detect the slightest hint of acridness or bitterness. When they took him up to the roof for his hour of exercise, he kept his body tense. Ready for some kind of attack. He didn't know how it would start or where it would come from.

"We don't know one another," said Britta, the guard who led him up to the cage on the roof. "But you don't need to look at me like I'm going to trip you up or something."

Teddy knew how he must seem to others. It was the new sensation within him, the new thought clogging up his brain.

Once he was up in the cage, he positioned himself as far from the door as he could, even if it was only twelve feet away, and then waited. He didn't know what he was waiting for, but something told him that the rusty gray door was about to open and that someone would come in. Someone who wanted to hurt him. Because they now knew that he knew. They had killed Fredrik O. Johansson. *They* were prepared to do anything.

He spent his nights lying awake. The same thoughts over and over again. He had called Emelie—you were always allowed to call your lawyer, regardless of any restrictions or isolation orders. He really wanted to ask her to get in touch with Kum—but didn't dare, the line probably had more people listening in on it than Assange's phone in the Ecuadorian embassy.

Eyes wide open. Teddy could hear his own breathing. The shouts and cries from the inexperienced idiots out in the hallway had stopped now; even those fools had fallen asleep after a while. There was no clock in his cell, and they had obviously taken his phone, but Teddy guessed it was sometime after midnight. The only dark hour of the day during June. Maybe he should read through the remand report Emelie had given him again—but there was no point. He had already seen everything there was to see in it, including the pictures of him holding a crowbar. He tried to breathe more quietly. He felt cold, stiff. Then he understood what was wrong with him. He suddenly worked out what this new sensation he was feeling was, something he had never experienced before. He—Teddy Maksumic—was scared. *Terrified*. For the first time in his life, he was afraid. Afraid for his life. For his unborn child's life.

It was crazy: he had kidnapped and beaten people, he had been arrested by task forces with their MP5s pointed at his face, he had gone to war with Kum, he'd been kept prisoner by crazy cops. He had been through more shit than 99.9 percent of the population, and yet he had never been scared, not *really*. Never to the extent that the smallest of sounds sent a cold shiver down his spine. Never to the extent that his breathing became unsteady at the very thought of having to sleep here. But now: he didn't even dare move in bed. All he wanted to do was listen—see whether anyone was waiting outside the door, whether they were going to come in.

———

He woke and realized he couldn't breathe. He gasped, gasped again, but he couldn't get any air. He tried to sit up, but something was holding him down, pressing on his back. It wasn't a dream. It *wasn't a dream.*

Someone was trying to strangle him from behind; there was someone sitting on his back.

He tried to throw himself to one side, but something tightened around his neck. He had to breathe; he needed oxygen. He tried to shout, but without any air, no sounds would come out.

His fingers tore at whatever was being tightened around his neck, but he couldn't get a good grip. His eyes felt like they were being forced out of their sockets. He thought of Emelie's bump.

Teddy flailed with one hand, but his fingers couldn't find a hold. He should have known: strangulation—the best way to make it look like suicide. Every year, at least one of the inmates would hang himself using his belt or sheet.

He threw himself around, trying to force off the person holding him from behind.

He gasped for a breath that never came, felt everything start to blur. How much longer would he manage? There was a rope digging into his neck. Cutting off his airway.

His head was going to explode.

He was about to disappear.

Air. Breathe. He could see a white light.

Images flickered past. Emelie's bump in the waiting room before the hearing, the way she carried the thick stack of remand documents. His hands searched beneath the bed. Found the papers—he had been reading them before he fell asleep.

Flashes of light in his eyes. Everything was blurry. He was on his way now.

He fumbled for the paper clip—there, he found it.

He tried to press against the edge of the bed, managed to grab the paper clip.

He had been playing with it earlier, bent it so that it was now a thin metal stick.

Then: his body was about to go limp, but with one last surge of effort he forced himself into movement. A throw, a blow, a stab: he raised what used to be a paper clip behind him, toward the person who was trying to take his life.

A popping sound, like water being spilled. He felt the unfolded paper clip pushing against something soft. Part of a body. His stab had hit its target. An eye? A cheek?

The grip around his neck loosened, a heavy body thudded to the floor. Teddy tore at the rope that had cut off his breathing. Threw himself to the other side, panting, coughing.

The man who had tried to kill him was already on his way out through the door. Teddy saw his back in the darkness, followed by his tall, rushing body in silhouette against the light from the hall-way as the door opened and closed.

Teddy tried to sit up, but he had to catch his breath first.

He heard the door being locked from outside.

He slumped back onto the bed. Drew in air.

Teddy pressed the alarm button, shouted and banged the wall.

He was, at least, alive.

The man had sneaked into his room while he slept. It came over him again, stronger this time, the feeling he had been carrying ever since they arrested him. The feeling he hadn't recognized, that he didn't think he had truly experienced before. It washed over him with full force: a purely physical effect in his body and head. He started to shake, trembling like a sick person.

The fear.

46

Nikola's palms were slipping on the wheel. His hands never normally sweated, but today it was like all of his sweat glands had been transplanted to the same place: between his thumb and index finger on each hand. He knew why. Bello was in the passenger seat next to him; they were moving the boxes of explosives that Isak ordered them to top off at regular intervals. Nikola wasn't just scared of the content of the boxes; they broke his back, too—heavy as concrete. A van: from Sjöbergsgatan to Selmedalsvägen, from Selmedalsvägen to wherever they were heading today, and so on. What normal person drove from one place to another with a vanload of *bombs*? It was an insane job, but someone had to do it. Bello had talked about it before: Mr. One was building up some kind of stockpile.

Once they were done with this, Bello had promised to show Nikola the telephone graveyard on the bottom of the lake.

Nikola held the wheel with one hand while he wiped the palm of the other on his pants. There were so many explosives in the back of the van that they would probably be given life sentences for planning a terrorist attack if they were pulled over right now. It was a joke: of all the bastards to do this job, it had to be him being forced to drive a van full of bombs around, despite almost being blown to pieces just last year. He couldn't help but think about what might happen if he braked or turned a corner too sharply. If someone crashed into them. Hägersten would see a fireball the size of the Globe Arena rise up on the horizon. The Stockholmers would think Putin had finally attacked or that ISIS had launched an assault on the southern suburbs.

Three hours later, Nikola broke the surface. He had bought a diving mask, a snorkel, and a waterproof flashlight in Södertälje. The water of the lake had enveloped him like a cold blanket, but it wasn't deep, only five feet or so, and it was relatively clear thanks to the rocks on the bottom. He could see better than he expected—a number of small black objects. Discarded cell phones. After just a few minutes underwater, he had fished up nine of them.

"I'm sure I dropped one of Mr. One's here in January. There was a bit of ice, so I gave the skates a spin, too," Bello said, pointing to one of the phones. "That's the one, the Samsung S5. I'm a thousand percent sure."

Nikola tried to smile—his friend probably hadn't gone ice skating since they had been forced to as eight-year-olds—but deep down, he was in a worse mood than earlier, when they had carried the boxes of explosives into a new, secret address.

He climbed up onto the rocks and wrapped a towel around himself. The air was warm, but he could feel his muscles shaking.

He wanted to call Roksana, to hear how it had all gone, whether there was anything he could do to help her. But something made him hold back: he had to finish this thing with the phones first. He had to find out who was really involved in the murder of his best friend. It was too big to leave hanging.

He watched a taxi pull up to the entrance below. He knew what the driver had for him: it was from Loke. Teddy's old friend from the slammer stepped up to help him time and time again.

Nikola went down, took the envelope, paid the driver, and tore it open. There was a postcard and a phone inside. The handwriting on the postcard was childish, almost as illegible as his own.

Hey, Cutie Pie. Believe it or not, you can work wonders with a
hairdryer and a bag of rice. I opened the phone, dried it out and
put it in a bag of Uncle Ben's best for two days. It still works, and
I've cracked the code, so you can check everything now. The code's
7586. Love&kisses / Loke

Nikola sat down at the kitchen table with the phone in his
hand—the phone Bello had pointed out. One of Mr. One's castoffs,
the one he had been using when Chamon was shot. Now Nikola
was going to look through it.

From the old poster on the wall, Al Pacino glared down at him.
Tony Montana was sitting at a desk with a gold watch on his arm
and a glass of whiskey in front of him. He had his beautiful wife and
everything was going well, but he still looked pissed off, bitter, and
tired of the whole thing. The darkness in Montana's eyes radiated
from the image and met Nikola's.

He had hit rock bottom in Dubai after Yusuf was killed, but
at the time he had still thought he was part of a family, a brother-
hood. He had thought that he'd found his place, despite all the crap
the cops were up to, despite having lost his best friend. He had
believed in a bond that was worth something all the same.

But they had fucked him. And the thing was that someone had
always been fucking him. He could see it clearly now, the pattern,
a line as straight as a fucking arrow stretching right from the very
start to now: the end. Though his grandpa had taught him to read
when he was five, though his fifth-grade Swedish teacher had told
him he was a "diamond in the rough"—he hadn't known quite
what she meant at the time, but his mother had explained that
it was something good, that it meant he had "huge potential"—
everything had gone to shit. He had never been a nerd, but nor
had he been one of the kids who fooled around most; he had just
wanted to live his life, to hang out with his friends. But the whole
class, the whole school—no, the whole area—had been condemned
from the very start. A problem area, defined by those who refused

to adapt. But adapt to what? They were still considered to have too much of an accent when they spoke, they were thought too loud or disruptive, but no one ever listened to what they were actually saying. Their drawings were seen as graffiti and vandalism no matter what they depicted. Their thoughts were considered medieval, violent, inciting fucking violence, even though no one had ever asked Nikola and his brothers what they thought they were doing. There was all this talk about everyone being born equal and the circumstances sending their lives in different directions, but it was bullshit—they were born *unequal* and the circumstances meant they were all pushed into the same life. They were like the fucking Angry Birds: you sent them flying with the slingshot, but everyone knew they would eventually come crashing down, that they would never reach heaven. The only question was how much destruction and damage they could do on their way.

Nikola opened Isak's phone using the code. 7586.

He saw the usual apps. Isak had simple tastes, just like Chamon: it was natural when he didn't hang on to his phones for more than a few weeks. Messages, pictures and camera, the actual phone function, WhatsApp, Vicker, Snapchat, Maps, and YouTube. He scrolled through the text messages but didn't find anything. Then he went through WhatsApp.

And he saw it. On the day they had attacked the gym, when Chamon's jaw had practically been shot off.

Mother. Fucker.

All that shit was still there, preserved by six months on the bottom of the phone graveyard—a message sent from Isak's phone.

He's here now. Come and get him.

Nikola read it over and over again. He tried to gather his thoughts, to see the bigger picture. He thought about the conversation he'd had with Isak when he went to visit Chamon in the hospital. How Isak had wanted to know how long Nikola would be staying by his friend's side, how the murdering bastards had arrived *after* the two hours Nikola had initially said he would stay. How they had found their way up to the ward far too quickly.

He knew two things. The first: Isak was the one behind Chamon's murder. Nikola didn't know why Mr. One had decided to order Chamon's death, but the boss was guilty, that was 1,000 percent certain.

The second: everything he had believed in now meant nothing. The only way was forward. He had to take down Isak. It made no difference how high the cost was. He had to do what he had to do.

At the same time: How the hell was he going to manage it? He needed to know more. Get more information. Find out whether anyone would be loyal to him.

He needed to talk to someone. And there was only one person who might be able to help: Simon fucking Murray. The pig.

47

There was some kind of fever burning inside her, only without her temperature rising above 99.5. It was as though nothing made an impression on her, like everything she saw and heard just ran straight off. Sometimes, she didn't even know where she had woken up—which might actually be understandable, given that she didn't even dare stay with Josephine any longer, and was moving from hotel to hotel. Sometimes, during the day, she forgot where she was going, and before she tried to sleep she realized she had forgotten to eat. The whole time: she had the feeling of being watched, like someone was studying her, listening to what she said over the phone. She knew that Teddy had been sleeping in a car, living on the run, but not only so that he could keep away from the police. Every time she turned around on the street, she thought she saw the same people slipping away. Every time she checked into a hotel, she had the feeling that the man with the Bluetooth earpiece, sitting in an armchair in the lobby, was staring at her. Maybe she was just being paranoid again, like she had been in the garage when she hit her head. She had thrown the alarm the police had given her down the drain.

Midsummer was only a few days away.

Someone had tried to take Teddy's life in his cell. It was insane, terrible—one of the worst things Emelie had ever heard of. Because even if she didn't hold the Swedish justice system above all else in the world, even if she was aware of its shortcomings, the easy remand orders and the long periods of isolation, she fundamentally believed in the overall system: Sweden was still one of the world's most just countries. Yes, there might be corrupt officers, and some might go too far at times. And yes, there were fights between inmates in their prisons, leading to serious crimes being committed—but this went way beyond any of that. The fact that someone locked in a remand cell, isolated and under full restrictions, could be subject to an attempted murder was unprecedented.

"We're aware that Teddy Maksumic has been talking about that, but no one here saw anything," the officer in charge told Emelie when she raised the issue. "He'll have to file a police report for someone to come here and talk about it." The officer's lips glistened as though he had just smeared them in oil.

Great idea, Emelie thought, *someone* who will probably try to kill him again.

"But you must have surveillance cameras in the hallway here?"

"Sure, I did actually try to check them when your client first started talking about it, but unfortunately there was nothing saved from that night." The cop's lips were glistening so much by that point that she could practically see her reflection in them.

"And you didn't think that was a bit strange?"

The so-called officer in charge pulled out a tub of some kind of lip balm: *For cold sores and herpes,* Emelie managed to read. "No, not really," he said. "It's almost always that way, sadly. The prison system's not what it used to be. And, you know, some inmates do actually try to kill themselves, a lot of them are suicidal, and hanging themselves in their cells is the most common way, unfortunately. So, we can't rule out that that was what your client was trying to do. We'll be checking him four times an hour now. So he can't try again."

Emelie was trembling when she stepped into the room where Teddy was waiting. The marks around his neck looked like small red bumps. She knew he wasn't suicidal.

She told him what the officer outside had just said.

"I can almost understand him," said Teddy. "Never in their wildest dreams would they believe what happened."

Emelie squirmed. "But they must know whether one of their employees got a paper clip in their eye? I'm going to try to find out."

They were sitting opposite one another in the little visitor's room where it felt like time had been at a standstill since the 1980s. The filthy linoleum floor, the scratched veneer on the rickety plywood table screwed to the floor, the old telephone with the curled cord—the kind you only saw in films nowadays.

"I spoke to Dejan. He's prepared to testify," she said. "But, as we've discussed, I'm not sure it'll help. There's a risk it'll have the opposite effect."

Teddy sighed: a long, groaning sigh. Emelie had never heard him sound that way before, not like that. She glanced up at him. Even though the strange cosmetic procedures had made him look different, she thought he seemed more tired than usual. As though beneath the firmer skin, there was an expression that hadn't been there last time they met. She immediately realized what it was.

"Emelie, I'm scared," he said, reading her mind. The last word seemed to leave such a bad taste in his mouth that he practically spat it out. "I would've been able to live with that in the past. But not now, not when I have two more people to worry about. I have to get out of here somehow. It's that simple. I have to fix everything. For your sake, and the baby's."

Emelie knew, in the same way she could usually tell when she was getting ill, that he was right. He had to get away from custodial prison.

Ten times a day, she tried to track down the Uber driver. When he eventually answered, she tried talking to him; he sounded like a young man from some Arabic-speaking country, and his vocabulary was limited to only fifty or so words in Swedish, even fewer in English. They met face-to-face: Emelie offered him a one-thousand-kronor note to talk. He could see the ride in his log. January 19, Gösta Ekmans väg, an eighteen-minute journey. The route was like a blue snake on the map in the guy's app. He had dropped off the customer at the crossroads of Regeringsgatan and Mäster Samuelsgatan. The only problem: that address didn't tell her much; it was in the very heart of the city. And even worse was that the phone number registered to the customer seemed to belong to a prepaid sim. She had tried calling it a few times, but the phone on the other end was always switched off.

Emelie studied the few documents relating to the ownership of Hallenbro Storgården that she had managed to track down. Suarrez Augustin Landman was the legal firm representing the companies that, in turn, owned Nordic Light Investment Group Ltd. via Paradise Nordic Estates Ltd., and so on. She had flashbacks, jolts of familiarity—the whole thing stunk of her old life in the world of corporate law. She did more research into the old companies Mats had had time to mention before he was shot in Oslo. Companies linked to the men he had met at the estate ten years earlier. She requested records from financial authorities in more than ten different jurisdictions. She called old colleagues at law firms around the world. She mind-mapped the whole thing on her computer: drew circles, rectangles, and lines. Common board members—lawyers who acted as gatekeepers for the real owners—addresses, dates when the companies were registered. She worked around the clock. The child inside her kicked. She drank milk and ate licorice. She spread out notes on hotel room beds. She held her bump, wrote as though her fingers were independent of her body, as though they had ten times more energy than she really had right now; she drank coffee with huge amounts of milk, called people in Hong Kong, Malta, and Panama. She made up cases, claimed to be calling from Leijon, claimed to be clued in. Sometimes she got answers, but more often they refused to say anything, maintained confidentiality. She paid for access to documents from a pedantically organized whistleblower system online. Several of the companies featured there, and you could also see the names of real people behind them. A pattern had started to emerge. It wasn't a pretty picture, but somehow she wasn't surprised.

Several of the companies had been established in Sweden, and the firm that had helped them get set up in various parts of the world was one that was all too familiar to her: Leijon Legal Services. Surprise, surprise—though possibly not.

She knew that Loke was working in parallel, using the trojan Teddy had managed to install on the police computer system before his arrest. "I'll find something, sweetie," Loke promised. "But you have to give me time."

All the while: she had to find something to get Teddy out. She weighed up calling on Dejan anyway: coaching him properly, going against all the ethical rules to come up with a story that would hold up, rather than cast suspicion on him. But it wouldn't work: Dejan had already been arrested once, when Teddy arranged to meet Nina at Slussen. They *knew* he was involved. Plus, the main hearing was at least a few months away—and she needed Teddy by her side now.

Who else was loyal to him? She thought about Nikola, but he seemed to have disappeared from Teddy's life. The thought rumbled through her mind: Who else was there? There had to be someone she could trust. She called Loke and Tagg—his old friends from prison—but they were unanimous in their advice: "Getting someone out of custody is impossible. The only time we heard about anyone escaping was when that gang leader the kids call the New Kum escaped from the roof in a helicopter. But that was insane."

There had to be someone else. She could think of only one more person, someone Teddy should really hate.

Kum was sitting on the other side of her desk, and he looked unimpressed. He wasn't even trying to hide the fact he was staring. "You should have better furniture," he said, gesturing toward Emelie's white Ikea desk and cheap chairs. "Clients like well-built furniture. It suggests stability and competence."

The upper section of Kum's face was completely motionless when he talked, unmoving, as though it belonged to another face or a different person. Emelie was convinced that Jossan would have called the mafia boss's forehead Botox smooth.

It had been easier to get ahold of him than Emelie had expected: he was registered to an address in Lidingö and had answered politely when she called his landline.

"I'm a lawyer. So this isn't entirely uncomplicated for me," she began.

Kum barely seemed to be listening; he ran a finger over the door of her document cupboard. "Is this Ikea, too?" he asked.

Emelie wondered if he was trying to provoke her somehow.

"Are you interested in interior design?" His forehead was as stiff as a waxwork. "By the way, I have a crib in my basement, maybe you'd like it?"

Emelie nodded, mostly to move the conversation on.

"But, before I give it away," said Kum, "and before I listen to what you have to say, I want to know whose baby you're carrying."

People could clearly see she was pregnant now, but Emelie hadn't yet told a soul who the father was. There was no reason for others to know: not while the child's father was being held on suspicion of murder. But Kum was her last hope.

"The father is the man who spent eight years in prison for doing something *you* told him to do."

Kum rocked back on his seat. "I suspected as much," he said—his face still so motionless that it didn't seem like a single atom could be moving there. "You sounded so desperate on the phone. You can have our playpen, too. It cost a fortune." A very faint smile spread over Kum's lips. Did he understand the gravity of Teddy's situation?

"I didn't want to meet so we could talk about secondhand baby paraphernalia," Emelie said. "I wanted to discuss the situation Teddy is in. He needs to get out."

Kum already seemed to know most of it. "You want me to help you get Teddy out of prison, in which case let me say this: you're a lawyer, and you have your rules to follow. If it ever comes out that you were involved in something like this, they'll revoke your license quicker than they always confiscate my fake disability permits. I assume you know this, and have taken it into consideration."

Emelie nodded again. She knew the rules of the game—she was taking an enormous risk that would ruin her job prospects forever if it all went wrong. Plus: being a lawyer wasn't just a job for Emelie—it was her identity. But she couldn't see any other way out.

Kum said: "I've managed many things in my life, believe me. For example, in 1999 I was shot by two hired dogs from Montenegro. They'd gotten ahold of a pickup that they were planning to transport my body in, to avoid leaving any evidence behind. I was standing by the parking meter in Hallunda centrum, this was back when I actually paid to park, and those idiots tried to sneak up behind me. But you don't become Kum by being slow. You have to have eyes in the back of your head, and I'd spotted their wound-down window when they first pulled into the parking lot. Those dogs tried a shotgun, like I was a fucking duck. Their first shot broke more than twenty-seven car windows—I read that later, in *Aftonbladet*—but by that point I was already taking cover behind a Saab '95. Anyway, you know, back then we weren't as used to drive-by shootings in this country as we are now, but I still carried my old Zastava M70 with me, from the war. I usually kept it in a special holster on the inside of my thigh, it could look a bit weird when I reached for it, but as I lay there under the Saab, really wondering why I hadn't written a will, I didn't give a shit if some Swede thought it looked like I was scratching my dick as I reached for my nine millimeter. So, I pulled out the gun and waited under the Saab. Have you ever tried to hide under a car?"

"No," Emelie replied, wondering when he would get to the point.

"No, didn't think so," Kum continued. "Anyway, it's not as bad as you might think. Yes, it's dirty and it's cramped, especially for a big guy like me, but it's also interesting. You really get to understand the geography of the car, its inner nature, if I can phrase it like that. And I remember thinking: if they get me now, I can die happy, I've lived life the way I've wanted to, I've never fucked with anyone who didn't deserve it, and I've gotten to see the camshaft of a '95. But those two dogs in the pickup deserved it more than almost anyone I'd ever met. So I rolled out from beneath the Saab."

The door opened and Marcus peered in. He was holding a tray. "Here's your coffee." He set down the tray of cups and the orange Stelton coffeepot that Emelie was suddenly proud she had bought.

"Thanks," she said, pouring coffee for Kum. "Sorry for the interruption. Please, go on."

Kum took a sip of coffee. "It doesn't matter."

"Yes, you were in the middle of something."

"It isn't important. All I really wanted to say with that little story is that I've managed a lot in my time, but that custodial prison is sadly beyond my reach. I can't help you get Teddy out. I just don't know how to do it. By the way, could I have some milk?"

She slowly got up, dejected by Kum's response, opened the door, and shouted for Marcus. Ten seconds later, he returned with a jug of milk. Kum stared at him.

Once Marcus had gone, he turned to Emelie. "Who was that?"

"That's Marcus, my deputy. He's basically been running this place over the past few months. Incredibly good."

"Loyal?"

"Very."

"Brave?"

"I think so."

"What's his surname?"

"Engvall."

"Not Maksumic?"

"No, what do you mean?"

"Have you seen the way he moves?"

"I've never really thought about it."

"Have you thought about his build?"

"What are you getting at?"

"I can't say he's especially like Teddy, facially, because he isn't," Kum said. "But the way they move, their build, they're practically identical."

Emelie poured milk for Kum.

"I don't know what importance his posture being like Teddy's has?"

"It could have all the importance in the world. And, if we're lucky, we've just cracked how to get your baby daddy out. But you'll have to trust your little lawyer. And probably offer him a serious bonus. A big fat one, actually, that's what I'd recommend."

TELEPHONE CONVERSATIONS 110–135 (SUMMARY)

To/From: Pierre Danielsson (co-suspect) and a number of other stockbrokers and bankers in Sweden, Switzerland, and England (named in relevant appendix)

From/To: Hugo Pederson

Date: 25 September 2006

Summary: As above. None of the transactions have yet yielded a capital return, but the speculative value now amounts to more than twenty-four million euros. It can also be noted that Hugo Pederson has entered into a purchase agreement for a property in Upplands Väsby, Stockholm, with a value of roughly 40 million kronor. The property has not yet been paid for, however.

TELEPHONE CONVERSATION 136

To: Pierre Danielsson (co-suspect)

From: Hugo Pederson

Date: 25 September 2006

Time: 09:34

HUGO: Man, this is all completely insane, completely insane.

PIERRE: What are you talking about?

HUGO: I agreed to meet Mats at Odenplan like they asked me. I told him I wanted to go through a few documents for that company on the Isle of Man, North Term Investment, you know. So we met there, nothing odd about that, but I knew that they were the ones who wanted me to meet him, so once I'd said good-bye to Mats I decided to follow him. He headed back to his normal job, walking over Barnhus Bridge, you know, between Kungsholmen and Vasastan. And what happens then? Well, I see a van pull up next to him, then two guys jump out and throw him in the back. See?

PIERRE: What are you saying? They threw him into the back of a van?

HUGO: Yeah, it's completely insane, it was just now. They grabbed ahold of him, threw him into the back of the van. I was only a hundred feet away. I saw everything.

PIERRE: Maybe it was a joke?

HUGO: It wasn't a joke, I can tell you that. I have to call the police.

PIERRE: Hold on, Hugo, why are you getting the police involved before you know what's going on?

HUGO: What the hell? Two giants have just kidnapped Mats.

PIERRE: Hugo, listen to me now. We have an enormous deal going right now. I'm not going to risk that by having the police bother our partners. So you're *not* calling the police. You hear me?

HUGO: But . . .

PIERRE: No, you're not calling the police. The only fucking thing you're going to do right now is go back to work and do what you usually do. Business as usual.

TELEPHONE CONVERSATION 137

To: Hugo Pederson
From: Louise Pederson (wife)
Date: 25 September 2006
Time: 10:40

LOUISE: Ahhh, how amazing!

HUGO: What?

LOUISE: You're so wonderful, Hugo, so cute. I really love you.

HUGO: What?

LOUISE: I heard from Fredrika who heard it from Calle that you've bought the estate. Just like I wanted.

HUGO: Ah, yeah, it's cool. I wanted it to be a surprise for you.

LOUISE: I understand that, but I couldn't stop myself from calling when I found out. You're so sweet, so considerate. It's going to be fantastic.

HUGO: Yeah, I think so, too. But we don't have access yet.

LOUISE: No, but that's just a formality.

HUGO: Yeah, for the most part, yeah.

LOUISE: Honestly, I feel all giddy, I've already started furnishing the great hall in my head, and decorating the bedrooms, thinking about the paintings in the dining room, the sound system in the TV room, and the billiards table in the boys' room. Plus which dogs we're going to have.

HUGO: That sounds good, Mousey. I'm happy you're happy. But we can't have any dogs, you know how I feel about dogs. I've got to get back to work now.

LOUISE: I understand. Kisses.

TELEPHONE CONVERSATION 138
To: Carl Trolle (friend)
From: Hugo Pederson
Date: 25 September 2006
Time: 10:50

HUGO: Hi, Calle.

CARL: Why are you calling me?

HUGO: Because I need you.

CARL: There's something wrong with you, you know that, right?

HUGO: A load of shit's happened, Calle, I'm in a really tricky situation. I want to apologize for acting like an asshole the other day. I was a real ass. I need you, you're my best friend, always have been.

CARL: So what's going on? You two been fighting again?

HUGO: No, nothing like that. I've gotten myself into business with the wrong people, let's just say that. And today, about two hours ago, a couple of gorillas dragged one of my consultants into the back of a van and drove off.

CARL: What are you saying? They grabbed one of your consultants?

HUGO: I think it's a kidnapping, and the guys who threw him into the van didn't look like much fun, like Slavic mafia. Honestly.

CARL: But you've called the police?

HUGO: That's the thing: if I call the cops, there's a risk it'll drag in a ton of people I don't want to be dragged into this, which means I won't be part of any future business, and then the whole purchase of the estate in Upplands Väsby will go to shit. Louise found out about it from Fredrika. She was ecstatic.

CARL: Sorry, that was my fault. I told Fredrika, but she promised not to say anything to Louise.

HUGO: You couldn't know. They gossip like crazy. But what am I meant to do?

CARL: Want to grab a coffee and talk about it?

HUGO: Sure.

TELEPHONE CONVERSATION 139

To: Hugo Pederson
From: Göran Blixt (boss)
Date: 29 September 2006
Time: 11:12

GÖRAN: Hugo?

HUGO: Yeah?

GÖRAN: Can you swing by the office this afternoon? I want to talk to you.

HUGO: Sure, but I've got a lot going on. What's it about?

GÖRAN: You can come in now instead, if you're busy later.

HUGO: I'm not at the office right now.

GÖRAN: No, exactly.

HUGO: What did you say?

GÖRAN: I said: no, exactly. You haven't been in much lately.

HUGO: I've been working from home.

GÖRAN: Okay. To keep it brief, let's just say that I haven't been happy with your performance over the past few weeks. You aren't here enough, which is one thing, but your reports also aren't up to standard, and that's not acceptable. Add to that the fact that you've been acting strangely, to say the least, over the past few days. I honestly don't know what you're up to, but we don't have room for anything like that at Fortem Capital, as you well know. I pay you to deliver, not to run around like a headless chicken.

TELEPHONE CONVERSATION 140
To: Carl Trolle (friend)
From: Hugo Pederson
Date: 29 September 2006
Time: 22:27

HUGO: Hey, Calle. You okay to talk for a bit?

CARL: Sure, sure.

HUGO: So, I still haven't called the police.

CARL: Why not?

HUGO: Nah, it won't work. But I have looked up some stuff.

CARL: Like what?

HUGO: Well, I saw the registration plate on the van that drove away with my consultant. It was a rental from OKQ8, so I called them and asked who rented the van, but they wouldn't tell me. So I called Gurra Hamilton, you remember him from school?

CARL: Yeah, yeah, he's on the board for the Swedish wing of OKQ8, right?

HUGO: Exactly. Anyway, five minutes later, the branch I'd called, called me back and told me who had rented the van. They gave me the guy's ID number and a copy of his driver's license and everything. So I looked him up, and he must be some kind of straw man because he's registered on, like, seventeen defunct companies and hasn't paid any tax for the past ten years.

CARL: Sounds like the ideal straw man.

HUGO: Right, but I went over to his place last night, with ten grand in a bag. The guy wouldn't say a word to begin with, but then I waved a thousand-kronor note under his nose and said there was more where that came from. After that, he told me he just let people use his name sometimes so he could afford his rent and old debts. I gave him two thousand more, and then he told me that he sometimes does work for really dangerous guys. "Kum's boys," he said. He wouldn't say another word after that, just sat there sulking, staring at the floor. But I'd managed to get in there, you know, and I'd gotten him to open a bottle of cheap wine. I nagged and threatened and played cute with him, but he really didn't want to talk. Eventually, I spread out six fresh thousand-kronor notes on the table and said that if he just gave me the name of whoever had rented the van, he could have those and as much again, so long as it checked out.

CARL: Did he tell you?

HUGO: Yep, I got a name.

CARL: Who?

HUGO: I've got no idea who he is, but apparently the guy's name is Najdan Maksumic. Goes by Teddy.

CARL: Okay, never heard of him.

HUGO: Of course not, he's a gangster. Anyway, I looked this Teddy up, and he's infamous, definitely part of the Slavic mafia, but I don't think he's a bigwig. In any case, I went over to his place.

CARL: Are you serious?

HUGO: Yeah, I did. He lives in Södertälje, in an apartment, but he wasn't home. I went back to the car and waited outside. Sat there all night, and half the morning, too. Göran even called me wondering where I was. He doesn't think I've been pulling my weight lately. Eventually, this Teddy guy turned up, he looked exhausted, big as a house, a real bruiser, you know? And I'm convinced he was one of the men who did the kidnapping. So, I reparked my car behind his once he went inside. A few hours later, he came back out and started the engine. And I followed him.

CARL: Shit, man, you're crazy. Why didn't you just call the police? You have a name now.

HUGO: I can't, I've told you.

CARL: So what happened?

HUGO: I followed him, stayed at a good distance but kept his car in sight the whole time. We ended up some way out of town, up toward Uppsala. There was another car parked there, a BMW, and after a few minutes another man came out, the other gangster type who threw my consultant into the van the other day. You see? I'm convinced they're keeping my man in that house.

CARL: Then you *have to* call the police. You did it, right?

HUGO: No, I didn't do it. I just went home.

TELEPHONE CONVERSATION 141

To: Pierre Danielsson (co-suspect)
From: Hugo Pederson
Date: 30 September 2006
Time: 01:34

PIERRE: You can't call at this time of day.

HUGO: It's up to you whether you answer or not. And you answered.

PIERRE: What do you want?

HUGO: I have to call the police about this Mats thing. I'm convinced he's been kidnapped, and I know who did it.

PIERRE: Get out of here. You're exaggerating.

HUGO: No, you get out of here. They might kill him.

PIERRE: But I fucking told you not to get involved. What's wrong with you? The whole deal might go to shit and you won't make a krona, the opposite.

HUGO: That's bullshit. I already have my positions. No one can take that from me now, the same way no one can take the shares you own from you. And we're in the same boat here, you, me, and whoever else is involved. No one wants to blow this deal. It's too big for everyone.

PIERRE: You sound crazy. Are you going to risk a deal worth, if I'm guessing right, more than 50 mill just for you, all because you've decided someone kidnapped a sweaty, criminal, money-laundering loser?

HUGO: You aren't listening. I'm telling you the deal won't collapse. There are too many of us banking on it now. I'm going to call the police.

PIERRE: Please. Please, Hugo. Wait until tomorrow. Sleep on it. You're making the biggest mistake of your life.

TELEPHONE CONVERSATION 142

To: Hugo Pederson
From: Louise Pederson (wife)
Date: 30 September 2006
Time: 03:10

LOUISE: Where are you?

HUGO: Sorry I didn't call, Mousey, I'm working.

LOUISE: It sounds like you're in a car.

HUGO: Yeah, I'm on the way to a meeting.

LOUISE: A meeting? At this time of night?

HUGO: Yeah, you could say that. I can't explain right now, Mousey, it's complicated.

LOUISE: I get worried when I don't hear from you. You usually let me know when you're going to be this late.

HUGO: I know, I know. I'll tell you everything later, I promise. Get some sleep now, and think about how great the house is going to be.

LOUISE: But when are you coming home?

HUGO: Soon. Two hours, maybe.

LOUISE: Who are you going to meet?

HUGO: I'll tell you tomorrow, I promise.

LOUISE: Okay, baby. See you tomorrow.

HUGO: Yeah, see you tomorrow.

TELEPHONE CONVERSATION 143

To: 112 (SOS Alarm/Police)
From: Hugo Pederson
Date: 30 September 2006
Time: 04:12

SOS: SOS Alarm.

HUGO: Hi, I'd like to report a crime.

SOS: Okay, and what is it that's happened?

HUGO: They've kidnapped a man, Mats Emanuelsson.

SOS: Kidnapped, you said? In what sense?

HUGO: I saw them drag him into the back of a van a few days ago. And I've tracked them down.

SOS: To where?

HUGO: Not far from Uppsala, the coordinates are 59.78 and 17.81 They're keeping him in a house there.

SOS: Aha, that doesn't sound good, but thank you for the coordinates. Just wait a moment while I jot that down. And who is it that's holding him there?

HUGO: I don't know for sure, but one of them is called Najdan "Teddy" Maksumic, I know that much.

SOS: And do you have any more information about this Teddy?

HUGO: No, sorry.

SOS: And how do you know what you've told me?

HUGO: I saw it.

SOS: You saw the victim?

HUGO: No, but I'm sure, I saw when they grabbed him.

SOS: And how did you find out the name of the perpetrator?

HUGO: I just know.

SOS: And what is your name?

HUGO: I'd rather not say, it feels really uncomfortable.

SOS: I understand, but it would be good for us to be able to get in touch with you, to know who you are.

HUGO: I've done what I need to do now. I've reported this crap and given you the address. That should be enough.

48

These were the shittiest days of her life, and yet Roksana had still forced herself over to the school hall in Kista, to hand over her cell phone, show *her own* ID, and spend more than six hours working on the various components of the aptitude test. For real this time, all her—no one else.

There was mathematic problem solving, quantitative comparisons, diagrams, tables and charts, word comprehension, sentence completion, and so on. Each section lasted fifty-five minutes. The math in particular went badly, she couldn't think straight, the stress blocking her thoughts, and it took her at least fifteen minutes to even read through the first question—fifteen minutes she couldn't afford to waste. She glanced at the other test takers around her: they were all hunched over, scribbling away with their sharpened pencils, focused—they knew what they were doing. Her thoughts veered wildly. The psychos' demands. The threat against her father. Z, who was apparently still being held for things to do with Our Land Club. She was going to fail, that much was clear. During the break, she went into the toilet and threw up.

She felt an enormous urge to go over to her parents' house immediately after the exam, but when she got there, no one was home. She called her dad and felt herself breathe a sigh of relief when he answered.

"Baba, where are you?"

"Your mother and I are going to the theater."

Roksana sat in their kitchen and listened to her father's music. Was he playing on any of these songs? Caspar came home and sat down to study for some exam. Roksana went into her old room, lay down on her old bed, and tried to watch YouTube videos— covers by Sofia Karlberg, Clara Henry doing stand-up, the kind of thing she had watched three years ago. She thought it would help her relax, to feel like she was twenty again. To forget all the crap. But it didn't work.

One million kronor. She was going to have to start trying to scrape the money together, but it was like she was paralyzed. The psychos were thinking of killing Baba, and nothing she could do would get rid of that thought—it whirled around her head like a centrifuge: blocking her senses, practically shutting her down. She couldn't smell, couldn't taste, didn't hear the vloggers or see their smooth faces on her phone, couldn't think of anything but her father's innocent vulnerability. And when the time ran out—that short-circuited her head.

She called Z: she still hadn't managed to get through to him since she was released. This time, someone did actually answer, but it wasn't him. It was his father.

"He came over here when he was released. He's going to be staying with us for a few days."

"Could I talk to him?"

"I'll tell him you called. Then we'll see."

The tone of Z's father's voice was clear: he wasn't particularly enamored with Roksana. She wondered what Z had said about her.

She tried Billie. "Billie, can I borrow some money from you?"

Billie's voice sounded cheerful. "Sure, how much?"

"A few hundred thousand?"

There was silence on the other end of the line.

Billie replied jokingly, in Norwegian: *"Kødder du?"*

"No, I'm not kidding. Z and I are in a really shitty situation."

"What happened?"

Roksana could hear one of Billie's partners in the background. "I can't talk about it right now."

"Gotcha," said Billie. "I want to help you, but I don't have a hundred thousand to spare. Maybe three."

Roksana sighed and they ended the call. She was still clutching her phone. She called the cute guy, who promised to lend her ten grand—as soon as he found a new job. She phoned a whole slew of old friends, but no one was especially keen to lend her any more than a hundred or so. She even called Ora Flesh, who said she could lend her a lot, but only if Roksana came over with at least twenty grams of K.

She dropped the phone onto her bed

Thought back to Tehran. To the back street that she, Leila, and Val had passed one evening, and that had been full of cars—Mercedes, BMWs, and so on. "What's going on there?" she had asked. It was the first time Roksana had seen Leila with a bitter expression: she looked insanely surly. "That's where the prostitutes go," she had said. "But now let's show you something else." Val had turned onto another back street. In the distance, Roksana could see cars and people standing in groups outside a building. Leila turned around. "This is Super Jordan." They had climbed out of the car. All you could see of the place was the light shining through a glass door. The shops all around it were closed. "Rumor is that the owner has a direct line to the mayor." The shop was no bigger than a newsstand, but it was full of people. Music Roksana recognized was playing in the background—the Rolling Stones. The shelves were full of cigarettes, bags of peanuts and other snacks, bottles of tonic water, soda, and strawberry drinks. The customers seemed to be avoiding eye contact with one another, and some were covering their mouths. Roksana had stared. But then she understood. There was no mistaking it: the smell of alcohol from the customers' breath had to be obvious even out on the street. "Half of north

Tehran comes here when they need something after midnight,"
Val had explained. Leila laughed. "The only thing you can't buy at
Super Jordan is your own success."

Roksana got up from the bed. It was over. She was having no
luck whatsoever—a complete loser. She was out of ideas. And it
would be her father who would suffer.

She should just take an overdose or something, bury herself
here, in her old room. Never return.

She thought about her cousins again. The way they spoke.
Their simple closeness.

Closeness.

She called Nikola.

49

He kept guard over himself all night, utterly determined not to make the same mistake again: to fall asleep in his cell. Virtually without any food: Teddy refused to eat anything but Kex bars or Snickers, wrapped in their original packaging—but he wasn't allowed to buy as many as he wanted from the kiosk; there were rules about that.

Emelie had tried in vain to track down a prison employee who had taken medical leave because of an eye problem, but the prison refused to give out that kind of information. Still, Teddy knew what he was waiting for. What was going to happen today.

"You've got a visitor," said one of the guards who peered into his cell at regular intervals.

The guard led him down the hallway. The smell reminded him of a high school.

Marcus was already waiting in the visitor room. Teddy had never seen him before, but Emelie had repeatedly insisted that he could be trusted. Marcus's face looked as though someone had powdered it—he was that pale.

"Has Emelie told you how this is going to work?" was the first thing he asked.

"Yeah, she was here yesterday."

Teddy couldn't help but admire her for getting her deputy to go along with this, and he had even more admiration for Marcus, who clearly had a deep sense of respect for his boss. Teddy had never heard of anything like it.

"Are you sure you want to do this?" Teddy instantly regretted giving Marcus an opportunity to back out.

Marcus crossed his legs. "It's okay. We've concluded that I'm not running any risks. It'll look like you've attacked me and forced me into it. And, as yet, surveillance cameras aren't permitted in these rooms."

There was a bag on the floor. Teddy knew the routine down at the entrance: the lawyers had to pass through metal detectors and put their bags through X-ray machines, but no one actually checked the contents of the bag, and it wasn't unusual for lawyers to have large bags with them—sometimes, the material from the preliminary investigation could run to thousands of pages.

"Everything's in there. The only thing I couldn't manage was a pair of scissors, because they're metal," said Marcus. "Did you manage to fix that?"

"Not scissors," Teddy said, holding up a yellow Bic razor. "But I got this."

None of the inmates were permitted to have razors or other sharp objects in their cells, but they were given a single use razor once a week, in the showers. The guards usually just brought in a box and let them help themselves—they had to be handed back once they were finished showering. Teddy had simply taken two.

Marcus pulled out a plastic bag containing a small towel, which he handed to Teddy. The towel was damp, and he started to dab at his beard—hopefully that would make the shave smoother. He wished he had a mirror, but that kind of luxury wasn't considered necessary in the visitor's room in prison.

Next, Marcus started to shave him. "I booked this room for two hours," he said. "That should be enough."

Teddy could feel the razor tearing at his beard, rather than cutting it.

"They're used to seeing you with facial hair in here," Marcus said, continuing to pull the razor in short strokes over his cheeks. First Kum's skin treatments and now a strange man just a few inches from his face, shaving him so carefully, it was like something out of a razor commercial. Marcus's breath smelled of coffee masked by toothpaste.

Forty-five minutes later, they were done. Teddy's beard was on the floor, and his cheeks were smooth for the first time in weeks. He was wearing Marcus's suit, tie, and shoes, and Marcus, in turn, was wearing his soft green prison uniform and had slippers on his feet. The icing on the cake was the wig Marcus eventually fished out of his bag: it was perfect on Teddy's relatively smooth head, and was roughly the same style and color as Emelie's supremely gifted deputy's hair.

Marcus smiled. "You don't look exactly like me, but we'll have to assume that the guards don't remember exactly what I look like."

"Is this going to work?"

Marcus grinned even more broadly now. "No, because you look exhausted, like someone who hasn't slept in a week."

Teddy rubbed his new face.

"But luckily, my boss thinks of everything," said Marcus. He held up a small bag.

Fifteen minutes later, they really were done. Marcus had primarily applied the makeup beneath Teddy's eyes, but there was also some on his forehead.

"Okay, that's as far as we're going to get," he said, putting the bottle of foundation back into the bag. "You're almost as handsome as me."

Teddy laughed for the first time in a long while.

Marcus sat down on the floor, and Teddy tied him to the table leg, gagging his mouth with a ripped pillowcase that he had smuggled out of his cell. Next, he hung Marcus's visitor pass around his neck, opened the door to the hallway, and shouted to the guard who was sitting fifty feet away, in his booth. "We're done in here."

The guard waved him over.

Teddy cast one last glance at Marcus. He nodded to him: good luck. Then he closed the door. Now he had to hope that they wouldn't immediately arrive to take Marcus—aka Teddy—back to his cell.

The hallway was empty. The glass in the guard booth glittered; he was going to have to pass it to reach the first door. He tried to walk like a lawyer would in these surroundings: confident in himself, certain he would never be locked up like his client but slightly stressed all the same, always en route to the next meeting. Almost immediately, he became acutely aware of his gait: never in a rush, always with his arms swinging by his sides—eyes straight forward. Oozing power, oozing self-confidence, oozing repressed aggression—it was ingrained in him. He had to get away from it. He sped up, held Marcus's bag as loosely as he could, and tried to look down at his shoes: there were surveillance cameras everywhere here, like flies on a warm summer's day. He didn't want them to catch his face.

He thought back to when he had been recognized just a few feet away from escaping the police station.

Teddy glanced around: there were postcards and various regulations stuck up on the inside of the guard booth. A bizarre insult: *postcards* from other guards who were free to travel the world. The guard sitting inside now was reading a newspaper. Teddy sped up. Said nothing as he passed the booth.

"Bye," the guard shouted after him.

The blue-painted metal door was heavy, unlocked remotely by the guard booth. Teddy had never been here before, a small room with three elevator doors, but Emelie had explained it to him: the elevators were operated by the central guard. At that very moment, there might be other guards looking down at him from the round, black eyes in the corners. He took a few steps forward and back—

another tip from Emelie: it would help them to spot him more easily and send down the elevator. He kept his face angled toward the floor the entire time.

The elevator doors plinged and opened. Shit, there was someone else inside. Teddy stepped in anyway. He could see the shoes of the other man: polished brown leather with brass buckles. He looked at the slacks: gray, pressed. "Hello," the man said.

Teddy had no choice but to look up. Gray eyes, shirt, tie. The man must be a lawyer.

"Hi," he said.

"Are you the new person at Ramblings?" The man was probably somewhere around fifty, the knot in his tie loose and his hair starting to recede.

Teddy could feel the sweat on his back. His suit felt uncomfortable, so itchy that he wanted to rub himself against the metal handrail inside the lift.

"No," he said. "I'm with Emelie Jansson."

"Aha, I don't know that firm. Do you work on anything but criminal cases?"

The display in the elevator showed floor three.

"Ah, no, just criminal cases. Plus the occasional asylum case," Teddy replied, hoping he sounded credible.

"I can imagine that type of case must have exploded in frequency in recent years. I should introduce myself, by the way. Patrik Wallin." The man held out his hand. "District commissioner."

Teddy wanted to hit the emergency stop button and throw himself out of the elevator—he didn't care if it would mean having to climb down the elevator shaft to get away. Of all the possible bastards, he was trapped in an elevator with a senior police officer. Though maybe it was better to be stuck with a high-ranking policeman than someone who actually worked on the ground: the risk of him being recognized must be lower that way.

"Marcus," was all Teddy said. He had no idea what Marcus's surname was. His palms were damp with sweat.

The elevator clattered and thudded to a halt. The doors opened.

"I'm sure I'll see you around," Teddy almost shouted, virtually running away from the elevator. He was still staring at the floor but gradually slowed his steps—a running lawyer would immediately draw attention to himself on the surveillance screens.

"Wait, Marcus," the commissioner shouted after him.

Teddy kept walking, as though he hadn't heard.

"Hey, wait."

Teddy didn't want to turn around, he didn't want to wait for the police officer whose footsteps he could hear a few feet behind him. But he did: calmed his breathing, turned around. The sweat was running down him as though someone were holding a showerhead beneath his shirt. He could see images flashing through his head: The darkness of the cell. The feeling of not being able to breathe. Fredrik O. Johansson's broken face.

"You forgot your bag," the commissioner said, holding out Marcus's leather bag.

The man winked. "It's not easy being new here. Easy to get stressed by all the locked doors and claustrophobic elevators."

Lock and key—Teddy wouldn't be going back.

He went down to the window in the central guard office. "Hi," he said to the guard, whose face was hazy on the other side of the reflective glass. He held up his visitor pass.

The officer pushed out a small drawer beneath the window, and Teddy placed the pass inside. The whole time, he was trying to appear as relaxed as he could. He told himself that Marcus was just Emelie's employee, that he had only been working on criminal cases for roughly six months. He shouldn't be a familiar face here, in other words. He might never have been to Kronoberg Remand Prison before.

Teddy thought back to when he was released after his eight-year stretch. Dejan had come to pick him up in his incredibly crappy BMW. The engine had sounded like a broken tractor, despite the fact that it wasn't a diesel, and the exhaust had put out a cloud of smoke like a bonfire. The metallic paint and the eighteen-inch rims had long since lost their sheen, and the only wing mirror was, for some reason, taped over. Teddy remembered wondering whether the car would even make it all the way home. He had thought that it might lose a wheel somewhere around Tumba, or that it might just rattle and die, leaving them sitting for hours in the freezing cold. He had glanced back at the prison as Dejan drove him through the woods, practically counting every tree. Trying to absorb the idea that he was moving farther away from his old life with every second that passed.

The officer said nothing. Just pushed out the drawer again. This time, there was a driving license inside. Marcus Engvall. Teddy picked it up. Clutched it tight in his hand, restrained himself from running.

The next heavy door clicked open.

He walked through the glass passage toward the street.

The last door clicked. He pushed it open with both hands. It felt easy, like it was made of paper.

He was standing on Bergsgatan. The sun was shining.

On the other side of the road was a Porsche Panama with matte black paintwork and matching rims.

The horn sounded, and Dejan wound down the window. Flashed him the world's biggest grin. "My friend, welcome out!"

Emelie was in the passenger seat beside him.

50

Nikola and Roksana met at Palm Village Thai Wok again. The woman who ran the place called Roksana "my new daughter" and gave them their meal on the house. "We had our factory down there," Roksy said, pointing her thumb toward the floor.

Nikola wanted her to smile as she said it—after all, it was completely insane that she had cooked up ketamine like some kind of crazy El Chapo Guzmán. He knew how much they had managed to sell at their club, how much they had made from the ticket sales, but he also knew they had lost it all.

After they ate, they went back to her place. The apartment felt empty, as though she were about to move out, but Roksana said that it was Z who had taken off. "He's gone to his parents in Tjottahejti."

"Where's Tjottahejti?"

"It's just something people say. Anyway, I don't care," she snapped. "All I know is that he hasn't called me, even though I've left him hundreds of messages."

"Has he dumped you?"

Roksana stopped dead—it was like a serious mannequin challenge. "We were never together," she said. "I thought you knew that. I mean, you hung out with us for three days."

Maybe he did know, maybe not. Because the truth was that he also knew two other things: one was that he felt something for

Roksana. Ever since they held hands after the club, he had been sure, and there was no kidding himself anymore—he was completely into this girl, for real. And yet, the second thing he knew was that the basic rule was still the same: whoever showed their hand first risked losing out. It was a simple principle he wasn't willing to compromise on. Telling her what he felt in his heart was a leap into the unknown. A leap he couldn't bring himself to take—that was why he told himself that she probably already had a boyfriend, that she was with this Z guy. That the reason there was no Nikola and her had nothing to do with his cowardice.

But now he needed to rethink. Now that she had explicitly told him that Z wasn't in the picture, there were no more excuses. Somehow, Nikola had understood something else: he had to take the chance with this girl—otherwise he would regret it for the rest of his life. He had already lost so much, but now that there was something sweet to gain, he had to do it right. For once, he *had* to fix it.

He leaned forward, pushed his mouth toward her face. He didn't dare look; he squinted, waiting for the laugh or the slap. But neither came. Roksana had leaned forward, too. They met in the middle. He wasn't even thinking about Chamon—he felt balanced.

Nikola turned over in bed. It was the next morning. The sheets were crumpled and had come loose around the edges, the result of last night's activities. Roksy lay beside him. She was still sleeping, curled up in the fetal position, with the covers half thrown back and her dark hair hanging over her face. Though the blinds were down, the room was bright: he could clearly make out the microscopic lines on her brow, the birthmark above one cheek and the long eyelashes that seemed to tremble with the regular movement of her breathing. Everything about her was still new to him, hadn't yet become routine. She might be the most beautiful person he had ever seen—not just because her face contained that mix of light and dark that he liked so much, but because she genuinely seemed to get everything he thought and said, without faking it. She didn't use her openness as a tool to get to him, not like all the counselors, social services hags, and staff in various detention centers he had met.

At the same time, all this crap was still raging inside him. Isak's betrayal. Mr. One: a man who ordered murders. Of his own boys.

A few nights earlier, Simon Murray had accosted Bello in a pub.

"I hear Nikola wants to see me," he had said.

Bello didn't want to talk to the pig, but he had still nodded and passed on Murray's suggested time and place.

They met by the gravel pit, the same place as before. The same grayish gloom. The same lame Volkswagen.

"Was that your gorilla who dropped you off again today?"

"If you mean Bello, he's not an ape. But I know you pigs call us that kind of thing."

The color of bastard Murray's face darkened. "I didn't mean that."

A machine whirred in the distance: they were working here today. Nikola had always thought the place was abandoned. He and Murray started walking.

Murray sounded almost out of breath. "So what do you want?"

"I wanted to talk to you about what you know."

"Why?"

"Because there's too much shit going on right now. I want it all to stop."

"I wonder. I think I've worked out most of it."

"What have you worked out?"

"You took out Yusuf and the other guy by mistake, because you thought he was behind Chamon's murder."

Nikola held off replying.

Simon Murray continued: "But now you think it was Isak behind it all. Am I right?"

Murray really had worked it out. Nikola had to say something.

"Why would I think that? I don't have anything against Isak. He's like a mentor to me."

Murray's voice had almost reached a falsetto by now. "Maybe he was, I don't doubt that, even if it is sad, because you could have chosen another way. But I don't think you're following Isak anymore."

"That's bullshit. You can't prove anything."

"You don't know that."

Nikola shoved his hands into his pockets. "Why do people become pigs? It's something I've always wondered. Why would you want to be involved the minute something bad happens? Wouldn't it be better to do something positive? There must be something about you people, something that draws you toward the shit."

Simon Murray's shoulders looked tense. "If you give me something, maybe I can make sure you get out of all this. So you can drop all this crap."

"No, it's you who needs to drop it," Nikola said, pulling out his cell phone. "I remember you thought it was incredible that Isak had been released even though the charges against him were ready and there was plenty of evidence."

"Yeah, that was magic, but what does that have to do with this?"

Nikola pressed play on the recording he had made of Simon Murray last time they met. The cunt's face turned even redder, the corners of his mouth drooping.

"Listen to me now. Just take it fucking easy," said Nikola. "Because you're giving me classified information in this recording. That's misconduct, and it's not at all good for you, even you know that. So, if you don't want me to send this to your bosses, I want you to answer one question."

Murray squirmed—now he knew why Nikola had wanted to meet.

"I want to know what the deal is with Isak." Nikola crossed his arms: demonstratively.

Thirty seconds passed. The sound of the road hummed in the background.

"You're a little asshole, you know that, don't you?" said Murray.

"Maybe, but right now one asshole is in a worse position than the other. So tell me what you know about Isak, why he was released."

"Okay, okay. If you delete that crap you recorded, I'll tell you what I know."

Nikola held out his hand. Deal.

Simon Murray's throat looked tense. "I only just found this out myself. I didn't know it when they dropped the charges against him, but I had the feeling it was something out of the ordinary. Isak has been an informant for local police for years."

"What?"

"You heard what I said."

Nikola had heard—but he still hadn't understood it. "Again please."

"Well, I said that I'd been looking into stuff and worked out certain things. Isak has been playing in our court the entire time, giving us information, building up a relationship with local police, squealing on whoever he thought he could squeal on, selling out whoever he felt like selling out. That's what Chamon found out: that your boss is an informant. Don't ask me how, but he found out Isak was a rat, as you say. And that's why Isak had to get rid of him. The attack at the gym was aimed at Chamon from the beginning, no one else."

Nikola had never listened to anything as carefully in his life, but he still couldn't make sense of it. Was this cop saying what he thought he was saying?

"What did you say?" Nikola asked. He had to understand. He had to hear it again.

They were standing opposite one another, roughly the same height. Murray—the police officer who had spent the past few years trying to send down Nikola and his brothers, who had been praised by the papers as "the police inspector who made it his calling to clean up Södertälje," the cop who always wanted to be righteous, honorable, *good*. Now Nikola wanted to know what he was really saying.

Murray repeated the same thing again. "And I think," he then said, "that after Chamon was attacked, he told Yusuf what he knew."

Nikola thought back to Chamon's words in the hospital, words his friend hadn't been able to speak but had written down: *You can't trust anyone. I want out.*

Shit.

It was crazier than he had thought. Isak—the boss—wasn't just a killer. He was also a rat. A traitor.

Now he really did have to take down Mr. One; it was justified on all fronts. But, in order to manage it, he was going to need help. The only problem was that he didn't know where he would find it. He couldn't talk to Bello: it was too much to ask for his friend to turn on Mr. One. The next person who popped into his head was Teddy. But they hadn't spoken in a long time, and his uncle was currently being held in custody. Nikola had been there; it wasn't a good place.

And yet Nikola had made a friend there, the guy who had spent his exercise hour in the neighboring cage: Kerim Celalî. The guy who had escaped by helicopter, been re-arrested, and then by some magic only been given three years by the courts. Kerim: the mafioso with more than nine lives. The guy everyone was talking about, who they called the New Kum, who seemed to be building an empire as big as the old one. Nikola counted the months and days. Kerim should have been given conditional release just a few weeks earlier.

Roksana opened her eyes. Nikola crept closer so that his face was near hers. When she blinked, he could feel her lashes on his. He was completely naked—even Chamon's gold chain and cross were on the bedside table. They kissed. He could see the fear in her eyes—last night, she had told him about the men demanding a million kronor in cash and threatening to kill her dad unless she delivered the dough.

"Morning, Roksy."

"Morning, Nicko. How long have you been awake?"

"A while. How're you feeling?"

"Yeah, you know. They want the money in three days, on Midsummer's Eve."

"I know. What are we going to do?"

"You've already done enough by lending me money. I need to try to convince my dad to lend me the rest somehow."

Nikola had given her all of his savings the night before: the 154,000 kronor that he always kept in two rolls, bound with rubber bands, in his pocket. But it wasn't a loan, like Roksy had said—he wasn't going to ask for it back. He thought about whether he should pawn the gold chain and cross—but they weren't really his.

"And you're sure you don't want me to talk to them? I might know who they are."

Roksana kissed the scar on his stomach: a physical reminder of the explosion he had survived. "No, it won't help. They've given me so many chances now."

"I'm coming with you, at least, when you go to meet them. No way you're going to see those bastards on your own."

"Z and I usually call them the psychos."

The psychos, Nikola thought: I'm just like them.

His phone beeped.

A Snapchat message: *Heard you wanted to meet. Just say when and I'll tell you where. /Kerim*

The New Kum was willing to see him—he had to seize this chance. Nikola got up and started to get dressed.

"When will I see you again?" Roksana asked.

Nikola hadn't thought that far ahead. He kissed her forehead. "I don't know."

"What are you going to do?"

Nikola knew the rules; he knew the law among brothers. But he also felt so good with this girl in front of him that he wanted her to know every inch of him.

"I'm going to war."

"What do you mean? War?"

"It's hard to explain."

He could hear how crazy it sounded when he used that word. War.

51

She was in her twentieth week of pregnancy, but she couldn't sleep at home. She would be giving birth in just a few months' time, and she was living under the threat of death. She was carrying an unborn child whose father's face was on posters all over town. *Billionaire's suspected killer escapes from prison. Suspected killer ties up lawyer in custody. Suspected murderer and former kidnapper pulls off most cunning jailbreak since helicopter escape.*

Emelie and *the suspected killer* were sitting in the entertainment room beneath Kum's villa with a laptop computer and stacks of papers and documents. Loke had finally come through with the information that, thanks to the trojan, he had managed to extract from the Police Authority's computer system. He hadn't sifted through it: that was Emelie and Teddy's job. Preliminary investigation reports from the old kidnapping case in 2006, reports from the Benjamin Emanuelsson case, material from the ongoing investigation Nina Ley was pursuing with her special unit. Emelie had already seen a lot of it, but there was also material she had never come across before: the ongoing preliminary investigation into Teddy and the murder of Fredrik O. Johansson, for example; other investigations Nina seemed to have carried out, investigations into Joakim Sundén—the cop who had worked for the bastards and who had been killed just under two years ago. In another world,

TOP DOG   461

she and Teddy might have been able to enjoy one another's company. But right now, they didn't have time.

They prepared, organized. Tried to understand the scope of the material, to draw up priorities. They read interviews, forensic reports, police memos. By looking at everything, they tried to see the bigger picture, to spot patterns. The network was bigger than she had ever realized: the range of those dogs became physical when she studied the mountain of material.

Every now and then, Kum came down with food.

"Emelie, what do you think of my *ćevapčići?*"

She loved the skinless lamb sausages, even if her appetite wasn't the greatest at the moment.

"The two of you seem comfortable down here?"

The place was nice, two big sofas, an enormous TV with all the games and streaming channels they could ask for, and two fold-up beds where she and Teddy tried to sleep at night.

Teddy said: "I'll always be grateful."

Kum started to head back upstairs. He paused midway and stuck his head over the railing. "A star lawyer and one of my best men. You two should be able to manage this. And you should be able to get yourself released, Teddy, right?"

Emelie wished she could agree with the man on the stairs, Teddy's old godfather. She just didn't know how they were going to do it.

In one of the police reports in the investigation into Fredrik O. Johansson's murder, Emelie saw that one of the surveillance cameras at the property had caught the dead man's Range Rover pulling away from the house after the killing. The police suspected it was Teddy who had taken it, but both Emelie and Teddy knew that it must be the man who had disappeared with the Samsonite case. The police had checked the toll booths and had tracked the car driving into central Stockholm forty minutes later.

Emelie thought about the fact that someone had taken an Uber to the same area after threatening Katja. Then she thought about the company documents she had seen for the estate, which had been drawn up by Leijon. She got an idea.

"I have to go out," she said to Teddy. "There's something I need to check in town."

She was standing by the entrance to the building that housed Leijon Legal Services. On the ground floor, there was a dry cleaner, a skiwear shop, and a 7-Eleven.

She stepped into the 7-Eleven and immediately recognized the same assistant who had been there when she worked upstairs.

"Hey, Gregory," she said, smiling so widely that her jaw almost ached. "It's been a while. How's it going?" She was glad he was wearing a name badge on his chest pocket.

Gregory seemed to recognize her—she had been a huge consumer of the self-serve mixed candy back in the day, after all.

"Pretty good. You not working for Leijon anymore? Don't think I've seen you here in at least a year."

"Yeah, yeah, I'm still there. But I'm trying to be healthier. They say sugar's dangerous, you know."

Gregory had freckles and still looked seventeen, though he was probably at least twenty-three.

"I have a question," said Emelie. "Or rather, the firm has a question. We were wondering if we could have access to the films from your surveillance camera on the front of the building."

Gregory picked his nose. "Why?"

"Uff, there was an incident a few weeks back, and we just wanted to check it out. It's not worth getting the police involved for such small stuff. I just wanted to check whether a certain person came to the office on a certain day."

"Aha."

"How long do you keep the films?"

Gregory's finger was even deeper in his nose now. "Several

months. It's all on the computer back here." He gestured to a door behind the counter. "You can check as much as you want."

Ten minutes later, Emelie had seen enough—finding the right clip hadn't taken long. 7-Eleven's camera also covered part of the Leijon entrance, and she knew which date she was looking for. On the same day the murder occurred out at Hallenbro Storgården, exactly 14 minutes and 12 seconds after Fredrik O. Johansson's car passed the tolls into the city, she watched a man enter the building pulling a Samsonite suitcase in the same color Teddy had described. In other words: Fredrik O's unknown friend had grabbed the case out at the estate, driven Fredrik's car into town, and then taken the case straight to Leijon.

There was only one problem: 7-Eleven's fantastic camera didn't cover the whole of the entrance. You couldn't see the head of the man pulling the bag. It was out of shot.

Maybe it was no longer in there, but just the chance that every-thing Fredrik O. Johansson had wanted to tidy up, everything he had wanted to hide, might be up there, within reach, meant that someone had to get in there. They had to try to get ahold of that crap. The evidence.

Emelie sat down at Jossan's kitchen table.

"What's really going on?" her friend asked. "I've seen posters with Teddy's face on them all over town."

"Yeah, it's a bit tricky."

"*A bit* tricky? You're involved somehow, right? It was your law-yer he tied up in the visitor's room?"

"I am involved. And you're right. It's not just *a bit* tricky. It's the worst thing I've ever been through."

Jossan pushed out her lower jaw. She looked skeptical—a look Emelie had never seen on her before. It scared her. Jossan clearly didn't feel like joking today.

"Just how involved are you?"

"Very. Teddy is the father of this little one, for example." Emelie patted her stomach.

Josephine looked like she had just found out that she herself
was pregnant with triplets. "Are you kidding? You said you didn't
know who the father was."

But then she laughed, back to her usual self. "Pippa, your kid's
going to be insanely cute. I mean, it would have been anyway, but
now that I know who the father is, I think it's going to be a baby
model. Maybe for Bonpoint or something. They make fantastic
clothes for little ones. Have you seen them?"

Emelie couldn't help but smile. "I want to come to the fortieth
anniversary party for alumni on Midsummer's Eve."

Jossan laughed again, but differently this time. "Nope, it's too
late, that's only three days away. I can understand why you didn't
say yes, but the RSVP date is long gone."

"I need to be there," said Emelie. "I have to get into the office,
take a look around."

"I'm getting the strong feeling you want to come to the party
and look around for a different reason."

"You could say that, but you don't need to know any more. Just
arrange it so I can come."

Josephine poked Emelie's stomach. "Okay, Pippa, I'll make sure
you get in, on one condition."

"What?"

"That I get to be godmother to the little cutie in your belly."

52

Roksana had dreamed things last night that she had never dreamed before. Or had she been dreaming? Maybe she and Nikola really had been flying over the roofs of Akalla on a motorbike, on one of the lightest nights of the year. Maybe they had turned off, across the forest, circling until they found a meadow where they could land, climb off, lie down, and look up at the brightening sky. But she knew it was a dream—because Nikola wasn't there.

Her life felt schizo right now: on the one hand, she had stronger feelings for the guy than she had ever felt before—an exhilaration that filled her with bubbles. But on the other, she wasn't anywhere close to meeting the psychos' demands, even if Nikola had lent her all of his money. She was genuinely considering asking her parents to visit Etty in Tehran, despite the fact her father had never been back. It was Midsummer in two days' time—her last day. The leader had announced that they would meet at five. Z was still refusing to get back to her—Roksana was thinking about going over to his parents' fucking house and dragging him out with her own two hands. The only problem was that she didn't know exactly where they lived.

It all rested on her. She *really* was screwed now. *Baba* was screwed.

She pulled the covers up to her chin. How could the apartment be so cold in the middle of summer?

She wondered why Nikola hadn't been in touch. The truth was that over the past twenty-four hours, he had answered his phone only once, and he had seemed preoccupied with other things and refused to say where he was or let her come to him. Despite the sweet feelings, irritation came creeping up on her. She was worried that she knew why he was staying away—he had said something about going to war. That didn't sound good.

She heard a key turning in the front door. Someone was here.

A moment later, she was sitting in the living room with Z in front of her. It felt good to have him back, even if she still had no idea why he hadn't called her. There was a suitcase and a cardboard box on the floor in front of him. He was wearing ripped jeans and a T-shirt which had to be from the U.S. election: a blue and red picture of hair standing on end, plus two combs. *We shall overcomb Trump,* it said.

"I'm moving out."

They hadn't spoken since he was released, and this was the first thing Z said to her. "I've promised my parents I'd leave Stockholm. Dad's found me work experience with some accountancy firm in Västerås."

Roksana looked down at his box. He had wrapped the stereo in towels and packed it away. "But what about the psychos?" Roksana asked. "We've got to get the money together to pay them. And we only have two days, otherwise they'll kill my dad."

Z studied her. His eyes seemed strange, as though he were looking at some K buyer or someone else he didn't know, as though she were no longer his best friend and roommate, as though everything they had been through over the past six months hadn't happened. *Two days.* It was insane. She didn't understand how Z could act so cool, but it had been the same thing all along, just pretending that it wasn't happening. This shit was constantly on her mind, like a cold, sopping wet blanket—*two days.* Then they would go after Baba.

Z closed the suitcase and taped up the box. Roksana didn't know how he was planning to move it all, though maybe he had borrowed Billie's car. She followed him out into the hallway.

"What are we going to do, Z? We have to come up with something."

Z had that look in his eyes again. He opened the door and moved the suitcase outside, placing it and the box on the floor in the stairwell. After that, he moved to pull the door shut behind him, leaving only a tiny gap. "I'm leaving now."

"Are you listening to what I'm saying? We have to come up with a way of scraping together the money."

"I've done my part."

"What did you say?"

"My dad helped me take out a loan. I've paid them 500,000 kronor. I couldn't do it anymore. They were threatening to kill my family, too."

"But we owe them a million."

"I know, but their leader said if I could give him half, then he was done with me. So I did. I don't owe those psychos anything now. I was about to have a breakdown, Roksana. But now I'm free."

Her head was spinning. Her heart felt wounded.

"But they still want five hundred thousand from me, right?"

Z started to open the door again. "Yeah, they want their money from you. But I've done you a huge favor. Now you only need to find half, not the whole million."

He looked away. Moved to pick up his bag.

"So you're leaving now. I thought we were in this together," said Roksana.

"We can't always stick together."

"Don't you have an ounce of pride?"

Z smirked. "Like Ester Nilsson says in *Willful Disregard*: 'I have no pride because pride is linked to shame and honor, and I'm shameless and have no concept of what others find honorable.'"

They often quoted Lena Andersson to one another, but did

he really think Roksana was going to laugh now? She was still in the doorway, trying to think of something to say. Z was going to leave—he had solved *his* problem.

"See you, then," he said, closing the door, an inch away from her face. She wanted to tear it open and say something to him, but she couldn't move. No, actually, she didn't want to say anything. She wanted to scream in his face. Spit on him. Hit him. Show him what honor meant.

Above all: she needed Nikola now, more than ever. But he wasn't here. Not even *he* was here for her when she needed him—instead, he was busy with his questionable lifestyle.

Anger bubbled up in her like lava.

They were pigs, all of them.

53

Kum's entertainment room, or rather his renovated basement, was Teddy's new prison. It was also his sanctuary. He no longer had to curl up in a car to sleep, and he and Emelie could now really get to work on everything without him having to hide behind dark glasses, face changes, and strange beards.

They had made a number of breakthroughs: they knew, for example, that Leijon Legal Services was involved somehow. Emelie was going over there tomorrow, but there was no guarantee she would be able to find the material that Fredrik O. had tried to clear out of the estate. The documents could be anywhere, if they even still existed.

They needed more. They continued to dig.

That evening, Teddy found something. Among the piles of material was a preliminary investigation into insider trading and tax evasion from 2006. It ran to more than seven hundred pages, primarily analyses of the deals and the market movements of different shares. But a significant portion of it also came from the wire tap of someone called Hugo Pederson, as well as three police interviews with him. The investigation itself had been shut down—the Economic Crime Authority didn't think they could prove that the deals really had taken place as a result of the exploitation of *information that wasn't publicly available*—so-called insider trading—and were probably put off by their terrible track record when it came to that kind of case.

What Teddy couldn't understand was why this investigation had ended up here. Had Loke included it by mistake? Teddy started to read through the documents, none of it making sense until he came to the last few sections: Hugo Pederson's logged phone calls. Suddenly he understood.

Once he was finished, he read through everything a second time. At the very end of the preliminary investigation, there was a long police interview with Pederson. Ninety percent of it was about the supposed insider trading. Pederson had gallantly explained that he and his buddy hadn't wanted to pay tax on the money they earned and that that was why they had used separate phones for their calls, but he insisted that all their deals had been carefully calculated and based on information that was known to enough people to be considered official. Teddy could understand why the ECA had dropped its case—it would have been difficult to prosecute Hugo Pederson, especially since he had made voluntary declarations and paid both his tax and the fines he was given. Toward the end of the interview, they had asked him about the kidnapping he had witnessed. Teddy felt the hair stand up on the back of his neck. He glanced over to Emelie from time to time, wondering whether she could see the effect that Hugo Pederson's answers were having on him.

She was half sitting on the sofa with the computer on her lap. She looked tired, but Teddy knew she was working, too.

Hugo was the man who called himself Peder Hult, something he also admitted in the police interviews. He refused, however, to name a single person from Hallenbro Storgården or to say who the contact who had invited Mats to attend was. The police officers had pressed him, you could tell from their questions—but this Hugo Pederson held firm. Teddy could see the link all the same: the man Hugo Pederson never mentioned must have been Fredrik O.

Johansson. But there was another active figure, from phone conversation 108. He read the tapped phone conversation ten times. He read the opening lines *twenty* times.

TELEPHONE CONVERSATION 108

To: Hugo Pederson
From: Unknown
Date: 23 September 2006
Time: 21:45

HUGO: Hello?

UNKNOWN: Hi, it's me.

HUGO: Who's that?

UNKNOWN: Don't you recognize my voice?

HUGO: Yeah, now I do, sorry. Hi.

UNKNOWN: I've got some questions about your consultant.

Hugo Pederson—aka Peder Hult—knew who he was talking to; he recognized the voice. He knew who had ordered him to make sure Mats Emanuelsson was in the right place to be kidnapped. But he had never given that name to the police.

Teddy searched online for a phone number for Hugo Pederson. He had to track the man down. But it was late: his call was met by an answering machine.

"This is Hugo Pederson. Please leave a message after the beep." He wondered why the guy was speaking English.

"Hi, I'd like to meet you as soon as possible. It's incredibly urgent and relating to the old police suspicions against you," Teddy said, leaving a phone number Pederson could reach him at.

Emelie had curled up her legs beneath her on the sofa. It almost looked like she was sleeping, but she opened her eyes. "Who were you calling?"

"I need to leave here tomorrow, too," Teddy said.

She glanced up from her computer. "You celebrating Midsummer without me?"

Teddy laughed. "You're going to a fortieth anniversary party."

"What are you going to do?"

"I have to visit the man who reported me to the police, the one who got me locked up for eight years. Hugo Pederson's his name, but he called himself Peder Hult, and I think he knows who has the documents you need to find at Leijon."

54

"Thanks for the licorice, I'll never forget that."

Kerim Celalî almost looked fat compared to how Nikola remembered him from prison: the last time he had seen the New Kum, he was being winched up through the hole he had sawed in the bars, to a helicopter hovering above the prison building, like some crazy *Independence Day* spaceship.

They were standing by the front of city hall, in the very heart of Stockholm, looking out at the water. "I live here now," Kerim said with a roar of laughter. "Can you imagine me in a place like this?"

"Do you like it?"

"No, not really. I miss Bredäng, but my lady wants to live here. She thinks it means something. But I say: you can take Kerim out of the 'burbs, but you can never take the 'burbs out of Kerim."

Nikola was happy he had agreed to meet him right away.

"You know"—Kerim grinned—"that candy you got to me when they locked me up again, it kept me alive. It's crazy that ten little pieces of salted licorice can keep your hopes up better than all the money, lawyers, and smuggled phones in the world. Those ten little pieces proved there were good guys out there, not just bastards who want to do me up the ass from every direction. So whenever you want to meet, my man, I'll always come. Running."

The whole of Södermalm was laid out in front of them: rows

of old buildings with towers and spires—it looked like something out of a fairy tale, the hill dropping off suddenly like some kind of huge barrier against the water and everyone wanting to get up there. Nikola had never been to city hall before, but he was aware of the place. The outline of the building was on the metro seats—it was the most important symbol of Stockholm, and he had no idea what they even did there.

"I'm guessing you didn't just want to check out the view with me," said Kerim.

"Nope. I've got a serious problem," Nikola said, explaining what he wanted. After ten minutes, he was done.

Kerim's front teeth were in bad shape, and they seemed to be smeared with something that looked just like licorice. "So you wanna be the new top dog? You want to take over after Mr. One?"

Nikola hadn't even thought about it like that. "I don't know," he said. "But I need your protection when I take that motherfucker down."

Kerim's smile disappeared. "What you're asking's not some small thing, my man, and neither's what you might end up setting off. But I respect you for your determination."

Something dignified sounding had appeared in the New Kum's voice. He was speaking more slowly and clearly, practically spelling out every word. "I respect you as a friend, too. But nothing comes for free. Not even friendship."

Nikola waited for what was coming. He knew he was selling his soul to Satan, even if Satan was being pretty friendly right now.

"I'll give you what you want. In exchange for a favor."

"What?"

Kerim cocked his head, and it looked like he was pulling at his earlobe. "We get jobs to order sometimes. If the money's good enough, we take them, keeps us on our toes. You help me with one of those?"

"What do you want me to do?"

"I don't know yet, but there's bound to be one soon. I've got a client who's really damn nervy right now, that's all I know. We just did a thing for him on the inside and it all went to hell."

"In prison?"

"Yeah, completely crazy, I know. I had a guy working there, but he's blind in one eye now."

"You want me to clip someone?"

"I don't know yet. I told you. One of us will be in touch when the order comes in."

"And you can trust your clients?"

"Yeah, for God's sake. We've done stuff for them before, not just on the inside. All you need to do is get ahold of a gun."

"I don't know."

Kerim straightened his head and stared at him. "If you're in, you'll get instructions about what you need to do. This kind of thing's in your blood, isn't it? Your uncle, everyone knows him, he was a legend when I was a kid. He was the king of kidnapping."

The New Kum: Nikola needed Kerim's backing. His protection.

He shook Kerim's hand. "Okay. Count me in. I'm in."

PART IV

MIDSUMMER'S EVE

55

The pre-drinks were served out on the roof terrace, with 360-degree views over Stockholm.

Emelie was glad that Jossan was there. She was Emelie's anchor. Though she had worked with the majority of the other guests, she felt like a stranger today. Josephine was her safe point.

It was a beautiful day. Emelie tried to hold her champagne glass as casually as she could. Every now and then, she raised it to her mouth and felt the small bubbles burst against her lips. She wasn't drinking—the movement was just for appearances. Her belly was straining, but she was wearing a loose-fitting dress and a cardigan over that, so people might not necessarily realize. If they did, they did. She was thinking about how she was going to make it into the heart of the firm's offices later—the hallways and rooms that weren't meant for either clients or former employees.

After a few minutes, Magnus Hassel rose above them all. Emelie couldn't see whether he was standing on a chair or a stool. He tapped his glass.

"Well, I just wanted to welcome everyone and say a few quick words." He was wearing a pale beige linen suit that seemed far too thin—Midsummer was always cooler than people liked to admit. On his head, he was wearing a panama hat that looked even stranger: as though he were on a beach somewhere in Italy.

"We're always thrilled to welcome former employees back to

our annual alumni gatherings, but this year in particular is very special. We're celebrating forty years. And when I talk to you, I realize that once you've been a part of the Leijon family, you always carry with you the special feeling we enjoy here at the firm."

Magnus raised his glass as though to give a toast, but none appeared. Instead, he continued to talk. Emelie knew all too well what this was about—buttering up their clients. When the chief counsels at Sweden's biggest companies needed to bring in outside legal services, Leijon wanted to be the first name to pop into their heads. And what could be a better connection than the chief counsel in question being invited to the party of the year? Still, it was crazy that they had decided to hold it on Midsummer's Eve.

Magnus continued to hold his glass high, keeping them all on tenterhooks. "That's why I'm so happy to be able to open our new top floor and roof terrace with you today," he said. "We don't just want Leijon to be the number one legal firm in Scandinavia, we want you to be able to feel that with every inch of your being, too."

On top of the world. The streets down below were empty, as though a deadly plague had struck the city. Midsummer's Eve: the most desolate day of the year.

They were served lunch outside, on the terrace. Leijon had even raised a modern interpretation of a Midsummer pole out there, made completely of aluminium. Emelie ended up between Anders Henriksson and a guy who had left the firm before she even started there, now a corporate lawyer with ExActor, an IT firm that tracked online traffic. "I've got shares in the company, so whenever I leave, I've calculated that I'll become Sweden's one hundred and twenty-third richest person," he said, raising his glass to toast with Emelie. Emelie wondered why he hadn't left yet, despite the fact that the guy had clearly been at his little company for more than eight years.

Jossan was diagonally opposite her, for which she was eternally grateful. When Anders Henriksson started talking about the wild boar hunting season which was about to begin, she launched into a monologue about how she had really wanted all of the food at the party to be vegetarian. "Mathias Dahlgren's new place, Rutabaga, is completely veggie, so that tells you what's in right now." Emelie didn't know whether she was joking or not, but she loved that Jossan could always bring her to the verge of giggles. But not today.

She couldn't understand how her friend could dare be so cocky. Though maybe she had been given good news. Josephine had been at the firm for more than seven years now, and everyone knew what the system was like at Leijon. It wasn't written anywhere in the promotional materials, on their home page, or in the brochures they handed out to the top students at universities, but the principle they abided by was informally known as *up or out*. If you didn't move up the pay scale, if the partners didn't acknowledge that you were still on the right track, you were expected to start looking for another job. You wouldn't be handed your notice or given the boot; it was more elegant than that. Job ads for corporate firms or positions with the larger state authorities would just start to be forwarded to your in-box, with no comments attached. But Jossan hadn't mentioned anything about any good news or suggested that it might even be in the works. Her friend had always analyzed, tried to predict what would be said, and worried for weeks ahead of development meetings.

The herring and potatoes they were served as the first course were sublime, and the slow-cooked prime calf ribs for the main were fantastic. Emelie didn't say much; she mostly smiled and tried to make herself uninteresting.

Anders Henriksson got up and made a speech in honor of the firm, giving an account of Leijon's history. "When this firm began forty years ago, Swedish lawyers could barely spell the word *transaction*. Today, we have alumni who teach at both Columbia and Cambridge, in legal English."

People clapped. When no one was looking, Emelie swapped the glass of schnapps that had arrived after Henriksson's speech for Jossan's empty one.

Lunch was coming to an end. Dessert consisted of strawberries and ice cream.

The terrace was almost empty now, with many of the guests having Midsummer plans with family and friends to head off to. The catering staff were cleaning up, and Josephine had said good-bye—she was going home to get ready for the evening.

Emelie could see the goodie bags lined up by the stairs down from the terrace—Leijon didn't cut any corners. She had shown her respect for her former employers, been polite, talked to both Magnus Hassel and Anders Henriksson. She had to go down—now. She watched Hassel from a distance, and when she saw him turn around to say something to a waitress, she moved toward the steps without saying good-bye. She grabbed one of the bags as she passed, and headed down.

She peered into the goodie bag: inside was a book about Leijon, a bottle of wine that was bound to be expensive and delicious, the latest edition of Legal 500, a copy of *Forbes* magazine, and an invitation to test-drive some new Volvo Cross Country car.

In front of her was the locked door to the firm's work space, an area that was out-of-bounds to clients. You needed a code to get inside, but Emelie had already managed to get that from Jossan before lunch.

"What do you need it for?" Josephine had asked.

"It's best if you don't know."

Jossan had studied her. "I don't like what you're doing. It goes against my principles to be disloyal to the firm. But, since I'm going to be a godmother, I'll make an exception."

Emelie glanced around, punched in the code, quickly opened the door, and stepped inside. The hallway was empty.

She had been there countless times before, but not at all over the past year. It was like going home to Jönköping, to her mother and father's house, to her old school. Everything was so familiar, so comfortable, and yet it felt alien and threatening all the same.

She wondered how she was going to find whatever had been in the Samsonite case. Her heart was racing like she had just finished a workout session. Her stomach felt uncomfortable, even bigger than it already was, like she was at risk of bumping into the artwork on the walls. She knew where she had to begin. The majority of the firm's cases were electronic now, which meant that the amount of filing they did had dropped. But that didn't mean a paper-free office—far from it. Many of the employees still preferred to print out draft agreements, summons applications, and so on. Many of them also thought it was more comfortable to have physical documents in due diligence folders than to scroll back and forth on a computer. The older partners in particular preferred working on paper rather than on-screen. In other words, almost all the lawyers working at the firm still had plenty of physical documents and papers in their rooms, but it was only the older members of staff who kept locked document cupboards.

To begin with, Emelie had planned to look in each of the firm's shared document rooms, or archive rooms, as they were known. That was where up to ten years' worth of old cases were kept—all in line with the Bar Association's rules for archiving documents.

The carpet in the hallway was soft and quiet; it was calm in here. Emelie's back ached; her stomach wasn't too heavy yet, but it still affected her posture. She opened the fireproof door to the archive room, stepped inside, and turned on the light.

The door swung shut with a thud. The air inside felt dry and old-fashioned: it smelled of paper, and it was silent. She glanced around: shelves from floor to ceiling, all full of cardboard boxes and folders, each marked with the codes the firm used to file their documents. She knew where she wanted to begin—she had seen the codes on the document relating to the company that owned

Hallenbro Storgården: the documents Leijon had been involved in producing.

She found the shelf after a moment or two, and spotted the box at the very top. There was a small step stool, and she dragged it over. The stool felt like it was wobbling as she climbed up. Maybe there was something moving in her stomach, too.

She placed the box on a rickety table, folded back the lid, and looked down at the stacks of paper: shareholders' and board meeting records, accounts opened, foundation documents for trusts in Hong Kong, correspondence with various legal firms and management companies. The documents related to around ten different companies, among them Nordic Light Investment Group. She already knew about the link to the estate, but these papers weren't especially dangerous—they weren't criminal in any sense. Plus, there had been a thin layer of dust on the top documents: that kind of thing took longer than a few weeks to build up in a closed archive box. She was sure: these couldn't be the documents that were taken away from the estate.

Suddenly she heard a noise. She paused. Listened. It sounded like it had come from the hallway. She flipped the lid of the box closed, pushed it away, and glanced around. Was there anywhere for her to hide?

It was too late: she heard the door open. She pressed herself against one of the bookcases and hoped no one would come any farther into the room.

But they did. She saw who it was: Magnus Hassel.

"Emelie," he said in a shrill voice. "I thought you'd gone home?" He didn't look as surprised as he should have. Not angry, either. He was just waiting for an answer of some kind.

She should have come up with a reason for sneaking around in there. Now she couldn't think of a single thing to say.

Magnus said: "Who let you in here?"

Emelie shook her head. She had to say something. "I'm here on my own. But Jossan wanted me to fetch something for her."

It almost looked like Magnus thought she was funny. "Why couldn't Josephine fetch whatever it was herself?"

"What are you doing in here?" Emelie countered.

"Confidentiality prevents me from telling you that."

Emelie didn't understand. Magnus should be agitated, angry. He should be throwing her out, possibly getting help from some of the others if they were still around, or calling security. And yet all he said was: "But what are you doing here?"

For a brief second, she thought about telling him everything. Laying her cards on the table. But at the same time: why had *he* just come in here, of all places? She tried to remember the person she had seen coming into the office with the Samsonite case on the 7-Eleven surveillance film. Could it have been Magnus?

He moved closer to her. She could smell schnapps on his breath; the shots on the terrace had clearly done their work. "Emelie," he said, in a darker voice this time. "I just thought that you shouldn't go without saying good-bye."

What was he doing? She knew she should feign indifference and leave, but she felt guilty at having forced her way in like this. "I have to go," she said. "I was just fetching something for Josephine, like I said."

Magnus was almost leaning over her now. "Yes, you said that, but I still don't understand. You can't just come barging in here. You don't work here anymore."

"I really have to go," she said again, turning away from Magnus. She knew she wasn't done here yet—she still had to find the contents of the suitcase. But with Magnus in the way, it was going to be difficult.

He was standing very close to her. A faint, possibly uncertain smile was playing on his lips. "Things got a bit weird when we met in the restaurant last time, I agree with you there. I've been wanting to apologize, but I didn't really know what to say. Maybe we can just start over from where we left off last time."

Emelie knew she should punch him in the face and run out of

the room, but with the little one inside her, she didn't know if she would manage it.

The room was warm and cramped, and she noticed that her breathing was quicker than usual. It felt like the walls were about to close in on her.

"It's fantastic, isn't it?" said Magnus. "I love working on days like this, when everyone else is so unproductive. Now that everyone's gone home, I was going to sit down with an old case and get some work done. But then I find you here, which leaves me both confused and happy."

Emelie glared at him. She was sure of one thing now, at the very least: Magnus Hassel wasn't all there.

56

Technically, it was too late for breakfast, but she was still standing in front of the fridge searching for something edible. It didn't take long, because the only option was some drinking yogurt Z had left behind.

She was thinking about the phone conversation she'd had with Nikola a few hours earlier.

"What are you doing?" she had asked. "Why can't we meet again?"

"I can't tell you everything, Roksy, even if I want to."

"Is it your war? Is that what's stopping you from wanting to see me?"

"There are just some things I have to do if I'm going to be able to live with myself."

"What do you mean?"

"I mean I've got to fix certain things if I'm going to be able to look myself in the eye."

"But you've already tried to do what you can, haven't you?"

"You don't know everything. I've tried, and kinda ended up with blood on my hands. But it went wrong."

"You'll be able to live with yourself no matter what happens. And Chamon isn't coming back, no matter what you do."

"Makes no difference," he said. "All those bastards are whores, even the ones I thought were my heroes. My uncle's not there anymore. My mom doesn't get a thing. The guy I thought stood for honor is the one who got Chamon killed. So when everyone else betrays you, you might as well betray them back."

Roksana had readied herself: she had to say this. "Nikola, I didn't know Chamon, but I know he wouldn't have liked you going after innocent people. You think you can get something back by hurting the people who've hurt you, but I think you'll just sink deeper into the shit. Because you know that with everything you do, you're really just abandoning the person you once were, the one Chamon liked. Do you get what I mean? Just because other people have betrayed you, you don't have to betray yourself."

Nikola hadn't replied. All she heard was a click. He had hung up.

He had left her. Again.

The drinking yogurt was too sweet for Roksana's tastes, but she drank it anyway. She got dressed and stood in the hallway, trying to get a handle on her thoughts: the anger, the confusion, the fear. The psychos wanted to be paid today.

A sound: her phone beeped. It was an email. *Test Result University and Higher Education Council. Click this link for your test result.*

2.0.

Oh my G.

Two point oh. She had actually gotten top marks. Herself, on her own. She would get into the psychology course now. She would get an elite education. And yet, what difference did it make—the psychos were going to do whatever it was they were going to do.

Maybe Nikola could help her somehow. She started searching the web on her phone. *Nikola,* she wrote, and then: *Maksumic.* There wasn't much information other than a picture from someone's Facebook profile, a few pages that seemed to be about his mother and plenty of things about his uncle, who had apparently escaped from prison. She tried a different search. *Chamon Hanna. Murder. Revenge.* That brought up different pages. Some kind of racist news site wrote about the fighting between Syrian factions in Södertälje. An article from *Aftonbladet* wrote about the growing violence in the Stockholm area and the increased use of firearms. Above all: flashback threads speculating about who had killed Chamon. She couldn't tear her eyes away from the gossip site's discussions. They speculated, guessed, thought they were on top of everything. But still: there were claims she couldn't let go. That the disappearance of another man, Yusuf, was linked to what had happened to Chamon. Her eyes latched on to one post in particular:

We are Yusuf's family. We promise a reward of 500,000 kronor to anyone who can give us or the police information about who took our beloved partner, son, and friend from us. / Magdalena and family.

Beneath the message was a picture. *This is the last photograph taken of Yusuf.*

The fire in Nikola's eyes. She heard his words from their phone call. "I've tried, and kinda ended up with blood on my hands. But it went wrong."

There was a reward waiting for anyone who could give information about what happened to Yusuf. A reward that could pay off the psychos' demands.

Maybe she should have realized. Nikola was who he was—he wasn't right for her. He was an egotistical idiot. He was some kind of fascist. And now she was convinced that there was a price on his head, that reward. Mixed messages: give up Nikola—and Dad could live. A guy she barely knew—against *Baba.*

She couldn't stop thinking about it.

She had heard Nikola mention names in passing, had met his friend when they were doing security for Our Land Club. She Googled like a madwoman, but she couldn't find much. The guy she had fallen for and his friends clearly didn't like being visible on social media. She went back to the page where the reward was mentioned. Read the text over and over again. Studied the photo of Yusuf: the last picture of a missing man. His face seemed relaxed, his eyes half-closed, as though he was about to fall asleep. Roksana could find only one other picture online: an old Instagram photo someone else had uploaded. There was something different about the new picture, but it was nothing to do with his appearance, expression, or hairstyle. It was his accessories: in the newer photo, Yusuf was wearing an enormous gold chain and a cross around his neck. She tried to zoom in. There was something about the chain and the cross. She had seen them before. She zoomed in further.

In that instant, she understood. She reached for the bedside table and picked up the gold chain and cross that Nikola had left behind after their night together. She held it in front of her—it was heavy—and studied the picture of Yusuf again. It was the exact same chain and the exact same cross that Yusuf had been wearing in the last picture ever taken of him.

Roksana lay back down on the bed. Turned off her phone. In a few hours' time, she would be meeting the Boss idiot. In a few hours' time, she needed to have the money ready. Otherwise her father would be killed. Baba would no longer exist, Mom's and Caspar's lives would be destroyed. She could barely breathe as that thought went through her mind.

Yusuf murdered—with a reward for anyone who could give information about his disappearance. A reward for the person who could link a chain and gold cross to a perpetrator.

The same word thundered through Roksana's head, over and over again: reward.

Reward.

57

The leaves on the trees on the avenue leading to the property were still pale green, as though summer was late to arrive in Kalaholm, despite being only twenty minutes north of the city. In the transcripts Teddy had scrutinized, he had seen Hugo Pederson's wife go on and on about this place ten years earlier. All the same, he hadn't been expecting a castle like this: three stories with a turret that had to be at least sixty feet high, a fountain in front of the building, and a parklike garden that never seemed to end.

"Seems like fancy people we're off to see," Dejan said as the Panama skidded in the gravel and pulled up by the fountain. "Who exactly are we meeting?"

"The guy who reported me and got me sent down."

Dejan rifled through the bag on the backseat. "Aha, it's like that. Good thing I brought all this, then. You can choose for yourself."

Teddy picked up the bag and peered inside. He saw a Mini Uzi and a Heckler & Koch MP5.

They climbed out of the car. To one side, by one of the smaller buildings, there were five other cars parked. Either Hugo was a collector, just like Kum, or else the Pedersons had guests today.

Teddy climbed the wide staircase to the castle door. Two bronze lions flanked the steps. The Mauler glared at them with suspicion, but then started licking their faces and sniffing their patinated green backsides.

No one answered.

"Doesn't look like there's anyone home," Dejan said, waving the MP5 in the air.

"Let's check out back," said Teddy. "And could you put the gun away?"

Behind the castle was an even bigger park, which opened out onto a lake. Cutting the lawns here must take weeks. Then it struck Teddy that in a place like this, they didn't cut the lawns themselves—they had staff for that kind of thing. The Mauler sloped off ahead of them, his tongue practically dragging on the ground. They could see a group of people in the distance, standing around a Midsummer pole. That explained the cars. This was probably a terrible moment, but Teddy was here now—he was suspected of murder, had escaped from prison, and was wanted across the entire kingdom. There was no going back.

Midsummer—the only time Teddy had ever celebrated it was when the guards had given them herring and low-alcohol beers in prison. It wasn't a Christian holiday—he knew that much—more something hedonistic. The Swedes raised tall poles covered in grass or similar, with leaf-clad rings. Somehow, it was obvious: the whole thing represented an enormous dick with the balls hanging at the top. And around that dick they danced.

At least that was what the Pederson family and their guests were doing as he and Dejan approached—they were hooting and jumping around the green pole. The women were, anyway. The men were sitting at a long table—they seemed to mostly be watching. Teddy couldn't see any children—they were probably still at the boarding school he knew the Pedersons' children attended, or maybe they were being taken care of by a nanny somewhere. Teddy could hear the revelers singing: "Little frogs, little frogs, so funny to see, no ears, no ears, no ears have they." No one seemed to care about the two strange men striding toward them over the grass. They probably thought that Teddy and freaking Dejan were here to cut the lawn.

He approached the table. The dancing continued around the pole. The grass was so green that it made his eyes sting. The people all looked the same; it was like their faces merged together in one big mix of pale features and the kind of wrinkles caused by sunny recreation on golf courses and chair lifts. Still, Teddy recognized him: Hugo Pederson, aka Peder Hult. He had seen only one picture of him, from a charity gala ten years ago, but the man looked the same. Hair slightly thinner than in the picture, but with the same side part and the same shade of blond.

"Hugo Pederson," Teddy said loudly.

The five men looked up at him in surprise, but no one got up. The white tablecloth was covered in beer cans and empty schnapps glasses. They had probably just eaten lunch; they were probably wasted.

"Or should I say Peder Hult?" Teddy said again, louder this time.

Hugo Pederson slowly got to his feet. He held out a hand and a smile lit up his face. "Hello, hello, who are you?" he said with crisp articulation—the way only incredibly self-confident people speak.

Then his tone changed. "As you can see, we're having a little private gathering here. You'll have to come back another day, whoever you are. What is this regarding, by the way?"

Teddy turned toward him. Tried to tell from Hugo's face whether he was joking. Did he really not recognize him?

"I tried to get in touch with you yesterday, but you never called me back. So now I just wanted to have a word with you, in peace and quiet." Teddy copied Hugo's familiar tone and placed an arm around his shoulders. He felt the man jump. "Could we talk eye to eye somewhere?"

"Like I said, we're trying to celebrate Midsummer here." Hugo's voice was firmer this time, as though to command the attention of the people around the table. "I don't even know who you are."

The Mauler was drooling.

Teddy felt like he was about to flip out. "We're here to talk about the old investigation into you. This place, for example, was bought with illegal money. Money you earned by cheating the system. Right?"

One of Hugo's eyes had started to twitch. "So it's those old accusations you're talking about? It's no secret that the Economic Crime Authority wanted to cast suspicion on me ten years ago, all my good friends know that, so there's no point trying to embarrass me there. They also know that the ECA dropped all that crap because I had nothing to do with anything illegal."

The little frog dance had ended. Small birds were twittering in the trees. Everyone's eyes were fixed on them. The women in their floral dresses and heeled clogs, and the men in their linen jackets and plaited belts: they had all lifted their sunglasses and were staring as though there was a play being acted out at the table.

A woman stepped forward. "Leave, please."

Teddy had Googled her. There were plenty of pictures: Louise Pederson, Hugo's wife.

"No, I'd like to talk to Hugo."

"You have no business here. Leave, before I call the police."

"Your husband already did that ten years ago," said Teddy. "He reported me and *I* was sent down. But what you don't know is that he *didn't* report who was really behind a network of pimping and child abuse."

Louise Pederson was staring at him. The men around the table were glaring so fiercely that it looked like their eyes were about to pop out of their heads. Hugo's face was still twitching. "Enough of this crap," he said. "We're calling the police."

Several of the men at the table stood up. Dejan shifted in the background. The women looked annoyed. Louise seemed more surprised than anything.

Then, from the corner of one eye, Teddy saw that Dejan had pulled out the MP5 from beneath his shirt.

KLAK-KLAK-KLAK. Three shots rang out in the air. Up into the blue sky. It sounded like he had aimed it straight at Teddy; his ears were ringing. What the hell was Dejan doing—did he think this was a Lebanese wedding or something?

Teddy gestured for him to lower his weapon, but Dejan started to shout. "Enough talk. Everyone get down. Take out your phones and throw them in front of you."

Teddy didn't know whether even he understood what had just happened: but within two seconds, there were twelve people lying flat out on the grass. Several of them were crying.

Hugo Pederson followed Teddy inside without another word.

The drawing room was like a museum. Teddy had seen so-called modern art before, particularly at Leijon, but he still didn't get it. He couldn't see the craft, the technique. In what sense was it admirable that someone had painted four thick lines onto a white canvas, or got a computer to arrange Japanese manga images randomly in a circle? Maybe it was to do with politics, maybe the works hanging on the wall in the Pederson family castle incited resistance, maybe there was a message Teddy just didn't under-stand. In all likelihood, it was something else: that they glossed over the simple and the dirty. They gave Hugo Pederson an aura of something he wanted to be.

Above the sofa was a framed black-and-white image of a lion—the only piece in the room Teddy could actually understand.

"Nice lion," he said, pushing Hugo onto the sofa. "That was your first piece, right? You bought it from Bukowskis?"

Through the window, Teddy could see the Midsummer pole and Dejan, who was still watching over the guests. He sat down next to Hugo, really sunk into the sofa. "Do you recognize me yet?"

Hugo's face was twisted. He looked like he was about to start screaming. "I know who you are. And the other guy, the one with the gun. You were in the van."

"Exactly. You saw us throwing Mats Emanuelsson into the back. That was the biggest mistake of my life. But then you saw me again, didn't you?"

"Yeah, by the house."

"And that was when you first called the police?"

Hugo didn't reply.

"Right?"

Hugo was silent.

"In the police interviews, you never told them that you knew who had ordered the kidnapping, did you?"

A string of saliva was hanging from Hugo's mouth when he eventually opened it. "Why are you really here?"

"I wanted to meet the man who made me spend eight years in prison."

The room was cool and silent. All the armchairs, sofas, rugs, and tables seemed to be color matched to the wallpaper and the works of art—or was it the other way around?

"Do you know what they try to do to you in prison?" Teddy held back as best he could. "They try to erase you as a person. They take away everything that makes your life unique: you can't plan your own time, you can't eat what you want, dress the way you want. You can't even shower when you want. Above all, they take away your opportunities for human closeness. Some people forget they're humans as a result. Some become even more like animals in there. Sometimes, it feels like I was dead for eight years."

Hugo stuttered. "I—I don't know what to say."

"You don't have to say anything. Because there's another story there, too. And it's that I'm glad you reported me, because nothing else could have made me stop. I changed in there. It really was like I was erased and born again. I came out a different person. And ever since, I've tried to atone for the fact that I kidnapped a man for the worst possible reason I can imagine."

"So what do you want from me? Why are you here?"

"I'm here because I want you to tell me who asked you to lure Mats to the place he was kidnapped. I want you to lay your cards on the table."

Hugo's mouth was like a line drawn with a ruler.

"You don't want to talk about it?"

Hugo Pederson didn't reply.

"You're not going to say anything at all?"

Hugo's lips were so narrow.

"That's not good," said Teddy, pulling out his phone. "Because I won't feel like I've atoned for what I did until all this is over. All of it."

Two minutes later, Dejan came in and set the Mauler loose. The dog sauntered over to Teddy. Hugo's eyes widened. Teddy thought about what he had read about this man's feelings toward dogs in the transcripts.

Teddy grabbed the lead and turned to Hugo: "This is the Mauler. He's a bull terrier specialized in eating people like you."

The Mauler pulled at the lead.

The Mauler yelped.

"Take the dog away!" Hugo shouted, hoisting his legs up onto the sofa.

The Mauler jumped up after him.

Bared his teeth.

58
***

Midsummer was a crappy day. But, at the same time, everything was fucked-up right now. The only glimmer of light in this dark Midsummer shit was that he had been with Roksana only a few days ago. Though, maybe that was about to turn to crap, too: when they last spoke on the phone, she had spent most of the call interrogating him.

Now he was at his mother's house, having lunch to celebrate the holiday. Grandpa was there, too. Nikola wished he was with Roksana instead, but that wouldn't work. He had to be on standby in case Kerim or the client got in touch, and he didn't want to leave Roksana in the lurch if they did. Plus: the hate was burning so fiercely in him right now that he was about to get himself worked up. He wasn't good for her now, that was just how it was.

Isak: the man who had ordered Chamon's murder. Isak: a rat—a pig informant. Nikola needed Kerim's blessing to take revenge. But first, he was going to have to do something for the New Kum—he wondered what it would be.

Later today, he and Bello were doing a job for Isak. It was a case of acting like normal so that the pig informant didn't realize that Nikola knew.

His mother had tried to mix traditions: there were bowls of her- ring and potatoes on the table, alongside sausages, ajvar, and sauerkraut. Grandpa insisted on eating only the Swedish elements: "It's Midsummer. I've never understood exactly what it is they're celebrating, but we should do it right." He raised a spoon of soured cream and chopped red onion to his mouth. Nikola was sure that wasn't what you were meant to do, but he didn't say anything— Grandpa was Grandpa, after all.

Mom raised her glass. "This whole business with Teddy is so awful. What they're saying he's done, everything being written about his escape. I'm just glad you're both here."

Nikola wondered if he should ask his uncle anyway: *Will you back me up if I go for it?* But no, Teddy was being hunted by everyone right now—and Nikola had no idea how to get ahold of him.

Grandpa sipped his beer. "I'm so sad for his sake. That he never learns."

Mom nodded. A constant complaint during Nikola's entire childhood. The bad path Teddy had chosen. Teddy's weak character. Teddy's way of showing that he didn't care about his sister or his father.

Nikola refused to believe all the media bullshit, and he remembered the conversation they'd had at Espresso House a few months earlier. He said: "Teddy's learned. He's changed, believe me. He's not the man he was."

"What has he learned?" Mom asked.

"More than me, anyway." Nikola didn't know what he meant by that last part.

An hour later, he was in the van, beside Bello. Standard job for late-afternoon Midsummer's Eve: transporting Isak's explosives, in other words. They had cleared out a stash site in Skärholmen and were now heading toward the main store.

"You think he's building an atomic bomb, or what?" Nikola asked. "We've never picked up this much before. That has to be several hundred kilos."

What was Mr. One up to? He wasn't just a dirty cop

informant—he genuinely seemed to be planning to blow Södertälje to pieces. Nikola thought about Roksy and the argument they'd had—what would she say about this? Boxes full of explosives.

"He sees what's going on in the suburbs and he's getting ready for war," said Bello.

Nikola paused. "What are you talking about?"

"You know what I mean. It's like a computer game. You don't have the most up-to-date weapons, you'll never win. Everything's getting shittier and shittier. When I started six years ago, shoot-outs were about as uncommon here as they are in the fancy villa areas north of town. But now . . . well, you know."

Nikola knew.

Oh, he knew.

Bello said: "Reckon we can pull over for twenty to grab something to eat?"

"I already ate, had Midsummer lunch with Mom and Grandpa. You ever had that?"

"Yeah, yeah, my old man loves fish. I'm hungry."

"I don't want to leave the van on the street, not with everything in the back. Can't you get takeout? I'll wait here."

And so it was. Steakhouse Bar was open. Bello stepped inside. Mr. One's regular. Chamon's favorite. Nikola stayed in the van.

He thought back to the beginning, to the start of all this crap. He hadn't known any other kids in the area at the time. They had only just moved in, but his mother had thought it would be a nice gentle start for him if he went to the youth club, which was already open, the week before school started. So, that Monday, she had dropped him off with a hairy teacher—or youth club educator, as they wanted you to call them—called Mikael, who said that everything would be just fine. Nikola hadn't understood how anything would be fine—all he wanted was to lock himself in the bathroom and cry, or to escape, forget about putting on his shoes and run barefoot home to Mom. He thought he would be able to find his way. Maybe. Or maybe not. Mikael had been sitting at a round table, and all of the other kids had crowded around him, watching as he drew a submarine. They all seemed to know one another, and none of them had said hello to Nikola. After what felt like weeks, when his mother came to pick him up again, he had told her: "I don't want to come anymore." "I'm sure it'll be better once school starts next week," she had replied. "The teacher'll look after you. I've talked to her. She's really nice." "I want to stay home tomorrow," Nikola had begged. "You can't, little man. I'm working." In that moment, Nikola had realized that nothing would be the same as before.

The next day, Mikael had sat down at the same table and drawn a plane. Everyone stared, rushed to tell him how good he was at drawing propellers. It went on like that for four days. By Friday, Nikola was crying before his mother even woke up. "Please, Mom, let me come to work with you. I promise I'll be quiet." He had felt like she might give in: there was something about the way her mouth twitched when his pleading was about to work. And yet she had said: "No, love, it's good for you to go, it'll make it easier when school starts on Monday." He hadn't wanted to let her go, had clung on when she dropped him off. Mikael had been drawing again. The other children either watched that or went off somewhere else. No one spoke to Nikola. He had walked around on his own, the loneliest boy on earth.

Behind the drawing room, there was a room called the cushion room. He had seen the boys who were starting first and second grade go in there. It was forbidden territory for the younger kids like him. They would probably beat him to a pulp if he set foot in there. Still, he had opened the door and peered inside. It was almost empty, the cushions covered in plasticky green covers and strewn about the room. There was a lone girl jumping up and down on a pile of them. Her dark hair rose upward with each bounce. "Hi," Nikola had said. He knew that he couldn't be friends with a girl, so he had just sat down in one corner and watched.

"Hi," the girl had said, continuing to bounce.

"Hi," said Nikola, getting up.

"You want to bounce with me?" asked the girl.

Nikola didn't reply, but he knew he wanted to bounce—despite the no-playing-with-girls rule. He climbed onto a pile of green plush cushions and got ready.

The two bounced alongside one another. They threw the piles of cushions into the corner, built obstacle courses, and jumped higher and higher. He and the girl.

After a while, the youth club educator had poked his head around the door and said: "Time to head home now, boys."

Nikola had stared at the girl in front of him: *boys?*

"What's your name?"

"I'm Chamon," said Chamon, whose hair might not have been so long after all. "I'm starting school on Monday. What's yours?"

"You can drive while I eat," Bello said as he sat down with the food carton on his lap. "We're circus performers. Juggling loads of stuff at the same time."

Nikola hoped Kerim would get in touch soon. He had spoken to Gabbe, Mr. One's old gun dealer, and gotten himself a piece. But mostly, he was preparing his head: everything he had done until this point was driven by burning fire. He had been pushed forward by a wave of hate. But now: now he would be instructed to carry out a task that he knew nothing about. Against someone he probably didn't know—that was new. Maybe he was crazy, but everyone had been pissing on him for so long now, it was his turn to piss back.

"Believe me," he said. "This is the last time I'm doing anything for Mr. One."

Bello's grin vanished. "There's something going on with you and Isak, right? All you've done lately is moan about him."

Nikola started the engine. "Yeah, there's something going on."

59

A memory. Emelie in the bedroom as a child. She had been reading *Harry Potter and the Sorcerer's Stone* for more than an hour, but she still couldn't sleep. Her mother had been sitting in the armchair, trying to go through a relaxation exercise with her—"Feel your body getting heavier, heavier"—but Emelie still hadn't been able to sleep, so her father had said that she could try getting into their bed. She had lain down on his pillow, beneath his blanket, breathed in his scent, tried to think about how good he smelled when there wasn't a cloud of alcohol around him. And yet: she hadn't been able to sleep. Her father had climbed in next to her, not saying anything, just stroking her back and resting his hand on her shoulder blade—as though he was protecting her from anything and everything. Embracing her. Suddenly it was like everything he had done and would do no longer mattered. Suddenly she could sleep.

Emelie could do with someone to protect her right now. Stuck in a fireproofed archive room with a metal door and an incredibly strange partner.

Magnus didn't want her here, but he kept talking about how sorry he was for the misunderstanding at the restaurant a few weeks earlier. He was, at least, not the person she had briefly feared he might be—he wasn't part of Fredrik O. Johansson's conspiracy, his network. He was just an ordinary, self-centered idiot. Just a simple loser.

Her phone rang: Teddy's name flashed up on the screen.

"It's me."

"I can see that."

"What are you doing?"

"I'm at Leijon."

Teddy's calm breathing on the line. Emelie's heart beating at three times its usual rate. Magnus staring at her.

"Hugo Pederson was more stubborn than I thought. He refused to name any names."

Emelie groaned.

"But, after a bit of four-legged persuasion, he gave me his phone," Teddy continued.

Emelie had almost forgotten that Magnus was standing next to her. She was just listening.

"And I saw a call to a very interesting number on it."

"A number?"

"Yep, the same number that booked the Uber from Katja's place, the one Fredrik O. sent a message to before he went to the estate."

Emelie understood. "So Hugo's been calling the same person who threatened Katja and who went to the estate with Fredrik?"

"Probably."

"Have you tried calling it?"

"Yeah, but no one answers."

"Maybe Loke can help?"

"Maybe. I'll call him. But you can also check the number where you are."

Again: Teddy's calm as he read out the number. Her own pulse at 180. She wanted him with her now. He must have heard something in her voice: "Emelie, is everything okay?"

"No," she said, weighing whether to tell him who was standing in front of her. For some reason, she decided against it. "But we can talk about it later."

She ended the call but kept her phone in her hand as she tried to work out what she was going to do.

Magnus's eyelashes were trembling. "Can you forgive my embarrassing behavior at the restaurant?"

Emelie didn't know how to reply. Magnus had to stop now. And she had to move on.

"Because this is what I'm thinking," he continued. "If we can just draw a line under that episode, you're welcome to come back to us here. I still believe in you. And you should know I've devoted my life to this place, I've built it up from the shabby little firm of amateur generalists we were when old man Leijon still ran the place to what we are today: the highest-ranked firm in Scandinavia, with the highest partner profit in the whole of northern Europe. And that's the ship I want you to join."

Emelie *really* had to get away now.

She breathed in and steeled herself—quickly stepped past him, toward the closed door. She tore it open.

Magnus started to say something: "What are you doing?"

Emelie slammed the door behind her—it thudded even more loudly than when she had gone in earlier. She picked up a sculpture of a boy in a swimming cap and goggles and pushed it beneath the door handle, blocking it—Magnus was trapped inside.

The silence in the hallway was almost unpleasant. She tried to calm her breathing. Then Magnus started banging. She could hear his faint voice on the other side of the thick door. "Let me out, Emelie, what are you doing?"

She needed to think clearly now, so she moved down the hallway. There could still be other Leijon employees around. The sound of Magnus grew fainter. She dialed the number Teddy had seen in Hugo's phone.

The call went through, but nothing happened, neither an answer nor a machine.

The carpet on the floor looked almost like silk as it glittered in the sunlight filtering through the windows. She held her phone in front of her, still calling the unknown number. She listened out for noises. Magnus was quiet now, as far as she could tell.

She passed Jossan's office; she passed her old room. The ringing continued at regular intervals. She walked past more of her former colleagues' offices. Her phone grew warm in her hand.

Then she heard it: a faint ringing farther down the hallway. She headed toward the sound. It grew louder. A phone ringing in someone's office.

She tried the handle. The door was locked, but she could clearly hear a phone inside. No one locked their door at Leijon; she had never seen anyone do it. Though the working culture was tough and you were expected to devote your life to the firm, the doors were always open. The assistant lawyers always had to be able to speak to one another or the partners if there was something they needed to know. The firm's decision always had to weigh more than individual employees' possible needs for privacy.

But she was sure: the phone she was calling was locked inside.

Emelie pulled at the door, but it was solidly built. Nothing happened.

She went over to the stairwell, down to the sixth floor where the handyman's closet—or the property maintenance department, as it was known—was located. She rifled through the tools and grabbed the biggest screwdriver she could find.

Back at the door: she forced the screwdriver into the lock and tried to pry it open. She pulled at it, tore, and hacked. She couldn't do it. Instead, she pushed the screwdriver into the gap between the door and the frame. She got ready and kicked. It rattled, cracked; the damned door opened.

Right then, she felt a kick in her belly.

The room looked just like she had expected it to: neat, tidy, incredibly impersonal—other than a picture of a woman on the desk, probably a daughter or new wife. She called the number again. She knew where she was now. This was Anders Henriksson's office. The arch-loser who had always been responsible for her development meetings, who had stopped Magnus Hassel at the bar in Ling Long.

She could hear the angry ringtone coming from a tall, brown cabinet. It was locked, and she broke it open using the screwdriver. Inside was a gray Samsonite suitcase. And, on a shelf, a phone was buzzing and ringing.

Emelie picked it up. Her own number was flashing up on the screen. She grabbed the handle of the Samsonite case: it was locked, too. She tried forcing the screwdriver into the lock, but she couldn't get a good grip. The case was clearly constructed to be difficult to pick. She was going to need better tools. And she couldn't stay here too long.

With the phone in one hand and the case in the other, she turned and left.

60

The police station in Täby didn't match the rest of the area. It was on what felt like a back street, to one side of the hulking great shopping center. She and Billie were holding hands. Roksana needed her friend right now—she had called her a while earlier, and Billie had come right away.

"That there's the temple of the repressed," Billie said, pointing toward the shopping center. "And the cult of consumerism demands complete obedience. Awareness of society's power structures is the one thing they don't sell in those otherwise so brightly lit places. Since that awareness is something money can't buy, they're not interested."

Standing in front of the heavy glass doors into the police station, Roksana felt a wave of nausea.

"Is this where they held you after Our Land Club?" Billie had possibly realized that Roksana hadn't exactly called her to go off on one of her political rants.

Roksana nodded. "Though they actually treated me pretty well," she said. "No fascist pigs. They were just doing their jobs."

Billie snorted. "They protect Nazis demonstrating on our streets, but they take your ticket money from a celebration of love. They're crazy."

Roksana knew who the real crazy people were. She had to find the money now.

The station wasn't open to the public today, but above a bell by the doors there was a sign reading *Emergency Help*. She pressed it.

"It's going to be fine," said Billie.

Ten minutes later, a woman in plain clothes opened the door.

"I'd like to speak to someone. Could we come in?" Roksana asked.

"You can talk to me, but we're pretty understaffed today, so you'll have to sit down and wait a while."

Billie glared at her. The policewoman continued. "The officers on shift are out hunting drunk drivers. Today's the most dangerous day of the year to be out on the roads."

They sat down to wait on one of the stone benches in reception. Roksana shoved her hand into her canvas bag and felt the cool metal of Nikola's gold chain between her fingers. A guy she barely knew versus her father. She didn't understand how it could be such a difficult choice.

After another ten minutes, a hatch in the reception counter opened. The police officer was now wearing glasses, and she was standing on the other side, behind the glass—lame, marking out her position.

Roksana breathed in and felt the chain in her bag again. "There's something I'd like to talk to you about." Her mouth was dry, her words catching on the roof of it, on her tongue.

The policewoman had switched on a computer and was standing with her fingers poised to type up whatever Roksana wanted to tell her. Billie seemed invigorated. She did a quick pirouette on the floor.

61

"I've never liked Stockholm by day," Dejan said. "This city has to be experienced at night."

"You're messed up," Teddy mumbled, thinking about how Dejan had fired the MP5 over the Midsummer guests' heads. Not that he wasn't grateful—if his gangster friend hadn't had his dog with him, Hugo would never have shown him his phone. And now Dejan was giving him a ride back to Kum's place.

"I mean," Dejan continued, "that everyone's so proud of Stockholm's successes, how beautiful she is with all the water, how clean, how safe, and all that crap. But the sexy thing is the depth of the place. The way nothing's how it seems. The fact that on those very same streets, *insane* amounts of coke are dealt every night, that the whores will go to any address you send them, that access to weapons from the Balkans has increased sevenfold over the last three years, that the police don't even dare go out to the districts."

"Quiet, concentrate on driving," Teddy said. Dejan was more screwed up than he had ever realized.

The touch screen on the Porsche dashboard was only half the size of the one in the Tesla, but everything else screamed German luxury.

He had just spoken to Emelie. She had managed to get ahold of the suitcase and a phone and was in a taxi en route to Kum's place, where they would try to open the case together. He was assuming they would find material inside that would enable them to round up and end the so-called network. With any luck, they would find a police officer who could help them, someone more trustworthy than Detective Inspector Nina Ley.

His child wouldn't have to be born into this. His child wouldn't have a father who was living on the run.

A memory: pre-slammer, pre-all-this-damn-shit. An equally cold spring. Teddy had taken Nikola to the amusement park, to Gröna Lund. He was maybe seven years old at the time. They bought wristbands and started on the left side of the park, where the rides for smaller children were located. The line had been long, and they spent twenty minutes in line for the Ladybird. After one ride, Nikola had wanted cotton candy. They went on the smaller free-fall tower and the teacups, the cotton candy like a thin beard around Nikola's mouth and a sticky mess on his fingers. Then he had wanted to head over to the "grown-up section" as he called it— and the bigger free-fall ride. They went on the roller coaster and the ghost train. Teddy was freezing, but Nikola had wanted to go on the Wild Mouse roller coaster; according to the brochure, you had to be at least forty-seven inches to get on, and Nikola was only forty-six. Teddy had said no. Nikola had begged. When Teddy said no a second time, Nikola had cried. "Please, Uncle Teddy. Please. You're the only one who does fun stuff with me, and Chamon's been on it, he told me. Do you want me to be the only one who hasn't been on the Wild Mouse?" They had gone into the bathroom, where Teddy lifted Nikola onto a toilet seat and pulled off his boots. He had folded two paper towels until they became stiff cardboard cushions and then shoved them into Nikola's boots. "There, now let's see how tall you are." They went back to the Wild Mouse, and Teddy had watched Nikola hold his breath as the entry guy measured him. But when their turn came around and they were finally sitting in the front car, Teddy had caught a glimpse of something else. He had stroked Nikola's cheek. "You okay?"

Nikola had nodded stiffly. The roller coaster cars screeched and vibrated and cranked their way thirty feet into the air, to the start. For a brief moment, they hung at the top, suddenly swinging downward, upward, around the sharp bends. They had been pushed outward by the g-force, heard people screaming, and Teddy had felt his stomach protesting. He had glanced over to Nikola and realized that he should have known better. His nephew's eyes were filled with terror. When they left the ride, it had all welled over— Nikola couldn't stop crying. Teddy had picked him up and carried him down the stairs to the exit. He had felt Nikola's warm breath on his shoulder, his tears on his neck. Nikola had been sobbing, huddled up—a small, wet fleck.

Children needed closeness. Children needed safety.

"Can I speak now?" Dejan asked.

Teddy was torn from his thoughts. "Yeah, yeah, of course."

"Those bastards you and Emelie are hunting seem to have no barriers, even worse than me. Just remember what they did in Oslo, how they locked you up in that abandoned prison last year."

"You're probably right." Teddy wondered what he was getting at.

Dejan braked and pulled up outside Kum's house. "So I doubt they're just going to twiddle their thumbs now, either."

"Definitely not."

"That's all I wanted to say. Stay on your toes, Teddy. Don't let the bastards hurt you or the people you love."

62

The Snapchat message had come in fifteen minutes earlier. It was short and to the point:

> Norr Mälarstrand 17, 4th floor, apt. 1405. Grab the woman there, but don't hurt her. Will send more instructions.

The New Kum had been clear—if Nikola did this, he could have his protection. It was finally time.

He was relieved that they just seemed to be asking for a kidnapping rather than a hit job, but he still couldn't shake off the bad feeling that had crept up on him.

He and Bello had driven straight to Norr Mälarstrand. Bello stayed in the van. They had decided that they couldn't just leave it anywhere. Nikola was glad that Bello was willing to step up for this. His friend was as loyal as a dog. But Nikola's body was still crawling.

He went up to the fourth floor and positioned himself outside the door. Söderlund, he read from the mailbox. Nikola had looked her up online. The woman living here was called Josephine.

He knocked on the door. Nothing happened.

He knocked again. Heard the padding of footsteps inside.

A woman wearing a dressing gown and with her hair twisted up in a towel opened the door. It looked like she had just taken a shower and was in the process of applying her makeup. She was pretty by the usual male standards, but she still wasn't Nikola's type.

He quickly forced his way inside and pulled the door shut behind him. The balaclava covering his face was itchier than the wasp sting he had once gotten as a child. Maybe the woman, Josephine, knew what was about to happen. Maybe not. It made no difference—everything went much more smoothly than Nikola had expected. He didn't even say anything as he raised his gun.

The apartment was luxuriously renovated. Recessed downlights on the ceiling, freshly sanded oak parquet, light switches that looked more like electronic devices than anything else. He sent a Snap of the woman as instructed. The whole time, she kept calm and quiet.

He got an immediate reply. *Drive her into the center. She's needed now.*

Nikola wondered how he was going to get her down to the van. Would she go calmly down the stairs, or would he have to tie her hands behind her back and shove her into the elevator? Could he let her sit in one of the seats, or did he have to throw her into the back of the van?

He had to act now.

He pointed the gun at her. "Just keep calm, otherwise I'll shoot your kneecaps." It was the first time he had seen her react. She trembled, as though a shiver had passed through her body. In that moment, he saw Roksy's face. Fuck—she was the best thing to happen to him in a long time—and now he was here, kidnapping someone.

Nikola looked at the woman again. What was he doing?

Honestly, what was he up to?

63

Driving through Stockholm was quick today. She had the Samsonite case next to her in the backseat of the taxi, and she could see the idyllic street that led to Kum's house ahead. Teddy was up to speed with everything, and she had even called Nina Ley—she didn't know any other officers she could contact about this.

"We've identified someone with a definite link to the network."

Nina had sounded almost absent. "What's happened?"

As quickly as she could, Emelie had told her about the suitcase that was taken away from the estate, about the bugging of Hugo Pederson, the number in his phone, and the case she had found in Anders Henriksson's office.

"A lawyer, you're saying?" was all Nina said once Emelie was finished.

"Yes, with my old firm. Leijon Legal Services. It's crazy."

"Thanks for that. We'll look into it as soon as we can. Probably tomorrow. It's not easy getting ahold of people today."

Emelie didn't know what to think—shouldn't the police be taking immediate action?

Suddenly the other phone rang. The one she had found in Henriksson's office.

A voice: "Emelie?"

"Yes?"

"I thought you'd left to celebrate Midsummer like all the others."

"Who is this?"

"Ignore that. You have something of mine."

"Who is this?" Emelie repeated.

"I think you know."

Yes, she did recognize his high, whiny voice. The voice that, ten years earlier, must have ordered Hugo Pederson to lure Mats into the kidnapping trap. It was Anders Henriksson.

"I've spoken to the police," Emelie said. "I'm going to hand over everything in the case."

"I don't like people taking my things," Henriksson said. "But, as luck would have it, I've also got something of yours."

"What do you mean?"

"If I'm not given the contents of that case, you'll never see your friend again."

"What are you talking about?" From the corner of one eye, Emelie saw the taxi driver turn around.

"I'm taking care of Josephine," said Henriksson.

Emelie gasped.

"I know you have the case," said Henriksson. "Meet me at Leijon and we'll resolve this without anyone getting hurt."

64

The leader was wearing the same leather hoodie as before; he was as fat as ever and seemed to be swallowing just as much phlegm. But he sounded much happier than she was used to. They met in the same hotel room.

Roksana unzipped the bag in front of him. The leader bastard looked down.

"Here's half a million in cash. Want to count it?"

This time, there was no one blocking the doorway.

The leader rocked back on his chair. "I trust you, little lady."

She got up. "So we're done, then?"

Billie was waiting for her down in reception.

The leader remained sitting. "Hold up a second. I'm curious. Where'd you get the cash? You said the cops had taken all your dough. Did you borrow it, like your guy Z?"

"No," she said.

"How'd you get it together so quickly then?"

"That doesn't matter."

"But I want to know."

"I'm curious, too. Why did you have ketamine in the apartment we rented? It's just been bugging me, you know?"

"Not everyone's as competent as you, little lady. The cops missed the ketamine when they raided the place. We already told you that, no? And the guy I sent to fetch the crap is a loser. He can't even tell whether a BMW's brakes are fucked or not."

Roksana had no idea what he was talking about.

"You, though, you deliver. You sold half a mill's worth in two weeks, that how you got the money?"

She thought about something Nikola had said to her as she opened the door into the hallway. "I can't tell you everything."

The leader watched her leave.

The only thing that mattered now was that the madman wouldn't hurt her father.

No, that wasn't the only thing that mattered. Nikola mattered, too.

65

They had no choice but to turn around. Teddy explained the situation to Dejan: "Someone's grabbed Emelie's friend Josephine, and they want to swap her for something Emelie has. You've kidnapped someone before . . ."

"So have you," Dejan interrupted.

"Yeah, but what should I do?"

Dejan sped up as they passed Sollentuna. "You should fuck those bastards in the ass."

Dejan parked illegally some way from Leijon. A minute or two earlier, Henriksson had texted Emelie the exact location he wanted to meet: the garage beneath the firm.

Teddy and Dejan had to walk around the building before they found the ramp down.

He texted Emelie.

Are you down there?

Yeah, I just got here. But no one's arrived yet, it's empty.

We're outside. Can you open the door for us?

No, don't think I should. He was clear that I had to be alone. Imagine if he sees me letting you in?

Teddy turned around and stared at the street. The shops were closed. People didn't want to be here right now. It was four thirty in the afternoon. He could see two young men walking hand in hand toward Stureplan. There was a van approaching, and it turned off onto Leijon's street. Teddy and Dejan took a few steps back, tried to position themselves around the corner of the building. He heard the van pull up in front of the garage door. It was going in— into the Leijon garage.

He heard the garage door slowly opening. The van rolled down the ramp.

One second. Two seconds. The door started to creak, making its way back down. "Stay here," he said to Dejan, before ducking beneath the door and creeping inside.

At first, in contrast to the brilliant summer day outside, everything looked dark. But after a few seconds, his eyes became accustomed to the dim light. The ramp led straight down, and Teddy saw the van come to a halt. He pressed himself against the gray wall.

He was convinced that Emelie's friend was inside.

66

Nikola parked the van in space number four, not far from the entrance to the garage, just like he had been instructed.

As he was driving toward Leijon, he had received a message containing the entry code for the garage, plus: *Drive inside. Park in space 4.* He did as he was told. He thought about the person in the back of the van, among all the boxes of explosives. It was *sick* that they had been driving Mr. One's deadly cargo at the exact moment he'd been given the order to do this thing for Kerim. But it was what it was.

I'm in position, he wrote as he turned off the engine.

The reply was immediate: *I know.*

This was creepy—whoever had ordered the job must be watching from one of the surveillance cameras on the ceiling. Seemed like a real bunny boiler—what kind of jobs did Kerim accept, exactly? Nikola thought back to the decisions he had made recently.

So what happens now? he wrote back.

The handover. You'll be given a phone and a suitcase, a Samsonite. Once I see that everything's right, I'll message you. You hand her over, then you drive away with my bag.

Honestly: this job really was sicker than a film. The client—whoever he was—could see everything. Like something out of *The* fucking *Hunger Games.*

67

Emelie could see the spot Henriksson had decided on sixty feet away. She thought back to when she had fallen and hit her head in the parking garage a few months earlier, when Teddy had driven her to the hospital and she had found out she was pregnant. This time, she wasn't paranoid—this time, there really was someone else there.

For a brief moment, she had genuinely thought they were about to bring the whole sad tale to an end. She was convinced that whatever was in the case would provide plenty of evidence against the network—the men who hated women. The phone had to be Henriksson's *secure* line. If the right police officer and the right prosecutor got their hands on that, they could charge him and the others. *They* would be arrested and convicted, and this nightmare would finally come to an end.

But not now—and all because that loser Magnus Hassel had contacted Anders Henriksson, who had now kidnapped her best friend. She and Teddy were going to lose. Anders Henriksson would take back the contents of the suitcase, destroy the evidence. No, she then thought, she and Teddy weren't the ones who would lose—that was Katja and all the other girls.

The sound of her own footsteps in the garage—Emelie heard them echo as though she were inside a musical instrument. She thought she could hear someone else moving around. In her hand, she was clutching Anders Henriksson's phone. She had called Nina Ley, but that was before she knew that Henriksson had Jossan. Now Emelie didn't dare contact the police: there was too much of a risk that Henriksson would hurt Jossan somehow, or that the exchange wouldn't take place. Plus, the police were still searching for Teddy.

Fifty feet to go. She could understand why he had chosen this particular spot: whoever was standing there could hide behind a pillar and still have a view of almost the entire garage.

She was holding the Samsonite case tight. What happened if Henriksson didn't hand over Josephine? The thought made her stomach turn.

There were two figures coming toward her. One of them was wearing a balaclava and was pushing the other in front of them: Josephine. Her friend had a black cloth bag over her head. She was moving oddly and wearing different clothes than earlier—was that a dressing gown? Emelie wondered if she was hurt.

She could barely bring herself to look and continued staring at one of the pillars in the distance instead.

The figure in the balaclava was holding a pistol.

What kind of man was Anders Henriksson?

"Stay there," the person in the balaclava said once they were thirty feet apart. "Put down the phone and push the case over here." Emelie vaguely recognized the voice—it was a man, but it wasn't Anders Henriksson, she was sure of that.

Suddenly she felt a pain in her stomach: as though her entire belly had contracted, tensed to the point of bursting. But she did as he told her: she paused and gave the case a slight shove forward. She placed the phone on the concrete floor.

"Now back up," the man said in a calm voice.

"I want you to let my friend go first."

"She's your friend?"

"You know she is."

"Then here you go," said the man, giving his hostage a shove and making Josephine jerk forward with her arms out in front of her.

Emelie remained where she was. The chill was moving upward. Her belly was as hard as a basketball. The cramp was almost unbearable. She staggered toward Josephine, whose wrists were bound together. The man in the balaclava had turned around and was heading back to his van. He had shoved the phone into his pocket and was pulling the case behind him.

Emelie tore the material from Jossan's head.

Only, it wasn't Josephine staring back at her.

It was someone else. A young man. Someone she didn't recognize. Or maybe she did recognize him: a dark-haired kid.

Damn it—Henriksson had tricked her. He still had Josephine—this was just a bluff to get hold of the bag.

The dark-haired kid said: "I recognize you. Weren't you Nicko's lawyer?" Emelie didn't understand a thing.

Then he said: "Relax. We never took that Josephine woman. Nikola wimped out. We had no idea she was your friend, by the way. But he has to hand over that bag and phone, otherwise there'll be trouble. Real trouble."

68

Only once she and Billie were in a taxi heading away from the leader did she finally breathe out. She had done it—she had managed to find the money and she had handed it over. It was incredible.

Billie laughed.

Roksana thought about the policewoman at Täby station who had been standing ready at her computer a few hours earlier. She had leaned forward, toward the hatch. "My name is Roksana, I'm here regarding case number 3232-K38909."

The police officer had tapped the digits into her computer. The station was as quiet as an exam hall. "Okay. And what is it you need?"

Roksana knew exactly what she needed. Billie had explained it to her when she went over to her place earlier that day. Shit—Roksana was so glad for Billie's chatter and awareness. She was super happy that Billie was taking the most unlikely of courses: law.

"I want to collect my bag and its contents," Roksana said, meeting the policewoman's tired gaze.

The police had seized the bag containing all of the cash after Our Land Club, but Roksana had been arrested on suspicion of accounting crimes and breaking alcohol licensing regulations, not the ketamine. The prosecutor had requested that some of the money quickly be sequestered, and a judge had also ruled on the matter in court: just over 1.5 million kronor should be held in

anticipation of a future ruling or decision—enough to cover any
potential tax obligations, fines, or fees. But that didn't mean *all*
the money in the bag. Billie had worked out that the prosecutor
couldn't possibly have anything to say about the rest of the money
Roksana and Z had earned legally from ticket sales. And the police
officer at Täby station had a duty to pay out *that* money.

Billie: a legal genius.

A few minutes later, the cop came back from the confiscation
room with Roksana's bag beneath one arm. "If I could just ask you
to fill in this receipt for your bag and your money."

Two lines to cross and sign.

Seized item number K38909-23 p1: Bag. Brand: Nike.

Seized item number K38909-23 p2: Cash: 1,404,400 kronor in notes.

It meant she had enough money to pay the psychos. The fact
she had even considered giving up Nikola to claim the reward was
madness—she was ashamed that the thought had even crossed her
mind, but the threat against Baba had made her crazy with fear.

The policewoman had handed over the bag of cash. "You have
a good Midsummer," she said.

69

Teddy saw everything. A young man had been handed over instead of Josephine, and Teddy recognized him: it was Bello, Nikola's friend. Thoughts were exploding through his mind like grenades. What was *he* doing here? Henriksson must have tricked them somehow. Teddy didn't know what to do—he just knew that he had to do something. Move. Act. Stop the Samsonite case from disappearing with the man in the balaclava who had handed over Bello.

Teddy stepped forward. He saw Emelie in the distance. She looked confused, and his instincts told him to run over and hug her, but there was no time for that.

"What are *you* doing here?" he shouted to Bello.

Bello looked as surprised as Teddy felt. "This shit's completely crazy. You need to talk to Nicko before he leaves."

Teddy's head was about to explode. Nikola? *Nikola?*

He ran toward the garage doors, the spot where he had seen the van parked as he sneaked in. The van had started to roll toward the ramp. Teddy didn't know what Nikola was doing, but his nephew was clearly planning on driving away. He couldn't let that happen.

Long strides. He wasn't thinking about anything. He was thinking about everything all at once. In his mind, he saw Fredrik O. Johansson tipping documents into the case out at the estate.

The garage doors slowly started to open. The van was waiting to drive out, its motor ticking over.

Teddy threw himself at the vehicle, tore open the driver's-side door. He saw his nephew's uncomprehending face and pulled him out.

"What the hell are you doing?"

They tumbled to the concrete floor.

Nikola shouted back: "What are you doing here?"

"You don't know what you're getting caught up in."

Teddy crawled upright. Nikola was standing over him. His nostrils were flaring. Eye to eye. Ten inches apart.

"*Ujak*, I've got no idea what you and Emelie are doing here. I've done everything as cool as I could," Nikola hissed. "I didn't know she was Emelie's friend, and I didn't even take her, I faked the whole thing and had Bello in the back instead. But I need that case. I'm not letting you have it. You don't know everything, Teddy."

"I know that you don't know who you're helping."

"I'm doing this for Chamon."

Teddy stared at him. His nephew: the boy he had rocked to sleep so many times, the boy he had taken swimming, to the amusement park, to football matches at Jalla-Vallen. Who he had never, ever wanted to hurt.

Right then, he heard a sound in the background. Teddy turned around. A metal door had opened at the back of the garage, and two people appeared.

One was dressed in police motorcycle gear, in a helmet with the visor turned down, and was holding a pistol against the other person's head. That other person was Anders Henriksson, and his face was as white as a painkiller.

Teddy recognized the cop: the helmet was the same make as the one the officer who shot Fredrik O. had been wearing.

"One of you has a bag belonging to Anders," said the motorcycle cop.

Teddy recognized the voice. It belonged to a woman.

Nina Ley.

"I want that bag," she said.

70

The past six months had been about as fucked-up as a life could be, but still: this was the sickest ever.

He had genuinely considered kidnapping that woman—he'd had to, to guarantee Kerim's protection. But he had changed his mind. Maybe it was Roksana's effect on him. *Just because other people have betrayed you, you don't have to betray yourself*—those words had bored into his mind and taken root in some fucked-up way. Or maybe it was Teddy: his *ujak* had done a U-turn in life. But that wasn't what Nikola was thinking about. It was how Teddy acted toward him. The way he had always cared. Always been there. Still: his head was chipped to pieces from betrayal. All he wanted was to fuck everyone back, but how was he meant to heal after that? He would just be deceiving himself again, and he really didn't need that. So, he had broken off the whole thing, left Josephine in her apartment, headed downstairs, and put a hood on Bello instead, who then lay down in the back of the van. All they needed to make sure the client was happy—and, by extension, Kerim—was the bag and the phone.

But now his uncle had turned up. And Emelie—his old lawyer. Plus a crazy woman in a motorbike helmet who radiated cop vibes and was holding a pistol against the head of a mega nerd who was probably the end client. What the hell was going on?

Teddy shouted for the cop to drop her gun, but she didn't listen.

"Put your hands on your head," she said to the client, turning to face Nikola and Teddy. "I want that case."

The client was breathing deeply, hyperventilating. In the background, the van was humming away, halfway out of the garage doors, the engine still running.

"What are you going to do?" Teddy asked.

The crazy cop wasn't speaking clearly, possibly because she was still wearing her helmet. "I'm going to end him. And then I want that suitcase."

She pressed her service weapon against the back of the guy's head. He was shaking. The concrete beneath him turned dark, his piss forming a small pool.

Nikola took a step toward her. Whoever she was, she had to cool down. She *had* to chill out.

"I don't know who you are, but you need to lower your gun," he said as gently as he could. "You can't shoot."

The cop's voice was less steady now. It vibrated against something inside the helmet, possibly because she was so angry. "Just give me the suitcase," she said, taking the gun off safety.

The clicking sound echoed like an explosion through the garage.

71

Confusion. Uncertainty. Madness. Things were happening too quickly. In too unexpected a form.

Emelie was staring at the motorbike officer who had appeared from nowhere with Anders Henriksson. Nina Ley.

Her brain was racing to assess the situation. The murder of Fredrik O. Johansson and all the other old men Mats had talked about—Teddy had discovered that five of them were dead and one was missing. Two had died of heart attacks and cancer, respectively, one had died in a boating accident, one had been killed by a robber in Brazil, and one had driven himself off the road. All within the space of eighteen months, it now struck Emelie. All since the abuse films were handed in.

The investigation carried out by Nina Ley's special unit was a failure from the point of view of the police force—no perpetrators had even been identified, never mind arrested. Emelie suspected she now knew why.

"Nina," she said. "It's time to stop."

The motorbike officer turned to her, still pointing her gun at Henriksson. With her other hand, she pushed back the visor.

Nina Ley's features looked squashed. "No, you're the ones who need to stop. You've done what you needed to do, now I'm taking over."

Suddenly, Nikola started to move toward Nina. Emelie didn't

understand what he was doing—he shouldn't approach her; it was too dangerous. But then again, everything going on right now was completely crazy.

Her stomach contracted in a painful cramp.

"I don't know who you are," Nina said, aiming her gun at Nikola instead, "but don't take another step."

And then: without Emelie having time to see how, Anders Henriksson got up and knocked the gun from Nina's hand.

A clattering sound.

Nina threw herself to the ground, grasping for the pistol.

But Henriksson was already making a run for it toward the garage exit.

Teddy shouted: "Grab him!"

Nina yelled something inaudible.

And then everyone started to run. Teddy. Nina. Emelie moved as quickly as she could, bent forward. Behind her, she heard Bello and Nikola shouting.

They came out onto the deserted street. The sun was blazing. It could have been a glorious late afternoon.

Henriksson hadn't made it very far, and Nina threw herself at him, the pistol back in her hand.

"On your knees!" she ordered, pressing the gun to his face. The man did as she said.

Everyone was standing still. A triangle of death: Teddy and Emelie in one corner, Nicko and Bello in another. On the ground in front of them, Nina and Henriksson formed the third point. A complete absence of movement. The van was still standing in the middle of the doorway.

The barrel of Nina's gun was pointing directly at Henriksson's eye.

"You can't shoot . . ." Nikola tried to say, but Nina didn't seem to hear him.

Emelie saw images. She and Josephine had been going to lunch a few years earlier when they had passed a crowd of people demonstrating on Birger Jarlsgatan. She couldn't even remember what they were protesting about, just the train of people streaming toward Norrmalmstorg like a huge, speckled snake. "Why are they all so angry?" she had asked. Jossan had clutched her designer handbag tight: "Because they believe in a different world. They think that if something's bad, you have to fight to change it. And demonstrating is their peaceful way of making their voices heard."

Emelie's gaze was steady on Nina Ley, and she took a step forward.

Nina didn't move. Nothing happened. They were all frozen in position. Other than Henriksson: he was trembling.

"Nina," Emelie tried again. "You have no right to do what you're about to do, regardless of the crime he's committed. He'll get his punishment, but not like this. There are peaceful ways."

Nina moved slowly. Lowered her gun.

Emelie could feel that the cramp in her stomach had let up slightly.

Tears were running down Henriksson's cheeks.

Nina looked stiff. Then she said: "No, because this is for Amanda."

She raised her pistol again.

She was going to shoot.

No.

From the corner of one eye, Emelie saw a movement.

Nikola had thrown himself at Nina.

Three shots rang out. Loud cracks that bounced off the buildings around them.

And then, immediately: Emelie was thrown back several feet. Flung as though she were made of paper. An enormous explosion, a sound louder than anything she had ever heard. The ground shook. The pavement trembled. Her ears were ringing. She saw tarmac. Tasted it. Her hands were on her stomach. The baby inside.

She tried to see. Squinted.

Nina Ley's body was on the ground in front of her: torn and deformed. She was still wearing her helmet.

Smoke was pouring out of the garage: something must have exploded. None of it made sense. But Emelie understood all the same: she saw the entire building start to crack.

The facade began to split. It looked like it was imploding, collapsing inward, like the images from 9/11. There was smoke and dust everywhere, chunks of concrete and glass. Stone and metal fell to the ground. It sounded like heaven itself was collapsing over their heads.

Leijon Legal Services had been blown to pieces.

Leijon Legal Services no longer existed.

Epilogue

To Emelie, in the event of my incapacitation.

The world turns on its own axis; spinning around itself, in other words. That's a dizzying thought, isn't it? That we're all in motion, all of the time, every second of our lives. When I was a child, I couldn't understand why we weren't thrown off the surface, or why we didn't at least feel the wind on our faces as the world turned. Later, once I was older, I realized that it should give us an interesting perspective: we're constantly seeing the same things, but always from different positions, and since we as spectators are constantly moving, we must surely, at some point, discover things no one else has seen, things it's only possible to glimpse from that particular angle, from that particular moment in time.

Emelie, I'm writing these words to you in a hurry. I don't know what's going to happen over the next few hours. Maybe I'll be dead. Maybe I'll be arrested. Maybe others will be dead. But there's one thing you should know from the outset: everything I've done, I've done for Amanda.

Amanda never got to join my journey. But I followed hers, her much too short journey. I was promoted to detective inspector four years ago, though, in truth, I've felt like a police officer ever since I was very young. Even in school, I thought of myself as someone who could put things right. But now I'm not so sure. Maybe I'm *no longer a police officer, perhaps I've been forced to become some-thing else. I've noticed something I wasn't aware of earlier. I've started solving problems in my own way. From a new angle, from a new position.*

We're at the beginning of the end of this nightmare. The nightmare that began for Amanda much earlier than I thought.

I've just realized that you and your partner have led me to one of the last pieces of the puzzle. You just called me to say that you have found a bag full of material from Hallenbro Storgården—hell on earth.

Back when I showed you the film clips during the interviews with Katja, I realized that you had recognized something. Perhaps you saw the similarity between me and my daughter, Amanda—but how were you supposed to understand the link? Amanda and I were always very similar. Not just in terms of appearance; we also shared the same strength of will. It's just that we put it to use in different ways.

You aren't bad people, you and Teddy Maksumic. You bear no responsibility for what has happened. On the contrary, I'm grate-ful to you for leading me to Fredrik O. Johansson. You have also suffered: I know they tried to blow your Teddy to pieces and that his nephew was injured as a result, I've found evidence as to who was behind this. I know that Teddy was arrested and mistakenly accused of what happened at the estate, and I let that happen. Forgive me, it was only temporary, it was only to avoid any dis-ruptions and to gain more time.

There is one man remaining that I need to deal with: I've long called him "the helper" because I didn't know his real name, but you have now led me to him. You and Teddy have been every bit as smart as I hoped.

So, I'm sitting here, alone on Midsummer's Eve, about to climb onto my motorbike. I've already contacted the relevant tele-phone company and know that he has been using his phone in the vicinity of Leijon Legal Services. Maybe he's still there. I'll find him: *Anders Henriksson. The helper. The lawyer who was with them from the beginning. Ever since Mats Emanuelsson was kidnapped. He may not have been directly involved in the crimes like Fredrik O. Johansson and the others, but he is guilty all the same. He was part of the machinery. He has made it possible.*

Amanda was one of the girls on the hard drive that Mats Emanuelsson handed in. She never told me what she had been through, but I had to watch as she and the other girl, Katja, were raped by four men at once. They urinate on my daughter, they force things inside her. They laugh when she cries out in pain and fear. I'll never be able to erase those thoughts, they're always there, like a film between me and reality.

For Amanda, there was no way out. I know that when she took her own life, she had tried. I know that when she ended her suffering, she actually wanted to live. But what they did to her had changed her soul, and buried it far too deep.

I couldn't save her.

When I began studying the films as the lead investigator a few years ago, I gained even more of an understanding. I never told anyone that my daughter was one of the girls. There was no point, doing so wouldn't bring Amanda back. Some wondered why the investigation never led anywhere, some questioned my and my colleagues' competence. But the investigation went further than they knew—just not in the way they wanted. I've taken care of everything myself. On the side. Without risking some pathetic Swedish court pretending that morals don't exist.

I'm sure you understand, Emelie, because you are carrying new life inside you. Every day and every night, every breath I endure, all I can think of is my daughter. And the more I've dealt with my nightmare, the more it has grown. Amanda wasn't alone, I've identified at least 25 of the 30+ girls who were abused. I've also tracked down the majority of the men.

Sometimes, I think that there's an image of the male sexual predator as being a lone wolf, a social outcast, perhaps someone with slight cognitive difficulties. And yes, some are like that. But the vast majority have proven to be the opposite. Just think of Göran Lindberg or the French presidential candidate Dominique Strauss-Kahn. All men with social skills, powerful men, men in high positions, with an insatiable appetite for damaging women, girls, children.

The network has been active for more than fifteen years now, and no one has ever suspected them, not even when the girls talked about the abuse with psychologists, counselors, and social workers. Their trappings of power protected them, their roots in society strengthened them. No one could believe it was true.

What I couldn't work out was how they knew you would be meeting Mats in Oslo, nor who had helped that rotten Sundén out in Håga the year before last—until I found the police officer, that is. His name is Patrik Wallin, the Stockholm district commissioner, and he is one of the perpetrators. I discovered his involvement by sheer chance, as I was reviewing who had searched for Teddy on the computer system after he escaped. Our system is intelligent in that sense—all searches are registered, as well as who made them. Even when they're made by high-ranking officials. Commissioner Wallin stuck out, he caught my attention. So, Emelie, if I only have a few hours left, it will be your job to make sure he is arrested.

The others are already gone. I gave one such a fright that he died of a heart attack. I drowned another while he was out on his yacht. I killed one on the street in Brazil. I drove another into a rock face and undid his seat belt just before we crashed. I strangled one in Switzerland, making it look like a suicide. He was actually the first to take up contact with Katja, the man she described in her interview. I've injected air into two men's eyes, making their hearts stop. I shot another in the face back at the place where it all happened: Fredrik O. Johansson. I know he was one of the men who did things to Amanda in particular.

I want you to know that they were all nothing but facade, they were all so weak. So empty. Amanda was stronger.

Amanda was greater than all of them.
I've done what I've done for her and for everyone they abused.
Now and in the future.

/ *Nina Ley*

Ikea with Roksy: he felt like a lion among a flock of sheep. Everyone was just walking around, perfectly normal, so happy and content, so interested in pale wood dining tables that cost 399 kronor. All the same, it was nice: his arm was around Roksy's waist—they were talking about starting a life together. Or maybe that was an exaggeration, but they were here to buy a bed. That was enough for him. Suddenly it struck him that everyone here probably saw him and Roksy as the most super average normal couple of all. They couldn't know that his arm was hanging in a sling beneath his jacket and that he was carrying a Sig Sauer in a shoulder holster.

"You know," said Roksy, "I think this place is ridiculous. But I still love being here with you."

It was a quiet day by Ikea standards, but there were still people peering into every single mocked-up room. This was Sweden in microcosm—only, they didn't reconstruct the cells, the prison hallways, or the tired school classrooms. Not that everything about Sweden was bad. Roksy had told him about the money she had gotten back from the police. She had sent a third of it to Z—even though he had let her down, she thought he had a right to it. A third had gone to repaying their loans and paying the handymen, DJs, and others who still hadn't received their money. The last third was hers, taxed and ready, since the prosecutor was already holding back anything she might owe. After paying off the psychos' money, she was left with roughly 100,000 kronor. "That should be enough to live off for a few months and to buy us a new Ikea bed," she said.

"When do I get to meet your parents?"

Roksy smiled. "They're not too happy with me right now."

Nikola felt his arm ache. The doctors had said that they didn't know whether he would ever be able to use it like normal again, but he was just happy he had survived.

They made their way to the bed section. Continental beds, sprung divans, mattresses: new words for a new life. At his mom's place, he'd had the same bed since he was a teenager, and he'd never given any thought to what kind it was. Teddy had bought the bed for his apartment.

Get five-star sleep in our continental beds, the ads said. *Dunvik, Vallavik, Lauvik.* He went over to one of the show beds and started reading the label. Everything was so chill.

He thought back to the explosion, caused by the cop lady's bullets. Her target had been the client—Anders Henriksson, Nikola had later found out he was called. But, because of his tackle, she had missed. He didn't really know why he had thrown himself at her—the old bastard definitely deserved to die. But if he had decided not to kidnap someone because it didn't feel right, clipping some old man by shooting him in the eye felt even less okay.

He had realized what had happened the minute he hit the ground—bombphobic that he was. The boxes had exploded—Isak's explosives, the boxes he and Bello had been moving around the county at regular intervals. The building above had come crashing down like a house of cards. It was so crazy that he could barely make sense of it, but as he and Bello ran away with ringing ears, they hadn't been able to stop laughing. He hadn't realized at the time that his arm might be permanently messed up—and not even because of the explosion. One of Nina Ley's bullets had hit him. He had read in the papers that she was dead: the crazy cop had fallen.

"Should we test it out?" Roksy asked.

Nikola couldn't quite drop what she had said about her parents. "Yeah, but tell me something first. Why are your mom and dad unhappy with you?"

"Because I took the aptitude test *myself* and got top marks, I guess you could say."

"Congrats, but that doesn't sound like something to be angry about."

Roksy explained. She had been over at her parents' house a few days earlier and had showed the university application page to her father. "I let my Baba read from the screen himself. *Admission decision: you have been accepted and are hereby offered a place in the psychology program.* You don't know him, but he was happier than I've seen him in years. 'This is wonderful,' he said. 'You're going to be a psychologist. I have to call your mother and let her know.' But I said to him, 'No, don't do that. Because I'm not going to take the course.'"

Nikola interrupted her. "Why not?"

"That's exactly what he said, only with more disappointment in his voice. I'll tell you what I told him: I don't want to start the psychology program. I don't think it's right for me. I've realized I want to do something else. I've been offered a night shift at Palm Village Thai Wok until I work out what, you know."

"What did he say?"

"The usual, that I'm losing out on a title and all that. But I'm sure he understands, Nikola. Deep down. I think he's a musician at heart. My grandmother in Tehran told me that."

A musician, Nikola thought. Like Chamon.

They lay down on the Dunvik bed. There was a plastic sheet covering the foot, preventing it from getting unnecessarily dirty. Nikola tried to relax and get a sense of what it would be like to actually sleep on it.

Kerim Celalî had been an inch away from punching him when he told him what had happened. They had met in a café in Bredäng. "So you screwed over my client? The guy who ordered the whole thing?"

Nikola had gone through the conversation with himself over and over again. He knew he had no option but to be straight with

Kerim. The media had done nothing but write about the bombing over the past few days, most fascinated by the fact that only one person had died and no one else had been seriously injured. How could the terrorists be so stupid, they said, to attack on Midsummer's Eve, of all days?

"I changed my mind," Nikola had said. "These things happen."

Kerim had raised his hand again. "I swear, I'll rip your head off. I'll fucking dance in your blood."

"Kerim, you don't need to worry. Your client's not going to cause any problems. I swear." He explained what had happened as concisely as he could. "How much were you meant to be getting for the job?"

"A hundred and fifty grand."

Nikola had given his money to Roksy, all of his savings from the past few years—but she no longer needed it. "Here," he had said, holding out a wad of 500 notes to Kerim. "A hundred and fifty thousand. It's yours."

Kerim had scratched his cheek. He really did resemble a young Tony Montana, when he was still living in the refugee camp.

"Nah," the boss had said, pushing the money back toward him. "You did the right thing, man, and you've messed up your arm. I didn't know what all that shit was about."

Kerim got up, walked over to the entrance, opened the door, and held it like that—signaling that Nikola was free to leave.

Nikola had shoved the wad of notes back into his pocket.

"Hey, Nikola, one more thing."

Nikola had turned around, wondering what was coming next.

"We're not bastards. We only go after people who deserve it," Kerim had said with a grin. "But you can leave the bombs at home next time, yeah?"

It was hard to get up with only one arm. Roksy was still lying on the bed: it almost looked like she had fallen asleep.

Nikola sat up and glanced around. The bed department in Ikea was practically the same size as half a football pitch. Maybe they could go over to Linda's tonight. Imagine being able to introduce Roksy to her: now that everything felt so good.

Then he saw the person he least wanted to see right now. There was a man lying on one of the beds next to them. *Dachri.* At Ikea, of all places—and in the bed department at that. Mr. One himself.

Isak was lying there, right beneath Nikola's nose. But he wasn't alone: there was a woman lying next to him, just like Roksy had been lying next to Nikola. And between Isak and his woman was a small child.

Nikola couldn't move: all he could do was blink repeatedly at his former boss. The tingling had started to appear in his head now—he knew what was coming. The woman seemed to say something to Isak, and he lifted the child up in the air. It was a baby, no more than a few months old—a tiny little thing that made the people around it smile and seem happy: the miracle of life amid all the shit.

Nikola hadn't heard that Mr. One had become a father, or even that he had a girlfriend. The boss clearly had several different lives that no one else knew about—he wasn't just a pig collaborator. But that wasn't the thing—the thing was that the man responsible for Chamon no longer existing, the man Nikola had sworn to take revenge on, was lying only thirty feet away.

He felt for the gun beneath his sweater. It would be easy: just walk over there and shoot that motherfucker in the face. One small squeeze of the trigger and everything would be in equilibrium again: Chamon against Isak—Isak against Chamon. It was cosmic justice. It was how it had to be.

That was when the first lightning strike appeared.

Nikola pulled his gun from its holster. Roksy was still lying on the bed with her eyes closed. Nikola went over to Mr. One and his family.

Isak was playing with the baby—his focus on the child. He held it up in the air above him. Kissed it on the forehead. The woman laughed. The baby gurgled with laughter again. Nikola couldn't see whether it was a boy or a girl. He paused three feet from the bed. His pulse was at 180 now. His head was pounding. He was holding the pistol in a loose grip by his thigh.

It would be so easy.

And so right.

Then Isak turned around. Looked straight at him. His eyes widened: he understood. He saw the weapon in Nikola's hand.

Nikola stayed where he was, his eyes locked on Mr. One's. Isak clasped the child in his arms, panic moving over his face. His breathing was unsteady.

Nikola bent down and almost-whispered: "You're a police informant. And you know what we do to rats."

Nikola could see that Isak understood. He panted: "No, no, don't do anything stupid."

"Why shouldn't I?"

Mr. One couldn't come up with anything.

"Give me one good reason why I shouldn't waste you right here and now." He pressed the gun to Isak's side. A light squeeze now, such a simple movement.

"Huh? Tell me why I shouldn't waste you."

Isak's bottom lip was trembling. "I don't know, but please, think of my kid. It's not right to do this kind of thing in front of innocents."

"Is that what you were thinking as they clipped Chamon while he was lying in a hospital bed?"

"Please, don't do this."

Nikola shoved the gun back beneath his sweater. "If you ever bother me, everyone's going to know what you are. You understand?"

"Yes, yes, just let me live."

"I don't execute people who can't defend themselves. I'm not like you. I'll never be like you."

"Yeah, I know."

"And one more thing," said Nikola. "You need to take care of Yusuf's widow. You need to give Magdalena whatever she wants. It won't bring Yusuf back, but you're going to help her anyway. Forever. You got that?"

"Got it, I swear."

Nikola turned around and went back over to Roksy.

She was sitting on the edge of another bed.

"Lie down here and try this one instead," she said.

The continental bed was higher, and therefore easier to get onto with only one arm. Roksy laughed and put an arm around him. "Imagine we're back at your place now," she whispered in his ear.

Nikola closed his eyes. Leaned back. Felt his headache dissipating.

He was calmer now. The lightning was gone. His head felt heavy, but clear all the same.

He was tired.

Relaxed.

He could sleep now.

Emelie was in her office, trying to work. Aside from the fact that her bump was constantly in the way now, she felt relatively good—though she still had too much work to deal with. There was a knock at the door and Marcus peered in. "Since you're working so much and have your phone off, your guy calls me. He's going to stop by."

"Thanks. Wait a second, Marcus," Emelie said before he had time to close the door. "I'm not going to be in the office much before long. *Again*, I suppose I should say."

"I guessed. Your bump speaks volumes."

Emelie laughed. "Well, you're used to holding the reins, right?"

Marcus laughed, too—he was a hero, looking after the majority of her cases during those chaotic months, and not least for having helped her save Teddy. Some of her clients had been irritated by her absence, but that was understandable: they had the right to demand full attention and availability from their *own* lawyer. Emelie hadn't been there like she should.

She went online to check the latest news. The papers were full of articles about the explosion at Leijon, and they finally seemed to be starting to accept that it wasn't a terrorist attack, more some kind of accident linked to a crazy police officer. Anders Henriksson was still in custody, and the police were investigating all of the material Emelie had handed over to them.

Everything but the letter from Nina Ley.

Nina: A lone avenger. A retaliator. She had been playing the double game until the very end.

Emelie had been worried about the baby, but after having everything checked over once and once more, the midwives and doctors were confident that the child hadn't been harmed by either the pressure wave or Emelie's fall to the ground. Magnus Hassel had left the building before the blast—the question was whether he would survive from a purely psychological point of view. His life's work no longer existed.

Josephine, on the other hand, had been deeply shaken by the young man in the balaclava who had threatened her in her own home. For obvious reasons, she couldn't work out what it was all about—and Emelie was probably never going to tell her. Though maybe she should? Maybe she should invite Jossan and Nikola over for matcha tea and energy drinks sometime?

When Teddy arrived at the office, they went out to buy a stroller. It was an entire industry, a science in itself. Though, at the same time, maybe it was the easiest possession of all to sell. Surely no parent wanted an unsafe stroller for their newborn child?

They were going to meet Dejan, who apparently wanted to

help them get it home, despite the fact that Teddy had a car of his own. "He's doing it to be nice," said Teddy. "It's important to him."

They were on the corner of Odengatan and Sveavägen, waiting for Teddy's friend.

"Mats Emanuelsson called."

"Incredible," said Emelie. "He can talk?" She thought back to Mats's bullet-torn body after the shooting.

"Yeah, apparently he's starting to feel better. He woke up from his coma and has been in rehabilitation for the past few weeks. He'll never be able to walk again, he said, but he's alive. And, in a way, his life is better now—he doesn't have to hide anymore. For the first time in years, he can actually live freely."

The air felt exceptionally clean for the middle of the city. Stockholm was, despite everything, a great town—possibly the best on earth. She pushed the stroller back and forth, tried to imagine how it would feel when there was a child in it.

Teddy's phone started to ring. He answered and gestured for her to put one of the headphones into her ear. She listened in on the conversation.

"Hi, Hugo. What do you want?" said Teddy.

"I, uhh, just wanted to have a quick word with you?"

"What about?"

"I'm reading about Anders Henriksson in the papers," said Hugo.

"Yeah."

"And the dead policewoman who killed the people involved in the network."

"Yeah."

"So I just wanted to make sure you didn't have a score to settle with me or anything. Either you or your friend with the dog. That neither of you are after me, if you know what I mean. Because I helped you as best as I could, I really did."

Teddy said: "Like hell you did."

"Yeah, yeah, I haven't done anything to either of you. You said yourself that you were grateful you were reported to the police, that it changed you."

"Yeah, it changed me. But you weren't exactly much help during those ten years you kept your mouth shut. So I want you to do something to make up for it."

"Huh, what do you want me to do?"

Emelie could hear the anxiety in Hugo Pederson's voice.

Teddy said: "I want you to give thirty million kronor to the girls."

"What? What do you mean? Which girls?"

"You heard what I said. Find out who they are and donate thirty million to them. It won't change what they've been through, but you have to do something. Otherwise the Mauler will be paying you another visit."

Emelie saw Dejan approaching from a distance. He had a particular way of walking: his arms swung slowly from left to right, right to left. The Mauler was skipping along beside him, without a lead.

She was skeptical about Dejan—she didn't really know him, but she instinctively sensed that he was a pig, something she had also mentioned to Teddy a few days earlier. The strange thing was how he replied: "Yeah, he's a pig. Probably one of the biggest assholes in northern Europe. But he's the friend I've got."

Possibly even stranger was what Emelie thought next: Dejan was a pig, but she could live with that—because she knew she wanted to live her life with Teddy.

The asshole friend approached. "Sweet stroller you've gotten yourselves."

"You don't know anything about strollers," said Teddy. "But you can test-drive it if you want."

Dejan looked like Teddy had asked if he wanted to lick poo. "Can't we just carry it over to my car instead? I've bought a new Range Rover Autobiography. It came last week. Insane amount of storage space."

"Strollers aren't dangerous."

Dejan's fingers touched the handle as though he wanted to check it wouldn't burn him.

"Get used to it," said Teddy. "Because you're going to be the little one's kum."

SWEDISH WOMEN'S WEEKLY
ELEGANT MINGLE AS
PEDERSONS START NEW FOUNDATION

Stockholm's society and financial elite gathered this week for the opening of Hugo and Louise Pederson's foundation, which will work to counter the trafficking and sexual exploitation of women. The charity dinner was held in the Hall of Mirrors at the capital's Grand Hôtel.

"I'll be auctioning twenty or so pieces from my collection," Hugo Pederson said proudly. *"The proceeds, in full, will go to the foundation."* Swedish Women's Weekly's *reporter on the scene can confirm that these weren't any old works of art: among the pieces being auctioned are several unique works by wildlife photographer Nick Brandt. The collected works have been valued at over fifty million kronor.*

Louise Pederson, dressed for the occasion in an elegant evening gown from Lars Wallin, was radiant. "We've got important work ahead of us. This is just the beginning."

Evil tongues have, however, criticized Hugo Pederson's business methods and suggested that he has profited from unethical practices. "He can't have earned that money legally," writes the anonymous finance blogger YourXmoney.

"Gossip is for losers. I've always paid my way. I'm a moral person through and through," says Hugo.

Johan W. Lindvall, 2007

NEVER FUCK UP

Stockholm Noir, Book Two

Translated by Astri von Arbin Ahlander

Mahmud is fresh out of jail, but he's forced to work for a brutal mob boss to pay off his debts to a drug lord. Niklas, a mercenary and weapons expert with an appetite for vigilante justice, is back in Sweden and plans to keep a low profile. But the discovery of a murdered man in his mother's building severely threatens those plans. Thomas, the volatile detective on the case, finding his efforts suspiciously stymied and the evidence tampered with, goes off the grid in search of the truth. But as these men cross paths and the identity of the murdered man is revealed, crimes and secrets bigger, deeper, and darker than a mere murder come to light.

Thriller

LIFE DELUXE

Stockholm Noir, Book Three

Translated by Astri von Arbin Ahlander

Jorge has a plan to pull off one final audacious heist and flee the country before the police close in. Meanwhile, Deputy Inspector Martin Hägerström, undercover as a disgraced cop turned corrections officer, is slowly earning the trust of Stockholm's imprisoned expert money launderer, Johan Westlund—a dangerous man to befriend, one who may demand more loyalty than Hägerström had planned on offering. And Natalie, the daughter of Radovan Kranjic, the Serbian crime boss who rules Sweden's underworld, is hurled into a chaotic struggle for control of her father's empire when an assassin threatens Radovan's life. Who will rise to power in the voracious hunt for money, prestige, and luxury to become Stockholm's new king—or queen—of crime?

Thriller

VINTAGE CRIME/BLACK LIZARD
Available wherever books are sold.
www.vintagebooks.com